FIND HER ALIVE

DIANE SAXON

Boldwood

First published in Great Britain in 2019 by Boldwood Books Ltd.

Copyright © Diane Saxon, 2019

Cover Design by Head Design

Cover Photography: Shutterstock

A CIP catalogue record for this book is available from the British Library.

Paperback ISBN 978-1-83889-258-6

Hardback ISBN 978-1-80426-162-0

Large Print ISBN 9781838894399

Ebook ISBN 978-1-83889-256-2

Kindle ISBN 978-1-83889-257-9

Audio CD ISBN 978-1-83889-404-7

MP3 CD ISBN 978-1-83889-259-3

Digital audio download ISBN 978-1-83889-405-4

Boldwood Books Ltd
23 Bowerdean Street
London SW6 3TN
www.boldwoodbooks.com

To Skye, my Dalmatian, without whom the real hero in this book may never have come to fruition.

1

FRIDAY 26 OCTOBER, 15:45 HRS

Felicity Morgan jammed her car into third gear and took the tight bend down the hill to Coalbrookdale with fierce relish.

'It's not right! It's just *not* right. I'm twenty-four years old, for God's sake, and still being told what to do!' She pounded the palm of her hand on the steering wheel and whipped around another curve.

'Not even *told*.' She glanced in the mirror, her gaze clashing with Domino's. 'Nope, she didn't even have the decency to speak to me.' She floored the accelerator and snapped out a feral grin as the car skimmed over the humps in the narrow road.

'She texted me. A freakin' text!' She shot Domino another quick glance and took her foot from the accelerator as the car flew under the disused railway bridge, past the entrance to Enginuity, one of the Ironbridge Gorge Museums.

Guilt nudged at her. 'I know. I know, Domino. We've barely seen each other since I moved in because of her shifts and my workday, but for God's sake. A text? Really? She must have been so peed off to send me a text. It's her version of not talking to me. She's done it all our lives.' Fliss blew out a disgusted snort. 'What the hell did you eat this time? Her bloody precious steak? One of her fluffy pink slippers? Hah!'

She appealed in the mirror to her silent companion. 'She said, "Don't forget to walk *the dog*.'" She pressed her foot on the brake and came to a halt, sliding the gears into neutral as the traffic lights halfway down the hill changed to red. They always did for her. Every bloody time. With a rebellious kick on the accelerator, Fliss revved the engine.

'She called you a *dog*, Domino. She couldn't even be bothered to write your name.' She stared at the big, gorgeous and demanding Dalmatian in her rear view mirror. Her lips kicked up as a smile softened her voice. 'How could I possibly forget to walk you?'

An ancient Austin Allegro puttered through the narrow track towards her just as the traffic lights turned to green on her side.

'Bloody typical.'

Domino raised his head to stare with aloof disdain at the passing Allegro and Fliss sighed as the driver's wrinkled face, as ancient as the car, barely emerged above the steering wheel.

'There was only once, a few weeks ago, I forgot to walk you. You'd have thought Jenna would have understood. I was hung-over from my break-up drinking bout. You, my darling, were suffering the consequences of a broken home.' She let out a derisive snort as she put the car into first gear and glided through the lights, back in control of both her temper and her vehicle.

'Not that you ever really liked Ed. You were just being empathetic. You sensed my...' she drew in a long breath through her nose, '... devastation. You sympathised with me. How was I to know you'd eat your Aunty Jenna's kitchen cupboard doors off while I was sleeping?' They still bore the deep gouged teeth marks. 'We didn't have any choice but to move in with Jenna. We couldn't stay with him. He was too mean. He wanted me to get rid of you. Said it was him or you.'

She flopped her head back on the headrest. Ed. The perfect gentleman, tender, gentle, an absolute charmer. To the outside world. Insidious, controlling arse to her. It had taken so long to realise his subtle intention to separate her from her mother, her sister, eventually Domino. The slick manoeuvres to keep her to himself. Unnoticed until her mother fell ill, when, in a flash, it all became clear.

'Poor Domino.' She glanced in her mirror to share the sympathy between herself and her dog as she slowed down to pass the stunning

Edwardian building she worked in on her right. Coalbrookdale and Iron-bridge School dated back more than two hundred years and had firmly entrenched roots at the centre of the Industrial Revolution. With the imposing cooling towers of the Ironbridge power station behind, they shared domination of the skyline from that angle.

She blew out a breath, making her over-long honey-blonde fringe flutter away from her eyes, just for it to land back again in the same place as she pulled the car to a virtual standstill to take a closer look at the school. Closed for the day, except the few lights in the left side of the building still burning for the after-school club.

A flutter of anxiety filled her chest. It hadn't helped that she'd had such a dreadful day at school. The kids had run her ragged as she held on to her sanity with barely a thread of control left.

Who would have thought teaching would be so hard? Yes, she'd appreciated, before she started fresh from university a year gone September, that teachers worked long hours, but who knew children could be affected by the phase of the moon? Until year six teacher, Sarah Leighton, mentioned it to her at the end of their particularly fractious and demanding day.

Why did they have to have a full bloody supermoon in term time?

She cruised to the bottom of the hill.

Perhaps she should have taken a leaf out of Sarah's book, gone home, poured a glass of wine and sulked in front of the fire until she was obliged to mark homework.

Instead, she'd been forced out of her own house by a text. Not that it was her house, and therein lay the problem.

'I love her to bits. I really do, Domino, but I'm not sure we can live together. Six weeks is probably the limit.'

Fliss glanced in the mirror as she drew up to the mini-roundabout while Domino sat bolt upright in the boot, his proud head close to the rear window as he gazed out at the driver in the car behind. The woman smiled at him, just as everyone did when they caught sight of him, compelling them to give him the attention he was convinced he deserved.

Attention Jenna never gave him as she'd never forgiven him. Nor Fliss.

The constant reminders wore thin.

As her temper surged again, Fliss whipped the car around the pimple of the mini-roundabout and then indicated left into the Dale End car park parents used when they dropped their children off at school.

Despite her annoyance with her sister, she spared the school building another quick glance, the side view hindered by trees, but nonetheless stirring an affection in her. Steeped in history, it lent itself nicely to the quiet Victorian Town. She loved it, with its small community and less than two hundred pupils. Pupils who on a normal day were wonderful. They'd chosen not to be today.

'We need to find our own place, Domino.' His ears twitched, and he cast an unconcerned glance over his shoulder at her use of his name. 'One closer to here, so I don't have to travel twenty minutes to get to work. It means I could spend more time with you. If we lived on our own, I'd need to get home earlier because Jenna wouldn't be there to see to you.'

She stopped the car in the middle of the car park to allow the elderly couple to cross over from the wrought-iron gates leading to the Victorian tearooms and smiled at them despite the mix of lingering annoyance and melancholy.

'I hate living on my own.' It made her nervous, for no particular reason. It just wasn't right to live alone. She needed someone to protect her from her unreasonable fear of the dark and her own vivid imagination.

Fliss's irritation cranked up again at the whine in her own voice as she circled her car around the almost empty car park and swung it with careless abandon into a space. She cut the engine and flicked the seat belt undone. Before Ed she'd never had such reservations. She was strong. She was capable.

Her shoulders sagged. She hated to be alone.

She shook off the self-pity, flung open the driver's door and slammed it behind her before she strode to the back of the vehicle. She wasn't alone. Not entirely. She had Domino. He was company enough. Surely.

'Wait!' she commanded as she opened the boot. She sensed the dog's urgency, his desperate desire to run free, but he'd do as he was told, she had no doubt.

She drew in a deep breath before she clipped the lead onto Domino's harness. She pressed her lips to his forehead as she fondled one silken, floppy ear before she stepped back to allow him out.

Bright and alert, all bunched muscles and restrained excitement, he bounded from the boot of the car and stood to attention, quivering in anticipation while she glanced at the people in the tree-lined park.

She zipped her coat up to her chin against the chill wind and hunched her shoulders, determined to move and keep the cold out.

'Which way shall we go, lad?'

Muted voices floated across, an open invitation for her to join the others in Dale End Park. She chewed the inside of her lip, undecided for a moment, before she turned from the company of the twilight walkers with their idle chit-chat which she normally relished. They wouldn't miss her, their unofficial dog meet was transient. If you turned up, you mingled. If you didn't, no one questioned it. A nice crowd, but she needed her privacy.

'This way, Domino.'

If she allowed herself into their sympathetic fold, she'd be tempted to whine about Jenna, and if there was one thing she couldn't stand, it was disloyalty. She huffed out a breath. Her anger with Jenna would pass. Until then, she'd keep to herself. Allow the solitude to blanket her.

She turned right out of the car park and strode out up the hill, past the small Co-op at the mouth of the Museum on the Gorge. It would be open until ten o'clock. Perhaps she'd nip in on her way home and buy that bottle of red wine.

Sodium lights illuminated the town to spread their warm golden glow as she lengthened her stride and marched along the narrow footpath, puffing out small bursts of vapour as her breath hit the cool evening air.

The Council had readied the flood barriers for erection along the Wharfeage, as the River Severn continued to rise after an unusually long, wet autumn. It threatened to break its banks early in the season, leaving a dull sense of foreboding for what the rest of the winter would bring. The town wallowed in an eerie quietness. The windows of almost all the premises overlooking the river dark, but for an occasional upstairs light on.

Breathless from her overexerted stride, she paused halfway up the hill before crossing the Ironbridge. A town in the summer overflowing with tourists keen to witness the birthplace of the Industrial Revolution, the Ironbridge dominated the landscape with its iron structure pioneered by Abraham Darby in the eighteenth century. The plethora of museums drew people from all around the world. Somewhere for the locals to avoid. As a tourist town, however, devoid of visitors during the winter months, most of the shops had already closed for the evening.

The car park in the little square opposite the Ironbridge was empty except for a single red car outside the Tea Emporium as the last of the patrons left for the day. If she'd been earlier, Fliss could have indulged in a fruit scone with jam and cream, accompanied by a cappuccino, or one of their thick, creamy hot chocolates. A treat both she and Jenna often indulged in as they watched the world go by from underneath the fluttering umbrellas outside all year long.

Her stomach let out a protesting wail as she turned her back on the café. She'd not eaten since lunchtime and couldn't wait to get back to Jenna's. She'd fling together a quick stir-fry in time for Jenna's return. Not that her sister deserved it.

The torrid waters of the Severn swirled beneath her as she crossed over the Ironbridge, deserted since the end of the summer and tourist season, much to her relief. Fliss wasn't in the mood for mad holidaymakers leaping at Domino just because they'd seen *101 Dalmatians* and believed they were all cuddly animations instead of big dogs who could give a powerful bite if provoked. Not that Domino would bite anyone. She reached down and scrubbed the top of his head and made his tail go wild. The big softie.

With high, prancing steps, Domino's strong muscles bunched and flexed as he matched his pace to hers, happy just to be with her.

Snatches of bad temper still curdled in her stomach and Fliss barely paused as she turned right off the bridge and hit the flat of the wide, disused railway track which led straight to the cooling towers, before unclipping Domino's jaunty red lead. She coiled it around her neck, clipped the end onto one of the metal loops along the lead, so it couldn't slide off, and headed after the dog.

As he veered off to the left, taking the narrower offshoot from the main path up into the woodland, Fliss automatically followed. She put on a spurt to get her up the first steep incline, blowing out white puffs of breath as the path rose in undulations until she was thirty feet above, and parallel to, the main drag. Glancing around, Fliss considered her mistake taking that route as dense vegetation crowded out the light to make it even more difficult to see where she was going.

She hesitated and peered down through the dimness at the wider trail. Already twilight, it would soon be an impenetrable black in the woods.

With a sniff, Fliss burrowed her nose deeper into her fleece-lined coat against the chill wind whipping through the Ironbridge Gorge and shrugged. Sure-footed, she was so familiar with the walk, the thought of negotiating it in the dark never bothered her. She wouldn't be too long, and where the paths merged at the base of the cooling towers, she'd return along the wider, safer path.

As the peace and quiet of the Gorge settled on her, she slowed her pace and breathed deep, allowing the rich, pungent aroma of the undergrowth to encompass her. Sharp scents of wet pine and dark wood smoke rose with snatches of damp soil and musky fungus to invade her senses.

Never one to hold onto her temper, she let it go and took in her surroundings. She squinted above her, way up the hillside into the thicket, in the hope she'd spot deer picking their way through. Too dark to make out any shapes, she turned her attention back to the narrow pathway.

Thrilled at the fresh crunch of leaves underfoot, she swiped at the piles of them with her boots, like she had when she was a child. Only the thick slide of mud underneath gave her a moment's pause. Perhaps it wasn't wise to kick the protective layer of leaves aside and end up on her backside, or worse still, at the bottom of the steep incline. Jenna would only give her hell. *What were you doing up there at that time of night? How come you slipped? Trust you to get into trouble.* Her sister's lecturing voice trailed through Fliss's mind, slowing her down still more.

Disappointed, she curled her fingers into the palms of her hands to keep them warm and ambled onward, her eyes straining to catch the quick bursts of Domino as he pounded in mad leaps up and down the hillside, the scent of deer in his nostrils.

A wild flash of white shot past her, so close the whip of air stroked her bare hands. The merry jingle of Domino's collar let her know exactly where he was as he tore through again, almost taking her off her feet.

'Slow down, slow down, you barmy dog.' God, but she loved him.

She laughed out loud as he charged by one more time. It wasn't worth calling him back. He wouldn't take any notice and it just made her feel stupid when she shouted for a dog that wasn't going to obey. Anyway, he was having fun.

She cast a quick glance up at the umbrella of trees and pushed away the regret of coming out here. It was good for him. He needed the exercise, and even in the dark, she was sure-footed, she knew the pathways. Besides, another twenty minutes and she'd be back onto the main track. Although it wasn't lit either, it didn't have the heavy layer of branches canopied over it to draw the night in.

'It's bloody freezing.'

She dug icy hands into her pockets and regretted leaving her gloves in the car in her haste and bad temper. She hunched her shoulders up to her ears as the bitter chill seeped bone deep. Mean and sneaky, it found the gaps in the neckline of her coat and filtered through to send ripples of goosebumps over her flesh. Damn, but she should have worn more layers. She kept enough of them in her car, but her temper had got the better of her.

She brought her nose out of where she had it tucked in her coat as Domino shot by once more and breathed a sigh of relief that she'd had the sense not to follow the even steeper route up to Patten's Rock.

Out of control, Domino flew down the hillside above her, clipped the side of her leg in his headlong rush and almost sent her over the edge of the path after him.

'Shit.' Her heartbeat spiked as she teetered on the edge, one foot slipping in the mud before she managed to pull herself back. 'Bloody dog, no sense of personal space. No sense, full stop.'

She dragged in a deep breath. For her own safety, she slipped her hands back out of her pockets for balance, just in case the dog side-swiped her again and pushed her over the edge. She narrowed her eyes and peered into the blackness of the Gorge while Domino careered through the undergrowth.

In her next life, she wanted to be a dog. Wild and carefree, with nothing to worry about. Tough and energetic, just like Domino.

Fliss pulled her phone from her pocket and swiped the screen to check the time and then slipped it away again. She'd better get a move

on before she couldn't even see the hand in front of her fa
the muted sounds of birds settling for the night, the di
voices and the occasional excited yip from a dog in Da...
directly opposite her on the other side of the river, peace settl...
around her.

Head down, she powered on, away from the soft lights of the town, deeper into the murky woodland, accompanied by the comforting thrash of Domino charging around.

One foot suddenly shot from underneath her and she slithered down a short, muddy incline. Arms spread wide, her spine cracked as she jerked upright and then came to a slippery halt as she grabbed onto the short stretch of wooden hand railing.

Still on her feet. Just. Heart beating in the base of her throat, she bent over from the waist and blew out a gusty sigh. Perhaps she shouldn't power on. Perhaps slow and steady was the means to stay alive.

Below her, Domino's enthusiasm quietened to soft snuffles and the darkness closed in. Above her, leaves rustled, and twigs snapped. She straightened, held onto her breath to listen. Something else moved amongst the trees.

Attuned to the peacefulness of her surroundings, Fliss angled her head so she could hear better. She blinked to focus on the shadowy woodland and waited. If there were deer, she was about to lose her dog if he decided to sprint after them, but the likelihood of deer getting so close wasn't too high, not even the bold muntjac. Not with the racket Domino made.

She sucked in a lungful of cold air, held it, her brow drawn low as she concentrated.

It didn't sound like deer. Not unless a whole herd had descended on them. Not a badger either. They would have just thundered past, oblivious of their surroundings. Busy characters, they tended not to stop for anything.

This was different, more rhythmic.

She tilted her head to one side to better catch the sound.

Footsteps. Definitely. Heavy footfall coming straight towards her down the embankment, from the higher pathway leading from Broseley. There was no hesitation in the steps, some slipping, some sliding, but whoever was there had to be confident of their ability and familiarity with the terrain.

'Hello?' Fliss burst out, her voice sharp and demanding, full of confidence she didn't feel.

In an instant, the footfall halted. A heavy silence descended from above, but Domino's movements still gave her some reassurance. A big dog, she'd never felt insecure with him around, knowing he'd protect her.

Doubt sent small shudders through her as her teeth chattered against the cold. Fliss peered into the darkness above her for movement as she strained to pick up any sound.

Nothing.

Perhaps it *had* been deer, or a badger. Badgers made plenty of noise, but what creature would freeze at the sound of her voice? Most would make off through the undergrowth.

As the wind shifted and swirled around her, she picked up the clear sound of the twilight dog walkers on the other side of the river in Dale End Park. The acoustics of the area carried their voices up the Gorge, the long valley emphasising their muffled laughter and dog-barking as though they were right beside her.

She turned her head to catch the sound of Domino, quieter now, closer, while he snuffled in the wet autumn leaves, unconcerned by anything other than the scent he'd picked up. She should be reassured by his closeness, but she couldn't dismiss the icy tingle which ran from her neck, down her spine and kept her still while she scanned the area above her and listened for something, anything.

Nothing.

'Domino.' Fliss hissed out his name as she stepped back to retrace her way along the path. She wasn't yet halfway along, and she considered it may be better to go back, rather than deeper into the woods.

Spooked, she focused on the area above her, determined to detect some movement. Her heartbeat throbbed in the base of her throat. She hitched in fast snatches of air as thinly veiled panic skittered through her veins. She tried to regulate her breathing, held it for a long moment, while she listened for further sounds. Concerned more at the unsettling silence above her.

She turned her head at the crackle of leaves as Domino moved closer.

'Good boy. C'mon, Domino. Good boy.' With a hushed croon, she bent from the hips and kept her face upturned to watch for any movement, her head tilted to listen. She groped for the dog's harness, soothing him while she stroked one hand along his smooth, warm body and took what comfort she could from his presence. With her free hand, she reached into her pocket for her mobile phone. Despite Domino's closeness, her icy fingers still fumbled while she clenched her jaw and pushed back the flutter of fear.

Clouds skimmed over the full moon to blot out the light. The damned dark. Always the subject of her nightmares.

She swivelled on her heel, released the dog's harness and swiped at the quick dial for her sister's number as she strode back the way she'd come as quickly as the narrow path would allow.

As though he sensed her discomfort, Domino matched his pace to hers and trotted along two steps ahead.

The phone gave a sharp trill at the other end. The fierce glow from the light heightened the density of the surrounding darkness as it closed in around her. Determined to tamp down on the panic, Fliss snapped her spine ramrod straight as she edged her way back along the path and waited for her sister to pick up.

Just the sound of Jenna's voice would give her confidence, although she was never going to admit to being frightened.

The signal slipped down to two bars and then dropped out.

From the sinister quiet above her, the dry crack of a twig broke through her thoughts and Fliss sobbed out a desperate gasp while she froze in her tracks to stare into the cloying blackness. There was someone there. Someone above her. Watching.

'Hello. Is anyone there?'

Disgusted at the quaver in her own voice, Fliss held her breath and listened.

Silence.

Domino circled around and came to stand by her side, and she reached out, touched his shoulder, seeking reassurance from his presence. His head came up and he scented the air.

She swiped Jenna's number again and prayed for the signal to kick back in.

Domino's low growl vibrated through Fliss's hand where she rested it, the short hair of his hackles rose under her fingers and he stood solid beside her. Every muscle in his body quivered to attention.

Heart knocking hard against her chest, Fliss inched the phone away from her ear to give her a better chance to listen to any further movement above. The phone pealed out its first ring and pierced the quiet. The glow from it blinded her to her surroundings.

'Dammit, Jenna, pick up. Pick up.' Fliss just needed to hear her sister's voice, stabilise herself once more. That's what Jenna did for her, she steadied her in her darkest moments. She'd ground her, make her see the unreasonableness of her worries without making her seem like a fool.

The connection failed again and Fliss stabbed a shaky finger at the screen. *Dammit. Connect.*

She drew a shuddering breath in through her nose and tried to still the rising fear.

As she debated whether to run or stand and face the dark presence, Domino's warning growl turned to a deep vicious snarl and terror froze Fliss to the spot.

2

Light from her phone bathed her pretty face in a soft golden glow while she stared right at him. Clouds skimmed over the bright white moon, then off again to leave a shimmer of silvery light casting through the shadowed woodland.

The man watched, raking his fingertips over the whiskers on his chin to make them rasp.

There was nothing for it, she'd left him with no choice.

'Stupid bitch,' he murmured under his breath.

It wasn't his fault. She'd provoked him. She should have gone on her way without looking at him. What the hell was she doing there, anyhow? Why couldn't she have minded her own business, instead of poking her nose up in the air to watch his every move? If just she'd walked away and let him get on with what he'd come to sort out, she'd have been safe. But now he had to deal with her and that fucking dog.

He hated dogs. Unpredictable bastards. His mother had had one when he was a boy. Some sort of fucking terrier. The worst. Whenever he'd come into the room, it had always growled. His mother had thought it funny, thought it was being protective. But the protectiveness stopped when he shoved a knife through its throat and buried it in a shallow grave in the back garden along with the neighbour's cat.

Animals. Nasty little bastards. They should all be destroyed.

He bent down, picked up a solid branch as thick as the top of his arm and weighed it in his hands. Without a clear view of the dog, he had no idea what breed it was, but from the amount of thrashing around, it sounded like a monster.

No fucking little terrier.

He altered his grip on the branch. Whatever the breed, it wouldn't stand much of a chance against him, if he caught it right. He may not be armed with a knife this time, but his weapon of necessity was a good one.

He smiled as the woman stared at her phone. He couldn't hear her words, but her mouth worked frantically as he imagined she cursed at the lack of signal in the area. There was never a signal in the Gorge, not a sustainable one at any rate.

Panic-filled eyes blinked up at him as she took her attention off the phone to scan the treeline where he stood. Stupid bitch couldn't take her gaze from him.

He drew in a calming breath. If only she hadn't stared, she'd be safe. It was her own fault. Not his.

He gave the bough another measure in his hands, forced himself to listen to his calming inner voice, *it's okay, it's just a little diversion to your plans, keep calm, you can deal with this* – his gaze never left the woman below. The wind whipped through the Gorge and he hunched his shoulders against the chill.

She turned to leave, stepped into the finger of shadow below. He couldn't let her go. She'd seen him. She'd know who he was. She'd be able to identify him.

Mind made up, he waited for movement below to estimate where the dog was and then he gathered his strength and launched himself towards the light from the phone, pulling his lips back from his teeth in a soundless scream.

As prepared as he was for it, thirty-eight kilograms of pure muscle took him by surprise as the dog released a ferocious growl and leapt up to meet him. A snarling mass of white, the man knew in an instant he'd underestimated his foe.

Terror streaked through him. He swung hard, gripped the solid branch with both hands and let instinct rule. The quick whip of adrenaline raced wild and free through his veins, instilling him with the strength he needed to accomplish the task. His shoulder jarred on impact and punched a sick jolt of pain through him. But satisfaction overrode the ball of nausea spinning through his stomach. The branch he held splintered in two, accompanied by a crack loud enough to be the dog's neck breaking. He hoped. Whether it did or not, the animal hit the floor like a sack of wet cement and flipped off the path, down the steep hillside. The body smashed through the undergrowth, cracking twigs and branches.

The woman's shrill scream chased it all the way as she shrieked the dog's name.

'Domino!'

A sense of achievement that he'd bested the creature rolled off him as the man squared up to meet the lesser of his enemies.

The crackle and groan of his shoulder didn't bother him as adrenaline sent a power surge through his system to disguise the pain. Wild laughter bubbled inside and he grinned.

Easy pickings.

A weak, pathetic woman.

He was strong.

Strong and dangerous.

Empowered by his success, he flung the remains of his branch to one side and stepped closer to the woman. His bare hands would be enough to deal with her.

Shock filled her eyes, huge and shadowed in a pale face, illuminated by the light of her phone and the glimmer of moonlight edging through the trees. She gave a slow blink and he grinned. Her bad luck she'd frozen instead of run. Silly little slag.

A wicked thrill pulsed through him to fill him with vitality. Surprise quickened the adrenaline spiking his energy levels. It felt good, this power he'd discovered.

His blood singing through his veins, he glared at her, punched his arm out to grab her as she stepped back. Her feet slipped in the thick, sticky mud. Surprised, he grappled with the sleeve of her coat, desperate to hold on to her as, with a sudden burst of unexpected energy, she flung her arms up. The hold he had on her loosened and, in desperation, she shook off his fingers and wrenched away.

Her shrill scream pierced his ears as she teetered on the edge of the path. He snatched at her one last time before she crashed down the Gorge, the same way as her dog, ear-splitting screams echoing around the valley.

Panic chased away his excitement and shock gathered in his gut as the fast smackdown of adrenaline left him with the shakes. He dipped his head to follow the sound of her descent above the frenzied crash of his heart.

'Stupid. Stupid.' He smacked the heel of his hand against his temple. 'They'll all hear, the fuckers.' Those walking their dogs on the other side of the river. 'Nosy, interfering bastards.' She'd ruined everything. Damn her. The bitch!

The echo of his furious internal scream reverberated through his mind.

Dizzy with rage, he started his descent, pounding downhill, slithering sideways through the thick undergrowth that snagged at his boots and threatened to upend him. But he had no choice. Help would come, and he only had a short time to sort out the matter he'd come to deal with.

At the sudden rise of voices, he glared across the river, anger pushing back the panic. Those bloody dog walkers would send help. They'd phone the police in response to the stupid woman's blood-curdling screams. Interfering fuckers, always reporting the locals for any indiscretions. Bloody dog walking neighbourhood watch.

A frustrated grunt stuck in his throat. She'd seen him. She'd be able to identify him. If she was still alive, he'd kill her.

Anger writhed in the pit of his stomach. If he had more time, he'd make her suffer, break her fingers one at a time, twist her arms until she cried out in her pain, yank her hair from her head, stab his cigarette butts deep into her soft flesh.

In his fury, he ground his teeth until his jaw popped, and then he skidded down the steep side of the hill, his feet skating through the perilous vegetation, barely getting purchase as he broke into a run, unable to put the brakes on.

He whipped the small torch from his back pocket and turned it on to scan the area. He shielded the arc of light with one hand, so it only glowed onto the ground.

He didn't have time for this shit.

He'd deal with her, but it would have to be quick and efficient.

3

FRIDAY 26 OCTOBER, 16:30 HRS

She slithered to a stop, choking on her own desperate gasps as horror clawed at her chest. Her world ricocheted in violent revolutions. Pain lanced through her knee from ramming into the brickwork of the ancient Severn Valley railway bridge. Partially buried beneath the hillside, the thick slide of black mud filled its belly from the entrance at the top of the short tunnel, to spew it out of the mouth at the bottom where it converged with the wider pathway.

Breathless, she barely paused before she whipped over onto her knees, ignoring the deep burn where the undergrowth had ripped her flesh. She scrambled around, patting the ground. She ignored the streaks of pain spearing the palms of her hands as the warm scent of blood filled her nostrils and a metallic taste coated her tongue.

'Domino.'

Desperate, she whispered his name under her breath as she reached out for him.

Her head still spun while crazy white lights slashed across her vision. Frantic, she swiped a hand along the brick edge of the partially submerged railway tunnel to centre herself, to picture where she'd landed and visualise an escape route. She raised her head, spared the slope a cursory glance. There was a lunatic up there but if she could grab Domino and make a run for it along the wide track, she'd hopefully reach the safety of the Ironbridge.

She groped around, grasped at leaves and branches in a desperate bid to locate Domino.

'Domino,' she hissed through clenched teeth. He had to be there somewhere. With trembling hands, she sought any heat source to hint at his presence. She'd plummeted down the hill right behind him, head over heels in wild rotations, enough to knock the stuffing out of her. She should have landed on top of him, but she could easily have tumbled in a different direction.

A desperate sob tore free of her tight throat. Where was he? He had to be near, she needed him. Needed to know he was safe. Her voice croaked out as she called for him again.

'Domino. Oh god, Domino, where are you?'

In the pitch dark, she focused, desperate to catch a glimpse of his bright white fur, but the moon was not on her side and hid its glow behind another rush of clouds.

A thrashing movement from above alerted her. She reared her head back and squinted up at the lighter skyline as the clouds parted and she caught a glimpse of the dark outline of the maniac as he moved on the pathway above. Her breath caught in her throat as he started his descent. He came towards her in a mad rush.

Panic clenched her stomach in a tight fist as she scrambled deeper under the recess of the tunnel, following the upward slope of it into the darkness. The pain of her damaged knee radiated through her leg. If she tried to run, he'd see her. Her only hope was to stay where she was. Hide.

She slapped one hand over her mouth to staunch the flow of wild sobs from bursting out, stop her breath from wheezing.

She reached out. Just a touch of reassurance he was there was all she needed. Alive. The man would go, she'd get Domino to the vets. It would be all right.

She fumbled around, grasped something solid. Cold. Waxy.

Bright white lights danced across her vision.

Partially buried beneath the thick carpet of wet leaves, branches, and twigs, Fliss moulded her fingers across the unmistakable contours of a person's face.

Her fingers trembled as she skimmed them over the nose, traced the outline of the lips and curve of the chin, down the neck. She smoothed her hands over stone-cold shoulders and down until she encountered the obvious definition of a pair of breasts.

The sick slide of horror turned her stomach to a churning ball of grease. She swallowed the nausea, but it still rose up her throat until she gagged. Unlike her sister, she'd never encountered a dead person before, but there was no doubt the waxen iciness she had her hand on was human flesh.

She snatched her hand back as a scream lodged in her throat. Fuelled by terror, her mind wiped clear of everything but the desperate desire to escape. Haste made her clumsy as she scrambled to her feet and turned back the way she had come, her priority no longer to hide, but to run. To escape.

The black shadow of a man stopped her dead in her tracks as he filled the entrance to the tunnel, flicked on a bright white flashlight to blind her and reached for her.

* * *

He picked out the pale glow of her face in the light of his torch and traced the arc of it down her body as she crouched in front of him at the mouth of the tunnel, her knees sunk deep into the mud.

The stupid woman had her dog's lead circled around her neck. Convenient for him, deadly for her.

As she stumbled to her feet, the squelch of mud dragging her back down, her eyes glazed in the bright gleam of his torch.

Fury, dark and dangerous, snapped through him. She'd ruined everything. It was her fault, she'd left him with no option.

Surprise leapt in his throat as she surged forward, took the first steps to run, but his adrenaline was still high and the savage animal inside surfaced. He grasped the red lead with his fingers and yanked hard until she slammed face first into his chest.

The thrill of power coursing back through his veins made him stronger, fiercer. He wrenched the lead, twisted it around his hand, one, two, three times, and grinned as she dropped to her knees in front of him, just where the little slapper should be. Surprise widened her eyes as they bulged, threatening to pop out of her head. He grinned with savage satisfaction as her pitiful snatches of breath gurgled through her throat and sent a stream of wild delirium rushing through him

The crack of her bones gave him strength as he wrangled the lead, wrapped it tighter around his hands with a solid, firm pressure while he allowed his fury to command him. He'd wanted to savour the moment, but she'd deprived him with her stupid, pathetic screams. She'd not have another chance now he had her under his power. Pleasure spiked while her hoarse gasps became weaker as he held on until the give in her body slumped her forward, a deadweight in his hands. Only to be expected. He'd broken her neck, felt the crack of it beneath his fingers. Stupid cow, with her useless ideas. Just like his wife. Why wrap a lead around your neck? It was an invitation to be choked.

He gave one last, vicious twist. Limp and lifeless, she left him with nothing but disgust at such an easy kill. At least his wife had given him years of satisfaction. She'd been strong and resilient, a scrapper. He sneered at the woman. This tragic excuse hadn't even put up a fight.

Untangling his fingers from the lead, he released her and allowed her body to slump forward over his feet, giving her a disgusted nudge with his boot. Silly bitch, she'd ruined his evening, then robbed him of the time he would have enjoyed making her suffer by letting out those godawful screams, which had echoed across the valley.

Straining to hear, he tilted his head to one side and listened to the familiar sounds of voices from across the river, pitched low with concern.

With the weight of the woman on his feet, he glanced down and pride edged its way through his annoyance. He'd killed her. He'd reflect on the horror in her expression later, give himself some satisfaction.

For a brief moment, he allowed himself a self-satisfied smile, to gloat over his conquest and then drew in gulp after gulp of fresh air, holding each one as control slid back into place.

He needed to move, get out of there before the police turned up. It would take them an age to reach him, unless there was already someone deployed this side of the river. Unlikely, but possible.

The muted ring of a phone filtered through to his conscience. His heart rate, almost back to normal, spiked up again while he scanned the area for the source of the sound. He kicked the weight of the body off his feet and circled around, his narrowed gaze focused on the ground. He traced his small flashlight over the area, scanning inside the tunnel where his dead wife lay, white and waxen under the partial protection of leaves. His lip curled with disgust. He'd no time now to do more to cover her, nor look for a fucking ringing phone that must have landed screen down so the light wasn't visible. It didn't matter, he didn't need a dead woman's phone. If just it would stop fucking ringing.

Flicking off the flashlight so it didn't attract attention, the man turned, his feet skidding in the mulch of leaves as he leapt over the other woman's body onto the old railway path below. He wiped his hands on his combat trousers while he considered his next move. He could drag her up into the tunnel too, place her next to his wife. Aware the insistent peal of the telephone had stopped, he peered into the darkness across the river. He couldn't risk any more time. He needed to get out of there.

As a familiar voice emerged from the undergrowth, every muscle in his body froze.

'Hello, this is Detective Sergeant Jenna Morgan. I'm sorry I'm not available to take your call, but please leave a message and I'll get back to you.'

'Fuck it.'

A long beep sounded in the darkness as he whipped his head around to stare at the crumpled form behind him, the rush of wild water spun through his head, making it reel.

Stupid cow, what the hell was she doing here?

He gave the body a vicious kick.

The soft sigh of a moan floated up to him and his pulse rate shot up. He listened for another sound, but there was nothing. He'd killed her. She was dead. She had to be. Perhaps it was just his imagination.

He leaned in, pushed the lead out of the way and placed two fingers against the side of her neck. The thready flutter of a pulse danced beneath his fingertips.

She was still alive. Fuck.

With a quick glance over the river, he made a decision as he squatted next to her body.

If he hurried, he could take her. Fate had possibly dealt him a good hand for a change. He could take her home.

Keep her.

He stared into the recess of the tunnel, focused hard but couldn't quite make out the naked body of his wife. He chewed his lip as he pushed the fine hair back from his forehead.

She'd be a replacement for Mary.

4

Detective Sergeant Jenna Morgan jiggled the car keys in her hand as she caught the attention of Detective Constable Mason Ellis. Her partner of choice loitered at the public service counter. She gave a quick jerk of her head to persuade him to follow her out of the main doors of Malinsgate, Telford's main police station.

As he caught up with her, she kept her voice low while they passed a group of vociferous teenagers, bouncing with overexcited enthusiasm, as they crossed the concrete moat that led to the station car park.

'We've had a report of a woman's screams heard in Benthall Edge Wood. Dog handler was already in the area, so he's picking it up. I think it's Sergeant Bennett.' Down-to-earth and old-school, Jenna had confidence that he'd investigate anything amiss with cool efficiency. 'We've been asked to meet him at Ironbridge car park, south of the river, and check it out while uniform take north of the river at Dale End car park. Apparently, the twilight dog walkers called it in. They're a bit panicked by all accounts.'

'Are they the lot you sometimes meet with the daft dally?'

'You know he's not daft. He's...' she struggled to find the word to describe her sister's gorgeous, dynamic Dalmatian. 'Ebullient.'

'Ebullient, huh? He ate your kitchen.'

Stirred to defend him, Jenna struggled to be generous. 'Not the entire kitchen. Only the doors.'

'Yeah.'

With a long, drawn-out groan, Mason stretched his body, arms above his head, as he walked side by side with Jenna towards the squad car. Jenna glanced up at him as he yawned until his jaw cracked.

She flashed him a smile. 'Sorry, pal. We nearly made it to the end of the day without going into overtime. Five more minutes and we would have been home and free.'

She should never have answered the bloody call. She should have let one of the other teams catch it. Now they'd be tied up for at least an hour on some stupid kids yowling in the woods. Little buggers should be home by now playing on their iPads or glued to some reality TV programme. It was the full moon with Halloween around the corner.

Jenna glanced at her watch and winced. Weariness had seeped through to her bones so deep, she just wanted to go home. Her feet ached like a bitch. With brand new boots, she hadn't envisaged leaving the station. It was supposed to have been a meeting and paperwork day. A boot breaking-in day.

'Do you want me to drive?' Mason gave her a lazy smile, a cocky quirk to his lips which meant he thought he knew the answer before she spoke.

'Yeah, actually.' She gained a small nugget of satisfaction as he twisted his head to a better angle to peer into her face and, she imagined, to judge whether she was taking the piss. She jerked a casual shrug. 'I've some messages to pick up. Gregg kept us tied up in some political meeting today. I lost interest after the first three minutes. I think it was to do with paper wastage.'

She slid into the passenger seat as Mason plugged in his seat belt and fired up the black, police issue Vauxhall Insignia.

'Toilet or printer?'

She snorted as she picked up the radio. 'Printer, but it sounded like shit to me.' She pressed the 'speak' button. 'Juliette Alpha 76 to Control. Over.'

'Juliette Alpha 76. Go ahead.'

'We're called to attend on the south side of the river at Benthall Edge. As we're on the north side, it would be quicker if we question the informants at Dale End Park as you already have the dog handler deployed on the south.' Clicking the button off, Jenna held on and prayed for the lesser deployment as she listened to static for a moment before the reply came through.

'Affirmative.'

'Thank you, Lord,' Jenna grinned as she slipped the radio back into its casing. 'I really didn't want to get my new boots muddy walking along the Gorge.' She flexed her feet in her boots and regretted yanking them on that morning. 'Jeez, it's probably only some teenagers scaring themselves witless over there. Halloween comes earlier every year.' She huffed out a sigh, taking her mobile phone out of her pocket, she dialled into her answerphone while Mason pushed to the speed limit along the Queensway dual carriageway.

The first two messages were people chasing for follow-ups, the third was two minutes of static from her sister, fully furnished with background noise. She'd probably pocket-dialled her by mistake. God only knows what the heavy breathing was about. It better not be her sister having sex. Chance would be a fine thing if Fliss found a new man to put a zing in her life, but Jenna really didn't need to hear it.

She tapped her finger on the screen and deleted the call as Mason took the turn off down Cherry Tree Hill and hit the speed bumps with a little more force than necessary. She grunted as she shot him a sideways look. 'This is why I don't let you drive, Mason.' She caught his wild grin and shook her head as she turned back to her phone.

The fourth call was her inspector demanding to know why she hadn't got back to caller one, who happened to be a local councillor.

With a heavy sigh, Jenna hit delete on that as she'd already winged the local councillor problem to one of her DCs asking them to report back to her. She tucked her phone in her pocket as Mason drew their police unit into Dale End car park.

She stepped out of the car and the cold bite of air had her sucking in her breath. It was downhill from now on. She hated winter. Fliss loved to curl up in front of a roaring fire with a glass of whisky and a good book. Jenna would far rather live abroad for six months of the year. Somewhere warm, bordering on hot.

As they approached the group of familiar people and dogs milling around, Jenna puffed out a sigh of relief as one of the 'old-school' uniforms, notebook in hand, questioned a lady with a small black Labrador slumped at her feet.

Molly. The dog was called Molly. Jenna hadn't a clue what the owner's name was, but they often saw each other when she and Fliss walked Domino. Jenna had come to know the dog walkers – a sociable crowd, always willing to let in another dog walker, imparting their knowledge and experience. She knew so little of their personal lives, but everything about their dogs. Little Molly who'd had two litters of puppies. Jenna had been tempted to have one herself, and then Domino had eaten her damned kitchen and put paid to her aspirations to own a dog.

Jenna scanned the others in the group. Hope, the black and white terrier, stood with her dad, a tall innocuous older gentleman with a shock of white hair. Ollie, the Golden Retriever, still bounded around, no amount of calmness influencing his mad dash, while his owner, a short, blonde-haired woman, chewed the side of her nail as she stood on the outskirts of the small crowd, her nervous energy pulsing off her.

Jenna recognised Henry, a retired police constable, with his three spaniels obediently at heel, faces turned to look up at him, full of anticipation as they awaited his next command. He stood apart from the crowd, solid, reassuring, and when she caught his gaze, gave her a calm wink. He'd wait his turn, knowing they'd get to him.

Another couple hovered, their hands linked together while Punch, the mottled Staffie, panted heavily, mouth wide open in a mawing grin.

A desperate relief washed over Molly's owner's features as Jenna approached.

'Hey, Domino's aunty.' The woman stepped forward, her fingers clenched together.

Jenna smiled in an attempt to ease the woman's anxiety. It wasn't something she'd noticed before; Molly's mum always exuded a calm assurance, happy to dole out words of wisdom on just about any subject.

'Molly's mum.' She touched the woman's arm in reassurance.

Scratching Molly behind the ears, Jenna scanned the group and then turned her attention to the Uniform, PC Ted Walker, one of the longest-serving police officers in Malinsgate. Loved his job and never wanted to retire. A damned good, solid PC.

She dropped her voice so her familiarity with the experienced PC only carried to his ears. 'What you got, Ted?'

Flicking back the pages of his notebook, PC Walker squinted in the dull orange glow from the streetlight. 'Several accounts. They all seem to be in agreement. The collective claim to have heard a woman's voice shouting a name south of the river.' He stretched his arm full length, his hand, spade-like, turned sideways as though he was directing traffic. 'Directly opposite this point.'

Jenna gazed at the bank on the opposite side of the river. If it had been full light, it was close enough to wave to people on the opposite side. Or holler to them as often happened. The lower pathway, a disused railway line, having long been taken up to leave a wide, flat track, curved around the hillside from Ironbridge car park next to the old Tollhouse, all the way through to the imposing cooling towers at the power station. She'd have been able to see that track in daylight, but the murky twilight closed in around it. Even in full sunlight, the narrow, upper pathway which followed the same route couldn't be seen through the dense thicket of trees.

She turned her attention back to PC Walker. 'Unusual?'

He nodded. 'It's unsettled them. According to the people I've questioned, this shout was followed by a lot of crashing noises and then a scream.'

'It made my blood curdle.' Molly's mum nudged closer, her chin almost on PC Walker's shoulder. His lips curved in a gentle smile and he gave her arm a reassuring pat.

As one of the local policing team, Ted Walker made it his business to know the residents, and this familiarity came as no surprise to Jenna. He'd know Molly's mum. The twilight walkers were always a great source of information. They witnessed many a trivial incident, reported a great deal of crimes. Kept the place clean of minor offences.

'Don't worry, Dina, the dog handler's just arrived. He'll look into it. We're taking it seriously.'

'I've never heard anything like it in my life. It was terror.' Reaching over, Dina took hold of Jenna's arm. 'Honestly, it really has me worried. The voice...' Her intense stare pierced Jenna's soul as Dina gripped her arm, fingers digging deep. 'Just before the screaming, I swear the woman shouted "Domino!"'

With a jolt, Jenna stared into Dina's eyes.

She shook off the fear that raised the hackles on the back of her neck and ignored the trickle of ice as it skittered down her spine. Dina's intensity startled her. The woman was seriously spooked.

As a trained police officer of nine years, Jenna knew people overreacted to situations. She'd also developed a good instinct for the truth.

'No one mentioned Domino before.' PC Walker flicked with furious concentration through his notes, scratched his head with the end of his pen, his broad brow furrowed into deep lines.

'No. The name didn't register until I saw you, but the more I think about it, the more I'm sure.' The woman's panic pulsed off her, sending a shaft of fear to ball in Jenna's stomach. It ran through her veins and try as she might to shake the feeling off, Dina's conviction was contagious. Jenna should know better. People's reactions wouldn't normally touch her, couldn't instill panic. She was trained to remain calm, but unease pricked at the sensitive skin on the back of her neck. The possibility that it could be her sister, or more likely Domino, in trouble stirred concern.

She squinted at the woodland beyond the river. Would Fliss be up there? Tempted to shout out her sister's name, just to test, Jenna clamped her lips closed. If Fliss was over there, she'd be fine. Physically fit, she was as sure-footed as a mountain goat as she climbed hills all the time, accompanied by the wild and wonderful Domino. She knew the Gorge pathways so well; it was almost a daily occurrence for her to walk them.

Still, the dark was closing in and if Domino had managed to do something stupid...

Jenna quashed the trickle of worry, stamped on it so she could focus. She glanced around, spoke to the crowd in general.

'Excuse me, may I have your attention?' As the voices fell away, Jenna held her warrant card in the air. There wasn't really a need as most of them knew her, but protocol demanded she introduce herself. 'Hi, some of you already know me, I'm Detective Sergeant Jenna Morgan and this is Detective Constable Mason Ellis. I assume you all know PC Ted Walker.' At the general murmur of assent, Jenna continued. 'Did anyone else hear what the woman shouted before she screamed?' She kept her voice flat, even, despite the flutter in her stomach.

Mason glanced over from where he'd taken up position. He raised his eyebrows, so she jerked her head in a 'come over' motion. His stride was long-legged and easy. His whole demeanour composed. She could always rely on him. Laid-back in any situation, he was almost comatose.

'I'm not sure, but it was screeched. Quite desperate.' A male voice grabbed her attention.

Mason's head swivelled in Henry's direction, then back to Jenna, a question furrowed his brow as Henry spoke again.

'Your sister's car's parked over there. But we haven't seen her tonight. Could it be her over there?'

Jenna blew out a long breath as her heart spiked. She hadn't noticed her sister's car, as they'd entered at the top end of the car park and walked through the main entrance into the park. Fliss would have parked her little white Peugeot, with its Dalmatian paw-print stickers strategically running along the bonnet, over the roof and sliding off the boot, at the lower end of the car park and entered through the river pathway.

Henry moved closer as the crowd parted to let him through. A figure of authority, he still commanded a certain effortless respect.

Holding onto her composure despite the lick of dread taking a stranglehold, Jenna took a couple of steps to meet him halfway. 'Hey, Henry, what you got?'

His tan and white Spaniel nuzzled its cold nose into her palm and, with an automatic move, Jenna ran her hand over the top of the dog's head to fondle his silky ears while the other two dogs sidled in to nudge at her knees.

Henry kept his voice low, below the general hubbub of the crowd. 'I'm sorry DS Morgan, I don't want to add to the drama, but that was no kids fooling around. Someone over there's hurt and the sooner the dog handler gets on it, the better.'

Jenna raised the Airwaves radio to her lips. 'Control, can you confirm if the dog handler has arrived at Ironbridge car park?'

'Affirmative, Sarg. It's Sergeant Bennett.'

Relief coaxed a smile from her as she turned to reassure Henry.

'The dog handler's over there.'

'Chris Bennett. Good man. I would have gone over myself, but you know what it's like.' He ducked his head and scanned the crowd. 'You may have ended up with a self-elected posse trampling all over there and that wouldn't do. I hope it's not your sister. I didn't catch the name that was shouted clearly enough, but Dina sounds pretty convinced.'

A spear of dread knifed through her stomach and turned her knees to water. 'Mason.' She was used to good, hard evidence and there was absolutely no evidence other than a slightly hysterical woman who believed she'd heard Domino's name. And Henry's cool conviction. The small nugget of doubt rolled through Jenna until it became a great boulder of certainty. 'Could it be Fliss?' she hissed in Mason's ear as he leaned in to catch her words. Her stomach quavered, sick nausea pulsing as her heart knew, knew without a doubt that her sister was in trouble. She was always in trouble. It had to be bloody Fliss, didn't it?

Concern wreathed his face as Mason drew her away from the group of people, dark gaze intense and piercing.

'Have you tried her mobile?'

She shook her head, disgusted that she'd not thought to do it immediately.

Jenna fumbled as she dragged her phone from her pocket, her icy fingers stiff. She punched in the quick dial for Fliss and waited. 'It's gone straight to answerphone.'

That knowledge pooled in her stomach, churning acid thick and oily until it clenched in painful contractions.

Mason's voice of reason cut through her worry. 'Okay. She may be out of range here, it's not always a good signal.'

She gave him a jerky nod, then tried again. Calm, she needed to keep calm, but deep instinct ruled and the sick conviction her sister was in trouble refused to be pushed away.

As Fliss's phone flicked straight to voicemail again, Jenna glanced up and caught the light of concern in Henry's gaze. She gave a swift nod and shot him a tight smile. 'It's okay, we're going over to meet the dog handler now.'

With a quick nod, the man shoved his hands deep into his pockets as his dogs shuffled closer to lean against his legs. 'There's a lot of ground to cover, and most of the light's gone.'

Mason scowled up at the darkening sky.

It would be even darker over the river in amongst the thick covering of trees. Jenna squeezed his arm. 'He's right, we need to get going. Thank you, Henry.' She raised her voice to speak to the rest of the crowd. 'We'll leave you with PC Walker. If you have anything more to add, please make sure you speak with him. He'll take names, addresses, phone numbers.' She glanced at PC Walker and he gave her a brief, calm incline of his head.

Jenna swivelled on her heel, scrunched her shoulders up to her ears and gave her hands a brisk rub against one another as she strode off through Dale End car park to the far end, where her sister's car was slewed into a parking space.

Mason peered in the windows. 'Looks like she was in a hurry.'

'Mmm.' Jenna tried the driver's door, but it was locked. 'Fliss is always in a hurry. I wouldn't expect her to park any differently.' And as a thought curled through her mind, she spat it out. 'I pissed her off earlier.' She chewed her lip as guilt wriggled its way through. 'I texted her. Told her to take her bloody dog out.'

Mason had worked with her long enough to know not to join in the condemnation of her sister. Fiercely protective of her, Jenna was allowed to criticise, but God help anyone else who did. 'Uh-huh.'

She stamped away from the car and headed back to their unmarked, black police issue vehicle. 'He stole my bloody bacon sandwich when I called home at lunchtime. I didn't even have time to make another one.'

'I see.'

'No, you don't see. I had to rush back for that stupid meeting. I never had time to walk him and he'll eat my kitchen again if he's not entertained.' She raised her hand to tug at her hair as she reached the car and glared at him over the roof. 'It's not enough. He doesn't have enough exercise. He's lucky if between us he gets two hours a day. He needs more. He needs three or four hours. Dammit, I was meant to walk him, but I knew she had an early finish today.'

Mason raised his eyebrow as he depressed the key fob and the door locks clunked open. "Okay."

Jenna slipped into the passenger seat and covered her face with her hands as her mind ran wild. It was her fault, she'd sent Fliss and Domino out and now something dreadful had happened to him. He'd hurt himself. Broken his leg or something or slid into the river.

When she raised her head, Mason's stare drilled into her, his face pale as the interior light cast a white glow over them. The panic inside her communicated with him.

He hit the start button and the engine fired to life as Jenna raised the radio to her mouth. 'Juliette Alpha 76. On our way to Benthall Edge Wood now. Inform Dog Handler we'll meet him.' Her fingers trembled so she could barely depress the talk button while Mason stabbed his finger on the blues and two-tone buttons in the centre console and whipped the car right out of Dale End car park, straight up the hill through the almost deserted town.

'Control. Acknowledged.'

As they passed the Ironbridge on their right, Jenna squinted into the distance. Her heart sank with little hope of seeing her sister and the handsome Domino trotting by her side over the pedestrian-only bridge.

Mason swept the car over the mini-roundabout and raced along the riverside as Jenna tapped her foot on the floorboards, wishing she was the one in control of the car. Almost a mile to the suspension bridge and then they needed to backtrack along the opposite side to reach the Railway Inn car park at the furthest side of the Ironbridge.

'Shit.'

Glancing sideways at her, Mason kicked down a little harder on the accelerator, took the bends faster than he should. Her shoulder rammed into the door as the car raced over the small suspension bridge and dodged around a sharp right-hand bend.

'She'll be fine. She probably knocked the damned stupid dog into the water.' But Mason's voice vibrated with concern.

Icicles rushed through her veins. Every step of her life was marred by a 'Fliss'. Her family had referred to incidents as 'doing a Fliss'. Why in hell's name did it have to be her sister again? She could be at home, wrapped in a fluffy dressing gown with a nice glass of New Zealand Pinot Noir in her hand, heating on and Domino lounging next to her on the sofa. But, no. It was Fliss. Fliss with her innocent green eyes and mass of curly honey blonde hair. Who would ever think she was a disaster zone?

'Almost there.' Mason pulled her out of her reverie.

'Shit.' She repeated as though there was no other word in her vocabulary. Her stomach clenched until she wanted to curl into a ball.

Jenna's instinct howled that Fliss was in trouble. She'd never been wrong before. Her sister. Prize candidate for getting into trouble. If anyone could find it, Fliss could.

She punched Fliss's number into her phone again and snapped it off as it went straight to answerphone.

Car screaming into the parking lot, Mason slammed on the brakes and sent it into a sideways skid, but Jenna whipped off her seat belt and leapt out of the car as it came to a halt, kicking up stones. Her terror escalated the more she contemplated the situation, adding wings to her feet as she raced, her legs eating up the short distance between the car park and the start of the woodland walk.

A quick shaft of relief slowed her pace as she spotted the dog handler already on the main thoroughfare. Sergeant Chris Bennett. Reliable. Experienced. Cool-headed. Exactly what she needed.

As he approached with Blue, his large Belgian Malinois police dog, Chris spoke into Airwaves. 'I don't quite know what we're looking for...'

'My sister,' Jenna interrupted.

'You don't know for sure, Jenna.' Mason's agitated tones interjected, but he was rattled too, every muscle in him vibrated with tension. She'd caused it with her uncharacteristic panic. 'It could be anyone.' She knew he didn't believe it. Maybe he wanted to defuse the situation, calm her down.

'I know.' She made a conciliatory effort, but she didn't agree.

Turning to the dog handler, she placed her hand on his arm. The dog growled low in his throat. Bloody thing had let her scratch his belly two days before. He was too well trained to bite unless he was given the command, but the mere sound of it had Jenna retracting her hand with studied care.

'Chris, I know it's my sister. She's in trouble. I feel it here.' Patting her own chest, she stared at each of the men. 'The twilight walkers said they heard Fliss's voice screaming Domino's name. Please.' God, if she was wrong, she'd be in the shit for wasting police time and resources. But she'd never been wrong about Fliss; every damned time that sister of hers was in a scrape, Jenna had known. Gut instinct told her now.

'Okay.' Chris touched the dog's head and Blue sat. Chris knew Domino, had helped with his training when Fliss first got him. He'd a soft spot for both dog and owner. 'What do you need, boss?'

Jenna took in a long pull of air. 'Right! Whether it's my sister or not, someone is along here, possibly injured, so the question is, should we deploy Air Unit One?'

She glanced between the two men. Chris kept his gaze firmly on her face while Mason sucked air in through his teeth.

The decision was hers.

'Right! Risk assessment. Is life at risk?'

Both officers inclined their heads.

Mason murmured, 'Possibly.'

Her heart kicked up a notch, but she held back the panic.

'Is the area accessible?' She counted the questions off on her fingers.

'No.' Mason glanced along the deserted woodland track. 'Not easily.'

'It's getting dark. The weather's setting in.' Chris tossed in.

'Yep.' Again, Mason agreed.

'What other resources do we have?' She looked to the others for their suggestions.

'Bugger all, unless you count Malinsgate. Twenty minutes away before they even start to look.' With a snort, Mason shook his head. 'They have to round up the resources first. They could be deployed anywhere, and how many will we get, how many do we need?'

That answered several of her questions.

'Is the air unit going to take longer than getting more resources here?'

Mason's flat-eyed gaze met hers. 'No, boss. Do it.'

She hauled in a long breath. 'Let's see how long they'll take from Halfpenny Green.'

'Ten minutes – fifteen tops if they're not deployed elsewhere.'

Decision made, she gave him a nod.

'Call it in, Mason.'

Aware of the dark blanket settling in around them as Mason spoke into Airwaves, Jenna spared the car a last glance before she set off, regretting the stupidity of not bringing a coat.

The radio crackled to life. 'Juliette Alpha 76 from Control.'

Her gaze met Mason's as he spoke into the Airwaves terminal. 'Go ahead, Control.'

'Air One dispatched. ETA seventeen minutes. Over.'

'Acknowledged. Out.'

'Seventeen minutes. A lot can happen in seventeen minutes. We can find her in seventeen minutes.' Chris regarded them each in turn and then twisted around to unstrap his dragon light from around his shoulder and flick the switch. A wide arc pushed back the darkness, illuminating everything in stark white light. 'I'm guessing you two don't have a torch between you?' Chris shot Jenna a dark look, her smart mid-grey suit and two-inch-heel boots earning her a raised eyebrow.

Jenna shrugged. 'Who'd have thought I wouldn't be confined to my desk all day? I didn't expect to be called out to the back of beyond.'

Clucking his tongue, he gave Mason the same perusal. Dark charcoal suit, white open-neck shirt, black shoes bulled to a high shine. You could take the uniform off the man, but you couldn't take away the training. Chris shook his head and Jenna could have sworn he bit his cheek to stop himself snapping out a comment about their apparel. Instead, he scratched the top of his dog's head, earning a wag of the tail. 'If your sister's out there, we're going to find her. Aren't we, Blue?' Leaning down, he released the dog.

Short, square and muscular, when Chris started to stride out, despite being long-legged, both Jenna and Mason were hard-pushed to keep up.

'Stay close. We don't want Blue biting either of you in the arse if we lose you in the dark.'

With a rude snort, Mason tucked his hands into his jacket pockets and hunched his shoulders against the cold. They all knew Blue was far too well trained to bite the wrong person and nowhere near as vicious as Chris would have liked him to be. A sheep in wolves' clothing, the dog was great at tracking, but attack was his weaker point.

Boots already sliding in the thick, sticky mud, Jenna huddled her arms around herself to keep out the chill wind as it bit its way through her jacket and T-shirt. She wished she'd put an overcoat in the car, but she thought she was just going to be on a paper chase. Damned if her mother wouldn't have told her to put a coat on the back seat, just in case. Jenna blinked away the sharp prick of tears. What would her mother think, if she was alive today? She'd scalp her for not taking better care of her little sister.

Jenna shook off the self-pity, irritated she'd even let it sneak through when she needed to remain focused. It had only been three months since their mother had died, and a sharp pain lanced through her every so often just to remind her she was human, and sorrow didn't always like to be ignored.

She scanned the area, following the wide crescent of the dragon light while Chris swung it back and forth to push back the black curtain which had dropped with a suddenness that took her by surprise. When had the dark nights drawn in? Only yesterday they were drinking wine in the mellow warmth and sitting out on the patio until the sun went down.

Jenna tucked an errant lock of her short, dark hair behind her ear for the third time and sighed as the mean wind whipped it back out again. She hunched her shoulders against the cold and fell in step beside Mason.

The main walkway was flat and straight, well maintained but for the thick, black mud the deluge of rain had churned up. The three of them strode through the tunnel under the railway bridge, mud sucking at their feet, making Jenna regret the pride she'd felt as she'd slipped her new boots on earlier, the small heel perfect for office work. Not so brilliant in the thick sludge.

She took a few trotting steps to catch up with the dog handler and her feet skidded, the long slide almost took her into the back of him as Chris paused to train his beam of light along the first winding pathway off to the right. It curled around behind them and over the railway bridge. Straight up the Gorge.

Jenna peered beyond into the dark. 'She wouldn't go up there. Not at this time of night. I would have thought she'd keep to the main drag, or possibly up the narrower path running parallel, depending on what time she arrived. Fliss likes to go up there to get a glimpse of the deer. She's really sure-footed normally, I don't think it would faze her, going along that path, she knows it so well. Definitely not that way though, it's too steep, too dark, and it's not the best of walks.' Shaking her head, Jenna continued straight on, determined, somewhere along the trail, her sister would be sitting down in a pile of leaves, crying over a turned ankle. If she was, Jenna would slap her stupid for making her heart stop. If she had the opportunity.

She stared through the white swathes of light as her stomach churned. Surely, if that was the case, Domino would charge out of the undergrowth at them. They'd hear something, movement of some kind, but complete silence reigned. The darkness had even silenced the birds.

'What the hell's happened?' Her low mutter went ignored by the other two.

Had Fliss lost her footing and slipped down the hill? There were only a few places on the walk someone could do that. Normally, the path was a safe one. Unless the stupid, dotty dog of hers had taken a leap of faith over the side of the old railway bridge wall further along and gone straight down the sharp bank. The bank that slid in a steep slope all the way to the water. Jenna had heard about a dog a few weeks earlier that had gone off the edge in a flying leap. The people on the opposite bank said they could hear the echo of the dog's legs snapping as it hit the ground by the river. The river had been low then; it had risen since with the amount of rain they'd had recently and was much higher. The flood defences were ready to be slid into place any time soon. If Domino had slipped, he would have gone straight in. No noise.

'You know, if Domino has leapt over the edge, Fliss is going to be down there, ferreting away, trying to find him.' Jenna glanced up at Mason. 'If she couldn't get a signal on her phone to call for help, she'd get on with his rescue herself. It wouldn't occur to her to run into Ironbridge to summon help. She'd put her own life at risk for him.' Jenna rubbed her fingers over numb lips because she understood. She'd do the same for him. The dog was special, he filled a place in her heart even though she bitched about him. 'She'd leap into the swirling waters.' Jenna's stomach gave a sick lurch.

The reason Fliss had left her ex was because he was so jealous of her relationship with Domino he'd tried to persuade her to get rid of him.

Jenna snorted.

Stupid move. It was one of the things that had made Fliss sit up and take notice of the way he'd been controlling her for the last couple of years while she'd been at university. The man had been a complete dick. His objection to Fliss visiting their mum in the hospital had been the final nail in the coffin of their relationship, so to speak.

Attention focused on the span of light, Jenna narrowed her eyes, searching for movement in the undergrowth, her ears straining for any sound, while her thoughts rambled around in her head.

Once Fliss had realised what was happening, she had dropped him like a hot potato. Served him right. Not that he believed it. He thought Jenna had something to do with it. They'd never liked each other and since Fliss had left him, he'd ranted frequently about Jenna, blaming her for the break-up. One moment he shouted down the phone, threatening to cut her out of his life for good; the next he sent flowers in an attempt to wheedle his way back into Fliss's life. Jenna was pretty certain Fliss had remained unswayed by his constant badgering. At least Jenna hoped she had. She wasn't so sure Fliss hadn't caved and met up with him a couple of times. Life had been a bitch since their mum had died. Perhaps she needed someone other than her own sister to lean on.

It wasn't fair. One day their mum was perfectly okay, laughing with them about the damned stupid dog, cheek to cheek with him as she snuggled him in. She'd loved him. Treated him like a baby. The next day, she'd collapsed with a blinding headache and double vision. The doctors said it wouldn't have made any difference whether she was in the hospital or not, the second stroke three days later was the one that killed her.

Dead. Her mum was dead and all she had left was Fliss.

The unexpected sting of tears hit the back of Jenna's eyes.

Her breath whipped out of her lungs and it took every morsel of her willpower to keep her knees from buckling under her.

Jenna had been devastated, still was. Every day was an effort to get through without the thought of her mum being there. Her heart had literally been broken, the tight squeeze on her chest only relieved when her mind was occupied with work. Work held her up, powered her on. Only in the quiet moments, the solitude of taking a bath, did she let the tears roll down her face.

Fliss had reacted differently. She'd left the man she'd claimed to love to distraction and moved in with Jenna. Nightmares had dogged her every night. Fear of the dark, of being alone, terrorised her, a re-emergence of her childhood phobias, and the only comfort she'd found was in the children she taught each day, Domino and Jenna. They'd always been close, but the death of their mum had pulled them in closer.

Fliss could still bug the hell out of her, but underneath it all, Jenna adored her. Her and her damned spotted dog, even if he had destroyed her kitchen. She'd forgive him everything, if only they found them both fit and well.

Jenna puffed out a breath and rubbed at her upper arms in an attempt to stave off the cold and numbness threatening to overwhelm her. There was no point dwelling on Fliss's problems. She just had to find her. Where the hell could she be?

As they passed the lime kiln and pathway up the hill to the left, Jenna shook her head.

'I think she would have stayed on the main drag. It's too dark up there.'

Chris stared up at the narrow path disappearing into the night. 'It wouldn't have been when the incident happened necessarily.' He ran his tongue across his teeth, making a sucking sound, then glanced down at the dog snuffling at his feet. 'Okay.' Decision made, he pointed back at the main path. 'It's the most likely place, so we'll start here. We can always move upwards if we don't have any joy.'

Jenna moved to the right to lean her hands against the exposed bridge wall, where, in the dimming light, it was still possible to look all the way down to the river. In full daylight, particularly in summer, you could stand at that point and see clearly the far side of the riverbank with Dale End Park. Jenna could almost hear the quiet murmur of voices from the twilight walkers as they gave their accounts to PC Walker. The acoustics of the valley lent themselves to channelling even the softest of sounds upwards.

Just above waist-height, the old bridge wall fell away on the other side, straight down the hill to the river. This was the place they'd heard her sister cry out. Directly opposite.

Jenna leaned over the wall and peered into the shadowed vegetation below. 'Chris, try here.'

The wide strip of light panned across the steep embankment, while Blue hitched his front paws onto the wall next to her, stretching up to look over the side while he leaned against Jenna and allowed her to curl her icy fingers into his thick pelt.

'Fliss?' she called, half expecting her sister to answer from the steep embankment below. Hoping. Dreading.

Silence. Not even a rustle of movement.

'I don't want to send Blue down there unless I have to, Jenna,' Chris murmured. 'It's straight into the river.'

'No, don't.' The prospect of her sister sliding down there filled her with dread and she wasn't yet ready to make the call on whether they should pull in the help to scan the river. She tried to tamp down on the dramatic, but the sick coil in her stomach sent a shiver through her. She dug her fingers deep into the comfort of Blue's coat, his heat curling around to warm her hands.

'Fliss!' Mason's voice boomed out into the night, and as Jenna jumped, she could only be grateful for the dark that disguised her fear.

The sound echoed around the Gorge. As most of Ironbridge would have heard it, Jenna sighed. The last thing she needed now was half the residents coming out to help. She needed to listen.

A heavy silence hung over them once more for several moments before Chris spoke. 'I can hear Air One.'

Jenna tilted her head and picked up the steady thwacking of the rotors in the distance, their approach rapid.

The radio hissed to life.

'Juliette Alpha 76 from Control. Air One, ETA one minute. Over.'

'Juliette Alpha 76, acknowledged. Over.'

'They need to shine their light down here.' Chris waved his hand across the entire hillside below them.

'They'd be better off using the thermal imaging. Let me tell them what we're looking for and where to start first.' Mason moved away from them both to talk to Air One.

With a hefty snort, Blue slumped down off the wall to stand next to Chris. Jenna instantly missed his warmth and wished he'd lean against her leg as he did to Chris. There wasn't much the dog could do unless they sent him off the edge of the cliff. If they wanted the helicopter to pick up thermal images, he needed to stay where he was while they calibrated everyone's positions, so they could detect any additional body heat. With a glum look up at the sky, Jenna considered they wouldn't even pick up her body heat. She was already a block of ice. She tucked her hands under her armpits and prayed hypothermia didn't set in before she found her sister.

As Mason spoke to Air One, a wide illumination moved over them, making the Gorge light up brighter than day. The downdraught from the helicopter thrashed through the trees to whip off the remaining leaves and fling them at them.

Jenna swiped at her face, shoving back her thick mop of hair whipping about her head. 'I can't hear anything now. If she's down there and calls out, we won't hear her. It's too noisy,' Jenna yelled above the sound of the rotors.

Chris dipped his head, his rugged features close to hers. 'If she's down there and okay, she would have already answered, Jenna. She needs us to find her, and the quickest way is thermal imaging.'

He was right of course.

Jenna blew out a gentle sigh. She was the senior officer at the scene, she needed to clear her mind and think logically. If Blue had heard or scented anything, he would have been off after it. He knew his job, but the hillside had been silent and eerie before the arrival of the helicopter, not even the sounds of disturbed animals.

She raked the hair back from her face and turned into the wind, so it could no longer thrash around her head.

'Juliette Alpha 76. Our thermal imager has picked up a form near you. Which way are you facing?'

Mason snapped the Airwaves to life. 'Air One, we're looking north towards the river.'

'Juliette Alpha 76, turn 180 degrees and walk eighteen feet forward.'

Mason turned first, but Jenna scurried to follow, the unsteady flutter of her pulse filling her ears to almost block out the sound of Air One. *Please, please let it be Fliss, let her be okay*, she found herself praying over and over as they headed to the opposite side of the track.

They peered up the hillside, squinting in the bright light of the helicopter. With Mason's broad shoulders blocking her view, Jenna moved another couple of paces along, desperate to see her sister. She didn't even know what she was looking for, what Fliss would be wearing. Would she have been sensible enough to have put on her waterproof, her jaunty red hat that matched Domino's lead? Fliss was far more practical than Jenna, but which coat would she have chosen?

'C'mon Fliss. Where the hell are you?'

'Juliette Alpha 76, take eight paces to your right.'

Following directions, Jenna leaned forward as Blue dashed in circles around them; from his obvious interest, he'd picked up a scent and, at the same time, inspired hope.

Jenna's heart stumbled. Stood right at the edge of the path, she scanned the lit-up area around her, unable to see anything that might give a hint of her sister's whereabouts.

'Below you, Juliette Alpha 76. Over.'

She could see nothing as they squatted to peer into the gulley disappearing beneath the line of the old Severn Valley Railway they stood on. The wide fingers of the spotlight unable to wriggle their way into the shadows.

'Go on, lad.' Chris sent the dog down first, then went over the edge, dragon light in hand.

Jenna followed, gingerly sliding on the wet leaves and fallen branches, muttering to herself as the heel of her boot gave a precarious wobble. She was going to kill Fliss for this. She'd make her buy her a new pair of boots when she got hold of her. 'If I break my ankle down here, I am so going to kick your butt, Felicity Morgan.'

Blue let out a series of short, sharp barks, filling Jenna with anticipation as she approached.

Let her be all right, please let her be okay.

There'd been no sound, she could be unconscious.

Whatever she was, just let her be safe.

5

FRIDAY 26 OCTOBER, 18:10 HRS

'Here!' Chris's voice boomed out even above the sound of the helicopter.

Jenna leaned on the dog handler's shoulder to peer into the vegetation while her heart pounded in her chest in rhythm with the whirring rotors. It took her a moment before her brain acknowledged what she saw. Covered in leaves and half buried beneath the brick tunnel, Domino's limp body lay motionless, the white of his fur barely discernible beneath the thick layer of mud and wash of crimson blood.

Dread consumed her as Jenna shook her head, horror warring with disbelief. So much blood. Swathes of it over Domino's coat, glossy in the brightness of the light.

'Oh, God.' She whispered as her stomach churned.

'Jesus Christ.' Shaking his head, Mason pulled out his radio. 'Juliette Alpha 76 to Control. We have a dog's body. Air One do you have any further heat ID down here?'

'Negative, Juliette Alpha. Only one heat source visible. We'll keep looking.' The helicopter moved off, the wide fan of its white light still illuminating the area, but Chris's dragon light was more effective where they crouched under the shadow of the bridge.

Chris straightened and called Blue from where the dog was sniffing at

Domino while Jenna slipped to her knees onto the thick carpet of mouldy leaves, oblivious of the wet soaking through her trousers.

'Oh my God, you poor baby. Poor Domino.' She reached out a tentative hand, stroked the leaves from Domino's still warm body and uncovered his face. She used the back of one muddy hand to swipe at the tears coursing down her cheeks. Poor Domino. Her heart clenched. He drove her crazy, but this was the last thing she'd have ever wanted to happen to him. She loved him to bits.

Chris held the light steady as Jenna ran her fingers over Domino, his body broken and twisted.

Surely, if her sister wasn't there, she must have gone for help. Why hadn't she used her phone to call her? Like a flash, Jenna remembered the static on her answerphone earlier when she'd picked up her messages.

'Mason. She phoned me, earlier. Fliss called me. She wanted my help and I wasn't there for her. Where the hell is she?'

Silent beside her, Mason scrubbed his hands over his face and shook his head.

She sank down and rested her cheek against Domino's soft, dirty skin. Fliss must have gone for help. She wasn't there. Air Unit One said there was only one heat source. Jenna curled her fingers through Domino's wet fur. Why would she have left him like this? She would have tried to lift him, move him onto the main track so they could recover his body with ease.

Unless she was hurt too.

Heart clenching, Jenna peered up into the broken darkness of the hillside above them, flashes of bright light from Air One illuminating the shadows and then moving on to plunge them into darkness again.

Jenna knew the terrain almost as well as Fliss did. Domino had probably taken them both off the side of the narrow path above, they could have slithered together, but Air One still hadn't found a trace of another heat source. Even if Fliss wasn't all right, if she was there, she'd still be pulsing off heat for some time.

Like the heat Domino was generating now, enough to warm Jenna's fingers as she lifted the heavy weight of him onto her lap, no longer caring whether tears streaked down her face as she laid her head against his limp body. 'I'm sorry, boy, sorry I wasn't there.'

The sturdy heartbeat of a living dog throbbed beneath her cheek. She reared back, whipping around to yell up at Mason.

'Call an emergency vet. Now! He's alive. Domino's alive.'

* * *

As he scooped Domino into his arms, Mason's suit jacket stretched taut across his shoulders. Strain lines slashed across his face as he bodily heaved the dog out of the trench as gently as the weight and size of a thirty-eight kilogram deadweight of dog allowed. As he carried him up the slope, slipping and sliding all the way to the veterinary van that had been brought as far along the walkway as possible, Jenna trotted alongside him, sharing in each grunt and groan Mason made for every step he took.

There was no other way to do it. Domino was a big boy. Impossible for the slight vet to carry out of there. The location of his body had hindered any equipment being brought in to help either. Vets weren't known to carry stretchers in their vehicles and speed was essential. They needed to get the dog tended to as soon as possible.

Mason's short puffs of breath became louder as he approached the van and Jenna wondered if her partner's legs would hold up. At the end of his strength, he managed to place Domino with such tenderness in the rear of the vet's van that tears pricked the back of Jenna's eyes and she could only hope the stifled sob that escaped her wasn't heard by anyone else. Mason curled his body over Domino's and smoothed the grime and blood from the dog's head, smearing it down Domino's neck with his filth-slicked hands.

Jenna crawled inside the van and sank to her knees beside Domino, her head close to Mason's. Her heart squeezed hard in her chest while she pressed her face into the dog's neck and sobbed for him, for Fliss, for herself, knowing Mason would say nothing, would never judge.

Stoic, Mason withdrew, leaving Jenna to cradle Domino while Sarah, the vet, got a line in. As she checked Domino's vitals, Sarah glanced up at them and nodded. 'He has a pretty strong heartbeat, all things considered.'

In the brightness of several more dragon lights brought in by the newly arrived back-up, bright crimson stood in stark contrast against Domino's white fur. Horrified, Jenna's searching gaze skimmed over the whole of him.

His fine coat was no protection against the trauma he'd been subjected to. His skin had unzipped from shoulder to hip.

Sarah gave a gentle prod. 'He's been caught on a protruding rock or branch.'

Jenna exchanged a look with Mason, knowing Fliss's situation was uppermost in his mind too. What if she'd slithered and slipped down too? What if she'd sustained injuries as life-threatening? Assumptions didn't help. They needed stone-cold sober evidence. Evidence she'd rather not find if she was being truthful. She'd rather just find Fliss alive and well.

Her attention on Domino, Sarah didn't bother to glance up. 'I think he's broken his jaw.' She took hold of his face with both hands to perform a gentle manipulation. 'Yeah. Broken. Poor soul.' She peered out of the van up at the now drenching rain. 'I'd better get him out of here.'

Jenna nodded as she stepped back. 'I'll ring you. Later. It may be much later.' Relieved that she already knew the on-call vet, Jenna allowed Domino to be tended to, knowing he was in the best hands.

Sarah climbed out of the vehicle and touched a gentle hand to Jenna's cold arm. 'I hope you find your sister soon, Jenna. I'm sure you will. Fliss won't be far from Domino.'

Jenna nodded, unable to push any reassuring words past the lump in her throat. She tossed a glance over her shoulder. 'We need to get back.'

Sparing Domino a last swipe of her hand along his warm body, Jenna turned, retracing her steps along the path to join the others.

Shoulder to shoulder with Mason and Chris, Jenna peered into the depths of the old tunnel. Breath restricted, her chest burned.

Two additional dog handlers and their dogs stood by, waiting for instructions. Jenna skimmed her gaze over them and the newly arriving PCs ambling towards them along the track.

How stupid was she? Each one of them was appropriately dressed in padded vests and waterproofs while she and Mason were drenched to the bone through their fine suits only suitable for office work.

She raised her hand, about to scrub it across her forehead when she remembered the mud and the blood from Domino smeared across it and dropped it back down to her side.

Mason nudged her shoulder to grab her attention. 'I know they couldn't find another heat source, but we really need to do a fingertip search in there.' He did rub his hand through his soaking hair and then stared at it as though he couldn't believe what he'd done. 'Where the hell else can she be?'

Jenna's heart fluttered in her chest and she took in snatches of cold air. She needed to take control. 'Okay.' She glanced around at the circle of faces, all fresh from the station having just started their shift. 'Let's go.'

'One moment, DS Morgan.'

Jenna raised her head to look beyond the group. Through the murky light, a large man approached, his long stride measured and sedate. Relief washed over her as her inspector approached. 'DI Taylor, sir.'

He inclined his head and handed her a padded jacket, passing another one to Mason. 'You'll need these.'

'Thank you.'

'I've been appraised. Let's get on with it.'

Unquestioning, Jenna hauled the oversized jacket on over her damp clothing, grateful for the protection it could provide against the wet and the downward draught from the helicopter.

Mason shrugged into his jacket and stepped across the divide, back-tracking to where they'd discovered Domino, while Chris let the straining dog off the lead again to continue the search, shining his dragon torch into the pitch blackness so Jenna could step across.

Her heels slithered in the sticky mud, threatening to give out under the strain. Jenna puffed out a breath, making a promise she would never leave herself unprepared for such an eventuality again.

Arms wrapped around her waist to generate as much warmth as possible, she pushed forward, Chris's strong hand under her arm to support her.

As Mason slid further down the slippery slope, radio in hand, Blue let up three further short sharp yips and had Chris scrabbling in the under-growth to reach him.

Four feet further on and under the brick archway, Chris turned the dragon light to banish the darkness and, in the illumination, caught the empty eye sockets of a cold, dead woman staring straight back at them.

6

FRIDAY 26 OCTOBER, 22:15 HRS

'Felicity Sophia Morgan! What did your mother tell you?' The strident tones of Felicity's ten year old sister rang out. *'Never, ever, **ever**...'* Jenna wagged her index finger in Fliss's face, leaned in closer. *'... ever, put anything around your neck. You could very well have choked yourself, my dear.'* The supercilious tone of her four years older sister did nothing but soothe as Jenna loosened the death grip of their father's necktie from around Fliss's neck and let her breathe again.

She'd only thought to try it on, but when she tugged the thinner end, it just became tighter, tighter, tighter until little black dots flashed behind her eyelids and the spit dried in her mouth as the breath lodged in her chest, unable to escape.

Jenna ruffled the blonde curls on Fliss's head, then ran her hand down the side of her neck to the painful burn encircling it. With a gentle touch, she smoothed her thumb over the injured area, pure sympathy welling in her huge, clear green eyes before she lifted her hand and gave a sharp, shocking tap to the end of Fliss's nose.

'You should always take notice of what your mother tells you.'

Fliss struggled to peel open her gritty, thick eyelids. The skin on her neck throbbed, swollen and painful. The air she dragged into her lungs stuck around the thickness of her tongue and the blockage in her throat. The echo of her older sister's voice still ran through her sluggish mind.

'You should have died.'

She blinked, wallowing in confusion at the dark bitterness of the voice penetrating her consciousness. She fluttered open eyelids too heavy to comply.

'Why aren't you dead?'

Shock reverberated through her system as brown eyes filled with bitter hatred peered past thick glasses into Fliss's face.

Who the hell was he?

Wild brown and grey eyebrows drew down as the stranger frowned at her, fury flashing to send blazes of fear dashing to her heart.

She whimpered as the stiffness of her neck restrained her from looking around to check out her surroundings.

'I heard your neck break.'

She was sure he was wrong. Her neck was stiff, but it wasn't broken. She'd know if it was broken. Wouldn't she?

'It sounded like the crack of a dry stick. Like the one I belted your dog with.'

Her heart contracted with the memory. Domino! Grief zoned her out for a long moment.

His mouth pursed as he breathed out through his nose, making a faint whistling noise. 'You should be dead,' he insisted. 'Of course, it's my own fault, I should have hit you with the branch as well. It killed your dog.' He said it in a matter-of-fact, sing-song tone, sending terror rippling through her and, from his tight smile, he seemed to be well aware of the shaft of pain slicing through her heart. 'But I didn't want to hit you with a broken branch. It would have been so untidy. A broken neck would have been so neat, but it's not. It can't be broken.'

He slumped back in the wooden chair, making it creak in protest at his rude treatment. Disappointment wreathing his features.

'I was so sure.'

He folded his arms across his chest, his brow wrinkling in deep furrows as he continued to stare at her. There was nothing she wanted to say to him, nothing she could say, as fury burned deep in her chest and her throat closed even tighter to send a wave of panic shuddering through her lungs. He'd killed her dog. Her baby. Her Domino. He'd killed him. He was probably about to kill her.

'Now what am I to do with you?'

He shook his head, crouched over her. So close she could smell his mint-sweet breath, see the wispy curls of grey-coloured hair poking out of his nostrils.

'Of course, it's all your fault,' he insisted. 'If you hadn't seen my face. If you had only carried on looking the other way. But I knew you recognised me. I could sense your recognition through the trees.'

She frowned in confusion, shook her head in denial. No, no. It wasn't true. She hadn't even seen him in the hazy light. She hadn't even seen his shadow until it was too late.

'Now, now, it's no good you telling me you didn't. It won't wash with me, young lady. It would have been stupid of me to have left you to identify me.' He considered her, inspecting her neck, slowly panning the whole of the swollen area with his intense gaze. 'If only you hadn't found *her*. Sod's law of course. How did you manage to slide your way straight into *her*?'

His gaze clashed with hers and sent an icy chill down her spine. He heaved a deep sigh. 'Why aren't you dead?'

He twisted his head like an enquiring bird.

'Like my wife'

Ripples of shock ran through her, but there was nothing she could do to stop the black clouds blooming in her vision, popping in puffs of white, just to form again and engulf her as the heavy weight of her eyelids proved too much for her to keep open.

Oh dear God. He'd killed his wife, just as he was about to kill her.

She needed to tell someone where she was. She needed to let Jenna know. Tell her the man had killed Domino. Tell her he'd killed his wife.

Revulsion skittered over her flesh as storm clouds rolled in. She could do nothing to still the tender stroke of his hand over her forehead. The last sound she heard as she drifted was his voice, gentled now, soothing.

'It looks like you were sent to me. Like Mary was. Sent for me to look after. Take care of.'

His voice smoothed over her. 'To keep.'

* * *

He craned his neck, all the time studying the woman he'd just acquired. Seemed like a fair exchange for his poor, dead wife. Fate, it appeared, had been kind to him. He'd never done anything illegal in his life. Not until now. He couldn't count his wife, everything that had happened to her had been her own stupid fault. He was a law-abiding citizen.

The man gentled his fingers over the raised, red welts on the girl's neck.

'Silly cow.' He scraped away blonde hair thickly coated in mud to reveal a face already starting to show dark purple bruising.

She was a pretty woman, Detective Sergeant Morgan's sister. He couldn't quite place her name, but he remembered her, even if she pretended she didn't know who he was.

He broke into a smile as he smoothed the dirt away from her sleek, arched eyebrows, the left one with a large lump forming above. He pressed it and watched her face with studied interest. Not a flicker, not a flinch. She was too deep asleep to feel any pain. He'd seen to that.

Proud of himself, he slipped the empty needle into a sharps box and placed it on the small medical trolley he'd brought into the cellar.

He studied her face.

Felicity.

That was her name. Felicity Morgan. Unmarried as yet.

He might rename her Joan. Perhaps, in time.

His smile stretched even wider as he stroked her hair again. He'd obviously given her the right dose, possibly even a little too much, but she'd live if she was meant to live. After all, he'd broken her neck and she'd recovered. She'd not died.

7

'... Seven, eight, nine, ten. Coming, ready or not.' Jenna's bright voice invaded the quiet of the warm afternoon. Fliss smothered her laughter as she scrambled into the abandoned refrigerator. Mum had made Daddy haul it out of the house into the back yard for the council to send someone to dispose of the week before, but no one had taken it yet. Her mother had complained. She said she'd complained, but Fliss knew it would be with such gentleness, they'd ignore her. People often ignored her mother with her soft voice and her kind, lavender eyes.

The door gave a gentle sucking noise as it closed behind Fliss. Oppressive silence engulfed her, drawing every sound from the world into the void, making her ears pop. No longer able to hear the gentle hum of the bees, the quiet twitter of the birds, her thrilled laughter dried up while she crouched in the bottom of the container and waited.

Time meandered by and still her sister never came. The stench of dirt and spiders rose to fill her nostrils while in the blackness, her body heated. She swiped her arm across her damp forehead and waited. In the dense quiet. So very quiet. She waited until the air became so thick, she sucked it in through parched lips in small panicked sips, her upper lip beading with sweat.

In the black, she pushed against the door. Heart fluttering in her chest like a wild bird, Fliss pushed and pushed, but it wouldn't give. She fisted her hands against the walls of the refrigerator, hammered so someone would hear. Pain burst through her arms, and no one came, but still, she banged.

Jenna would hear. She had to.

Tears streaked Fliss's face, trickling down her scorched, burning cheeks. Blind panic filled her lungs and burst out in an ear-piercing scream reverberating around the walls of the hot, tight enclosure so only she could hear her cry for help.

As the door burst open, Fliss fell forward into the cool, fresh air and the open arms of her older sister.

She sobbed, hiccupping in great lungsful of air while her heart threatened to explode from her skinny chest. She burrowed her nose close into Jenna's soft warm neck, inhaling the familiar scent of safety, relief turning her legs to jelly and even though she wanted to pee herself, she pressed her thighs together and kept it in.

'What did your mother tell you?' In a sly mimic of their mother's voice, Jenna placed one hand on her hip. 'Don't go near the old fridge, girls, it's dangerous.' She waggled her finger in Fliss's face, then smoothed away the tears from her cheeks. 'And what did you do, Felicity Sophia Morgan? You didn't take notice, did you?'

Jenna's cool fingers swiped the hair out of her vision, and she placed pecking kisses on the end of Fliss's nose as she clucked her tongue and smiled down at her, waiting for the gulping sobs to subside. She stroked her forehead and leaned closer. Her breath held a strange hint of sweet mintiness.

'You should always take notice of what your mother tells you.'

Fliss's eyes popped open as the systematic stroking continued. The dream burst in an explosion of bright white lights, which vaporised into the atmosphere to leave her weak, her mind sludging through thick cotton wool.

Confused, she gazed straight into myopic dark brown eyes hidden behind thick black-rimmed glasses, while she struggled to recall where she was.

She blinked the man into focus. His mouth stretched into a sickly-sweet smile which oozed sympathy, while dead eyes gazed at her with idle curiosity. As she opened her mouth to speak, he centred his intense stare on her lips, willing her to make a noise.

Nothing came out except a small expulsion of air. Not even a croak. Pain radiated through her entire body, setting her skin on fire.

The man leaned out of her vision for a moment. When he returned, he held a glass of water in his hand. A pink candy-cane straw bobbed out of it. With the tenderness of a lover, he positioned the straw between her lips and nodded encouragement.

'Drink, Felicity.'

She took a cautious sip. The cool slide of liquid relieved her burning throat, while she made a slow, thorough inspection of the man's features.

Did she know him?

She couldn't recall him.

She wanted to shake her head, rid herself of the thick clouds stopping her from thinking clearly. She didn't understand. He seemed to believe she should know him. He knew her name and yet she had no recollection of him. Her brain was listless and vague and the harder she attempted to iden- tify him, it seemed the more her head ached.

Closing her eyes, she stopped sipping.

'Just a little more.' His voice nudged.

His voice. There was something about his voice. A vague nasal whine to it. Something familiar, but she couldn't place it. The effort was all too much.

Her lethargic brain could no longer hold onto her thoughts and pain shoved thick black bubbles to wash away her vision. She heard the groan inside her own head but knew the sound had not escaped her heavily swollen throat.

'Felicity Sophia Morgan, what did your mother tell you?' Jenna grasped her hand a little tighter than she expected and Fliss reared up to look at her sister. Staring back down at her, Jenna smiled and as Fliss watched, the smile morphed from Jenna's natural straight-toothed grin to something sweet and sickly. Jenna's eyes, normally a beautiful clear green with a random scatter of dark hazel pigmented dots, became darker, almost black. Desperate, Fliss yanked her hand from her sister's grasp, fear skittering across her skin to make her flesh crawl. She drew in her breath to scream. Jenna squeezed harder and then stabbed her nail with studied viciousness into the back of Fliss's hand.

Jerking up, Fliss wrenched her hand away from the source of pain only to pull up hard against the restraints around her wrists. Confused, she stared down at the police issue handcuffs tethering her wrists to the thin metal frame of the camp bed she lay on. She turned her head, stared into the eyes of the man sitting on a chair next to her. Eyes reflecting the dead expression of a shark.

'That's better,' he soothed. 'You'll soon feel the benefit of the painkiller I administered.'

He smoothed his fingers across the back of her hand, smiled sweet and sickly to make her stomach lurch as nausea clawed its way up her throat.

'Did you know I was meant to be a doctor? My mother told me if I worked hard, that's what I'd be. And I worked so hard.' He nodded and gave the impression it wasn't Fliss he spoke to as his gaze centred on the wall behind her.

Fliss tried to concentrate. The information he gave her might prove useful if she escaped. When she escaped.

He blinked and moved his attention back to her. 'I tried so very hard, but they wouldn't let me. Even the paramedics didn't want me.' His mouth tightened. 'I think they were jealous because I had more experience. That I'd completed a year of doctors' training when I came to them.' His distant expression cleared, and he smiled again, baring crooked teeth. 'You're in such pain, my dear. We can't have that now, can we? It's my duty to take care of you.' He rubbed his thumb in a hypnotic circular motion against her skin, which only served to increase the sick feeling roiling in her stomach. 'I think it must be my lot in life to keep you.' He shook his head. With a rueful smile, he sat back in his chair and gave a vague wave of his hand over her body. 'A replacement for the loss I've suffered. Fate plays a funny part.'

He raised his hand to his own face. The dull rasp of his fingers rubbing against the whiskers on his chin drew her attention. Everything he did was methodical, repetitive, deliberate.

'She was very ungrateful, you know. My previous wife. And then she was gone. Fate certainly played a part there.'

Fliss closed her eyes and drifted up, up, away, his voice a thin, reedy sound. 'You were very heavy. I hadn't expected to have to toss you in the boot of my car. Mary was much smaller and lighter.' The bitter sigh he let out echoed around her mind. 'You've caused me so much inconvenience. I was there for Mary, not you. It's your fault I had to leave her behind. You gave me no choice. If we're lucky, nobody will have taken any notice of your attention-seeking and I'll be able to return tomorrow. I don't think anyone will find her. She was quite well hidden, if you didn't look too closely, and let's face it, who does?'

Fliss couldn't stop the flinch as he stroked his fingers along her cheek.

'When you're feeling stronger, we'll have to clean you up a little, but I think you'll be fine for now. After all, if you didn't die of a broken neck, then you're not going to succumb to some silly little infection, are you?'

She strained her neck to raise her head enough to peer down the length of her prone body while her mind drifted a mile above her. Her coat had been removed and she lay on her back. From what she could see, her upper body appeared to have been fairly well protected by her fleece-lined coat and long-sleeved T-shirt, but from her waist down, her jeans had been viciously ripped and lay in tatters around her limbs. The hot burn of scratches pulsated across her skin, but at least she knew the cause.

Memory flooded back. Beneath the thick layer of dried mud, Fliss could make out the congealed mass of blood where brambles and tree branches, stones and undergrowth had ripped into her as she had tumbled down the steep incline of the Ironbridge Gorge in the same direction as her dog. Domino.

She flopped her head back onto the thin pillow, all the time keeping her gaze steady on him. After all, she needed to know for sure.

'Domino.' She forced the dry rasp from her engorged throat.

The man's eyebrows shot up; his brow crinkled. 'Yes, well. Unfortunate, but we had to dispose of him, didn't we?' His voice gained the sing-song pattern he'd used before, more to soothe him, she decided, than herself. 'We couldn't risk getting bitten, now could we?'

Fliss gave a small jerk of her head to indicate he should come nearer. As he leaned in close, she opened her dry lips and ground out through clenched teeth. 'I'll never forgive you!'

8

The drizzle had started hours earlier. Exhaustion had set in not long after. Having already been on duty since six the previous morning, Jenna barely had the energy to drag her body up the empty, brightly lit staircase of Malinsgate Police Station. Her footsteps echoed in unison with Mason's. Her quick survey of him told her he didn't look any fresher. Not even his normally boyish humour could overcome the deep worry lines that appeared, bracketing his mouth and deepening around his eyes to give him a haunted look of such aged weariness, Jenna couldn't help but wonder how hard her sister's disappearance had affected him.

Chief Superintendent Gregg came to his feet as they entered the conference room and crossed straight over to Jenna, reaching out his hands to take hold of hers. A large man with a broad chest, he towered over Jenna. Approaching retirement, his years of experience sat comfortably on his shoulders. His steel-grey hair had been swept straight back from a high forehead. His bright hawk-like gaze drilled into hers.

'Jenna, I'm sorry. I'm sure this is a terrible shock for you. I'm informed your sister is missing.'

Leading her over to one of the small, uncomfortable, brown leather armchairs, Gregg guided her into it, taking the seat next to her without letting go of her hands.

A petite woman in uniform placed a cup of hot black coffee on the table in front of her. Jenna glanced from the coffee to the police officer and back to Gregg. She didn't recognise her. Raven black hair scraped back in a neat bun, chocolate eyes and smooth coffee toned skin. A newbie who looked no older than twelve. A lifetime ago since Jenna had been so young.

Jenna's lips moved. No sound came out and she shook her head. Pulling her fingers out of Gregg's gentle grasp, she raised her hand to her mouth, closed her eyes and allowed the intense feeling of helplessness to wash over her. Just for a moment.

The chair groaned as Gregg settled himself in it, and Jenna's eyes shot open to watch as his large body spilled over the top of it. Blinking back the tears, Jenna leaned over and picked up her coffee. She blew across the top of it and watched the ripples form and steam puff upwards.

'Report.' Gregg's strong tone, filled with command, resonated in the large conference room. She suspected he had a strong desire to keep her from falling apart so she could deliver her report and concentrate on the most important element: her sister's disappearance. Not her own feelings.

Jenna nodded abruptly. She needed normality. He gave it to her.

'We responded to a call at approximately 16:35 hours.'

She glanced up at Mason, who leaned against the wall by the door, for verification. At his nod, she took a sip of the hot, weak coffee and continued.

'Dog walkers in Dale End Park – the twilight walkers – called in the sound of a woman screaming on the south side of the Gorge. After liaising with PC Ted Walker, we met with the dog handler, sir, Sergeant Chris Bennett, with his dog, Blue. We called in Air One.'

'On what grounds?' Gregg's bright gaze pierced hers as the vertical furrow on his forehead deepened.

Fear, instinct. Neither of which were professional enough answers. Mason shuffled his feet while he paced across the room, coffee cup in hand, to loom over the back of her chair.

'We deployed them because of the information received. The woman's screams, combined with several other factors, such as my sister's car in the car park and a number of walkers saying they heard the name of Fliss's dog being called. Domino. The woman screamed Domino.' She clamped her lips together for a moment as the shake in her voice threatened to spill into sobs. 'We carried out an instant risk assessment and made a decision based on facts. Time of night, resources available, risk. It's all recorded, sir.'

Jenna flicked a worried glance at Mason.

Instinct. For her, it still boiled down to instinct.

Jenna waited for Gregg to call her on it, but instead, he dipped his head, the steel grey of his hair shimmered under the electric lights. 'I've already listened to the recording. I'm comfortable that you made the right decision under the circumstances.' He paused. 'Fliss. Your sister?'

Jenna nodded, every drop of saliva in her mouth had deserted her. While she met his eyes, she took another sip of coffee, dropping her gaze so she no longer had to meet his.

He drew in a breath through his nose. 'Continue.'

She wrapped her fingers around the coffee mug to disguise the shake in them, but not for one moment was she mistaken to think he'd missed it.

'We discovered a badly injured dog...' she stopped, the air stuttered at the back of her throat. 'Domino... and the body of a woman.'

'The dog is your sister's?' Gregg enquired.

'Yes, sir. Our... her Dalmatian.' A shudder rippled through her.

'The body is not your sister.' It was a statement, not a question.

'No.' Thank God. She clipped her cup onto the desk, placed her hand over her mouth and breathed deeply.

'Has the victim been identified?'

She met his gaze again. 'No, sir.'

'Was it the victim who screamed?'

'No.' She shook her head, Jenna hauled herself upright in the chair, only just noticing how damp her clothes were, how filthy her skin was. 'She'd be hard-pushed to. The body had been there for some time. SOCO are talking ballpark figure of twenty-four to thirty-six hours. Rigor mortis had started to relax, particularly in the face. Eyes missing. No evidence they'd been taken pre-death, but the probability is they were taken post-mortem.' Not usually given to squeamishness, she had to swallow past the bile in her throat. 'By animals.' She grimaced at the thought of the woman's eyes being plucked out. The woman who could have been her own sister.

Jenna rolled her shoulders. The damp had soaked through her clothes to make her skin itch. 'The victim was female. Short. A little underweight. Estimated age range at this point, around thirty-five. More information when the post-mortem has been carried out.'

Jenna huffed out as she glanced up at Mason, who'd moved to lean against the meeting table, cradling his coffee, she assumed, to pull in as much heat as possible. He looked like shit. His smart suit, since he'd removed the squad jacket, soaked through, muck and blood covering his entire upper body. Smudges of dried mud smeared up his face and into his hair. If it had been any other case but this, she'd have taken the piss at his loss of composure, but she had everything to be grateful to him for.

Guilt riddled her, but she had a job to do. She had to find her sister. She bowed her head and stared at the blank screen of her iPhone. There was no use pestering the vet, she'd said she'd have Domino in surgery for some time. Still, the need to phone rose as Jenna's breath quickened. If only Domino survived, it would mean Fliss still had a chance. They were connected.

She pulled herself back to the present and realised Gregg waited with patience for her to continue. Picking up her cup, she took another gulp of sweetened, black liquid, and relieved her dry throat before she continued.

'Domino was removed by the vet. SOCO arrived, cordoned off the area. Two lines, an inner, around the victim's body and where Domino was. They covered the area in a tent to stop the rain from washing away any forensics. The outer cordon is keyhole-shaped. There's evidence both the dog and possibly my sister slid down from the upper pathway. There seem to be several slide marks. SOCO followed them up the hillside to a point almost directly above the body. They must have gone straight down. Through everything. Rocks, branches, brambles. We have no idea what would have caused them both to take the dive.'

She closed her eyes, pictured Domino's split skin and felt her stomach pitch. She'd caught sight of a bone protruding through the flesh and sinew. His body had hundreds of other smaller lacerations. Crimson daubed his beautiful white coat in crude abandon, highlighted by the overpowering white lights hastily erected by the team.

It was difficult not to think her sister had suffered the same fate. Jenna shook her head, covered her mouth with her fingers and rubbed her numb lips. Where the hell was she? Where was Fliss? Why hadn't she been at the bottom of the incline alongside Domino and the dead woman?

Jenna's stomach clenched. *Where are you, Fliss?*

The firm squeeze of Mason's hand on her shoulder helped her to centre herself and continue. 'The cordon goes twelve feet above the upper path and either side of the slip marks at present. They can't do an awful lot more until daylight in looking for further evidence. We're due to meet there at 07.00 hours. We left them to remove the victim's body. They'll be some time, forensics have to do their thing.'

Nodding, Gregg narrowed his eyes and peered closely at Jenna. 'And your sister?'

Placing her cup on the table, Jenna gave her cold, damp thighs a vigorous rub, trying to get the circulation going. Lifting her hands, she gave a helpless shrug. 'We don't know, sir. We didn't find her there and it was difficult in the fading light to track any evidence. Air One used up all its airtime and had to return to base not long after Domino had been evacuated. We have no idea where she could be.'

Looking at Mason, her throat started to tighten up again. She wasn't sure if she could even think about her sister as a victim at the moment. She couldn't risk falling apart right now. She blinked away the sting of tears, watched as Mason placed his coffee cup on the table and straightened.

'Sergeant Morgan phoned her sister's mobile, sir. We heard it ring.' Instantly recognisable as Fliss's theme tune, 'Cruella de Vil' had blasted out into the night air, her iPhone lighting up from under the wet leaves. 'Three feet from where we were standing, six inches from the dead body, sir.'

Jenna had sunk to her knees to retrieve it and Chris had shouted to leave it until SOCO arrived. The pain had been unbearable to not pick up the phone, not touch what belonged to her sister.

Both men had waited in silence for her to compose herself before she'd picked herself up out of the wet leaves for the last time that evening.

Mason plucked a leaf from the collar of his jacket and dropped it into the wastepaper basket. 'We've sent units around to Jenna's house where she lives with Fliss. Nothing. Checked with hospitals. Nothing.'

'Would she go to a friend's house?' Gregg enquired.

Before Mason could answer, Jenna interjected.

'No, sir. Fliss would always come to me. There is nowhere else she would go, no one else she would go to.' She was adamant. 'She has plenty of friends, but no one as close as us. The only priority for her would be to get Domino rescued. She loved... *loves* that dog. She would not have abandoned him willingly. Something else happened.'

'What? Has she slid into the river?'

At the shake of her head, Gregg reached out, touched her arm.

'She couldn't slip directly into the river from there. There was the main pathway first, then the bridge parapet. She would have literally had to climb over the wall. There was no reason for her to, and no evidence anything like that had taken place. The foliage doesn't appear to be disturbed further down, although forensics will check there thoroughly in the morning. At the moment, the river is so swollen, there's no footing down there. The towpath is entirely covered in water.'

Gregg chewed on the corner of his mouth, his face twisted. 'House-to-house?'

'Yep, in progress. It didn't take long to get through the first batch of houses closest to the bridge. I can't see her going any further, she wouldn't bypass the closest houses if she was in a panic to get to a phone for help, but the uniforms are working their way up the bank on the other side. There're only a few houses on the Benthall Wood side. One person thought they heard a scream, but sometimes kids run through the woods. It's not unusual. Especially this time of year, with Halloween just around the corner.'

There was a long pause, while Gregg took in the information. 'Jenna, what do you think happened to your sister?'

Seconds ticked by as they stared at her. Jenna choked back the bile that threatened to scald the back of her throat as the words she'd held back poured out thick and hoarse.

'Assuming the naked woman has been murdered, I think whoever did that has her.'

'You think we have a murderer out there?'

Any hope she'd clung to of finding Fliss disappeared like thin tendrils of smoke.

'Well, someone dumped a naked body at the bottom of the hill. I don't think she got there under her own steam.'

Silence blanketed the room.

9

Anger churned with an acid burn in her stomach. She stared in the bathroom mirror at the deep lines of strain either side of her mouth, recognised the rage reflected in her own hard, glassy expression. She studied the fine lines surrounding her tired eyes, the vertical frown line which cut deep between her eyebrows, and the pale waxiness of her skin. She was going to look like a sullen, bad-tempered child if she didn't do something about it.

It seemed so unfair though. Her sister was missing for God's sake. She needed to look for her, but they'd sent her home at two thirty in the morning with a police escort – the female officer who had been in the conference room. She didn't even know her. She guessed that had been the idea. Anyone who had known her would probably have helped her slip out of her house and go looking for her sister.

Reason took hold. It wasn't an escort. Gregg had the best intentions when he'd sent someone to accompany her. He'd never suspected her of slipping out of her own house to look for Fliss. It was simply protocol. It was support. She had no one else.

She met her own gaze in the mirror, hiccupped through an inward breath. She had no one.

Mum.

Her mind screamed the tortured word. If only her mum was here. She'd know what to do, but Jenna had no idea.

So, she'd had a long, hot shower, scrubbed all evidence of the night's events from her body; but she couldn't rid her mind of them. When she'd fallen into bed, her body had dictated that she sleep. An uneasy sleep besieged by blood and black clouds, the dark, churning waters of the River Severn and Domino's blood-covered body.

Jenna peered closer at her own tight face, then routed around in her make-up drawer. She slapped on a good dollop of moisturiser, the one Fliss had bought her for her last birthday with a flippant laugh as she told her she was getting older and she needed to look after her skin. Jenna studied herself for a moment, she needed some anti-wrinkle crap around her eyes and mouth too. Surely at twenty-nine, she shouldn't need to use it already. Fliss insisted she did, but what the hell did she know? She was still a child.

With a soft sob, Jenna dabbed a small amount of anti-wrinkle cream on, patted it over her skin while the smell wound its way through her senses to remind her of her sister who used it all the time. Fliss's not-so-best-kept secret.

Quick puffs of air served only to make her chest ache while she ran a critical gaze over her handiwork.

'Crap.'

Purple smudged beneath her eyes, making her green irises bright and glassy. Her cap of short, thick hair emphasised the paleness of her skin.

Nothing for it but to cover up with foundation. Not something she normally bothered with for work, she had no option, she needed to hide the dark blemishes and brighten up her cheeks with blusher. Because there was no way she was about to face her team and others – strangers enlisted in to help – looking like shit. As though she couldn't handle a case, just because it involved her sister.

She gulped in air and grabbed the tube of foundation, dotting a little on each waxen cheek, her forehead, her chin and then her nose.

Once she started, the routine of applying make-up soothed, and by the time she'd finished, her eyes had lost their insolence and had started to simply look haunted. As she met her own gaze in the mirror, pain cramped her stomach. 'Oh God, Fliss. Where are you?'

'Sarg?'

The urgent rap on the door had Jenna almost jumping out of her skin.

'Yes?' Her voice was sharper than she intended, but the woman had scared the living daylights out of her.

'Are you all right in there?'

'Yes.' Irritation sparked. Of course she was all right, she was in her own bloody home. What did the woman want? She had every right to get herself ready, didn't she? Prepare herself for the day.

She drew in a lungful of air, blew it out again as fury flashed back at her from the mirror. 'Yes. I'll be with you in a minute.' She choked back the torrent of abuse she desperately wanted to hurl. 'Just give me... a minute.'

'I've made coffee.' The police officer's muffled voice came from the other side of the door.

Jenna jerked open the bathroom door with such suddenness the woman almost fell in.

'What?'

Her dark eyes widened with shock, the PC blinked at her. 'Coffee. I've made coffee for us both. And a piece of toast. I hope you don't mind.' Chewing on her lip, she stepped back into the hallway, knuckles exposed as she wrung her delicate hands together. 'I'm sorry, but we need to leave in fifteen minutes for the meeting.'

'Fifteen?' Jenna stared at her watch. Where had the time gone? She must have been in the bathroom for over an hour. She'd sat on the loo seat for most of the time, stared into the mirror for the rest of it. Head completely empty. No wonder the officer had been concerned.

Jenna raised her hand to push back the choppy layers of her brown hair and grab hold of a little composure. 'Coffee would be good. Thank you.' Forcing herself to be reasonable, Jenna followed the woman through to the kitchen and accepted the mug of thick, black liquid. 'I'm sorry, I don't think I caught your name last night.'

'Donna. PC Donna McGuire.' Sitting down opposite her, Donna took a sip of coffee, wet her lips. 'I'm sorry about your sister. It's terrible.' Her soft, Scottish brogue soothed Jenna.

'Thank you. I know.' With a nod, Jenna leaned back in her own chair, not really knowing what to say. She'd always kept her own counsel. She wasn't really used to opening up to others. Her little sister was the only one who ever knew what she was thinking. Her and Mason. 'I'm sorry if I was rude. It's...' Breath shuddered through the burn in her chest. 'It's not easy.'

Donna nodded, took another sip of her coffee while her gaze skittered away from Jenna's. She picked up a slice of buttered wholemeal toast and nibbled at the corner. 'I understand.'

Fear and hard-to-control fury bubbled just below the surface, threatening to emerge in a screaming, teeth-gnashing geyser. Understand? It was a term Jenna had used herself, a million times. But how the hell could anyone understand? Instead of replying, she turned her face to the window and took a deep gulp of the hot coffee so Donna couldn't see the spitting fury in her expression.

The police car Donna had brought her home in the previous night was parked in her drive where Fliss normally dumped her stupid little car.

White, with huge black Dalmatian prints all over it. A damned humiliation which Fliss thought was a hoot when she stuck them on. Especially when Domino stared at people in the cars behind. He sat up straight like little Lord Fauntleroy, with a haughty stare out of the window. All he needed was a monocle.

Stupid bloody dog.

A sob caught in her throat.

On the practical side of things, no one would ever want to buy or steal the car.

Jenna choked on a small hiccupping sob. Poor Domino. Who the hell would want a Dalmatian print car other than Fliss? Unless they had a cow fetish.

Sarah, the vet, had phoned sometime in the middle of the night. Jenna frowned as she tried to remember what time. She barely remembered the call. Just that Domino was out of surgery and in recovery.

She touched her fingers to the deep ache in her temple. She needed to phone the vets' as soon as they were open, check on him again. Pain cramped her chest. Fliss would never forgive her if she let anything happen to him.

At least the police vehicle wasn't parked at an angle. Fliss couldn't park for shit, but Jenna would far rather see the car half-mounted on the pavement than know it was currently with SOCO undergoing a thorough examination to check if there were any clues.

They wouldn't find anything. They knew that already, but it had to be carried out. No sense in leaving out one step and finding out later down the line she'd returned to her vehicle and left some kind of evidence. Evidence which would be contaminated by the biggest shitload of rubbish SOCO had ever encountered.

Despite residing at Jenna's, Fliss lived out of her car. Take-out coffee cups, tissues, sweet packets and half the contents of her wardrobe were in there, scattered around so she had to dig for anything she needed.

Jenna glanced down at her hands cradling the mug of coffee. Paper-dry skin already from the elements. At least Fliss could always find gloves in her car. They may not be a pair, but Fliss always insisted on keeping her hands protected and her hands were always soft. And warm.

Jenna sucked in a breath of air. What if she wasn't warm now? What if wherever she was, she was freezing cold?

The sharp sting of tears threatened while a leaden weight pressed on her chest.

Slow and controlled, she placed the mug on the table, blinked to rid herself of the impending tears and forced a tight smile. 'I should ring the vets' again before we go.'

'I already did.' Donna flicked out her notebook. 'Your sister's dog had to have ninety-seven stitches down his side. His jaw was broken. Not as bad as Sarah had thought at first. They managed to fix him up during a four and a half hour operation. They've kept him lightly sedated because they were worried about his brain swelling after the blow to his head. You can visit him this afternoon if you would like. Let them know before you go.' There was a moment's awkward silence as Donna closed her notebook and waited for Jenna to say something.

'Domino.'

'I'm sorry?' Donna leaned closer as though she couldn't quite hear.

'My sister's dog.' Jenna smiled as she thought about him. How much she adored him, despite her continual moaning about him to Fliss. All she wanted was to have him back, so she could nurse him, cuddle him. Cry over him. 'He's called Domino.' She squeezed her eyes closed for a moment to stop the tears. 'When he was a puppy, he only had a few spots. Fliss thought he looked like a Domino.' She dipped her head, sucked in a long breath and sighed it out while she picked at a fingernail still with ingrained mud under it, despite scrubbing her fingers through her hair in the shower. Jenna shook her head with the memory of the leggy little pup. Adorable little thing, who'd grown into a monster, far too big for her compact three bedroom house.

She ignored the slice of toast Donna had buttered and cut into triangles for her and jerked up from the chair. She made her way over to the kitchen sink to throw the dregs of her coffee away. She rinsed the mug and set it upside down on the draining board while she stared out of the kitchen window at the grey light and the depressing drizzle, searching for something innocuous to say to keep her from thinking about the day ahead.

'You know Dalmatians get their spots like chickenpox.' She flicked Donna a sidelong glance as the woman brushed the crumbs from her fingers, still chewing the last of her toast as she crossed the kitchen to join her. She probably wasn't really interested, but Jenna continued anyway. It soothed her to talk a pile of shit. 'From birth, the spots come out every few weeks in crops, like a rash, until they're about two years old.' She watched Donna place her mug in the sink and wondered absently why she hadn't washed it. It was something Fliss did. It bugged the hell out of Jenna to find an unwashed mug in the bottom of the sink.

As Donna walked away, Jenna automatically picked up the mug and washed it under the hot water, ran the soapy dishcloth around the rim to make sure she'd removed any germs. Cold sores. She hadn't noticed one on the police officer's lips, but you never knew. That's how she always got them, if a mug wasn't washed properly. She gave it a final rinse before she placed the mug on the drainer. 'Shall we go?'

Donna brushed delicate fingers over her perfectly defined lips, self-consciously brushing away a stray crumb as she nodded her agreement and followed Jenna into the hallway.

Jenna slipped her old flat-heeled ankle boots on. Her new ones were still covered in mud from the slide down the Gorge and she had no interest in cleaning them or finding out if the heel had given way. There were far more important things to deal with and it was time to focus on them.

She pulled the door closed behind her and followed Donna down the garden path, her attention on the woman's neat little bun at the nape of her neck, shoulders square, posture perfect, and straightened her own shoulders, disgusted at the creak and groan down the entire length of her spine. When did she get to be old? It had started when her mother died and snowballed the moment she realised Fliss had gone missing.

At the click of the unlock button, Jenna opened the car door and slid into the passenger seat.

The drive to the station was only fifteen minutes but it gave Jenna the opportunity to sulk again. After she'd given her report to the Chief Super last night, he'd told her he wanted her to go home, wash, eat, sleep and report for duty at 09:00. She tried to argue that she was due to meet with the search teams at Ironbridge, but he would have none of it.

'You will shower, you will eat, and you will sleep, that's an order, Sergeant. There's nothing more you can do tonight. You're done. We need you tomorrow. The scenes of crime officers won't be able to do anything until daylight, and you can't do anything until they've done their job. So, go home. When refreshed, you will answer more questions. Jenna, you will be needed, and you will be on top form.' Gregg showed a measure of why he had been promoted to the position he was in. Leadership and command came naturally.

She had followed his instructions. She'd showered at length, but it hadn't washed away the fear; ate, so to speak; slept fitfully. She couldn't claim to feel refreshed.

She glanced out of the window, desperate to get back to the search instead of wasting more time by going to the station. She could be looking for Fliss. She needed to find her sister. Where the hell could she be? Jenna refused to believe she'd been swept away by the river. But the alternative didn't bear thinking about. What if someone had her, was holding her captive? What if she was injured? What if... Jenna's mind raced in ever-decreasing circles. She needed to get to work. There was no point making assumptions. She needed facts.

The forensics guys would already have been at the site at first light to conduct a fingertip search. She comforted herself with the thought that they would be getting on with the investigations while she had a debrief in the conference room at the station, and as she was in charge of the investigation, she would join SOCO later.

10

SATURDAY 27 OCTOBER, 08:10 HRS

The man stared at Felicity while he scooped porridge into his mouth, scraping his spoon over his lips to swipe away any that may have missed his mouth. Still out of it, her purple-hued cheek lay flaccid against the greying pillow, her limbs sprawled over the narrow cot bed.

He glanced around the room. He'd not used it for several months, ever since his wife had become more... receptive. The heavier she'd become as the baby grew inside her, the more compliant she'd been.

He'd obviously made a mistake by letting her have more freedom and ultimately it had resulted in her demise. He'd learnt his mistake from that. One he would never make again.

Stupid woman, with more thought of escape than survival. He'd adored her. He told her every day how much he loved her as he stroked her tender skin and tended to the minor abrasions she seemed to have accrued. Such a clumsy woman. She always had something wrong with her, brought about by her own stupidity, her clumsiness, but he'd cared for her, kept her safe. Helped her to give birth.

The pungent smell of damp wrinkled his nose. He'd need to replace the mattress and pillow if Felicity was to stay. Maybe bring a small rug down to give the place a homely feel. Although with the likelihood of flooding, it might be better to leave it until spring. If she survived.

He chewed the porridge, counting to twenty in his head before he swallowed while he contemplated the corpse-like state of the woman. He'd overdosed her. She was obviously lighter than he thought when he hefted her through the Gorge the previous night. She'd felt like a lead weight. Perhaps he was getting weaker, but he'd assumed she was half the weight again of his wife. That's what he'd based the dose on.

He filled his mouth again and then placed his bowl on the floor as he crouched down beside the inert body. Her flesh was cooler than it should be but still felt tepid to the touch. He pushed his fingers against the side of her swollen, blackened neck and pressed to find a thin, thready pulse. Perhaps she'd die, and all his efforts would be for nothing.

With narrowed eyes, he studied her neck.

Her skin warmed beneath the heat of his fingers as he cupped his hand around her throat. Her lips parted, and she expelled a light breath triggering a shot of lust which fired through his veins to make his own breath come in short, excited puffs. She wanted him. Even in her sleep, she wanted him.

He trailed his fingers down her chest, nudging aside the soft cotton of her T-shirt, teasing aside her lacy black bra, his heart hammering as he slipped his hand inside and cupped her breast in his palm. Smaller than his wife's large, balloon-like breasts, Felicity's barely filled his hand, her small nipple hard against his palm.

A bead of sweat broke out across his forehead as he licked his lips, his penis hardening, so he shuffled onto his knees to a more comfortable position, pressing himself against the metal-framed cot. He closed his eyes and gave a gentle squeeze of her breast. Ecstasy setting his skin on fire.

Fliss whimpered in her sleep and his eyes shot open as he whipped his hand away, guilt and disgust mingling.

He shouldn't touch her. It was wrong. She was a dirty little slag. His lip curled in self-disgust as he stared at the blood-stained remains of her clothes. She was injured. Damaged. Imperfect.

In a swift move, he lurched to his feet and backed away from her, his foot clipping the porridge bowl he'd left on the floor. The loud clatter shook him, rattling through his system like an alarm. He blew out in short, sharp pants in an attempt to centre himself.

If she died, he'd have to get rid of her body. Fate would make the decision, but he could help keep her alive.

He glanced at his watch. Time was running out. He had to go. He'd be late for work and he really needed to be there.

He snatched at the musty smelling blanket on the bottom of the cot, jolting her feet so she let out a pained groan. He shook out the blanket and threw it over her, and then tossed her jacket on top. He swiped up his empty bowl and scurried from the room, locking the door behind him, her soft sigh haunting his every move.

11

SATURDAY 27 OCTOBER, 09:05 HRS

She didn't feel like talking. Not the idle chat she'd normally have with her colleagues anyway. Most of the officers in the room had no idea why they were there yet. Rumours spread fast and furious as they always did in the station. Most of them inaccurate. When they dealt with rumours, unlike dealing with their jobs, they tended not to check the facts out before they passed their little titbits on. So, she sat in the corner, choosing a table instead of a chair, at the back of the room, well away from them all.

Mason, rumpled and weary, ambled over and handed her a cup of coffee. Her third of the morning. She was starting to think her rapid pulse might be better served by not feeding it any more caffeine, but she needed something to keep her occupied. If she'd been a smoker, she would have lit up by now. Several times.

She reached out and touched the sleeve of Mason's suit, the concern in his eyes worrying her.

He wrapped his fingers around hers, gave them a squeeze. 'Have you heard from the vet?'

'Yeah.' She nodded. 'I managed to get hold of Sarah. She operated last night. He's holding up.' Relief wallowed in her stomach. 'His jaw wasn't as bad as they thought at first. He lost a hell of a lot of blood.' She shuddered as the vision of Domino floated back to her, so covered in his own blood it had virtually obliterated the white fur. 'He'll be in a few days, but she tells me there's no reason he shouldn't recover.'

'Poor bastard.'

She bumped her heels against the table leg, tapped her fingernails on the side of the thick stoneware mug while she watched the hands of the clock on their slow rotation. Gregg had instructed 09:00 prompt. He was unusually late.

She raised her hand to rub her already weary eyes, stopped herself and dropped her hand onto her knee. She'd almost forgotten she'd put make-up on. It wouldn't be the best look, black smudges like a panda before the day had even begun. It may have been a mistake. She'd probably have to wash it off when she had her break. If she even had time for a break.

She placed her coffee on the table next to her, ran the nail of her index finger across the back of her other hand where the flesh had been torn and scratched the night before in her haste to get through the undergrowth. She should have had gloves on, then she wouldn't have scratched them. Christ, she should have had a proper coat on, then she wouldn't have almost died of hypothermia. What would her mum have thought?

What would her mum have thought about her not looking after her younger sister? She'd always watched out for the little wretch. Never in her life had she known anyone get into more trouble than Fliss. If 'trouble' had a face, it was Fliss. It wasn't because she went looking for it, necessarily; it just always found her.

Awareness of her surroundings returned as silence descended on the room. Jenna raised her head, studied Gregg as he stepped through the doorway ahead of another man. Sharp, she snapped upright, her police-trained eyes quick to assess the stranger. She stared at his oversized feet; size thirteen, she reckoned. Jenna's gaze tracked up his very expensive char-coal grey suit, made to measure no doubt, too precisely fit to his tall frame to have come off the peg. Taller than Gregg by a good couple of inches. Broad chest covered in a crisp, white cotton shirt. Old-fashioned cufflinks. Pearly grey tie, definitely silk. Too well turned-out to be a police officer. No officer she knew could afford clothes of that standard, nor would they be seen looking so stylish for duty. Maybe a wedding or a funeral. Even then... they were expensive togs.

She shuffled off the edge of the table, stood tall so she could inspect him over the heads of the other officers, a worm of unease unfurled in her stomach.

Shoulders back, spine straight; he stood like an Army officer. He dressed like a lawyer. Style immaculate. Colours, boring. Had to be a solicitor. What was he doing with Gregg?

Dark chocolate brown hair had been sheared a little too close above his ears. Immaculate but severe. Jaw, square. Nose, straight. If she was asked to identify him, she'd have no trouble, he was distinctive. Cheekbones, hmm, nice. Eyes... watching her.

With a jolt, Jenna shot her attention back to Gregg, but unable to resist, she slid her gaze back to the stranger. As her gaze locked with his, his eyes crinkled at the edges as though he was about to smile, but his mouth remained in a straight line before he moved on to make a perusal of the rest of the officers in the room.

With a nervous lick of her lips, Jenna dipped her head, sure he'd been able to read her thoughts. It wasn't her thoughts that were inappropriate, her mind was clear-cut focused on her sister's well-being. It was the deep, visceral pull in her gut that concerned her.

Mason sidled closer and propped himself against the table, one leg swinging so the table gave a precarious rock as she slipped back onto it.

'Who is he? The slick prick.' His gruff whisper accompanied a sharp nudge with his elbow.

'How would I know?' She kept her voice low, head down while she made a pretence of scrolling through her iPhone messages.

'When he looked over, I assumed you knew each other.' He turned more fully to face her, bumped her with his broad shoulder. The table rocked harder.

'Never met him before in my life.' She gave a disinterested shrug in the hope he'd lose interest, but heat rose in her face.

'But...'

'Ssshhh...' The sound came out sharper than she had intended, and half a dozen officers turned around with enquiring looks on their faces.

Gregg cleared his throat and, to her relief, in a synchronised move, every head swivelled to face him. 'Thank you for coming. I apologise for being late. Let's get down to business.' Gregg scanned the room to ensure all attention was on him and his visitor. 'This is Chief Crown Prosecutor Adrian Hall. I've asked him to attend due to the complexities of this case.'

Jenna allowed herself a small cynical smile. Right first time. Solicitor. High end. Pain in the arse. Always were, these types. He looked too young, she estimated thirty-five, to be such a senior lawyer. Possible, but he'd have to be one hotshot lawyer if that was the case.

He'd come in, read them all the small print on rules and regulations and the guys on the ground would carry on regardless and get the job done. What the hell was Gregg thinking to bring in an outsider? They knew what had to be done, they just needed to get on with it. Complicated it may be, but not damned complex.

With resignation, she crossed her arms over her chest and waited for the lecture to begin.

'Sergeant Morgan.'

She almost jumped out of her skin and the table threatened to topple over, its legs scraping across the floor tiles as she leapt to her feet.

'Jesus, I thought you were going to salute.'

Ignoring Mason's snarky murmur, Jenna stepped forward. 'Sir?' Heat scorched her cheeks, she *had* almost saluted.

'I know this is difficult for you, Sergeant, but I'd appreciate it if you could come up here and brief everyone on the current situation.'

Expecting it, Jenna stepped to the front of the conference room and in a smooth, professional repetition of the report she had given Gregg, she relayed the information from the previous night. She paused only for one heart-stopping moment to clear the tightness in her throat which threatened to choke her when the soft gasps of pity reached her ears as she imparted the information regarding Fliss's disappearance and Domino's severe injuries.

She allowed the silence to hang in the room after she told them of the dead body. She let it sink in before she continued.

'I spoke to SOCO just before the meeting commenced and they confirm there is no evidence to suppose Fliss slid further down the embankment. They'll continue their search along both sides, but it is very obvious where both Fliss and Domino came down the first descent. Samples of clothing, hair, skin, and blood...' She took a steadying breath. 'DNA samples weren't hard to find in the area they'd tumbled down. There's no reason to assume it wouldn't be as evident if she had continued down the next incline. And she'd have had to get herself over the wall on the opposite side of the main walkway.'

She scanned the room, Jenna knew not only would these people, her friends and colleagues, do their professional best, but now they had a vested interest in solving this case. She was one of theirs and, by association, so was her sister. She allowed herself that small nugget of reassurance before she continued.

'There is no evidence she went into the river.' She locked gazes with several officers she'd known since she'd been a young, newly qualified PC. Their silent support strengthened her resolve. 'What they did find was evidence of someone else coming downhill from above Fliss's position, directly at her. There are footprints beside a tree where someone stopped for a short time, where their boots sank into the mud. SOCO has a good imprint. They are going to try and trace the make and size of the boot. Initial thoughts are possibly UK size eight or nine. Could be male or female. Fliss wears a size eight in walking boots herself, so...' she shrugged, watching the faces of her colleagues.

'Her boots were a good make, quite unusual, Italian, which made it easier to track her. Her footprints show her route all the way along the upper path, where she stopped. There seemed to be a scuffle there, but the dog wasn't so easy to trace as he'd charged...' Knowing him, she could picture the frantic rush as he raced all over the hillside, kicking up his heels in wild abandon. 'Charged all over the place, scuffing up leaves and making slide marks in various places. But when he fell, the long slide down is obvious. Traces of skin, fur. They found the branch they think split him open, dropped on that upper pathway. It has skin, fur, flesh, blood attached. He may already have been unconscious when he fell.' She paused, swallowed while everyone stared, no longer sympathetic but attentive and eager for the details.

'Where Fliss went down, the skid is more obvious, the heels of her boots dug in, we assume to try and slow her slide down. She was conscious. This is the point at which we believe the dog walkers on the other side of the Severn heard her second scream.' She paused to make sure she still had the room's attention. No one moved, every one of them had their gazes fixed on her while she scanned around, held the gazes of those she knew well, moved on to engage the others.

'No tracks came out at all after the fall. Heavy footprints from the other boots show on the main pathway. They are currently tracing these, but unfortunately a lot of the evidence has been ruined by the amount of activity from all of us last night – Mason, myself, Chris the dog handler and Blue.' She shrugged. 'We had no idea at that point that this was a crime scene. We believed there'd been an accident.' She narrowed her eyes to stop the sharp prick of tears. 'The vet drove her van along the main concourse. SOCO put a more extensive cordon around; in fact, basically, they've restricted the entire hillside, so they can try and trace the other footprints and see where they originated. As I said, he appeared to have come from above Fliss, so he may have come over the top from Pattern's Rock, Broseley or Red Pool. They're trying to trace him back to a vehicle. At this stage, we have no idea.'

Frustration and fury rolled together, but she held them down. 'He may have come on foot, in which case, if he was carrying my sister he wasn't going to get far.' She knew the only way her sister would have gone was if she'd been unconscious and he'd carried her. 'At five foot eleven inches, around nine stone six pounds, at least that's what she admitted to me.' A thread of humour rumbled through the room. 'The offender would need to be strong. There was no evidence of anyone being dragged.' Which could mean she was dead. Her mind stumbled over the thought, but she refused to turn from it. Every possibility had to be investigated. Perhaps he'd tossed her into the water after he'd killed her. It was a long reach and he'd have to be exceptionally strong, but something worthwhile checking out.

Reluctant to admit her thoughts, she flicked open a folder, took out copies of a photograph of her sister and passed them around. It had taken her some time earlier in the morning to find one Fliss wouldn't have objected to. She could hear her sister's voice in her head. *'Oh Jenna, look at my hair, it's a mess. Why would you choose that one? I'm squinting into the sun on this one. For goodness' sake, do you want me to look dreadful? That's my fat side. If it's going to be the last photo of me circulated, at least have the decency to make it a good one.'*

In the end, she had picked one of Fliss and Domino. Head and shoulders of both. Almost cheek to cheek, but a good clear likeness of Fliss. She heard the 'aahhs' and 'awws' mainly from the female officers, she assumed because of the dog.

'As I said, five feet eleven inches or one point eight metres, and nine stone six pounds, about sixty kilograms. Not terrifically heavy, but tall. If someone carried her out of there, he must have been pretty fit and strong, despite his small feet.'

She let the silence hang heavy in the air, only to be broken by a fresh-faced young PC raising his hand as though he was still in the classroom. At Jenna's acknowledgement, he dropped his hand back down to his side, flushed to the roots of his strawberry blond hair and stuttered out his question.

'What about the body you discovered, Sarg?'

Relieved to side-track from the subject of her own sister for a moment, Jenna spoke to the room in general but directed her gaze back to the youngster several times, locking eyes with him, taking in the intensity of his stare. The interest. The passion.

'We currently have no information on the body. Other than the description I've already given, there's nothing. Naked, no visible identifying features, no jewellery, nothing. No missing persons we know of immediately who fit the description, but we will need to conduct a thorough search. We'll be checking with other Forces to see if anyone further afield can identify her. There was nothing on her to indicate where she came from. So, either she was murdered and dumped there – strange place to dump a body – or she was murdered there and stripped of evidence on site. It seems very cold and calculated if that's the case and means the person we are dealing with may well have known how to cover their tracks. Forensics should be able to confirm whether she was killed on site or dragged there after the fact. I'll let you know when the post-mortem takes place.' She paused, allowed the team to absorb the information they had been given. 'Any further questions?'

She skimmed her gaze around the room, watched for their reactions, aware of Gregg moving to stand beside her. His steady, stoic support was welcome as the team turned their attention to him.

'Thank you, Sergeant Morgan. You all have your packs.' He slipped Jenna's actions book from her fingers and turned to the room. 'I want you out there. SOCO are doing their bit. They've an enormous job to complete and time is of the essence. It's quiet this time of year in Iron-bridge, but it won't have been entirely deserted. Somebody, somewhere, will have heard something, seen something they thought was just "off" at the time. If you jog their memories, we may well turn up evidence. Feed it through.' He indicated a lean, dark-haired man near the door. 'Frank Bartwell is lead intel analyst on this case. If you have information, pass it to him.'

Frank's shoulders hunched as the attention of the room centred on him, but Gregg continued.

'There will be witnesses, people in the area. PC Walker has supplied names and addresses of the dog walking group he questioned last night. For anyone who doesn't know, they're the twilight walkers. They've been a great source of information in the area whenever there's an offence. Normally minor. They walk their dogs, they chat, they know things. I want them questioned again. Other than that, was there anything suspicious? A person acting out of character. A husband arriving home with blood on their clothes. T.I.E.' As the young PC's hand shot up in the air, Gregg nodded at him. 'Trace. Interview. Eliminate.' The hand slipped back down again. 'Anything else?'

With the rumble of excited voices to cover him, Gregg turned to Jenna. 'Could you please wait in my office for me?'

She opened her mouth to query his instruction and stopped herself as she stared into his calm deep eyes filled with solemnity and wisdom, which brooked no argument.

With a slight incline of his head, he turned back to the room and grabbed their attention once more. 'Detective Inspector Taylor will take the lead on this case...'

'But, sir,' Jenna interrupted, only to have Gregg's attention wither her to the spot.

'My office, Sergeant.' His voice was gentle, but there was no mistaking the look in his eye that commanded compliance. With a sharp nod of her head, Jenna stalked to Gregg's office.

Three minutes of pacing seemed like a lifetime and as Gregg walked through the door, Jenna almost leapt at him.

'Take a seat, Jenna.'

She flung herself into the nearest chair as fast as she could, sat ramrod straight, fingers linked to stop them twitching, feet flat on the thin marble grey carpet tiles, gaze straight ahead.

'This is a very difficult situation, Jenna. Unusual, to say the least.' Gregg leaned against his desk, crossing his arms over his chest. 'I can't tell you how very sorry I am about your sister.'

She was silent, waiting. For fuck's sake, she should have seen it coming, but she'd not given it a second thought, all her focus on Fliss, Domino and a Jane Doe.

'I can't let you work on this case.'

Tension grabbed her throat, choking her. She knew at any moment she was going to be incapable of speaking, that the tears she had been holding back so desperately were rising and if she started, there would be no consoling her. So, she sucked it in and drew her body even straighter.

'Sir...'

'Jenna, you can't possibly be on this case. It would compromise every-thing. You know. You have been in the force for how many years? Eight, almost nine? We need continuity of evidence. We need absolutely every-thing cut and dried. We cannot risk catching the murderer and him getting off because he can claim you've tampered with evidence. We can probably get away with your initial findings simply because you weren't aware at that stage what you were looking at and you were in the constant company of Sergeant Bennett and PC Ellis, but we can't risk any further involvement in the case by you.'

'That's bollocks, sir...'

Shaking his head to stop her going any further, Gregg let out a gusty sigh.

'If I may...?' The deep tone of Adrian Hall's voice had Jenna whipping her head around to face him as he leaned with casual negligence against the closed door of Gregg's office. His arms were also crossed over his chest. She hadn't even realised he was there.

One eyebrow shot up as her gaze clashed with his. The stranglehold on her throat released and anger roiled thick and black in the pit of her stomach. Anger at this man, this stranger, who was going to pacify and reason with her. It wouldn't work, she'd damned well investigate. She'd find her sister.

'I have to be on the case. There is nothing going to stop me investigating this,' she ground out.

With an indolent shrug, he pushed away from the door and took a step towards her. His sheer size should have intimidated, but Jenna wasn't about to let him or anyone else overwhelm her. She had a job to do. Her sister to find.

'I *can* stop you.' His smile was tight and brief.

With an insulted gasp, she opened her mouth ready to blast him off his big feet if required, but he raised his hand in a stop motion and moved his attention back to Gregg.

'May I suggest something?' Unruffled, it appeared, his voice poured liquid calm into the room.

She frowned at him as he moved across the office towards her.

'A compromise.'

He folded his huge frame into the small chair opposite hers, crossed one leg over the other. He hunched over and steepled his fingers, tapping them against his mouth as he stared at her, dark gaze intent in his study of her before he flicked a look at Gregg's puzzled face and then back again. He dropped his hands onto his thighs and tapped his knees with long fingers.

'Chief Superintendent Gregg asked me to advise on the case because of the complexity of it.' He leaned closer, his gaze so intense all thought of arguing went out of her head and her one focus was to listen to what he was to say. 'An unidentified body is always complicated, admittedly. Add into the mix the involvement of your sister and her dog, and we have a puzzle. Sergeant, taking into consideration the participation you've already had with this case and the knowledge you carry regarding your sister, her dog, the area and your discovery of the body, I would say the last thing we need to do is remove you from this case. We don't need a hostile witness.'

Looking up at Gregg, Adrian leaned back in his seat, making it groan in protest. 'I believe if there's going to be a challenge in court, it will happen regardless. From Jenna's description of the entire incident from start to finish, she has already, technically, compromised the crime scene.'

Offended, Jenna reared back and spat out. 'I have not compromised the scene.'

'Sergeant, technically, and if the courts so decided, you will have already compromised the scene just by being there. Forensics will pick up your fingerprints for elimination purposes, a stray hair, a nail end.' He raised a finger as she opened her mouth to argue and silenced her with the quick rise of one black eyebrow. 'However, and here is my point, if you are removed totally from the investigation, then, in my opinion, from a Prosecution point of view, we also endanger the case. We effectively remove the continuity of evidential information. The short of it is – we need you, Sergeant.'

Jenna turned her head from Adrian to Gregg and back again while the tension in her chest eased, and she gave a slow nod of her head.

'I don't agree. In my opinion, Sergeant Morgan should take compassionate leave and go home.' Gregg paced across the room, turned his back and rested his hands on the windowsill as he stared out at the thick cloud of fog that engulfed the station. 'If I allow Jenna this, not only does it endanger the case but also her career. It could damage her reputation irretrievably. There are too many scenarios that could end up with her getting suspended. If it goes to court, she could lose her job.'

'But if you don't allow her to stay on the case, you end up with a hostile witness, because I have a feeling your sergeant here will not just sit back and watch the case come together.' Adrian flicked a look at her and this time his smile quirked in genuine amusement and, she suspected, a glint of admiration. 'I think Jenna is of more use to us onside.'

'I can't disagree.' Gregg turned to rest his backside on the windowsill, before running a hand through his thick, steel-coloured hair. 'I have no doubts about your professionalism, Jenna, but how do we keep you out of trouble?'

Her entire life on the line, she sucked air in through her teeth. The best it appeared she could do was listen to these two men discuss her future without any input from her. The decision was in the balance and she thought if she contributed now, it may just tip that balance in the wrong direction. So, she held her tongue, gazed at the Chief Crown Prosecutor and hoped he could come up with a resolution agreeable to them all. Without knowing him, she had an inexplicable desire to put her faith in him.

The vague tremble in her core which had threatened to shake her apart since Fliss's disappearance balled in the pit of her stomach.

'If we let you do desk duty, we still have the same problem. Any piece of information you handle regarding this case, or these two cases, because, as it stands right now, we have no idea if the body of this woman is linked with the disappearance of your sister. It could be an amazing, twisted coincidence. But it will be checked into.' Adrian stood. He buttoned the jacket of his perfectly tailored suit, without a crease in sight; the man looked like a male model as he towered above her. 'The only way around this, I think, is if you are shadowed for every moment you're on duty. And when you're off duty, nothing to do with the case is to happen. You have no communication whatsoever with the station or anyone in it.'

'She has a partner, DC Mason Ellis...' Gregg waved his hand in the general direction of the meeting room, but before he was finished Adrian shook his head.

'Can't be a police officer. It could implicate them, especially as she's his senior officer.' He pushed fingers through his thick hair, paced across the small office to the cold, unused coffee maker in the corner. He ran an absent finger across the dust on the top, remained silent for a moment longer before turning to face them both. 'It needs to be someone entirely impartial. Someone not connected with the sergeant.' He placed his hands on his hips, his eyes darkened with intent, making Jenna's world narrow in on him. 'I would suggest it's me. I do it.'

At Gregg's lifted eyebrows and Jenna's frown, he continued.

'I can't see any other way.' He spread his hands wide, as if appealing to the room in general, a trick she suspected he used often in court. 'If you're shadowed by me, everything you do, every movement you make is monitored and recorded, then we can work this. I have to be on the case anyhow, it's just going to take up a lot more time than I thought. The quicker we can get the case solved, the better it is for my workload.'

Cynicism curled her lip. 'Give me five minutes, Adrian, I'll hop out there and identify the murderer and... while I'm at it, I'll just track my sister down in the local supermarket and drag her back home like a naughty schoolgirl, just to oblige your workload.'

'Jenna!' Gregg's hawk-like stare did nothing to stir any shame.

Adrian glanced at Gregg and shrugged her remarks off.

'I need coffee and twenty minutes to clear my diary. Can I use your office?' It wasn't a request, but it sounded polite enough. The man exuded authority. As Jenna came to her feet, ready to leave, he pinned her with a stare. 'The only way for this to work, Jenna, is for you to be with me every minute you're in the station or on police business, otherwise there will be holes in your evidence.'

'Will I be able to pee in private?' She couldn't stop the quick lash of words.

He narrowed his eyes at her, shifted his weight as she lowered herself with studied care back down into her chair.

'I need a coffee and you need to stay with me until I clear everything with my office. You can't work the case, but you can be on hand to advise and inform. Possibly even suggest.'

At the short, sharp rap on the door, they all turned as Mason strode into the room, looking for all the world like he was about to take a swing at someone, chest puffed, shoulder's back. He just needed to roll up his sleeves and he'd look like a bare-knuckle fighter with his broad shoulders and rugged features. Not much younger than her, she had no doubt he would always have her back.

'Sergeant?' He addressed her and only her. If ever she needed a hero, Mason was her man. But she didn't. Not today. So, she smiled at him and waved him deeper into the room, indicating the chair the Chief Crown Prosecutor had vacated.

'Have a seat, Mason, we're just about to have coffee.'

The other two men in the room remained standing and she noted with a twinge of amusement that they had both casually crossed their arms over their chests. Declining her offer of a seat, Mason stared down at her. The testosterone in the room nudged up a notch.

Jenna leaned back in the chair, glanced at the three men, all of whom appeared to only want the best for her, and yet she wasn't in the mood to watch them squabble. She simply felt weary.

'Chief Crown Prosecutor, Adrian Hall, has suggested he accompanies us on our duties in order to give credibility to any further evidence and maintain the continuity and integrity of the case.'

'Just a minute.' Adrian interrupted. 'There's no reason why I should monitor PC Ellis and in fact it could quite possibly make my workload untenable and cause undue restriction on the investigation of the case.'

'But, she's my partner...' Mason attempted to butt in.

'Is there any reason why you should be closely monitored by a senior Court official, PC Ellis?' Steel threads ran through Adrian's voice as he pinned Mason with a stare, hard and accusing. 'Do you have a relationship with either Detective Sergeant Morgan or her sister that we should know about?'

Mason's chin came up, brilliant blue eyes connecting with stony brown ones. 'It's *DC* Ellis...' he pointed out, his voice deep and unusually loud. It wasn't often she witnessed Mason getting flustered. '... And no, Chief Crown Prosecutor. I have worked professionally with the detective sergeant for over three years. I know her sister and we have all socialised together, but I do not now, nor have I ever, had a sexual relationship with either of them.'

Adrian's lips twitched up at the edges while heat raced up Jenna's neck. 'Good, that lets you off the hook then. No monitoring for you.' Dismissive of Mason, he dipped his head to check his phone.

Gregg, however, had not yet had his say. His quiet voice, in direct contrast to those of the younger men, grabbed everyone's attention without a quibble.

'Adrian, I haven't yet agreed with your suggestion.' He picked up his telephone and dialled. 'Lesley, would you mind bringing four coffees in please.' Gregg circled to the back of his desk, sat heavily in his chair. 'Sit.' He commanded and as both men hesitated, he looked each in the eye.

'Take a seat, gentlemen, you do not come into my office for a pissing competition with each other. Now, *sit*.'

Jenna ground her teeth. Couldn't they see she just wanted to get on and find her sister, every minute lost meant they were less likely to succeed? The first seventy-two hours were the most crucial. After that, the chances of finding any missing person became slimmer. She didn't give a flying fuck who monitored her, who partnered her. All she wanted was to find her sister.

The desire to pull her hair out by the roots and scream blue murder almost overwhelmed her, but she reeled it in, biting down hard so nothing came out of her mouth.

'Jenna, I apologise. I'm sure the last thing you need now is internal arguments.' Gregg glanced at the other men in the room. 'You will respect Jenna's rank and her personal position here.'

He paused for a moment while Lesley brought in a tray with coffee, milk, and sugar; waited patiently while she served them all and thanked her graciously as she pulled the door shut behind her while Jenna tapped her fingers and restrained herself from jumping up and running from the room.

Gregg raised his cup of heavily sugared white coffee and took a sip. 'Adrian, as you can imagine, I'm not happy about this situation. However, as far as suggestions go, I think you're right. If Jenna is removed completely from the case, it nullifies everything that went before the discovery of her missing sister.' He placed his cup down, tapped his fingers on the desk. 'I have to agree though, if Mason and Jenna stay partnered, it's a waste of highly qualified and experienced resources. No matter how busy Jenna becomes, she is still going to be restricted by being monitored and by the hours she's going to be allowed to work because of the monitoring.' Gregg's index finger tapped with a little more vigour than required. 'I think what we initially need to do is a handover session, so all material evidence is accounted for and Jenna follows through with gathering of information this morning at the site of the incident. From there, Jenna, if you're comfortable, you can pick up other cases.'

Jenna found herself nodding with enthusiasm. 'Yes, sir.'

'However,' he continued, 'if at any time you become overstressed with the workload, the situation, the emotional pressure, you are to take time off, seek the guidance from Occupational Health and, above all, keep me in the loop. Is that understood, DS Morgan?'

'Perfectly, sir.' She'd agree to anything if only he'd let her out of there, so she could get on with her damned work and find her sister.

As though he could read her thoughts, Gregg trained his gaze on her for a long moment until she squirmed in discomfort and was forced to nod again.

'I understand, sir. I do.'

Satisfied, he nodded once and turned his attention to Mason while Adrian spoke in lowered tones into his phone. 'So, DC Ellis,' Gregg held the man with his stare, 'you need a new partner, and I have just the man.' He picked up the phone, dialled once more while a small smile kicked up the edges of his mouth. 'Lesley, send PC Downey in please.'

'PC Downey?' Mason spluttered 'He's got to be all of twelve.'

'He's almost twenty-one and I think his age is irrelevant.'

'He doesn't even shave.'

The finger Gregg had been tapping on the desk halted and pointed directly at Mason. 'You have a new partner. Or a disciplinary. Take your pick.'

The door edged open and the young officer who had raised his hand in the conference room peered around it, eyes blinking in a rapid flutter. His Adam's apple did a ferocious dance in his skinny neck and Jenna wondered if he was about to turn tail and run down the corridor to find his mum. Either that or pee himself where he stood. She caught Adrian's sly grin before his gaze slid to hers and she knew from the quick wiggle of his eyebrows he'd had the same thought.

'Sir?' PC Downey's voice warbled as Gregg held him immobile with his sharp stare.

'PC Downey. How would you like to be assigned to plain clothes for this murder and missing person's investigation?'

A deep red flush swept up the young officer's scrawny neck and spread in a wild slash across his high, sharp cheekbones. 'Yes, sir. I mean, I would, sir. It would be an honour, sir.' He bobbed his head in short, rapid motions and Mason tapped his fingers to his creased forehead, his lips curling. Jenna could almost hear the string of fuck words reeling around his mind.

Gregg leaned back in his leather chair and raised a hand to stop the outpour. 'DC Ellis, take your man, teach him well. Keep your sergeant informed.'

Expression flat and dead with none of the amusement Jenna would have expected, Mason surged to his feet and paced to the door, towering over the young PC. He cast a last disgruntled glance over his shoulder at them before he flung open the door and disappeared into the corridor beyond, leaving PC Downey to follow.

As the door swung closed behind the new team, Gregg gave his crinkled forehead a weary rub, his attention focused back on Jenna.

'Sergeant, it's been a long day already.' He glanced at his watch; a quick flicker of surprise dashed through his widened eyes and Jenna checked the time on her phone. The day had hardly begun. 'Go sort yourself out while your partner makes his plans. Keep me informed.'

She drained her cup of coffee, it might be the last one she had the opportunity to grab for the rest of the day.

As she made for the door, Adrian finished his phone call and trailed after her as Gregg's voice stopped her once more. 'Jenna.' As she turned and met his gaze, the sympathy she'd been trying to avoid filled the slate-coloured depths of his eyes while his voice soothed. 'I'm available to you twenty-four hours a day. Whatever you want. Get Lesley to give you my private numbers.'

She blinked at the quick prickle of tears that threatened, while he settled back in his chair. His calm grey eyes were once again blank. The brief nod of his head dismissed her.

12

'Fliss, I just don't know how you manage to get yourself into these scrapes. Honestly, can you just, for once, try and avoid trouble?'

Fliss watched her thirteen year old sister dab firmly at her knee with antiseptic wipes as she sat on the kitchen counter at home. The blood was thick and sluggish, and her knee hurt like hell. She'd normally swing her leg, but she held it stiff to stop the pain. The rhythmic throb of it vibrated through her pulse. It wasn't her fault the bough of the tree had been too fragile to bear her weight. How was she to know it would snap and dump her on her knees on the patio slabs below?

'You're going to get hell from mum. She loves her apple tree, and I think you just ruined half her crop.'

Fliss sniffed and instantly choked on a mouthful of blood.

Full and snotty, her nose pulsed so she could barely draw in air. Desperate to breathe, she opened her mouth, hissed at the sharp sting of her cracked lips as they stuck together while the metallic taste of old blood filled her mouth. She managed to part her lips, thin slivers of skin stretched to catch on her teeth, but she sucked in as much oxygen as she could through her mouth. The sound of her gasps filled her head, the strange clucking noise that came from her own throat roused her.

She cracked open gritty eyelids to take in her surroundings in a cautious sweep of the room as memory flooded back. Pain returned in a persistent throb to take her hard-earned oxygen away. The pop and crackle of her neck muscles sounded as she strained to raise her head to get a better view of her prison.

She scrutinised the small square room in what she assumed was a very old house. Silence hung dense and oppressive. The thick, white painted stone walls would block out most sounds. Her best guess was she was in a cellar. Even if she had the ability to shout, no one would be able to hear her through those walls. Panic gripped a tight fist in her stomach and shot icicles through her veins. No one would hear her. Dear God, how was Jenna ever to find her?

She twisted her head, inspected the walls while she ground down the fear, the ball of nausea stuck in the base of her throat and she swallowed it back. If there was one thing she'd learnt, there was no point in panicking. It only made things worse. This time, she couldn't rely on her big sister to save her. She had to save herself, which meant she had to remain alert, completely aware of her surroundings.

With soft, slow pants, she controlled her breathing, willed her heartbeat back down to a normal rate and took her time studying her prison. Jenna would look for her. Of course she would. She'd have the entire frickin' police force whipped into a frenzy, searching every house in the neighbourhood.

What if she wasn't in the right neighbourhood? What if she was miles away from the Gorge and her sister was looking in the wrong place?

Panic slithered under her skin.

She stared up at the ceiling. Control. She needed control. And she needed to assess her surroundings. Start again. Take a look.

There were two doors. One, straight in front of the bed she lay on. She scanned the thick oak wooden door lined up directly between her feet. The other door was on the adjoining wall to her left. Again, thick oak, but this one had a frosted glass window panel. Both had locks she imagined had been engaged.

A vague recollection pricked her subconscious as she recalled the grating of an old key turning in an ancient lock when her captor left earlier.

Fliss dropped her head back to the hard surface of the bed to rest her neck, the tendons too taut for her to keep her head up any longer.

She willed her sluggish brain to engage. If it was still night, she had no idea what time it could possibly be.

Iciness engulfed her feet and the foetid smell of the blanket reached through the stuffiness of her nose. Chilled, despite the cover, Fliss shivered. At least it meant she didn't have serious hypothermia, didn't it? Had she read somewhere that if you shivered, your body was still reactive? Maybe shivering was the first sign of hypothermia and she'd die anyway. That would be shitty after surviving so far when poor Domino was dead.

Warm tears slipped down her temple to trickle into her hairline. Domino. The sharp crack of the stick hitting Domino echoed in her mind. He'd killed Domino. She sucked her bottom lip into her mouth and clamped her teeth down to stop herself from crying out. 'Mum, oh Mum.' Dark shadows floated in front of her eyes as her mind drifted, unhinged. Her mum had loved Domino, doted on him.

Disorientated, Fliss stared up at the bare bulb which hung from a straight wire in the ceiling. Bright white, it made her brain ache. The sensation of being hung upside down circled and the blood rushed to her head, filling it so completely she could barely think, barely breathe. The tightness in her chest pressed down as the walls closed in on her, just as the sides of the old fridge had trapped her so she knew she would die through lack of oxygen. As the memory blossomed, panic rose fast and venomous.

Fliss lay for a moment, eyes closed to concentrate on her composure. She wrestled down the fear that threatened to break free until she screamed like she'd screamed when she'd been trapped in the fridge. But this time she wasn't a child, and there was no Jenna to rescue her. She had no option but to rescue herself.

Determined to remain calm, she waited until the frantic pulse in her throat slowed and forced her brain to think through a logical and practical solution.

He wasn't here. She knew he wasn't here. She could feel it in the blanketing silence of the house. Sense it, rather than hear it. No movement, no echoes, no sounds. Perhaps he had left her to die. Alone. All alone. Her biggest fear.

Ruthless, she clamped down on her terror again, forced herself to reassess. Thick, white stone walls. Soundproof. Heavy oak beamed ceiling. One bare bulb. Two heavy doors. One external. The other internal. The likelihood was she was in a house somewhere near where she had been taken, but that covered a whole host of places. Ironbridge had around a thousand houses scattered about, and then there was Broseley, Coalport. Just looking at the thick walls of her prison made her think Ironbridge though. The paint on the walls was bright white as though it had been newly painted, with a faint tide line approximately four foot-high around the room. Flooding caused that.

Claustrophobia lodged in the back of her throat and threatened to swell up. She didn't want to drown. The Severn was near to breaking its banks. Ironbridge had the flood defences at the ready. What if it flooded? How close to the river was the house? She couldn't drown. What an undignified way to go.

Escape was her only option, but uncertain if she had the energy or the ability to move, she gave a tentative wriggle. Every bone in her body screamed with pain. Well fuck. Fuck-a-duck. How the hell was she supposed to get out of this?

Her hands were cuffed on either side of the single metal-framed bed. With a cautious rattle, she tested the hold. The old-fashioned metal hand-cuffs gave her a small radius of movement, not enough to escape. If they'd been the modern plastic zip ties, she wouldn't have a hope in hell of getting out of them, but with these, she could try.

Jenna propped herself up on her elbows and glanced down while she gave a wary tug on the restraint, twisting to manoeuvre her hand from the cold steel of the cuffs. She squeezed her thumb as close to her little finger as possible, scrunching up her palm to make her hand a tight ball, and wriggled her wrist back and forth. The handcuff slid down her wrist, over the first thumb joint... and stuck fast.

The effort too much, she flopped back onto the pillow, too exhausted to move. Her head swam, and the swirling acid ball of nausea threatened to rise up her throat and choke her. She was going to die. He'd not come back for her. She'd either freeze to death, die of starvation, or drown.

For an eternity, she lay still, until she pushed back the clouds of dizziness and the queasy roll in her stomach. She propped herself on her elbows once more, turning this time to the left.

Horror left her weak. She sucked in a sharp wheezy snatch of air while she stared at what should have been her left hand. She let out a low moan, unable to process what her brain told her was there. A grotesque twisted and swollen purple and black rubber glove which appeared to be on the verge of exploding. Only it wasn't a rubber glove. It was her own bloated skin.

She edged towards it, tugged on the restraints on her right arm as hard as possible without cutting off her circulation and peered for a long moment at her left hand. It wasn't hers. It couldn't possibly belong to her. She couldn't feel it. There was no pain, no sensation, just a disassociated numbness.

Her eyes burned, and she blinked away the wash of tears and focused on the sight of her hand. Her brain commanded her fingers to move, but they didn't. It was some kind of sick joke, it had to be. She collapsed back onto the bed, a black wave rushed over her vision. She was going to lose her hand. Then she was going to die. One way or another she would die. Hypothermia, drowning, gangrene, rape, murder. Could she scare herself any more?

She quelled the panic, forced herself to remember. The man had grabbed her as she had turned to run, and his hand had wrenched at Domino's lead which had been draped loosely around her neck. She could visualise her hand pressed between the lead and her own throat, paralysed with shock at what she had just discovered in the undergrowth. She remembered the sharp violent wrenches as he had choked the life out of her. She heard again the snap and crunch of bones as he'd twisted harder. Bones in her hand. Not her neck as he'd believed.

She stared at the ceiling. Eyes unblinking as she remembered. Oh God, he'd thought from the crackle and snap that he had broken her neck. He thought he'd killed her. He'd been wrong. Unbelievable pain had shot through her hand and she had been helpless to do anything as her life force rapidly faded. Black waves consumed her.

She closed her eyes, blinked in the brightness of the single light bulb still glowing inside her eyelids. She had no idea how much time had passed since she had fainted, her brain too sluggish to care, a distant fogginess still insistent on damping down her ability to think.

With a dispassionate glance, she took in her fat, swollen hand again. Sure it had distended even more, she inspected the tightly stretched flesh surrounded by the stainless-steel handcuff. There was no room for movement, not a spare millimetre between her wrist and the handcuff. Even if there was room to move it, her fingers still didn't obey. The purple-hued flesh spilled over the sides of the metal. If it continued to swell, she'd lose her hand. It may already be lost. Yet she couldn't dredge up the energy to care.

She panted through her mouth, her nose so blocked that when she swallowed it shot pain into her forehead.

Her gaze skimmed to the door, straining to listen to the silence beyond. How much longer would it be until the man returned?

Fliss wallowed through the washes of black, contemplated the idea of an escape plan, if only the marshmallow listlessness would move on. She allowed her eyes to drift closed, her brain tangled with the desire to sleep. Just sleep. The vague memory of the injection he'd administered poked at her consciousness just to be swallowed by the thick clouds. He'd seemed to know what he was doing. What normal person kept needles and pain serum in their own home?

13

'Wanker!' Mason tossed a narrow-eyed stare over his shoulder at Adrian as young PC Downey struggled to keep up with his long-legged stride. Mason punched a thumb in Adrian's direction. 'What kind of entitlement makes him think he can use his own fucking car for police business?'

Jenna shot a quick grin up at Mason almost hanging over her shoulder, so he could growl in her ear. It had been funny, even under the circumstances.

She gave a quick sweep over Adrian's vehicle, a smart, black Range Rover Autobiography LR SDV8. Practical, comfortable, warm and overwhelmingly gorgeous. She couldn't blame him for trying his luck.

Mason took her by the elbow and guided her away as Adrian ducked into his car to retrieve various items he evidently couldn't live without. 'Fucking Duty Inspector Connelly was having nothing of it. Did you hear?'

'Shh.' Jenna lowered her brows while she kept an eye on her unwanted guest.

'He told him in no uncertain terms that, as a civilian, Chief fucking Prosecutor or not, he wasn't fucking insured nor authorised to drive his own vehicle on police business. And when he tried to fucking wangle a bit more, Connelly said he wasn't allowed to transport an on-duty police officer in pursuit of her duties.' Mason tipped his head back and let out a hoot of laughter. 'Fucking funniest thing.'

She had to give Adrian credit, he'd tried his best while she'd tapped her foot, ready to go. Mr hotshot lawyer had approached the Inspector with several different attitudes; reason, persuasion, dogmatism. All to no avail. If she hadn't more important matters on her mind, she probably would have taken the unholy piss out of him too.

Instead, she jiggled the keys to the police issue Vauxhall Insignia.

'We'll see you over there, Sarg.' Mason called out as he took out the keys for another vehicle from his pocket, his lip curling in a sour smile. 'Just got to run the kid back home to change out of his uniform.'

She raised her chin in acknowledgement and sighed as she waited for Adrian to catch up with her.

In no rush, he ambled across, overcoat slung across his arm, iPad and phone in his hands. She cruised a critical gaze over him, finding it difficult to find fault. Ill-prepared the night before, she'd shrugged into a thick, warm overcoat as they came out of Malinsgate Station.

She pursed her lips, tossed a quick glance at a rain filled sky and hoped it held off as long as possible before it soaked them all to the skin. She patted her pockets to reassure herself that her gloves were safely there for when she needed them and opened the rear door to slip her wellington boots in the car.

It was going to be a long day.

Although the same height as Mason, Adrian seemed to have more difficulty fitting in as he squeezed into the passenger seat of the Insignia, his long legs folded, his knees almost touching the dashboard. Her lips twitched at the sight of his discomfort. It was almost pitiful. Almost.

'I prefer to drive.' His low rumbled objection reached her ears as she turned the key and listened to the well-used engine roar to life.

'Me too.' The flash of her smile fell from her lips as guilt pricked her.

She shot the man another glance. 'Entitlement', Mason had called it. Everything about the man screamed entitlement. From his perfectly manicured fingernails to his Gucci leather shoes.

Jenna sobered. She had far more important things to think about than whether or not he bought his shoes from TK Maxx or Harrods. *Fliss.*

She'd said so little in Gregg's office because, quite frankly, she couldn't care less what arrangements they thought they were making. It made no difference. She'd find her sister, regardless. With or without their permission. She'd never stop looking, not until her dying breath.

She focused on the road ahead, blinked away the wash of tears.

Irony had succeeded in raising a response from her though. This huge hunk of a man, who'd exerted his power insisting on their enforced partnership, now suffered the consequences of his forcefulness by being squashed into her car.

'Nice vehicle you have back there,' she murmured, more to distract herself than him.

'Yes,' he grunted back.

She changed gear and knocked his knee with the side of her hand, his answer barely a distraction from her all-consuming thoughts. *Fliss.*

Her belly filled with a tight, clenching desperation. Where was Fliss?

'So, what's the plan of action?'

Aware he'd moved closer, so he could watch her, Jenna gave a shrug. She'd simplify it for him. 'We're going to find my sister. We're going to find the killer. Then, we're going to see what the connection is.' She shot him a quick glance and then turned her attention back to the road.

'Okay.' His low rumbled voice filled the car. 'And in the meantime, how do we achieve this?'

She changed down a gear and took the bend onto the suspension bridge with a little more gusto than she'd intended. 'We do grass-roots police work, which entails door-to-door, asking questions, finding answers, lots of walking, research and a lot of cups of tea.'

'Tea? I'm more of a coffee man myself.'

Another ripple of amusement took her by surprise, but he was in for a shock. 'I think you'll find you get what you're given, in what you're given, when we're visiting people. Unlike in your world where the cups are most likely bone china, we accept what's offered.' He'd probably never come into contact with the kind of people she worked with. 'We take the dirty mug with the chipped rim, the grey tea with the sour milk and just ask for three sugars to disguise the dirty dishwater taste.'

She sensed his delicate shudder of disgust and resisted the temptation to smile. Not with amusement, but with a strange satisfaction that she'd managed to make him cringe.

She changed gear and knocked his knee yet again. 'Sorry.'

He attempted to shuffle away from her.

'You can put the seat back, you know.'

His lip curled. 'I believe it's as far back as it will go.' He huffed out a breath. 'You do know you're not going to be taking part in any door-to-door, any coffee drinking, any information gathering, don't you?'

Startled, she jerked her head around to stare at him. 'What do you mean?'

'I mean that's precisely the kind of thing to compromise this case. The only thing you're doing is handing over your knowledge, reviewing information gathered and expressing your opinion. There's no way you can actually take part in the investigation. I thought I'd made it abundantly clear.'

He hadn't made it clear. She had to find Fliss. Who the fuck did he think he was?

She whipped the car through the wide curving arc up the hill in the direction of Broseley, noting Adrian's wild grasp at the door handle, and then she deliberately slewed the car around the final bend and shot down the straight towards the Ironbridge car park.

She allowed herself a vicious smile as he shifted his weight from his left buttock to his right while she pulled the vehicle into the car park. The sight of the skid marks across the tarmac Mason had made the previous night as they'd raced across it made her lose her smile again while fear washed over her.

As she turned off the engine, Jenna turned and quirked an eyebrow at the man next to her, waiting for him to speak.

Knuckles white, he extended long fingers and gave them a wiggle. 'Have you ever been on a police driving course?'

She shot him a feral grin. 'Of course. How do you think I got to be this good?'

Before he could reply, she flung open the door and leapt from the car as the sharp reminder of why she was there slammed back home.

Adrian unfolded himself from the passenger seat, which gave her a brief moment to compose herself as she pulled the keys from the ignition with fingers of ice. His dark gaze rested on her across the bonnet of the car, and she realised he'd deliberately moved to give her a moment alone.

She opened the back door of the car, pulled out her wellington boots and tugged them on, placing her flat-soled ankle boots in the footwell. She fastened the buttons of the thick, black woollen overcoat her mother would have approved of and forced her shaky hands into a pair of red leather gloves Fliss had bought her the previous Christmas.

'Looks like someone was in a rush.' He indicated the marks through the thick layer of mulched leaves and mud the weather had inflicted on the area in the last few days. She chose not to answer, instead, she closed the door and stabbed her thumb onto the remote key fob to lock it behind them. More than she had been able to do the previous night.

The caffeine she'd poured down her throat had done nothing to slow down the rapid pace of her heart, but her mind was sharp, focused. She had no idea what had made her think her sister was in danger the previous night before any evidence had even presented itself, but she had. It had been pure impulse, not a police officer's professional deliberation of the circumstances, but a sister's deep, abiding instinct borne of her close connection to Fliss. The same instinct which told her her sister was still alive. That someone had abducted her.

She'd lived her entire life looking out for her little sister. Perhaps it had all just been preparation for now; for this moment. She hoped to God she was up to the job.

Much warmer than she had been the night before, Jenna stood in the dim watery light and let her gaze cruise across the Benthall Edge Wood hill. The Ironbridge stood stalwart to her right, a handful of visitors straggled across it, huddled in their coats, noses red, insisting on taking photographs of the famous landmark. The birthplace of industry.

'Did you manage to get hold of the vet?'

Jenna continued to scan the area with a critical eye as she ignored the gentle sympathy in his voice and answered the question. 'Yeah, Domino's awake. They've splinted his lower jaw. The vet says it's more of a fracture than a complete break. It should take six to eight weeks to heal.' She rubbed her fingers over her brow as she studied the far side of the river. A slow drizzle reduced visibility, leaving the entire town in a dull, grey mist. She turned on her heel, the deep ache in her chest was for Domino. 'He'll have to have a feeding tube for a while.'

With Adrian matching her stride, Jenna marched towards the Tollhouse. She cast her gaze side to side, aware of Adrian's intense observation, but her attention was on her surroundings.

Jenna saw nothing out of place. Forensics were up in the cordoned-off hills, but she needed, for her own piece of mind, to review escape routes now, before any more visitors contaminated a possible scene. She came to a standstill at the gated entrance to the Ironbridge. With Adrian silent beside her, Jenna breathed in the chilly air coming off the River Severn and noted the faint wisps of fog spiralling their way down the valley. She paced onto the bridge, did a one-eighty on her heel to look back up at the woods.

'He couldn't have taken her over the bridge. Someone would have seen.' She turned in a slow circle, scanned the area, taking in The Tontine pub on the opposite side of the bridge. Two police officers emerged from the front entrance, flicked their notebooks closed and moved on. More police officers trooped up the hill as they conducted house-to-house enquiries. If it hadn't been her own sister missing, she'd have had to admire the quick flood of officers who'd volunteered to take part. It wouldn't make any difference to them who was missing. They were trained to help, to volunteer, to commit.

She cruised her gaze over the hillside. Where? Where could her sister be? Where could he have taken her?

'She can't be up there. It would be too impractical. Too difficult to take an unwilling or unable person all the way over the bridge, up the hill.' She cast her gaze back and forward, peering up at the vista. 'Impossible.' She knuckled her fingers into her forehead. 'It doesn't matter how strong a person was, there's no way they could carry a body all the way up there.' She flopped her arm back down to her side. She scanned the area again. 'Nor would Fliss go willingly. Would she?'

With a shake of her head, Jenna continued to talk to herself. She was aware of Adrian's presence, his broad shoulders and wide chest were unmissable, but it wasn't for his benefit she spoke out loud. She needed the process to keep her sane.

'He couldn't risk anyone seeing him. Even at this time of year when it's really quiet. Most of the tourists would have gone back to their B&Bs or hotels. But he couldn't guarantee that. There...' She pointed at The Tontine. There were other houses stacked up the hillside, but she concentrated her attention on the pub. 'He couldn't risk being seen from there. So...'

Retracing her steps, Jenna ignored Adrian as she strode past him.

'He had to have a car. Why would you pick someone up, carry them some distance...' she pointed down the woodland track, '... if you didn't have transport?' Looking along the short length of the car park they had just drawn into, there was nothing to immediately grab Jenna's attention. 'Fliss didn't walk out of there under her own steam. She had to have been carried.'

'What if she was dead?'

Jenna whipped her head around as Adrian spoke. 'Dead?' Aware of the sharp challenge in her voice, Jenna scowled at Adrian, tempted to poke him in the chest.

'If he'd already killed her. What if he just...' He shrugged his shoulders, stared past her, down the track she'd been looking at. '... Carried her body so he could dump it further along? So, you don't find everything at once. Or perhaps he thought if he hid her separately, you wouldn't have discovered either of the bodies.'

'That's bullshit because my sister is not dead.' She ground her teeth, flexing her jaw as she glared back up at him, daring him to continue, willing him not to.

His steady gaze met hers for a moment before he turned to watch the approaching police car.

14

Mason didn't seem to have as much trouble unfolding from the confines of his own police issue car, in fact, he leapt out of it with an agility that surprised her. Perhaps it was relief he didn't have to sit in it any longer. Brow furrowed, he hunched his shoulders as she strode towards him and his new, temporary partner.

PC Downey slid himself out of the car at the same time, looking even younger than he had in uniform. As he reached inside the vehicle, the pair of jeans he wore hooked under the top of his underpants at the back with material so loose it seemed as though his arse hung down to his knees. Layers of T-shirt, hoodie and jacket clung to his skinny frame and with the woolly black beanie pulled low on his forehead, Jenna wouldn't have been surprised if he'd actually been arrested by Mason instead of partnering him.

From the sour look on Mason's face, her ex-partner wasn't terrifically impressed himself.

'Hey.' Jenna kept her face neutral as the young police officer approached her but gave him a quick assessment before her attention returned to the surrounding area again.

Ryan raised his head and grunted, all attitude and teenage punk. Jenna wondered if he wouldn't have been better off back in uniform. The lad seemed to have lost the sweet innocence he'd had earlier that morning. Perhaps Gregg had made a mistake.

'He smells oily,' murmured Mason as he passed by her and started walking towards the Forensics team further down the path.

'Oily?'

'Yeah, like someone slicked him down with, I dunno, that stuff they stick on their hair. Oily stuff.'

'Pomade?'

Mason whipped his head around, eyes filled with horror. 'Fucking... what? Fucking pomade. You have to be kidding me.'

'I kid you not.'

His shook his head, mouth twisting in disgust.

With a twitch of her lips, Jenna fell in step. She flung a brief glance over her shoulder as Adrian engaged the kid in conversation. She wasn't sure she'd ever been so young, so thuggish, but it would be good to think the young man was trying to make something of himself.

'Perhaps it's his aftershave,' she suggested helpfully to Mason.

'He doesn't shave...' Mason grumbled back, flicking a spiteful look at the boy's smooth cheeks, '... and if he does, the aftershave's gone off.'

She tossed another glance over her shoulder at the errant PC. 'Didn't he have a suit?'

Mason stopped abruptly and stared at Jenna as though she was an idiot.

'You are joking, aren't you? I ran him home. He didn't even have a wardrobe. He picked those up off the floor, for Christ's sake. They'd probably been there three weeks.' He stabbed his finger at her. 'If we're looking for dead bodies, perhaps his flat is the place to start.'

Jenna flicked up an eyebrow. Mason seemed to have moved on from being pissed off earlier with Gregg for assigning the Chief Prosecutor to her to being pissed off he'd been partnered with a kid. Perhaps he was permanently pissed off. She'd just never noticed before. She'd assumed it was attitude.

Mason stopped his tirade. 'I'm sorry, that was tasteless. This is Fliss we're talking about.' He picked up his pace and glanced over his shoulder as they left Adrian and the young PC behind. Shaking his head, he ran his fingers back and forwards across his mouth. 'She's a really nice kid.'

'Kid? You do know how old she is?'

'Twenty-three.'

It was Jenna's turn to stop. Her reply was hesitant, suspicion niggling in the back of her mind. 'She's not a kid. Not any more.' Although she'd always be her younger sister.

'You're right. Twenty-three. She's a woman.' His voice turned gruff.

Jenna glanced up at him. 'Mason? Is there something you're not saying?'

Mason shook his head and stepped to one side to let Jenna pass him by. Adrian was talking quietly to PC Downey. He didn't seem to have a problem with his get-up, but it might just cause a riot when they got back to headquarters. PC Downey looked more like a druggy than CID.

Half amused, she shook her head and then noticed Adrian watching her from beneath lowered brows. Did he regret the decision he'd made to allow her to stay on the case? Would it be his decision to take her off, or did Gregg have the final say?

She scooped her fingers through her choppy brown hair while she assessed the scene before her. She could have fallen apart. She could have screamed and shouted, but despite the pain arrowing through her, she knew she had the strength to carry on. Whether it lasted was yet to be seen, but she was damned if she'd show any weakness in front of the others.

As they reached the cordoned area, lengths of barrier tape stretched up the hillside from the main walkway through the trees to the narrow path above to define the territory they needed to search and investigate. A long, narrow, white canopy had been erected on the main thoroughfare to protect the area from the rain, but Jenna assumed it just wasn't feasible in the woods to cover everything.

She blew out a soft sigh as she scanned the vicinity. The area was vast. Despite the large team drafted in to help, it could take days to carry out a thorough investigation. Control, preserve, record and recover. The process had been drilled into her since her first green days on shift.

'What happened to DI Taylor?' Mason interrupted her reverie and she answered without taking her gaze from the scene.

'He's reviewing the information with Frank, setting everything up. I need to report back to him when we get back, then he'll come out and take a look later.'

Adrian moved closer to her as they approached half a dozen people in white personal protection equipment.

Reluctant to step inside the cordoned area at this stage, Jenna waited.

A tall, skinny guy separated himself from the group. A mop of thin greying hair flopped onto his forehead above the glasses perched halfway down his long angular nose. He gave a brief nod and held up gloved, muddy hands as an apology for not offering them to shake.

'Mason. Jenna.' He turned warm grey eyes to Jenna and her heart melted. This man always invoked a feeling of security, of calm solemnity, a father figure she'd never had. 'Sarg, I'm sorry about your sister. We'll do the best we can to help.'

Jenna met his quick, sympathetic look before she nodded and turned her head.

'Adrian, this is Senior Forensic Scientist Jim Downey.' Both men nodded rather than lean in for a handshake. 'Jim, this is Chief Crown Prosecutor Adrian Hall. He's here to keep an eye on me. Make sure I behave myself.' With a bitter twist of her lips, she smiled at Jim and then turned to introduce the younger man. 'Of course, you know Acting DC Ryan Downey.'

Jim flicked a curious glance Adrian's way and then swiped his gaze back to the kid. 'What in hell's name are you wearing? I thought they'd just made an arrest and brought along a criminal to my scene.'

Ryan's new-found confidence rushed out as a bright red blush took its place.

'Dad!' Ryan kicked at the mud beneath his feet, his spine curved over in a long sulk, and then shot a resentful glance at his father while Jenna tried to smother her laughter.

'Go see your mother later, she'll sort out some clothes for you.' Jim held his arms wide. 'Do you see anyone else around here wearing grunge gear?'

'No, but...'

'You've been assigned to CID, not undercover on the Drug Squad.' Jim raked his gaze over the younger man. Unable to hide his pride, his lips twitched in a reluctant smile. 'Congratulations on your secondment, son.'

He turned away from Ryan to face Mason, who did little to contain his own amusement. With an embarrassed cough, Jim indicated with a wave of his hand they should follow him through the inner cordon.

They dressed in the pale blue Personal Protection Equipment in silence and when they were ready, they headed along the main concourse behind Jim as he strode through the thick mud, blackened from the days when steam trains were used to transport thousands of tonnes of coal every day to the power station in the distance. Long since decommissioned, the land still bore the marks of the Industrial Revolution.

Jim turned his head to speak as they approached the collection of white tents.

'Right, well, so far, we've contained the area. An absolute nightmare of a job. We've only just finished. We've not removed the body. I've collected as much evidence from her in situ as possible. We have to be mindful we don't contaminate any evidence, especially with the rain washing mud and leaves down the hillside. They've managed to barrier it off as efficiently as possible, but if we have a deluge, we're in trouble.' He glanced up at the pewter sky and shot Jenna a pained look. 'We have to pray the rain holds off for a while longer.'

He came to a standstill and drew his hand in the air to indicate the wide swathe of area they'd quarantined. 'I have a number of my people up there carrying out scene recognition.' He turned to Adrian to explain, 'At this stage, we touch nothing. We use our eyes and only our eyes. Equipment is camera, paper, pen. We need to gain an understanding of the extent of the crime scene. We have one chance only to perform an untainted search before the evidence is washed away by the rain, swallowed by the mud.'

He turned his back and took another few steps to the entrance of the tent, picked up a long, thin cane. He stepped to one side and indicated for them to look inside.

Jenna took a long moment to study the scene, so very different from the night before when they'd wallowed around in the rain and the mud with only the dragon lights to illuminate the area once Air One had moved on. Powerful though they were, there was no substitute for daylight.

As she stepped back, Adrian moved forward and ducked his head to get inside the tent. Jim hunched his wide, bony shoulders against the cold and rubbed his acrylic gloved hands against each other.

'What we have so far is an unidentified female, I'd guess early thirties.' He squinted at Jenna. 'Although she could be much younger. It looks as though she's had a tough life. I'd say there's considerable evidence of abuse. She's white, pale brown hair. We'll send her to the morgue when we're ready, post-mortem will be carried out later today, possibly this evening. Pathologist has been informed and is making his way from London. From first observations, I'd say she has a broken neck. We'll know for sure later if that was the cause of death. I would say so. We fingerprinted your sister's iPhone last night. There only seemed to be one set of prints, we assume they belong to Fliss. We got it off to IT who are checking it out now.' He shot Jenna and Mason a quick frown. 'Bloody police officers trampled half of my crime scene last night trying to get a dog out.'

He removed his muddy gloves, bagged them and pulled on a fresh pair. 'However,' he paused and pointed up the hillside to the higher pathway, 'we have a pretty clear indication from the tracks up there and beyond the path what may have transpired.'

Handing gloves to each of them, Jim pointed a finger at his son, his grey eyes intense. 'Don't touch a thing!' He turned to indicate along the path. 'Best guess at the moment. There are tracks leading from further up the hill, where someone has come down quite controlled, sideways to keep from sliding, deep footprints where they paused for a while behind a tree, the mud let him sink in, obliging us with perfect prints. Then he came straight down to where it looks as though your sister was standing. The imprints from her boots are deep and clear in the mud. Loads of dog tracks all over, so that confuses matters. We all know he's a bloody lunatic, that dog of your sister's.' He wrinkled his nose in disgust and irritation stirred in Jenna's stomach. He'd ruined a crime scene, but in her eyes, he was a hero. He'd suffered horrific injuries and if he died...

Unable to consider the thought, she tuned back into Jim.

'We managed to eliminate other footprints, both human and dogs, because they were different. Fliss's footprints weren't difficult to identify and the Dalmatian's are distinctive.' He crouched down, pointed to one with a long stick. 'Large, catlike almost, with no fur between to smudge the imprint. Not many walkers up here after the rain, so we were fortunate.

Quite a bit smudged by the presence of so many leaves, but there are distinctive prints in patches of mud.'

He moved, flowed his arm around the area. 'Then we have slide marks right down to where Domino supposedly landed. We don't know for sure as someone's size elevens walked all over my bloody crime scene.'

He cast a scathing look at Mason and waited, but if he thought he'd get some kind of apology, Mason acted true to form and gave a careless shrug.

'Domino was alive. He needed to be sent to a vet immediately. We didn't know at the time we were dealing with a crime scene. We were working under the assumption he'd had an accident.'

'Some bloody accident. Poor lad.' Jim snorted his disgust. 'So, we know more or less where he landed, but then it looks at the moment like someone else fell too.' He swept his arm to indicate the slope of the wooded hillside. 'There are more slide marks, intermittent, as though the person was rolling and bouncing.' Jim glanced at Jenna.

Blood drained from her head leaving her weak and light-headed. She clenched her jaw, determined not to show any weakness, but noticed how Adrian watched closely as Jim continued.

'From the initial observations, no forensics yet, it looks like your sister slid down the hillside and then, on hands and knees, crawled up into the tunnel, right over the body. The deceased has clear fingerprints on her face, neck and shoulder. Obligingly, someone dipped them in blood and mud before they applied them to the corpse. We're getting them checked against the prints on Fliss's iPhone.'

Jenna closed her eyes, ground her teeth together as she tried to swallow. She cleared her throat and squared her shoulders. 'Continue.'

'There is one clear footprint on the body. We're double-checking, but we believe it's the same as your sister's prints above. As the body had been there for possibly twenty-four hours from the state of rigor mortis, we're assuming your sister had no idea she was there as she scrambled through the mud.'

Jim waved his hand in the vague direction of the site, shook his head with disgust. 'So many bloody footprints in there, we can't tell what happened.' He flicked his fingers to indicate higher up the hill. 'It's clearer up there. Larger footprints keep coming down the hill, still controlled, still sideways, but faster and a little more slide to them. Right to the site.' Jim let them absorb the information. 'Any questions?'

Ryan eyed his father, raised a tentative hand as though he was still in school.

'Son?'

'Was she alive? Sarg's sister. Was she alive when he took her?'

Jim cast his gaze around the rest of the crew. 'I can't give you that information. She wasn't moving is all we can surmise.' In the silence, he waited for further questions, but when there were none forthcoming, he waved them on to follow him. He strode away back towards the car park, coming up short as he reached a small area to the right-hand side, cordoned off with red and white crime scene tape.

'Here. We think he put her down. Maybe he had to readjust his hold on her. We don't believe there was a struggle. We need to conduct a thorough search, but here,' he pointed, 'there's soft imprints in the mud, not just footprints, but clothing. And here.' He used his stick to point again. 'The shrubs here have been flattened.'

Jenna's heart stuttered, and she voiced what everyone else must surely be thinking. 'She couldn't be dead. There was no logic to him carrying her if she was dead. Why risk it?' Jenna circled her gaze around the group. 'There's already one dead body. Why wouldn't you leave another? You have nothing to lose at this point. No. She had to be alive.' She couldn't believe anything else. Wouldn't allow herself to.

Jim reached into his inside pocket, pulled out several small plastic evidence bags. 'I've plucked a few things, simply because I could see them and with the weather closing in again, I don't want to lose stuff I can clearly see.' Handing out one each to Jenna, Mason, and Ryan, he gave them a moment to inspect the contents. He flicked his finger to indicate Jenna's bag. 'Long, blonde hair. Caught on this bramble. Fits your sister's description. But we need DNA.'

'I'll arrange that. Her hairbrush?'

'That would do.'

Nodding at Mason's bag, 'Clothing fibre, red. Again, we'll see if there is any DNA on it.'

Jenna swallowed as her mouth went dry. 'She had a bright red coat. To match Domino's collar and lead.' She slipped the bag from Mason's fingers to get a closer look. 'I'd hazard a guess that's the same material.' Her heart squeezed tight. They didn't need DNA, it belonged to Fliss.

'And, finally...' Taking the small evidence bag back out of Ryan's hand, Jim showed it to Jenna. With shaking fingers, she slid it from his grasp, rubbed her own fingers across it. A small silver locket.

Adrian stepped in for a closer look.

Jim's voice gentled as she stood perfectly still while she studied the locket. 'We know it belongs to your sister. We already checked inside. There are three photographs. Your mum, you... and Domino.'

Jenna's soft pants were the only sound in the quiet of the woodland. Adrian slanted his gaze over to Mason, and Jenna turned to see why, realising from the stiffness of his frame that Mason suffered almost as much as she did.

Unable and unwilling at this point to take the implication in, Jenna paced away, took a moment, rubbing her thumb across the plastic encasing Fliss's locket.

'Mum bought it for her twenty-first.' Her mum who'd been gone such a short while. Jenna closed her mind off to the pain stabbing at her chest. She'd not even come to terms with that emotional rollercoaster and she had to deal with this one. She could only hope she had the strength within her. 'It damned near cost a fortune.' With a last stroke of the necklace, Jenna handed it back. 'Was that the only one you found?'

'Only...?'

'Necklace.' She touched her fingers to her throat. 'She always wore two. The locket Mum bought her, and the angel I bought her for her eighteenth. She never wanted to take it off.' She stopped as her throat tightened against the words that needed to be said. 'I bought it to protect her.'

Jim cleared his throat roughly. "There was no other necklace. Not yet. We'll keep looking."

Helpless, Jenna turned on her heel, she glanced at each of the men in their varying degrees of discomfort, held Adrian's gaze for a long moment, clear determination filling her before she turned her attention to Jim. Professional. The only reason she could stay involved in the case was if she remained professional. If she fell apart, she'd never find her sister. Her mother was dead and gone. Fliss still stood a chance of being found if they acted quickly. First twenty-four hours were the most important. Half that time had already gone.

With steely determination, she met Jim's sympathetic gaze and pulled her own inner strength right out of her boots. 'What next?'

Jim indicated further down the pathway and they walked in silence for several minutes.

He reached inside his jacket pocket and took two further evidence bags out. 'We think he put her down here again. Just before he came out to the car park. Maybe he needed to check there wasn't anyone around. Maybe she was just too heavy for him. Either way, this is where we found the chain from the locket. They obviously became separated. It may have caught on her clothes, it's considerably lighter than the locket.' Holding it up, he showed it around. 'And something else. A gold wedding band.' He handed this to Jenna while he watched and waited.

'This isn't hers.' She frowned as she handed it back and turned to walk away.

'No, I assumed that from the size of it. Your sister is tall, long-limbed. This ring is quite tiny. We think it may have belonged to the deceased.'

She swivelled around, tilting her head slightly to one side. 'How?'

'Don't know.' Shrugging, Jim took the evidence bags and put them all back inside his white overalls, except the one with the gold ring. 'But the victim had a wedding band mark around her finger and no wedding band. The size would be consistent with her finger size. Her fingers were quite small.'

Jenna's head spun with the possibilities. 'So, either *he* took it because it's identifiable and dropped it when he placed Fliss on the floor, or what's the possibility Fliss had hold of it, as she touched the body, and she dropped it?'

Mason stepped in to take a look. Jim nodded his head, jiggling the packet in front of them.

'Indeed. We'll have it fingerprinted. Plain gold wedding ring. Initials and date inside.'

'What?' Jenna demanded, closing in on Jim to take the bag from his fingers and stare at it.

Jim leaned over, waggling a finger above the ring. 'It has a date: 14 March 2008. And initials.' He took the evidence from Jenna and held it close to his eyes, screwing his face up as he peered through his half-moon glasses. 'MS and FS by the look of it, although the script is very ornate, so it could be something else.' He squinted. 'Could be a B. MB and FB. I dunno. Heh.' He lowered the ring. 'We'll give it to the Intelligence Unit and see if they can come up with anything.' He weighed it in his hand before stuffing the bag back in his pocket. 'Good lead though.'

Jim stopped as they reached the boundary of the car park, indicating their surroundings. 'No further evidence, no more footprints. Anything that might have been there was covered by all the activity when the Services arrived. We don't know if he had a car because the vet drove hers down here, destroying any evidence, or if he lived locally and simply carried her home. Difficult to tell, but I do know he couldn't have carried her far.' He pointed at the ground where footprints had been cordoned off. 'She was too heavy for him, you can see from the way his right foot goes over to the side every couple of steps, and besides, it would be too noticeable in this area to carry someone far.' Nodding towards the overlooking houses rising above the car park. 'You'll see if anyone noticed anything when they finish their door-to-door.'

Jenna nodded, scanning the hillside once more. 'He had to know he had limited time after Fliss screamed. He had to assume someone would call the police. The dog walkers in Dale End said it sounded...' She paused to drag in a laboured breath. 'Blood-curdling.'

Stripping off his gloves, Jim extended his hands to Jenna, wrapped both of his around hers when she reached out, his warmth seeping through the thin layer of her vinyl gloves. 'Jenna, I'm sorry. Best of luck. You know if you need anything, my love, you come to me.'

She dipped her head but never made any attempt to withdraw her hands from his, feeling the easy affection which came from years of knowing each other. 'Thank you, Jim.'

Glancing around, she gave his fingers a quick squeeze before she dropped her hold on him and stood in silence for a moment before Jim turned.

He shook Adrian's hand, his gaze narrowed in quick assessment as though he needed to take the measure of him. He clenched Mason's big fist in his for a brief moment before he turned and gave an affectionate scrub of his knuckles across his son's head. 'Get a suit, boy.'

Ryan bobbed his head in acknowledgement, his Adam's apple jerking as he made rapid swallowing noises, dark crimson rushing up his neck and into his cheeks to leave them flushed and mottled under his pale skin. 'Yes, Dad.'

Already preoccupied with the next step of his job, Jim strode off up the path towards the crime scene.

Mason drew up alongside Jenna as they made their way back to the cars. She tucked her chin into the collar of her coat, keeping her voice low. 'I'm going back to the station. I'm told I'm not allowed to join in any house-to-house or questioning of witnesses. I'm only here to keep the glue sticking in the right places.'

Mason glanced over his shoulder at the Chief Prosecutor. 'Wanker.'

She ducked her head to study her robust boots. 'You're going to have to find a more suitable name for him.'

As she raised her head, Mason patted her on the shoulder. 'It's good enough for now.'

She gave him a reluctant smile. 'He doesn't seem so bad. I guess his intentions are noble.'

Mason's stillness drew her attention. 'Don't go all soft on him, now, will you? He's not on your side, but I am.'

Before she could reply, he turned away and wandered towards his car as PC Downey scuttled after him and Adrian caught up with her.

'He doesn't like me.'

She kicked up a smile. 'Mason? Eh, he doesn't like anybody.'

15

SATURDAY 27 OCTOBER, 18:00 HRS

The man rubbed eyes scraped raw by contact lenses. He fucking hated them, but he hated his thick-lensed glasses even more and refused to wear them to work. They made him look like some kind of geek with his thin, straight dark hair and swarthy skin. He raised his fingers to his stubbled cheeks. He looked scruffy enough by the end of the day without squinting at everyone through bottle bottom thick lenses. Not only did they age him, but the weighty frames dug into the dip at the top of his nose to leave a thick red ridge, like a scar. He'd considered buying new ones with thinner frames, but they could never thin the lenses down quite enough for his prescription to fit into the type of frames he'd appreciate wearing.

It was his mother's fault. The opticians told her. If she'd taken him when he was younger, they would have corrected his vision at any early age while he was developing, but because of her fear of any kind of authority, she'd failed him. She'd always failed him.

He glanced at his watch. There was nothing more he needed to do. He'd kept his head down all day, but it seemed everyone needed him. The office bustled, but he'd handed over his workload before he was due to leave. Damned if he was about to work overtime. He had better things to do.

He flicked the screen off on the PC he'd worked on. Everything neatly filed, all information collated. Tomorrow he'd give the project more of a structure. He pushed to his feet and made for the door.

'G'Night all.'

He blinked in the harsh lights of the corridor and made his way down the stairs, a hint of anticipation trickling through his veins. He'd not allowed himself to think about her all day, deliberately turning his attention away from the woman who was now his wife's replacement. Soon. Soon he'd see her. He'd tend to her wounds, make her better and she'd be grateful.

On his way out of the door, he raised his hand. 'Bye, Ben. See you tomorrow, mate.'

Relief swept over him as he slipped into his car. He could take the contact lenses out and drive home with his glasses on.

His stomach gave an angry growl and he realised just how busy he'd been during the day. Too busy to eat.

He reached for a packet of breath fresheners and popped one in his mouth as he checked his mirror and then pulled away from his parking spot, a quick thrill of excitement pushing away his weariness.

16

SATURDAY 27 OCTOBER, 19:40 HRS

'My tummy hurts, Jenna.'

'Well, you should have taken notice when Mummy said to go to the loo before you came out. Don't you dare wet yourself!'

'Jenna, it hurts so much, please. I need to find a toilet. Please, Jenna.'

Fliss blinked once, twice. She could have sworn her sister had been in the room with her. Her voice had been so real. It hadn't seemed like it was just in her head. It had been the shriller tones of Jenna's younger self she'd heard.

The pain in Fliss's stomach increased and she flexed her legs as much as the restraints allowed, pulled in her pelvic floor muscles. God, she was going to wet herself. She wanted to jiggle around as she used to when she was a little girl and she'd waited too long to go to the loo. She'd always done that. Always been too occupied to think about such things as going to the toilet. Now, there was nothing more important, and it made the need all the stronger.

She had to have been on her own for hours and although she dreaded the return of her captor, she also desperately longed for him to come back and rescue her. Rescue her! How could she even think that way? He wasn't going to rescue her. He was probably going to come back and kill her.

She waited in silence. Nothing but the sound of her own breathing to fill the empty cavern of a cellar. Desperate to pee, not even the welcome diversion of her drifting mind could help, her ears labouring to hear a sound, any sound.

Then she heard something, the faintest noise. A shuffle in the dimness of the white painted room. She held her breath and listened harder. Strained to hear. Less of a sound than a vibrating hum she could vaguely feel through the metal bed. She stared at the solid wooden door, it seemed to be coming from that direction. She angled her head slightly to catch the sound better, but it stopped abruptly as though it had been switched off. Resting her head back on the thin pillow, Fliss stared up at the ceiling and gave herself a minute to think.

Could it be a car? She tried to sniff the air for evidence of fumes, but her nose was still so blocked, filled with blood and snot so as to constrict her breathing, so she had to suck air in through her lips. The metallic taste in her mouth a persistent reminder of what had happened.

Christ, she'd probably broken her nose. Her sister was never going to let her live this down. She'd had quite a neat nose. A little on the long side, but at least it had been straight. Aware she could see it, she peered down the length of it. She hoped it was just swollen, or the break had been clean, and it would heal straight again. Knowing her luck, it would develop a lump, or be bent. She'd look like a witch. If she even managed to get out of there. If she lived.

She shifted uncomfortably, the pressure in her stomach growing. Glancing down at her injured hand, she studied it for a moment before deciding it hadn't swollen any more, but it was still being squeezed by the handcuff. She had ceased to feel any pain there at all. She knew she should care, but somehow, she couldn't summon up the energy.

She raised her head, tilted it to catch any further noise while she stared at the door. There had to be a garage through there, and the other door must lead into the house. This was the information she needed to help her when she escaped. And she would escape. She needed to be free from her restraints, acknowledged, but right now she had to think positively.

The familiar scraping sound of a key turning in the lock caught her attention and she squeezed her eyes closed as the internal door swung open.

'Hello, my dear, nice to see you're awake.' His myopic stare already peered through thick lenses close to her face as she blinked her eyes open. He blinked back at her, slowly sending a quiver of revulsion to tighten her swollen stomach.

'Toilet.' Her voice rasped out, barely audible.

'Oh, you need a drink, my dear.' He raised his hand, stroked her forehead.

Her stomach clenched. 'No.' She virtually squealed through her constricted throat, thrashed her head from side to side to rid herself of his touch and make him understand her desperation.

Without warning, he fisted a length of her hair, yanked her head up to his. Nose to nose, his flushed face wobbled as small eyes beyond his glasses bored into hers. Pain shot through her scalp as he tugged harder and the clench in her stomach convulsed as his sickly minted breath puffed over her face.

'Don't...' He wrenched her head sideways, following her movement so his face was in line with hers. 'Ever...' He screwed his fist into her long hair until his knuckles bruised her scalp. 'Say no...' He shook her head, bouncing it against the bed until her brain hurt as it rattled against the inside of her skull. 'To me...' Spittle flew from his wet lips to spray her face. The tear of her flesh burned as a hank of hair parted from her scalp. 'Again.'

She closed her eyes against the fury in his red, flaccid face as tears streamed down her temples. She squeezed out a desperate apology.

'I'm sorry. I'm sorry. I need the toilet.' But she knew it was already too late. Raw humiliation coursed through her as the quick scald of her own urine spread from between her thighs.

From his instantaneous stillness, she could tell he knew what she had done.

'I'm sorry,' she whispered again and blinked through the wash of tears.

His nostrils flared as the stench of ammonia rose. He leaned back to stare at her with barely controlled horror, his mouth pinched tight, his nostrils white with disgust. He narrowed his eyes to stare at her for a full minute before his whole face relaxed and a nauseatingly sympathetic look washed over him again.

'Oh, my dear. I didn't know you were incontinent.'

Horrified, she tried to correct him, but his expression sharpened, his fist clenched in a painful twist in her hair to choke the words in her tight throat mid-denial.

'We'll have to do something about that, won't we?'

Unravelling her hair, he flicked his fingers until he shook loose the hank he'd torn from her head. His eyes gleamed behind the thick glasses as he watched it fall to the floor. He wiped his fingers against each other, his mouth twisted in a tight line of disgust.

A flick of horror crossed his face as he ran his gaze down her body and encountered not only the urine stains but, she imagined, the dark crimson of her period as another cramp seized her lower belly and the warm flood of it coated her inner thighs.

He stumbled to his feet, revulsion creasing the deep grooves around his taut mouth. He dashed towards the door, his voice constricted as he tossed words over his shoulder.

'You dirty bitch. Dirty. Dirty bitch.'

Nausea burned a hole in the base of her throat and the wild flutter of her pulse pounded in her ears like a gush of torrential rain. He'd wanted to kill her. It had been right there in the manic gleam of his dark eyes.

She twisted her head to look at the door he'd gone through. She needed to escape. He'd not locked it behind him, but there was nothing she could do about it. She was too well tethered to the cot.

Exhausted, she rolled her head against the flat pillow, misery seared her as her urine and blood turned cold and clammy across the back of her jeans and down her thighs, soaking through the mattress.

Humiliation clawed at the anger she held deep inside. How dare he? To treat another human in such a way. When she escaped, and she would escape, she was going to make him pay. Jenna would make him pay.

She wasn't a victim. Her body may be held prisoner, but her mind was free.

Fliss heaved air in through her lungs and brought herself under control. The throbbing pain from her head intensified as adrenaline and blood surged through her and hate blackened her vision.

The sharp metallic rattle cut through the black haven she'd retreated to, jarring her nerves until she jerked her head up to watch as the man came through the doorway, tugging a stainless-steel medical trolley behind him.

Dread turned her veins to ice and she could barely breathe through the constriction in her chest as she skimmed her gaze over the contents of the trolley. Long, silver, sharp. Oh, dear God, what was he about to do to her?

'Here you are, my dear. We'll try this first.' He raised what could possibly be an incontinence pad for her to see from the second shelf of the trolley. 'Mary left them behind when she departed. She couldn't control her bladder either. I'm sure she won't mind if you need to use them.'

Memory came in harsh flashes. The body. She'd touched a body. She'd held the woman's hand in hers while the iciness of it had seared itself in her own flesh.

Her stomach cramped again as her gaze flew to his and the simpering smile spread across his face.

'Yes, my dear. That was my wife you met. Silly woman obviously had no idea what was best for her.' His eyes crinkled at the corners. 'She ran. I thought she understood, I thought she'd learnt her lesson.'

He raised his hand and Fliss forced herself not to flinch, to remain completely still as he stroked her mud-caked hair back from her face, so she had a better view of him.

'You see, she'd been mine for so long. I was her keeper. Then she wanted to leave.' He smudged his thumb beneath her eyes, stretching the delicate skin there. 'I couldn't allow it. We were good together. She was obedient.' He dug his thumb into Fliss's cheek, pushed hard until the flesh ground into her teeth, his gaze distant with memory. 'Until Friday morning when she was no longer obedient.' He trawled a glance over Fliss as though he'd just remembered she was there. 'She ran. For no reason I could think of. Ran naked through the woods. She'd rather run naked than stay with me, it seemed. Stupid woman. She slipped and broke her neck. I'd followed, but there was nothing I could do to help. She was already dead.' He leaned closer. 'I knew she was safe there. No one could have found her. I had to go to work first, then I brought my car. I walked the high path, so no one would see me.' He slipped his fingers down her bruised neck and the whimper she let out shamed her as he applied a little pressure, sharp eyes watching her all the time, pleasure flickering through them at her response.

'And then you came.' He pressed his thumbs deeper, his wet lips quirked up at the edges while she choked, desperate to pull in air as the tears trickled from the corners of her eyes, down her temples and into her dirty hair.

'Please.' Shamed, she willed him not to kill her. She wanted to live.

His smile spread, sweet and condescending, and he replied as though she'd spoken her thoughts out loud. 'I shan't. Not yet awhile. Not unless you disappoint me.' His gaze moved lower to study her neck. He reached out while she lay frozen beneath him, his fingers clasped at the tiny angel at her throat. 'You're my angel. Sent to me from heaven to replace my dear wife.'

He dipped his head and every nerve ending in Fliss's body tensed to snapping point as he lowered his face into her neck. He fumbled for a brief moment and came away with the delicate necklace she'd had around her neck. The one Jenna had given her for her eighteenth birthday. The one she'd bought, she said, to protect Fliss. Torn between that and the locket her mother had given her for her twenty-first, Fliss had worn them both ever since.

He dangled it in front of her face, the silver angel sent tiny sparks of light to dance in the air and give her hope. 'My angel now.' He slipped it over his head, and it disappeared as he tucked it into the neck of his jumper, dispelling all hope.

There was no longer any fear, just a flat well of weariness and despair.

Fliss closed her eyes and allowed the billowing black clouds to engulf her as the slippery eels of nausea writhed in her stomach. A minute, that's all she needed to regroup, then she was going to kick his arse for him. Without letting it show, she allowed herself a smile inside. Jenna would approve. She'd tell her to stiffen her spine and not expect to be rescued every time something went wrong. She was responsible for her own fate.

The sharp tug on the cuff of her jeans had her eyes springing open. The effort to lift her head proved almost impossible, but the distinctive sound of scissors cutting material forced her to strain her aching neck.

He glanced up, his gaze met hers without him stopping what he was doing, the steady grind of the scissors against the thick material of her jeans grated against her skin. 'Relax, I'm just going to see to your wounds.' He smiled and zipped the scissors further up, slicing up the side of the seam to her hips. 'It's okay. I know what I'm doing.' He applied pressure and snipped the waistband with what appeared to be a pair of industrial scissors. She flopped her head back onto the pillow, the effort to keep it up too much. 'I trained to be a doctor, you know. For a full year. And then a paramedic.'

Fliss wondered if it was her imagination, but she could have sworn he'd already told her. Perhaps he was proud of the fact that he was a failed doctor. Her head reeled as she attempted to imagine him as anyone's doctor. He claimed his wife died accidentally, but his dead, hollow eyes had pierced her soul when he'd stared down at her.

She forced her eyelids open while he moved to the other side of the bed, took the metal trolley with him and started on the other leg of her jeans. As he came to the waistline, he paused, and she turned her head to see what had caught his attention. He clipped the last piece of material and then placed the scissors on the trolley before he rolled his rounded shoulders down so his face was level with the side of the cot.

He sucked air in through his teeth, made a quiet clucking noise while he took her broken and bruised hand in his as though it was the most precious of china. 'Oh, my dear, you should have said something earlier.' The fanatic gleam in his expression shot a visceral pain into her gut. If she could have curled into a protective ball, she would have, but the restraints on her ankles inhibited her from any movement.

He smoothed soft fingers across the back of her swollen hand and sent shivers of revulsion through her. Currently, she could feel nothing, but he was going to hurt her, the maniacal blackness in his soul told her. He placed her hand on the edge of the bed, patted his pocket and removed a set of keys, the sharp jingle of them knifing through her nerves.

Surprised at the efficiency with which he unlocked the handcuffs, Fliss studied her hand, a peculiar sense it wasn't hers distanced her. Blackened to her wrist, the indentation from the cuffs dipped deep into her flesh.

'You must have broken it when you slid down the hill. I never noticed. I've been a tad... preoccupied.' He cupped it in his own pudgy, soft white hands, but as there was no sensation other than a deep throb from the flow of blood in her wrist, Fliss didn't attempt to remove it. She'd not broken it sliding down the hill, he'd done it when he'd tried to choke the life out of her with the dog lead. She narrowed her gaze to study him while he was preoccupied. If she told him, he'd probably kill her as he seemed to believe fate had intervened to rescue her.

Sod fate, her own hand and a desperate desire to live had accomplished the task.

She pushed back the insistent waves of tiredness to watch him closer. With repulsively tender movements, he straightened each of her fingers, using his own to investigate the swelling, palpating her purple flesh. Perhaps he had no intention of hurting her and the manic light in his eyes was because he wanted to care for her in his own twisted way.

The violent wrench of her hand soon disillusioned her of that notion as she almost shot off the bed while pain more excruciating than she'd known before sent flames licking up her arm. Her entire body spasmed and the scream that emerged from her throat was low and guttural, an animalistic cry for help. A cry no one could hear.

'There, there. I'm just putting it right.' He gave another sharp yank on the next finger and she pressed herself back on the bed, body arched to repel the pain while she sucked in deep breaths through her open mouth and dug her heels into the thin mattress. 'It's okay, just relax.'

Once more, he twisted her hand; this time the grind of bone against bone had her clamping her jaw closed, desperate whimpers clawing past her damaged throat. Stop. She just needed him to stop.

'It was so very remiss of me not to have tended to this earlier.'

The black clouds she'd fought so hard against raced in to obscure her vision and block out the pain.

17

SATURDAY 27 OCTOBER, 19:40 HRS

Head in hands, Jenna sat on the hard-plastic chair opposite Adrian in Malinsgate Police Station canteen. She'd not eaten since first thing that morning and the vast quantity of coffee she'd consumed earlier had taken its toll. The fine shake in her fingers was evident when she'd picked up her cup a few minutes earlier, almost spilling the black liquid. She thought he'd not noticed, but then caught his expression. If he told her to cut down on the caffeine, she'd probably take his head off, but he remained silent, and then pushed his chair back and disappeared from the room.

She took advantage of the silence while no one was there and allowed her mind to empty of all thought until he laid his hand on her shoulder. She whipped her head up, prepared to fight if he told her to go home.

'You need to eat.' He pushed a sandwich towards her.

She stared at it for a long moment before reaching out. His offering was some kind of speciality bread stuffed full of ham and lettuce. 'Where the hell did you buy this? There's nowhere to buy anything here.' She looked around at the stark whiteness of the room with its basic melamine topped tables and plastic chairs. 'It's only somewhere to sit while we eat.' The days had gone when she could walk in and have a full roast meal, subsidised by the Force.

'I went out earlier when you were in the incident room. I figured you couldn't get into too much trouble under DI Taylor's keen eye.'

'He's a good man.'

She smiled, the brief flicker of pain gave way to the desperate need to eat.

He slipped into the seat opposite and gave the sandwich another nudge until it touched her elbow and forced her to move. She dipped her head, hesitated just long enough to convince herself she really needed to keep up her strength, then pulled it towards her.

He picked up his own sandwich, took a bite while he watched her with narrowed eyes as though it was important she eat.

She took her time to chew and swallow, her appetite gone as soon as it had made itself known, but she forced it down and took another couple of bites before she spoke.

'I thought we would have found her by now.'

Surprise flickered over his face at her confession, and he leaned in closer, elbows on the white topped table. 'Why?'

'I don't know.' She took another bite, forcing it down as it turned to dust in her mouth. She glanced around the mostly empty canteen. 'I just thought it all had to be a mistake.' She laid down her sandwich to pick up her coffee, took a sip. 'It was the locket. Seeing that seemed to make it a reality.' She gave a jerky shrug. 'I don't know why, but I understand now why people want to hold on to something personal of the missing person.' She gave a rapid blink, her mouth pulling down at the corners.

Wariness flickered over his face and she wondered if he could deal with it if she cried. Whether he'd put a comforting arm around her or run like hell. Now wasn't the time to test the theory.

She pulled in a shuddering breath, picked up her sandwich and took another taste of it. He'd almost finished his and he'd had double the amount she had. She struggled just to take each bite. Each nibbling mouthful. To act normal when her world had fallen apart.

'You know, our mum died a few months ago. Back in July.'

It wasn't discomfort on his face, but pure sympathy, giving her heart a deep wrench. She should shut her mouth. Stop talking, but somehow, she found she couldn't. Easier to talk to a stranger than someone she knew; Jenna discovered the emotional tap had turned on.

'It was sudden. So sudden. We had no idea. I've never had anyone close to me just die. It was the three of us, always. We're so close. *Were* so close. Nothing defeated us. Not Fliss's unbelievable trait of finding trouble, nothing.' She broke off a corner of the bread and stared at it, unable to put it in her mouth. 'When she was gone...' She flicked a look up at him. 'Mum, when she was gone, I promised her I'd look after Fliss. She's my little sister, I've always looked after her.' The sob hitched in the back of her throat and threatened to turn into a wail.

'Hey.'

Jenna glanced up as Mason shuffled his frame into the small plastic seat next to her and slapped a limp, white plastic breaded sandwich onto the table in front of him.

Shoulders too wide for the space, he nudged Jenna over, oblivious of the desperate emotion bubbling just under the surface, threatening to spill over in a horrible mess. 'Are you going to eat that or interview it?'

She bestowed him with a weak smile and pushed some more of the sandwich into her mouth, then spoke around it. 'Dear God, what did you do to *him*?'

Mason snorted into his coffee cup as he took a huge swig and then swallowed. 'His mother got a hold of him. Apparently, Jim texted her.' A wicked chuckle rumbled through his deep chest and he nudged Jenna like a school kid, raising another reluctant smile from her as Ryan slipped into the seat next to Adrian.

Wafts of cheap aftershave almost made her bring what little of her lunch she'd eaten back up as Adrian turned his head to inspect the youngster, who stared at the three of them, challenge in his bright blue eyes. His hair had been slicked to his head; the comb marks still evident. The white shirt with its starched collar stuck out, far too loose for his scrawny neck, while the plain blue tie had a knot the size of a tennis ball.

Adrian spared Mason a quick glance while he pushed the last of his sandwich down his throat in between small snorts of laughter, his wide shoulders shaking.

The boy's suit had obviously come from his father's wardrobe. Too wide in the shoulders, the sleeves came over the back of his hands almost to his knuckles as he reached for his meal.

Heaped high on a plastic plate, the mountain of food vaguely resembled a chilli con carne, but Jenna wasn't quite sure and her stomach hitched in protest at the greasy smell. It didn't seem to matter to Ryan as he bowed his head and scooped forkfuls of the Sainsbury's microwave meal for two into his mouth.

'No rush, Ryan. We've got twenty minutes.'

The kid raised his head and grinned at Mason. 'Enough time for a pudding, then.'

Jenna picked another piece of sandwich off and put it in her mouth. 'Don't you get fed at home?'

Ryan grinned. 'Sure I do, I call in at Mum and Dad's on the way home. She'll have dinner ready, but I need food now or I'll keel over by the time I'm off tonight.'

Jenna met Adrian's gaze, grateful for the distraction, however brief. Her mouth twitched again, and she pushed the last of her food into her mouth, surprised she'd managed to eat it all without her stomach rebelling. 'You're right. We need energy.'

Ryan grinned at her and wolfed down some more of his dinner while Jenna caught the quick flash of relief on Mason's face as she dusted her hands off and screwed up the packaging from her sandwich. She chose to ignore it. She didn't need the man turning soft on her. She'd melt in a puddle of self-indulgent pity if anyone showed her more than a lick of compassion.

The day had been too long and unkind.

The sweltering heat in the station still failed to melt her frozen emotions. She recognised it as shock, had seen it in so many others. Countless over the years. Faceless in their anonymity. She empathised on a level she'd never suspected herself capable of with all those victims she'd patted on the knee, laid a comforting hand on their shoulders, while her heart had truly never understood. Could never have understood until this moment how they felt when she broke the news of their loved one's demise. A car crash, an accident, a murder.

Until this moment, she may have thought she understood, but she never had. She'd never imagined the searing, soul-deep pain they'd suffered.

She knew now and wished to God she didn't.

With no ability to change the past and no chance of predicting the future, a woman in command of her own fate, so she'd always thought. She'd forced food into her mouth, with absolutely no interest, knowing she had to keep up her strength for the sake of her sister. Emotionally paralysed while others took control.

Mason swept fingers through his short, spiky hair. The lines around his mouth had deepened, his brow lowered. Always the clown of the shift, his change of temperament sucked any life out of the air.

Jenna always suspected Mason had a thing for her sister, and from the lines of worry slashed over his face, she guessed it ran far deeper than he'd ever admitted. An honourable man, despite his wild good humour, he would never have made a move on her little sister while she was with Ed.

Ed.

She whipped her head up, pushed her chair back as she stood.

Mason's gaze snapped to hers. 'What?'

'Ed.'

The chair legs scraped across the floor like nails on a chalkboard as Mason surged to his feet.

Ryan leapt to his at the same time, stuffing the last bit of food in his mouth with no idea what was going on, but sensing the urgency. 'Where are we going?'

Heart hammering, Jenna was already halfway to the door.

'Whoa. Hold up, Jenna. Where do you think you're going?' Adrian was there before her, his hand on the door to prevent her from opening it.

'Ed.'

Eyes cool, shoulders relaxed, he kept his hand on the door and ignored Mason's step forward. 'Who is Ed?'

'Fliss's ex-boyfriend.'

Dark eyebrows rose to crinkle his forehead. 'And you've only just thought of him now because...?'

'Because she hasn't been with him for...' Jenna racked her brain to think how long Fliss had been living with her, '... almost three months.'

'Okay.' Adrian dropped his hand from the door and crossed his arms over his broad chest, effectively blocking her exit. 'So, why now?'

Mason closed in. 'Because Fliss started getting texts from the twat last week.'

Unsurprised, Jenna shot Mason a quick look. They'd always been on the same wavelength, that's why they worked so well together. The moment she'd mentioned Ed's name, he'd known. She'd grumbled about Ed's texts when he'd sent them to her sister and Mason had half-jokingly offered to bury the guy for Fliss.

'I see.' Adrian raised a hand to his knitted brow. 'Okay. Mason, Jenna, let's go and speak with DI Taylor and I'm sure he'll deploy someone to bring him in for questioning.'

Panic at the loss of control skittered over her skin. 'No, I...'

The sharp shake of his head stopped her mid-sentence.

'No, Jenna. You won't do anything. This is exactly what would compromise this case.'

The logic of it seeped through her determination to track down Ed. Stupid of her to even think that way. She'd always wanted to get the prick in a small room and beat the shit out of him for what he'd done to her baby sister. He'd scraped away at Fliss's self-confidence, made her doubt herself by telling her she was stupid, not worthy of his love or anyone else's.

Jenna stepped back with a quick nod and waited for Adrian to open the door.

'I'd suggest you keep away from him too if you already have knowledge of the ex-boyfriend.' He addressed his remark to Mason, then stepped through the doorway into the brightly lit corridor beyond. 'Let's speak with the DI.'

Then she was going to visit Domino. Damn that dog, but if it hadn't been for him, Ed may well have destroyed Fliss completely, but Domino had taught her sister self-respect and love of another being far deeper than Ed could ever understand.

Tears filled Jenna's eyes, not for the first time since Fliss had gone missing. She'd held it in, remained stoic in her approach, but if Domino died, she was going to kill him. Fliss was going to need Domino when they found her, and they would find her. Jenna's heart told her so. It could accept no less.

She marched along the stark hallway, heels clicking on tiles dulled with age and the harsh treatment of many a footstep. Aware of her following, she paused to rap a quick, respectful knock on the Inspector's office door before she let herself in.

Old-school, DI Taylor came to his feet and made his way around the desk to greet her, a quick flick of surprise crossed his features as the other three men shouldered in to stand beside her in the cramped room. Taylor peered over the top of his glasses at them all before he guided her to the only visitor's chair in the room, his hand a gentle firmness in the centre of her back.

'Jenna. How are you holding up?' Raw whisky scraped at his words. A man of long, hard service, he'd started his career in the Army and moved on, spending his earlier years in London, witnessing far more than Jenna could imagine in his time before he moved to the quieter realms of Shropshire. 'You have something for me?' He wasn't the kind to hold her hand, but the touch on her back was his gentle reassurance he would stand by her and give her every ounce of support he was capable of.

She settled into the chair, while Taylor made his own chair creak with indignation at the sheer weight of him. 'Fliss's ex-boyfriend, Ed Pendleton.'

Taylor picked up his pen, wrote the details down on the paper in front of him, ignoring the computer by his side. 'Address.'

She reeled it off. She'd been there countless times before Fliss had made the decision to leave the loser.

As a thought occurred to her, she gave a quiet cough and waited for Taylor to raise his head. 'Has anyone accessed her phone yet?'

At his slow nod, a shudder ran through her. They'd listened to her sister's last call. The one Fliss had made to her. The one she'd missed.

'Can I listen to any of it?'

'Sorry, Jenna, but you're not allowed access to that kind of information. You know that.'

'Was there anything from Ed?'

'Yeah. We were about to ask you who he was.' He held up a hand before the words she held in her mouth could burst out. 'They weren't nice. You don't need to know the details, but we'll get him in for questioning right now.'

'Can I be there?'

'No, Jenna, it would be inappropriate.'

'But I can help. I can suggest questions.'

'And you can compromise our case.' He kept his voice gentle but firm, to leave her in no doubt of his professionalism.

Frustrated, she slammed her arms around herself to hug in the anger and the fear.

'We'll keep you informed of any progress.'

'I can go, can't I?' The ice in Mason's voice slithered down her spine, but it appeared that Taylor, with his years of experience, was unmoved.

His gaze took a slow perusal over her partner before he nodded. 'You can of course watch, Mason, but you won't be involved in the questioning of Ed Pendleton.'

'But...'

'That will be assigned to Salter and Wainwright.'

Jenna glanced up at Mason as he towered over her on one side while the kid – whatshisname, her mind went blank for a long moment while she stared at him as he twitched with excitement – Ryan, that was it, Ryan. His long willowy form swayed next to her like a sapling in the wind, while Adrian's shadow dominated the corner of the office. Solid.

It's what she needed. A team. Her team. She lowered her head, gazed down at her arms wrapped around herself and slowly loosened them. She'd always been a team player and at this time, when she least of all wanted to be alone, they'd closed ranks around her, to protect her, help her, support her.

When she raised her head, they were waiting. She pushed herself up from the chair, tugged her jacket into place.

'Salter and Wainwright are good officers. I'll wait to hear of any progress.' She took a deep breath. 'Thank you, sir. I appreciate everything you're doing. This is not an easy case for anyone.'

Taylor nodded, the swirl of understanding lit his eyes. 'I'll keep you apprised of progress, Jenna, have no doubt.'

With a glance of approval, Adrian swung open the door and she slid by, tossing a look at Taylor over her shoulder. 'I'll be in my office. There are other cases to deal with while I'm waiting.'

She wasn't sure she had the ability to deal with anything else, but what the hell else was she supposed to do? She could take time off, go home, sit in an empty house and worry about her sister. Or she could clear her head, look at her caseload and get on with her life while she could. At least if she was there in the station, she'd hear of any progress.

Aware of every single person casting her sympathetic glances as she strode along the hallways, down three flights of stairs and into her office, she shut the door behind her and leaned against it.

The light knock made her sigh with impatience, determined to ignore it. Five minutes. That's all she needed, just five minutes to bring her emotions back under control. The gentle rap sounded again and, with a sigh, she stepped away from the door and let it swing open. It appeared no one was prepared to allow her five minutes alone.

Surprised the whole gang wasn't there, she stared at Adrian. 'Where've they gone?'

His serious eyes met hers with far too much understanding. 'To see if they can track down Salter and Wainwright so they can get in on ground level, as Mason said.'

She turned away, the empathy in his gaze was too much, her throat thickened as she swallowed. She glanced at her watch to distract any attention he may pay to her. She'd put in a twelve hour day, and even the clean-cut Chief Crown Prosecutor had started to show signs of exhaustion.

She may not want to, but she needed to head home. There was nothing further she could do.

18

Stomach cramping, Fliss groaned as she ran her gaze around the empty room. How much longer would the man be? He'd been gone a lifetime and whilst he seemed to have cleaned her wounds up while she'd been out cold, he'd not left her anything to eat. Her stomach griped again in protest.

Mortified that he had stripped her legs bare and left them with a thin blanket over the top, revulsion skittered through her at the thought of what he may have done while she was unaware. Her only consolation was the revulsion he'd shown when he realised she bled. As though she was dirty.

She glanced down the length of her body, kicked aside the thin covering and studied the state of her naked legs. Relief swamped her at the sight of an over-large nappy – incontinence knickers – covering her lower half. The quick flood of embarrassment heated her cheeks at the humiliation.

She didn't feel any different. There was no longer any throbbing pain from all the abrasions, and her hand had stopped its insistent pulsing. She chanced a look at it, managed to pull herself up onto her elbow to peer down at the injured limb.

Confusion stole through her mind, making her thought processes stutter to a halt. Her arm, from the tips of her now pink fingers through to her elbow, had been encased in what she assumed was a plaster cast. She fought to remember what had happened just before she blacked out and the surge of pain in her hand reminded her of what he'd done.

What the hell was he? He said he'd trained to be a doctor and a paramedic. He'd set her hand, plastered it. Her gaze cruised over her naked legs. Her pulse raced along with the thoughts in her mind. He'd been so angry, violence threatening to explode one moment and then suffocatingly obsequious the next, as though he couldn't be kind enough to her.

He wasn't bipolar, that was far too simplistic for his personality traits. Perhaps schizophrenic was the only way to describe him.

Fear popped the sweat out on her freezing skin.

Each gash had been stitched and abrasion treated, every area tended to with neat precision. Not the work of someone who didn't know what they were doing, but with skill and a meticulous care. She sucked in and found her breathing less constrained, her nose less constricted. Had he also cleaned her face up? She frowned and pain shot the length of her nose. He'd broken her nose. And fixed it again.

Humiliated, she screwed her eyes closed. She had no memory of him fixing her, touching her body with revolting familiarity.

Neck aching from the effort, Fliss allowed her head to flop back on the thin pillow. The bright white of the ceiling arched over her head. Low. She thought back to when the man had come into the room. He hadn't had to duck at all. Hard to judge height when you were lying flat, but he couldn't be too tall. In fact, quite a delicate build. If she was free, she could take him. She was strong enough, and although he wasn't young, maybe in his early forties, he seemed like a... geek. She was fit, healthy, stronger than him, wasn't she?

Tears gathered, and she let out a bitter laugh. If she was free...

He'd left the single bare light bulb burning, whether for her benefit or not, she didn't know, but there were no windows, no natural light, not even seeping in from the gap around the two ill-fitting doors.

She rolled her head, cruised her gaze around the room, the stale mustiness of it filling her nostrils. The river, she could smell the river, and the tide mark from what she imagined was recent flooding came to just over halfway up the walls, leaving a dull grey smear of mould.

She screwed her eyes shut and worked her way through the fog in her brain. She had no way of knowing how long she'd been out cold originally but... the tideline. The evidence of rising waters. She had to be close to the river, close enough for the flood waters to invade the cellar from time to time. Relief swamped her. She was near the river, not too far away from home. She pulled in breath after breath. She was close to home.

She raised her plastered arm, placed the heavy weight of it on her stomach as it registered in her mind that her arm was no longer cuffed to the bed. Her ankles were free, and she could, if she wanted to, sit up. She tested the cuff on her other wrist, far too tight to slip her hand out of, but it enabled her to roll over onto her side and lever herself up into a sitting position.

Dizzy nausea swept over her in an ugly wave, almost knocking her on her back again. Sheer willpower kept her upright as she ground her teeth and hung onto the edge of the bed with her one good hand while she swayed, the floor coming up to meet her, then retracting at an alarming rate.

Fliss tempered her breathing and, by dint of sheer determination, managed to stay upright until the room stopped spinning.

Her stomach clenched in a violent protest against the lack of food while her gaze settled on the back of her undamaged hand. Bones stark under parched skin and blue veins sunk deep below the surface. Not only had he deprived her of food, but she was in desperate need of water. She was dangerously dehydrated.

If he didn't come back soon, she was going to die from dehydration. She could only assume he'd gone to work. The rapid flutter of her heart slowed down for a moment while she concentrated on her breathing, then raced off again as soon as her attention strayed.

The pain in her face almost distracted her attention from her swollen, dry tongue. As she glanced down, she became aware of the sight of her own cheekbone in her eyeline, distended and blue. She couldn't remember each knock she'd suffered, but the one on her cheek throbbed like hell.

She raised her right hand only to have it jerk to a standstill as the handcuffs gave a metallic rattle to remind her she was trapped.

With detached observation, Fliss studied them, wriggled her hand, only to regret it as the weight of them gave a sharp bang against her wrist bone in a cruel reminder she was his prisoner.

She rolled forward to stare at the handcuffs again, felt the swell of dizziness push her further over, but clenched her jaw and leaned down anyway. She could hardly hurt herself more than she already had, but she needed a closer look at the cuffs. Her sister had exactly the same pair from when she'd first joined the force. They were never used any more because they had been replaced by plastic ties.

She wriggled the fingers on her good hand, compared them to the dirtier pink stubs she could see poking out of her cast, her mind a constant marshmallow sludge as she trailed her gaze over her legs once more. No wonder she was unable to hold on to a single strand of thought. Except for the dull ache which filled the empty cavity of her chest. Beyond the sickness came a sharp shaft of pain to drag a wild sob from the depths of her soul.

'Domino.'

She dragged in a hiccupping gasp, the burn in her chest sending it tighter while she struggled to blow out again without a keening cry emerging from her lips. He couldn't hear her; she didn't want to risk the man hearing her. He'd know then how terrified she was. He'd know he'd hurt her. She couldn't bear the thought of him gaining sadistic pleasure from her pain. And he would, she'd watched it in the dark swirl of his gaze.

'Domino.' Her voice a dry croak, she was careful to lie herself back down on the metal cot, wriggling her legs to coax the thin blanket back over herself while tears slid down her temples and she hiccupped in small sobs. 'Domino.'

He'd saved her life, saved her sanity from one man who believed he should control her body and soul, just to sacrifice himself to a man who now had total control of her.

She gave a dry swallow. Except he didn't. Just as Ed had controlled her body, and for a time her thoughts, her soul had still been free and, with Domino's help, she'd set the rest of herself free too.

But Domino was no longer there. The man had killed him. She forced herself to remember, delved into her own dark memories. The loud crack as the man hit her Dalmatian, the wild thrashing through the undergrowth as Domino had flipped over and over into the darkness where she could no longer see him. He'd not made a sound. Not even a quiet whimper. There'd been no further movement, only from the man.

She slammed her eyes closed, she didn't want to remember. The tears dried and still her muscles refused to relax until her mind acknowledged what it needed her to remember. The body. She'd been unable to see it in the dark, but she'd held the hand, slipped the ring off the shrunken finger into the palm of her own hand and held on.

'*Stupid bitch*,' he'd grizzled as he'd taken the final step down before bright lights filled her vision, and then nothing. Nothing until she'd woken a prisoner in a cell.

19

SUNDAY 28 OCTOBER, 08:00 HRS

'Juliette Alpha 76, this is Control.'

Jenna snapped up the radio and depressed the speak button. 'Juliette Alpha 76 receiving.'

'We've had a report of a disturbance on Benthall Edge, are you available?' The operator's monotone voice dragged across the Airwaves.

Jenna bumped the heel of her hand against her forehead. 'Jesus, don't they know I'm not available for enquiries like this? What are they thinking of? Benthall Edge.' It could be information about her sister, or her sister's abductor. It could be her sister, for crying out loud. And she wasn't allowed to go. Although the temptation to simply snatch up the job almost got the better of her. She slanted a look at Adrian. She swore he could read her thoughts. She gave a heavy sigh before she depressed the talk button. 'Negative Control, try Juliette Alpha 24.'

The sharp trill of the telephone almost had her leaping out of her black leather boots.

She grabbed the receiver, held it to her ear, her voice sharper than she intended. 'Sergeant Morgan speaking.'

'Sergeant Morgan. I have a woman at the front counter who'd like to speak with someone.'

'Is no one else available, Len?' Irritation laced her voice as she ground her teeth at the interruption. She hadn't even been to the incident room yet. She had no update on her sister since she'd left the previous evening and lack of sleep made her snappy.

'Quite honestly, Sarg, no. Everyone else is tied up on... other cases.' Her sister's.

'What about uniform?'

'I think she'd rather see a female, plain clothes.' His voice dropped. 'She's here to report a rape.'

'Her rape?'

'Yes, Sarg.'

Jenna closed her eyes and pressed her hands over her eyes. What the hell was going on? Why did everyone suddenly want her to deal with stuff? She could have sworn they had a conspiracy to keep her distracted.

She drew in a calming breath; grateful Len couldn't see her.

'See her into interview room one, I'll be there in just a minute.' She surged to her feet, slamming down the telephone as she charged to the office door, the idea of a self-indulgent cry no longer an option.

Aware of her shadow beside her, she marched along the corridor, listened to the slap of her boots as she raced down the stairs, almost grateful for the diversion. There was nothing productive she could do for her sister right now, so she might as well try and make someone else's world a little better.

She nodded at Len on her dash through, but his nasal voice halted her mid-stride. 'Interview one is occupied, I put her in three.'

'Thanks, Len.' He knew she never liked two, she found it too small, too claustrophobic.

'Sarg?'

She stopped again, turned to face him. For some reason, Len always had the ability to irritate her. His slow, insistent perfectionism did it. It wasn't his fault, in fact it made him a genius at his job on the front counter. Precision was exactly what they needed, but so many times, speed would have been a little more important. She raised her eyebrows as she waited, impatient for him to speak.

His cool gaze swirled with sympathy as he peered at her over the top of his glasses. 'I'm sorry to hear about your sister. I hope they find her alive.'

Slam.

Just like that, her mind flew, and her heart thundered. Alive. She'd never allowed herself to believe Fliss could possibly be dead. Never. She wasn't dead. Jenna would find her.

Light-headed, she forced her frozen lips to move. 'Thank you.'

She knew it had been nothing but concern that made Len say that, but pain sliced her heart. She swivelled on her heel and let herself into interview room three, leaving Adrian to decide whatever the hell he wanted to do, but he wasn't coming in with her. This was her scene. It had nothing to do with her sister and he wasn't welcome inside.

She closed the door and leaned against it.

Dark, haunted eyes greeted her, and she wondered what the young girl saw as she stared back at her. Not too dissimilar a look, if the pain Jenna felt in her heart was reflected in her expression.

She shoved aside her own emotions and straightened her shoulders.

'Hello. I'm Detective Sergeant Jenna Morgan.'

She reached out her hand, enclosed the young woman's icy one in hers. It wasn't always the right thing to do, to touch someone, but Jenna sensed this girl needed the human contact.

She dug deep to find the compassion in her soul to deal with another's pain when hers was so wracking. She consulted her notes. 'Estelle, would you like to tell me what happened?'

* * *

Sunday 28 October 13:15 hrs

Adrian had gone. She couldn't expect him to hang around while she interviewed her rape victim and arranged for a sexual offences liaison officer to take over from her, but she was unprepared for the rush of disappointment when she realised he wasn't there. Already his quiet, supportive presence had made itself felt.

He'd been outside the interview room when she stopped for a comfort break the first time and dogged her footsteps down the hallway while Donna had sat with Estelle. By the third break, he'd removed himself to the comfort of her office, where he'd raised his head to acknowledge her as she drew open her desk drawer and grabbed a small bar of chocolate.

She checked the obvious places, but with no further time to spare, she dragged her phone from her pocket and stared at the time. If she wanted to be in on the arrest, she needed to get a move on. And she did want to be in on the arrest. It meant locating the frustrating Chief Prosecutor while everyone else rallied. She'd given them thirty minutes to get everything they needed, but she needed something else. Something more. She needed to know whether there'd been any progress with her sister's case. The new case she'd caught had been a welcome distraction, but several hours had passed since she last checked in on the incident room. She slipped into the almost empty room.

'Hey Frank, how's it going?'

Not much taller than her, Frank's wide, bony shoulders rounded in a slight hunch and his waistline had thickened, expanding each year she'd known him. She touched the sleeve of his woollen jacket. His slicked-back hair had thinned recently, giving his broad forehead a wider appearance.

He rubbed his hands together, gaze firmly fixed on the incident board. 'Nothing. There's nothing going on. Nobody saw anything, no evidence, no leads.'

She stepped closer, narrowing her gaze to see what he could. Efficient at his job, she knew there wouldn't be a piece of evidence out of place, but there had to be something, a hint, a lead. 'How can we have nothing? Surely...'

His sigh was heartfelt. 'Essentially, we've got nothing to go on. It's a perfect dead-end.' The hint of admiration in his voice drew her attention. 'Sorry, Sarg, I know it's your sister, but this man is clever. He's covered his tracks and when he hasn't, he's had them covered for him. A mixture of great planning and a good dollop of luck.'

She gazed up at the board again. 'Do you believe he's the murderer and the kidnapper?'

With a sharp nod, he met her gaze. 'Inevitably, he has to be.'

She stared at the information in front of her. There was nothing new. No more evidence. 'Any updates on the door-to-door?'

'Nothing fresh. No reports of a disturbance apart from a couple of people who heard the initial scream, but never thought to call it in. They're feeling guilty now, though.'

She nodded as she flicked through the file to see if anything new leapt out at her. 'CCTV?'

'Nothing beyond the initial sightings. No CCTV beyond the Bridge.'

Disappointment scratched at her conviction that Fliss was still alive. 'Has the victim been identified yet?'

'No.'

'What about the press release?'

Frank slipped a page in front of her and she skimmed through it.

BODY FOUND IN WOODLAND AT IRONBRIDGE,
   POLICE SEEKING WITNESSES

At 16:35 on Friday 26 October, police received a call from a member of the public reporting they could hear screams from what appeared to be a female in the wooded area on the Broseley side of the Ironbridge.

Police attended and, following a short search of the area, located a body partially covered in the undergrowth just a short distance from the riverbank between the Ironbridge and the cooling towers at Ironbridge power station.

A police spokesperson said,

"At this time, details are still limited. We know the deceased to be female, but we do not know the timescales in which the body may have been there. A post-mortem will be carried out in due course.

The scene has been cordoned off and detailed searches will be undertaken until we are satisfied that all evidence from the scene has been recovered. We would request that the public and media refrain from visiting the area.

We are seeking any witnesses who may have been in the area between the hours of 15:00 and 17:00 and heard any screaming or other event which may lead us to identify the person and or trace other witnesses.

Current investigations show that a woman in her twenties has been reported missing from the same area and although we are not currently connecting the incidents at this time, we would request the public remain vigilant. The description we have for the missing woman is 5'11', slim build, long blonde hair. No distinguishing features. Last seen wearing a red jacket and jeans walking a large Dalmatian.

In addition, we will be checking for any outstanding missing person reports and request that if anyone has not heard from a relative or friend and is concerned for their welfare but has not reported them as missing they should get in touch with us.

The investigation is being led by DI Taylor."

Standard. Impersonal. Clinical. Professional.

Jenna nodded. 'Thanks, Frank.'

Frank turned away from the board and stepped into her space, dark eyes filled with torturous pain, mouth turned down at the edges in agonising sympathy. 'Len told me you caught a rape case. How did it go?'

She hadn't time for his over-sympathetic pity especially when she suspected it was more to do with her sister than the rape victim. It was hard, when she knew he cared so much, but sometimes for the sake of self-preservation, you had to turn off certain feelings.

She took a moment before she replied. 'As well as can be expected.'

'Was she telling the truth?'

Jenna blinked at Frank, taken by surprise by his line of questioning. 'Yeah, yeah, definitely. I've raised a warrant for the suspect's arrest. We'll get it sorted.'

'Was it someone she knew?'

'Yeah. It normally is. He was her boyfriend.' Jenna raised a hand, flicked her hair back and made for the door to the stairs. She needed to get on with her work, not spend time looking over an incident desk she wasn't even allowed to be involved in. She should never have come in, she had enough to concentrate on without taking time out every five minutes to check on progress on her sister's case. She swung open the door.

'Oh, Sergeant Morgan.'

She paused, repressed the desire to huff at him. 'Yes, Frank?'

White light poured down from the harsh ceiling lights, casting his face into shadow, so his eyes were obscured from her view. 'I'm sure they'll find Felicity soon.'

Her throat tightened. 'Fliss. We call her Fliss.'

She let the door whisper shut behind her, aware, as she took the stairs up two at a time, of Frank's observation through the interior windows which displayed the staircase all the way to her office.

It wasn't Frank's fault. Everyone knew Fliss was missing. There was no getting away from it, but Jenna's hands were tied, there was nothing she could do until they questioned Ed, the little shit. They probably already had. She just had to bide her time until they saw fit to let her know what progress had been made. She'd chase them down later after she made her own arrest.

In her office, she lowered herself into her chair. She'd left the door wide open as it normally was, not to show she was coping, but so she'd see the moment Mason and Ryan came back from observations. She could hardly leap on Salter and Wainwright, but she'd tweak young Ryan's ear to get him into her office and Mason would saunter in, all relaxed and casual despite the worry in the depths of his perceptive dark blue eyes.

She raised the paperwork for the arrest of Stuart Roddick, made the calls she needed to make. Kept notes on the system, more than normal as she knew with the distractions, she'd possibly miss a step, forget something in the process.

Her sister was her sister. But Fliss was someone else's victim. Professionally, nothing to do with Jenna. Jenna needed to put her faith in Salter and Wainwright that they would do their duty on Fliss's behalf. DI Taylor called the shots. She was theirs now and Jenna had to have faith they'd do their best for her. Jenna may badger them, poke at them, pester them, but she had her own victims to stand for and the young woman she'd left in the care of SOLO was now on her way to hospital to undergo tests. The boyfriend would be arrested shortly and brought in for questioning and the one thing she had to do for the sake of the victim she stood for was remain alert and engaged.

She swiped her fingers through her hair, she needed...

Adrian walked through the open doorway, a takeout cup from her favourite coffee spot clutched in each hand. He raised one, a dark eyebrow flicked up.

She wiggled her fingers. 'Gimme.'

His mouth twitched into a smile as he handed one cup over. She lifted the lid and inhaled. The rich aroma of real, strong, dark coffee hit her senses and shed the blanket of tiredness which had threatened.

'Yes, you're a lifesaver.'

He plonked himself into the seat opposite and peeled the lid off his own coffee.

'What have you got?' She stretched her neck to get a closer look and he tilted the oversized cup towards her.

'Full fat gingerbread latte.'

'You're kidding me? You go for that crap?'

'Sure, but I didn't think you would. You strike me as a straight up, bring it on, full-strength, black, unsweetened kind of girl.'

She flung herself back in her seat, took a studied sip of her straight up, black coffee. 'I always drink it black in the station, otherwise that shit might kill you, but I wouldn't have minded a cappuccino.'

'Boring.'

She smiled, caught the scent of his gingerbread latte and almost admitted how good it smelt, that had she been in the coffee shop, she may well have tried it.

'So, what's happening?' he asked.

'I caught a rape.'

'I got that.'

'Yeah, she's gone for tests, I'm just getting together scenes of crime and they'll be ready just as soon as I've had this coffee.'

He took a deep pull of his drink, pleasure wreathing his face as his serious eyes met hers. 'You don't need me to keep tabs on you. You're going to be tied up with this for the next few hours, and I need to trust you to get yourself off home straight after without any further connection to your sister's case. Can I do that?'

A ripple of disappointment that he was leaving her made her hesitate before she took a sip of her coffee to disguise how she felt about not having him around. She'd come to feel comfortable with him, supported. She raised her cup to him. 'Promise.'

His gaze bored into hers as though he wanted to assess how far he could trust her. 'Good. I have things I need to see to for a court case.'

'I'm sorry. I'm keeping you from your work. You must be swamped.'

'I volunteered, so don't apologise. It's interesting to say the least, but yes, I have to touch base and make sure I've got all the files I need from Birmingham Crown Court.'

Expecting him to be impatient to get off, Jenna held still, but he made no move to get up, instead he reached inside his jacket pocket and pulled out a small plastic bag filled with miniature muffins. He tugged it open, took one out and slid the bag over the desk to her, pushing the entire mini-muffin into his mouth and grinning around it.

She'd thought he was a strait-laced person. It just went to show; you could never judge a book by its Armani suit.

20

There were times when an accusation rang false, when everything about a victim's statement grated on the nerves and pushed doubt into the mind. Not every woman told the truth, not every man accused was guilty. But the mean-eyed man who swung open the door and leaned with challenging insolence against the frame vibrated guilt and anger.

Jenna had known before she met him, absorbed the man's character and attitude from his victim. The woman he'd taken to lunch twice and dinner once, then demanded payback in the tight confines of the front seat of his car, which he'd driven down a dark lane before he cut the engine and twisted a hank of the woman's hair around his fist.

She let the ball of nausea curdle in her stomach while she kept her face neutral, her eyes flat and uncompromising.

'Stuart Roddick?' At his nod, she held out her warrant card for his inspection. 'I'm DS Jenna Morgan. I'm here to arrest you for the rape...' The flash of his hand knocked her ID from her fingers to send it in a rapid spiral to the ground.

If she hadn't been so tired, she knew, her reaction would have been different. She would never, she thought to herself later, have bent down to retrieve her ID. She should have cuffed him first, handed him over to the others behind her before she made another move. She hadn't misread the situation. She knew without a doubt what he was capable of. She wasn't just responding to a spiteful accusation but evidence from a battered and beaten woman who'd suffered untold damage from the animal in front of her.

She could only put it down to the distraction, to the fog in her brain that only allowed her to concentrate on the whereabouts of her sister, but she knew her mistake the moment she made her move. His hand had been fast to flick away her ID, his knee even faster as she leaned down to retrieve the wallet from the ground.

Pain exploded in a bright profusion of colour as her head snapped to one side, her cheek pulsed, making her stagger backwards down the two steps she'd mounted to his door. Her mind grasped at the mad rush of bodies charging past her as she reeled, breathless.

'Bloody hell.' She raised her hand, stared in blank confusion at the crimson streak of blood across her palm, then touched her fingers to the corner of her lip again. He'd split her lip. Bastard.

She raised her head, not an ounce of sympathy emerged as he was held by the two uniformed officers. Left cheek squelched against the grubby wall just inside his front door while they whipped cuffs on him.

'Are you all right, Sarg?'

'Yeah.' She nodded, swiped at blood dribbling down her chin, then nodded again while she retrieved her warrant card from the ground and mounted the two steps back up to Stuart's door, humiliation and fury roiling together in a black cloud. 'As I was saying, I'm here to arrest you for the rape of Estelle Rogers...' She shoved her warrant card back in his face until he squinted and then reeled off the rest of his rights through lips that thickened while she spoke. When she'd almost finished, she added assault of a police officer to his charges. 'Take him to the station.'

She raised her hand to pull the door shut behind them while the uniforms shuffled him into the back seat of the police vehicle. Movement halted her as a young woman descended the stairs.

'What's he done this time?'

The woman stepped forward into the light, a delicate hand rested on her distended stomach. Pretty close to full term, Jenna estimated as her gaze met that of the pregnant woman's.

'Rape.' She skimmed her fingers over her own tender cheek. 'Assaulting a police officer.'

The woman nodded, a regretful smile kicked up one side of her lips and she took her hand from the bump, fluttered it in a nervous wave, her brown eyes wide. 'Will you hold him long enough for me to get away?'

Jenna's gaze met the young woman's, all thought of her own injuries pushed to one side as she studied the other woman, frail and frightened. 'Don't you want to press charges?'

'No.' The soft auburn of her curls bounced around her young face. 'I want to get as far away from him as possible so he can no longer harm me. Us.' She rubbed the curve of her belly. 'I just want to escape.'

21

Escape.

Was she capable? Could Fliss escape from wherever she was?

Jenna hadn't been able to let the pregnant young woman escape. Much as she would have liked to from a personal viewpoint. It wasn't personal and she couldn't allow it to become so. The desperate woman played a vital role in the prosecution of Stuart. They needed her evidence.

Gillian Falmer. It hadn't been easy, but she'd managed to persuade the details from the young victim, coaxing a statement out of her. Jenna never saw the bruises until Gillian stepped out of the dingy hallway into the weak winter sunshine. Large, faded to yellow fingerprints in a necklace around the woman's slender throat.

Her heart broke for her.

She'd allowed the uniforms to take Stuart, put him in a cell and hold him while forensics could do their part. Divest him of his clothes, take swabs. They'd have to keep him overnight before she interviewed him.

As for Gillian, she'd left her in the understanding care of SOLO overnight. They'd make her comfortable, advise her until Jenna could also take her statement.

She closed down her computer, pushed away from the desk. She was too tired to think straight, and she suspected that if Stuart knew, he'd take full advantage.

She wrapped her scarf around her neck, paced through the main office and dashed down the three flights of stairs. The weather had turned frigid with the setting of the sun and while she had the desperate desire to go and join the search for her sister, she knew she wouldn't be allowed. It would be wasted energy trying. Energy she needed to save. She needed a good night's sleep so she could think straight the following day. Straighter than she'd been able to so far.

She pushed open the glass panelled door at the bottom of the stairs, raised her chin to acknowledge Frank who stood in the foyer.

'Goodnight.'

'Goodnight, Sergeant, you've had a long day.'

'You too, Frank, when are you off home?'

'I'm going off now, same as you.'

She paused at the heavy outer door of the station. 'I'm sorry, Frank. With everything that's happened, I forgot to ask how your wife is.' The woman had been sick forever, but every so often Jenna remembered to enquire. Uncomfortable with asking, Jenna was aware Frank had it tough as the woman's sole carer.

Weary, red-rimmed eyes blinked at her. 'She's much better, thank you, Sergeant. A different woman altogether.' A genuine smile wreathed his face and Jenna's heart relaxed a little. At least someone had good news.

'That's good to hear. You take care driving home, the temperature's dropped, I suspect it's turned icy by now.'

'Thank you, Sergeant. I will. You drive carefully too.'

She stepped through into the icy blast of northerly wind, strong enough to suck her breath away. When did it get so cold?

She slipped into her old car, the one she'd kept because it belonged to her mum and somehow it still seemed to smell of her. Jenna turned the key twice before the engine decided to kick in. She'd have to buy a new one sometime soon, but it wasn't a priority when she could take comfort in the closeness of her mum as she drove home.

While she waited for the heater to warm up, she dialled the vets and got a quick update on Domino. Progress it seemed, in the animal world, was fast and he'd be ready to come home in a few days. She wanted him there now, the deep connection with Fliss had to bring her comfort. They'd know further details tomorrow.

Jenna rubbed her hands over her face, then blew out a breath before she pushed the gearstick into reverse and pulled out of the parking space. The one advantage of working late was the decided lack of traffic around the Telford Town Centre on a Sunday evening. Almost a ghost town, it didn't take Jenna long to negotiate the roads, slip onto the dual carriageway and make her way home.

Exhaustion pushed her upstairs as soon as she let herself in the house. That and the cold, enough to put icicles in her veins. After the heat of the station, her house chilled her to the bone. Not just the temperature but the absence of her sister.

She crept into Fliss's bedroom and stared at the bright, jaunty bedcovers daubed in crimson poppies, and gave in to the ache in her chest as she crawled onto the bed and wrapped the duvet around herself.

If Fliss had been there, she would have had the heating blasting out enough for Jenna to curse her about the waste of energy and racking up the bills, so Jenna threatened to make her pay more than her one third share. She'd taken pity on her when Fliss had left the low-life scum and not charged her a full half of the bills.

Jenna curled her body in a tight ball and blinked away the tears in the dark. She wouldn't charge her anything at all if only Fliss would come back. She'd give anything to have her here but bartering with fate didn't work. Fate dictated its own passage, as they'd both learned when it came to their mother's death.

The low growl of her stomach reminded her she'd had nothing to eat since lunchtime, except the mini-muffin Adrian had brought her with her coffee, but she had no interest in food. She just wanted her sister back.

'Oh, Fliss. Where are you, Fliss?'

22

'Where are you, Fliss?'

Her eyes shot open, but the bright white light had been turned off, leaving a heavy black shroud over the room.

The sound of her sister's voice still echoed in the emptiness of her mind. Sure Jenna was there, Fliss lay as still as she could, straining her ears for the slightest noise. There was nothing. Not the dull reverberation of the car coming back, not the grating scrape of the key in the door.

She was alone.

Her stomach tightened to remind her she still hadn't eaten, but the chill in her feet and ankles made her curl up into a tight ball. She was going to freeze to death before she died of starvation.

The temperature in the room had dropped considerably since she'd drifted off to sleep. There'd been warnings on the news before she was taken that an Arctic blast was due in. They'd considered themselves lucky to have had such a long, mild autumn, but winter was about to hit hard, and it may just be Fliss was going to be one of its victims.

Her teeth chattered in the dark, dispelling the echo of Jenna's voice, but the memory of the dream still lingered. Not a dream, but a memory.

'Fliss, where are you?'

'I'm here. Come and see what I've got.' Excitement sent shivers over her flesh, *so she pulled the tiny puppy in close and gave him a cuddle, his plump, warm body writhed in her arms until she put him down, leaving a cold empty spot where he'd been.*

'Oh, Fliss. How could you?'

The disappointment in her sister's voice couldn't chase away the thrill of having the sweet little thing crawl over her lap. 'I couldn't help myself. I've always wanted a dog.'

Jenna settled on the carpet next to her. 'But a Dalmatian? What possessed you to get a Dalmatian? They're crazy.'

Fliss ran a light hand over his plump, velvet body and grinned as he squirmed around, trying to settle down in the gap where she sat cross-legged. 'I thought he was perfect. They don't shed as much as other dogs.'

Jenna swiped him from her lap and held him in her arms while she inspected him. A reluctant grin spread across her face as his pink tongue took sly licks at her face and her laughter filled the small kitchen where they both were sitting on the floor. 'Oh my God, he's beautiful. What are you going to call him?'

'Spotty.'

'No, you can't.'

The thrill of annoying her sister sent a ball of laughter through her. She couldn't help herself, she found it irresistible to tease her, just to see the horror on Jenna's face. She was always so damned serious. 'I'm joking. I thought maybe Domino.'

Jenna snuggled the wriggling puppy, buried her face in his neck. 'That's a good name. I like it.' She smiled as she sniffed the top of his head. 'He smells like a baby. He's beautiful. And you're irresponsible.'

Fliss laughed, knowing the puppy had won her sister over. 'I thought the timing was right for a puppy. Mum will love him and at least he'll always have one of us around, with your shifts and me working days.'

'Oh, no.' Jenna passed the puppy over, his warm tongue smothered Fliss's face, making her laugh again as Jenna struggled to her feet. 'Nope. He's not my responsibility. You got him, you look after him.'

'But, Jenna...' Her voice took on a whiny plea.

'No, Fliss. This is yours.' Her sister flicked her fingers at the puppy and then grabbed a mug out of the kitchen cabinet. 'What's the betting he'll be nothing but trouble?'

He'd been barely any trouble at all.

And then the man had killed him.

A soft sob burst from her lips as she tried to hold the sound in, the fear in, but the sinister chill of it all soaked through her.

Her toes were like icicles and she could no longer stop the mad chatter of her teeth. She was going to die. Then Jenna would be left alone, no mother, no boyfriend, no dog, no sister.

Grief tore at her, not for her death, but for the sad and lonely life her sister would lead.

The faint aroma of car fumes snaked through her senses, while a vague tremor rumbled. He was back. The man had returned.

Perhaps now he'd kill her.

Perhaps now he'd save her.

She closed her eyes to wait.

Bright torchlight flooded the room casting back the darkness in a wide swathe.

She'd never heard the man come in over the clattering of her teeth, but he was there, and she couldn't help curling into a tight ball to protect herself against the cold and the fear.

'Bloody light bulb's blown. Left you in the dark.'

Warm fingers smoothed the hair back from her face, forcing her to open her eyes and blink him into focus, but the spasms still wracked her body, so her muscles contracted in a hard, painful pull, elastic bands ready to snap.

'Oh, my dear. I'm so sorry. I got caught up with something and never realised how cold it had become.' The weight of a thick cover pressed down on her, but as she tried to snuggle in deeper, the man tugged her up, wrapping an arm around her shoulders to keep her upright. 'Here, drink.'

The scald of it didn't stop her from gulping down the tomato soup while he held it against her lips. Her head rested on his shoulder. Weak and pathetic, not even pride could persuade her to refuse the hot liquid. It slid down her bruised throat, dribbled from her lips, but she didn't care. He'd take it away just before she had enough anyway, so she needed all she could get as quick as she could. She didn't want to die, and the delicious warmth of the soup would help her survive.

He tipped the cup away from her lips, dabbed them with a tissue. 'Slow down, you're going to choke.' The sliminess of his voice sent a violent shudder through her, but she still accepted the soup as he brought the cup back to her mouth. Grateful for anything to stop the grinding ache in her stomach and give her the energy to think just so she could formulate a plan to escape.

The man obviously worked. Though she had no idea where. Her senses told her it was night-time, but she had no idea really, no idea how long she'd slept each time and no way to tell whether it was day or night.

As she drained the last bit from the mug, she leaned her head against his bony shoulder, weakened with relief as his warmth soaked into her body and the cocoon he'd wrapped around her started to heat her up.

'What time is it?' Her voice barely croaked out of her lips and stuttered to a halt as his narrowed gaze studied her with a cold detachment, chilling the bones that had just started to warm through.

'It's time for you to sleep again. Sleep heals.' His tight smile brooked no argument.

'Thank you.'

A glimmer of pleasure skittered over his face, satisfaction, it appeared, at her submissiveness.

'My feet...' she needed to swallow before she could continue, but he brought his head in closer to listen. Aware of the greasy smell of his unwashed hair, Fliss gulped once more before she forced the words from her lips. 'My feet are still really cold.'

He tightened his lips as he straightened away from her, laid her head back down on the chilly pillow. Much as she wanted him to leave, she also needed his help if she was to survive, and if he left again for several hours without seeing to her needs, she may be dead by the time he came back.

She mustered up a smile of her own, trying to make it genuine, while his hard gaze wandered over her face.

He gave a swift nod and then disappeared. The snap of the door let her know he'd left the room and relief flooded through her as the warmth of the soup spread from her stomach outwards. She tucked her face into the thick downiness of the duvet he'd thrown on her, wrinkled her nose at the faint scent of mildew. It didn't matter, the stench of her own urine still permeated through the mattress. Perhaps she would survive, if only she could get warm enough, if she could wriggle under the quilt and keep herself covered. Only her handcuffed arm remained outside and the cold of the metal against her skin served to remind her she was captive.

Torchlight flooded the room again and she peered from beneath the covers to watch him change the light bulb in the low ceiling. As he flicked on the light, the bare bulb illuminated to chase the shadows away. Silent still, he disappeared, then returned with a sharp metallic rattle and bump.

'I hope you appreciate this, young lady, because I'm only doing it out of the kindness of my heart.'

Sickened by him, she still managed a quick nod and a faint smile in case he took away the mobile radiator he'd hauled in behind him. Grateful for it, she mumbled through her still chattering teeth. 'Thank you.'

'You're a polite young lady.' He straightened from plugging in the heater, stared down at her, his brows pulled low. 'Not like your sister. She's terse. Very terse.'

Fliss's heart stumbled in her chest, but she lay immobile, determined not to react to the man. He knew her sister. There was nothing about him she found familiar. Nothing she could recall about him jogged her memory. He wasn't a police officer, that was for sure, but perhaps Jenna had arrested him.

Fliss almost jerked upright as the thought zapped through her dull brain. Of course. It had to be someone Jenna had arrested. Who the hell else could it be?

She forced her muscles to relax, watched him potter around the room. Her stomach clenched as he snapped on acrylic gloves, a vague recollection of him doing this previously circling in her drug-dulled mind, just out of reach so she couldn't quite grasp it. Earlier, when he'd shoved a needle in her, maybe when she passed out.

As he approached, his smile turned saccharine. 'You're very lucky. I kept these from when Mother needed them.' He raised a pair of incontinence pants and placed them on the side of the bed.

He slipped a pair of scissors from the same pocket, cut off the incontinence pants she already wore, ones he must have put on her while she was unconscious, and slid the bloodied, soiled ones off her. His face crumpled with disgust as he dropped them into a plastic bag. The touch of her own cold, wet pee sent a shudder of revulsion through her as her naked backside settled onto the urine-soaked mattress, filling her nose with the acrid smell of ammonia and mould.

She screwed her eyes closed and tried not to cry out as he tugged a fresh pair of incontinence pants up her legs. Beyond humiliation, Fliss raised her hips to allow him to pull them into place.

She peered at him through narrowed eyes, compelled to observe his obvious distaste in her bodily functions. Not a young man, possibly in his mid to late fifties. Older than she'd thought at first. His upper body strength was huge as she knew from the way he'd carried her along the trail, but she was fairly light, and he'd run out of steam. After the first time he put her down, he'd barely been able to haul her into the boot of his car. She couldn't remember how he'd got her into his cellar. She'd been out cold by then.

She avoided any eye contact with him as she watched him wheeze again, the effort of changing her pants taking its toll. When he finished, he threw the thin blanket over her near nakedness and dumped the duvet on top. Her teeth rattled as she shivered, scared to move in case he saw it as a criticism.

A T-shirt and a pair of incontinence pants was not nearly enough to keep out the cold air that sneaked in around the edges of the single duvet, but at least the incontinence pad formed a barrier between her skin and the wet patch on the mattress.

Interested in his movements, Fliss observed him as he moved away to the other side of the small cellar. Exact, neat, leaving everything in its place with precision.

He disappeared again, and when he returned this time, he had more food. Her mouth watered at the enticing, spicy aroma. Her stomach growled in anticipation.

He slumped into the chair next to her, shovelled a forkful of food into his mouth and spoke around it. Little bits of rice splattered over her, while she recoiled into the covers, desperate not to let him see her revulsion.

'I let my dinner get cold because of you.' Dark accusation glared from angry eyes.

'I'm sorry.' She'd learnt well how to say that phrase when she'd lived with her boyfriend. It had taken her far too long, and too many fallings out with Jenna, before she realised how cowed she'd become by a man who had professed to love her, but in the end had demonstrated nothing but sneering contempt.

This man didn't love her either. He was probably about to kill her, and her words of apology were well thought out, contrived to earn his kindness and a little bit of time.

He filled his mouth several times more, chewing each mouthful thoroughly before he swallowed, but he nodded his head to acknowledge her words.

Fliss's stomach rumbled again while he devoured his food. A takeaway. The pungent aroma of Indian food filled her nostrils and cramped her stomach, the soup barely lining the vast emptiness there.

The fork clattered as the man got to his feet and shoved the bowl onto the chair he'd been sitting on. He swiped his forearm across his mouth before he patted his pockets and pulled out a packet of chewing gum. He inspected it for a long moment before he placed it back in his pocket without opening it.

'It's time for bed.'

Fear gripped her as he swept his gaze over her and the distinct feeling he meant to get into bed with her tore through her. If he decided to rape her, she was powerless. Up until that point, the thought hadn't occurred to her. Nothing he'd done had made her believe he was about to rape her. Kill her, yes, but rape had not entered her mind, but a flicker of something dark entered his expression as he contemplated her.

She held in the desperate whimper while his black glare centred on her face.

'I'll see you in the morning.'

The light blinked out and he was gone. Her limbs turned to water and she let out the quiet sob she'd held back. The cuffs rattled as she tried to curl into a tighter ball, warmth at last reaching her lower limbs.

He'd dragged the heater close to the side of the bed and Fliss risked one foot out of the covers to grope around in the dark and touch the radiator. Despite its size, heat pulsed from it, too hot to rest her foot against, but the thought of it there, keeping the worst of the iciness from the room, filled her with a sense of comfort. A comfort she knew she shouldn't feel while she was held captive, but at least she hadn't been raped and at least she wasn't going to die. Tonight.

The savoury smell of the man's leftovers reached out with tempting persistence and wouldn't let her settle. Although she had become accustomed to the dark, she still couldn't see anything at all, but she stretched her shackled hand out and touched the arm of the small wooden chair he'd been sitting on. With small tugging movements, she brought it closer to the bedside, careful not to make too much noise as it scraped inch by inch across the stone floor until she wedged it right up against the bed.

Hand shaking, Fliss crawled the fingers of her tethered hand along the seat as far as they could go. Relief swept over her as they encountered the bowl and she dragged it closer. After she tried to reach out with her plastered arm, only to find it uncooperative, she gave up. She swung her legs over the side of the bed and leaned down, the chain gave a protesting rattle, but she twisted her arm, so she could get closer to the bowl.

Wary in case she tipped it over the edge of the chair, Fliss used the end of her nose to locate it. Pain seared between her eyes as she encountered the rim far sooner than she'd imagined. The nose she suspected broken definitely had to be. Tears streamed down her cheeks and she paused, allowing the initial agony to disperse to a dull, throbbing ache.

Face inside the bowl, she tried again. With cautious movements, she stuck her tongue out and licked at the food. In ecstasy, she closed her eyes and dabbed her tongue against the korma coated rice, swallowing with ease until she encountered a piece of chicken she managed to push around the inside of the bowl until she could pin it against the side and grasp it with her teeth. She ignored the spike of pain shooting through her face for the sheer pleasure of the food.

Slow and restrained, she picked at it. Determined to ignore the ache from her damaged nose, Fliss chased the fork out of her way with the side of her face as she managed to get every last morsel she could from the bowl. She had no idea when her next opportunity to eat would come along. She needed energy to get out of the cellar. She was damned if she was going to die there, cold, hungry and alone.

Exhausted, she slipped back under the duvet, swiping her face against the covers to remove the stickiness from her mouth and cheeks. She jiggled until she had the quilt pulled over her and she could once again curl up and savour the warmth and the pleasure of a full belly.

She fluttered her eyes closed. Jenna wasn't coming for her this time. She had no one to save her but herself. So, tomorrow. Tomorrow she'd have the strength to think of escape.

23

MONDAY 29 OCTOBER, 06:15 HRS

'You little bitch!'

Agony tore through her as he yanked her hair from her head and brought her crashing out of the weird dream she'd been floating in. A pained yowl shot from her mouth until the man cracked the back of his hand over it and made her swallow the blood that spurted from the split lip he'd caused.

'Bitch!' He hauled her around, jerked her from the bed, her legs tangled in the thick covers, so she stumbled. Her knee smashed onto the cold, stone floor, sending shooting pains up her thigh. The scream of protest paralysed her throat in fear of further retribution.

He was mad. Totally off his freaking head barmy.

'You stole my food. You greedy cow.'

Comprehension ran through her as her gaze darted to the empty bowl, the stickiness of the korma sauce still crackled around her swollen mouth. Who would have thought he'd mind? She'd had no idea he'd even notice, but then, staring into the wild fury of his gaze, he could well have done it deliberately as a test.

His hand tightened in her hair and he forced her head further down, so she had no alternative but to stare at the empty dish. He wrenched her head lower still and she shot out her injured arm to save herself, only to let out a squeal of anguish as her fingers bumped the slate tiles and fire shot up her arm whilst the wrist on her other hand was almost dragged out of its socket by the icy metal of the handcuffs.

'I'm sorry.'

'Thieving bitch!'

Tears filled her eyes as he forced her face into the bowl, pressed her nose against the base until pain powered through her head.

'Don't you ever,' he growled in her ear, 'ever, steal my food again.' He twisted her head back, his black eyes blazed into hers. 'Do you understand me? Do you, you fucking slag?'

'Yes.' Her voice shamed her with its high-pitched squeak, the pathetic mewl.

Desperate to keep her balance, she shuffled on her knees, but the grip he had on her hair made it impossible to move. She closed her eyes and swallowed past the tenderness of her swollen throat.

'I'm sorry. I thought you'd finished. I won't do it again without asking.'

As he relaxed his fingers from the fiery burn of her scalp, she opened her eyes again to stare into his taut features. The deep slashes bracketing his mouth smoothed out, his dark brows lifted, his tight lips relaxed. 'If I had more time, I'd make sure you understood your lesson.'

She tried to nod, but her scalp, so tender, halted any further movement in case he pulled at her hair again. 'I'm sorry. I've learnt my lesson. I promise.' He pressed his lips together in a straight line as if considering what she had to say. 'I never understood the rules. I'm sorry.'

A little smile accompanied the satisfied glint in his eye as he released her and came to his feet to tower above her.

Unsure whether to move or not, she stayed where she was, head bowed.

'Up you get, Felicity.'

She stumbled to her feet, using the shackle on her arm to keep her balance in an effort not to put weight on her broken hand. Dizzy with relief, she managed to haul herself back onto the bed and waited, trying to gain her equilibrium while the man stared at her in silence. She kept her head down, unwilling to meet the fury flashing at her.

She cleared her throat but waited for him to speak.

The man adjusted his glasses. 'I've a lot to do today. Clearing up.

Preparing.' She kept completely still, reluctant to let him see the relief glimmer in her eyes. 'It means you'll be alone most of the day and all of the night. It'll give you time to think about your behaviour. I'll not tolerate it, you know.'

Optimism sprang in her heart. His threats didn't matter. He was about to leave her again. This time she had far more energy and her mind was considerably clearer as the drug he'd administered wore off. If only she had the time to figure out how to escape, how to release herself from the handcuffs, while he was away. All night. She had all night. How was she to tell what was day and what was night though? If she escaped too soon, he'd catch her. He'd probably beat her to death, going from her previous experience with him, if he caught her in the act of escaping. She had to make sure she acted as soon as he left and not mistake the timing. She'd concentrate. Bide her time.

She resisted the temptation to let out a gusty sigh and blew out slowly instead, anticipation almost getting the better of her. She was going to escape.

He placed his fingers under her chin and raised her head, so she had no option but to look at him. 'I'll change your nappy now.'

Revulsion skittered through her veins. He was going to touch her. The feral gleam in his eyes sent shivers down her spine.

'Lie down.'

There was no resisting his command. His obvious enjoyment of what he was about to do to her cramped her stomach. She lay back on the bunk, squeezed her eyes closed tight until white sparks flashed in the blackness.

Cool air wafted over her naked skin as he sliced the side of the pants and drew them away from her body. She automatically lifted her backside from the mattress to help him as he slid it from underneath her. She only hoped she wasn't going to throw the contents of her stomach up all over him. She couldn't imagine the retribution she'd suffer if she soiled his neatly pressed chequered navy shirt and spotted blue tie.

Soft fingers smoothed over her flesh to send a flash of butterflies to dapple her skin. She squeezed her eyes tighter, the ball of nausea heating her stomach and threatening to explode through her mouth. She swallowed several times, aware of the removal of his hand. The crackle of the incontinence pad startled her out of her trance-like state, and she flashed open her eyes only to regret it as she met his manic gaze.

As he grinned, his yellow stained teeth flashed. 'Oh, don't get your hopes up, lady, I haven't time for that right now.'

He nudged at her bottom for her to lift it up again and slipped the incontinence pants over her hips. He stroked his fingers down her thighs, touching each of the bandages he'd applied the previous day, and making her skin skitter with fresh revulsion.

'You're still cold, I see. It's probably shock from your nasty fall, and the break you've suffered, but I'm sure you'll be fine.' To her relief, he flipped the covers over her and tucked them in around her chest, leaving her arms uncovered. 'Now I know you can cope, I'll leave you some water. I brought you porridge, but I don't think you need it since you ate all my dinner.'

The desire to plead with him rose, but she tamped it down, knowing he would only gain sadistic pleasure from withholding the food from her the more desperate she appeared.

'Perhaps,' she croaked out, 'you could leave it for later. In case you're needed at work for longer than you anticipate. Or when you leave for the night.' Porridge was hardly going to sustain her for the rest of the day, but if she could eat it once he left, then make her escape, at least she'd have food in her stomach to give her more energy. Anticipation had fired her up, and adrenaline would give her an extra boost once he left. She needed the opportunity to escape and he was about to give it to her.

'You're right. I'll leave it here.'

She turned her head as he placed the bowl of porridge and flask of water on the chair beside the empty bowl. He rubbed his hands on his black trousers in the first nervous gesture she'd witnessed before he picked up the empty bowl and left the room.

Fliss stared at the flask with its plastic straw poking out of the top, neatly placed above and to the right of the porridge bowl, a silver spoon in perfect position between the bowl and the flask. He'd just given her the timeline she needed. Morning had come. He'd had his breakfast and given her some too. Which meant, if she could concentrate and keep a handle on the time, she'd be able to pinpoint exactly how much time she had once he left for the night.

She'd hear him go, smell the fumes from his car.

She craned her neck to look at the medical trolley he'd brought in previously, studied the precision with which he'd placed every single item on it. None of them touching the others. The guy had OCD. He couldn't help but remove the dirty bowl. An interesting snippet she filed away in case she needed it later. Not that she had any intention of being around later, but when she escaped, she needed to be able to identify the bastard so her sister could arrest him.

Her sister. Fliss screwed her face up, regret hammering at her heart. Jenna would be devastated. She'd think she was dead. Mum was dead, Domino was dead, and Jenna was all alone.

Tears pricked the back of her eyes. How would Jenna cope on her own? No matter how much fuss Jenna had made when Fliss had moved in with her, Fliss knew her sister loved having company, knew she hated to be alone. It was why she'd wheedled her way into Jenna's home instead of getting a place of her own. They both needed each other since their mum had gone.

Fliss blinked away the hot scald of tears that blurred her vision.

'Mum.' Her breath hitched in painful gasps. 'Mum. Please, please help.'

To conserve her energy, Fliss lay her head back and drifted in and out of consciousness as time shimmered past.

The sharp clack of the man's leather-soled shoes warned her he was back. It wouldn't be for long and then she'd be left alone so she could plot her escape and get out of there before he returned.

He gave little irritating sniffs as he inspected the small trolley, rearranging items until he was satisfied they were in the right order.

'I see you haven't eaten your porridge. I do hope you're not sulking.' Deep disappointment furrowed his brow.

'No, I...'

'I thought I'd bring you a sandwich, but I can see it would only go to waste.'

'Please, I...' She clamped her mouth shut on her words as his gaze sharpened on her face. She couldn't risk him losing control again. She just needed him to go.

A worm of doubt writhed in her stomach as he picked up a small vial and a needle. Her battered, swollen mouth dried up as he filled the hypo-dermic, tapping the side and squirting out a little fluid before he turned to her, a placid, condescending smile on his face.

'You didn't think I'd leave you alone all night so you could play, did you?'

'I...'

'Shhhh. It's okay. There's nothing for you to concern yourself about. Don't worry, I'm fully trained.'

Fliss scrunched her brow as he pushed the needle into her skin.

Soft, black clouds floated around her to encase her in a warm, floating sensation where her fears evaporated, and the man's face filled her vision for a moment before darkness took him away.

24

MONDAY 29 OCTOBER, 06:30 HRS

Jenna shoved one last piece of toast in her mouth, choked down the free-range eggs she'd scrambled. No appetite, but she knew if she was to keep up her strength, she needed to eat, and she needed her strength because she had to find her sister.

Another shit night's sleep.

She pushed herself away from the kitchen table, rinsed her plate before she stacked it in the virtually empty dishwasher. That was another thing about Fliss that had bugged her. Instead of putting her crockery in the dishwasher, she left it in the sink, and then the bloody dog got up on the side and started licking at the dirty dishes.

A strangled sob broke from her as she turned away from the dishwasher. She wouldn't care if only Domino was okay, if only Fliss would come through the front door.

She wiped her hands, snatched up her bag and coat and slammed out of the door as fast as she could, leaving behind the accusing silence.

As she pulled the car up outside the vets' practice, she sucked in several deep breaths, unsure if she could bear to see him. She'd phoned three times the previous day, but they'd told her there was no point her visiting because he was still heavily sedated.

Her heart ached as she stepped inside the quiet reception at just after seven in the morning. She needed to get in and out before they became busy. Get on with her own work.

'Morning. I'm Detective Sergeant Jenna Morgan. I'm here to visit Domino.'

The flicker of surprise in the young veterinary nurse's gaze served to remind Jenna she wasn't there to arrest anyone, merely to visit the damned dog. She should never have whipped out her warrant card, but her mind hadn't engaged. The woman in pale blue scrubs probably thought she was an arse of epic proportions. Jenna gave her a tight smile. 'Sorry, bad night.'

The soft touch of the woman's hand against Jenna's arm almost brought her to her knees. Unsure she could cope with sympathy, Jenna swallowed hard and ducked her head so the nurse didn't catch the gleam of tears that had sprung from nowhere.

A gentle lilt of Irish wound around the nurse's words. 'I understand. Come through to the kennels. Domino's doing well. He's a strong boy.'

Jenna weaved through the narrow passageways behind the nurse, sucking in deep breaths of air, unsure if she'd be able to cope when she saw what a mess her sister's dog was in.

The nurse swung open a door and gave Jenna room to peer past her into the dimly lit room. 'I'll leave you alone with him.'

Jenna stared down at his limp, lifeless body and wondered how they could have told her he was stable. He looked dead.

With a sharp crackle and pop of her knees, she crouched down.

Her fingers shook as she reached out. Surprise rippled through her at the satin heat of him, the sturdy beat of his heart as she stroked her hand over the length of him and felt the life pulse through the palm of her hand.

Hope fluttered. If he could survive, surely her sister could.

Jenna laid her head against Domino's shoulder instead of cheek to cheek the way he liked it. His face was too much of a mess. There was barely anywhere she could touch with all the stitching and bandages.

The scald of tears ran into his fur and she pulled away, desperate to wipe them from her cheeks as the vet knocked on the door before sliding through the narrow gap she'd created, obviously used to animals trying to escape.

'It looks a lot worse than it is, Jenna.' The cool, calm tones of the woman helped to dry up Jenna's tears, and with one last swipe, she turned to face the vet, keeping her hand lightly on Domino's neck.

'What's the prognosis?'

Sarah stepped closer, hunkered down on the floor next to Jenna and touched Domino's shoulder with fondness. 'Most of the cuts and abrasions are superficial, they should heal relatively quickly. Except for this one.' She indicated the long zipper of clamps from shoulder to hips. 'We'll have him up today. He was lucky, the break in his jaw is what we'd call favourable. It'll take a few weeks to heal, but he'll be as good as new. We've wired it, you'll have to take care with him, especially in the first few weeks. Knowing Domino, he'll be full on straight away. He'll want to charge around like the idiot he is. So far, we've kept him a little bit sedated for his own good.' Sarah's lips curved with affectionate humour while she ran her hand over him again. 'You can probably take him home tomorrow.'

With a fast jolt, Jenna realised Domino was her responsibility. She jerked her head up, faced Sarah. 'I'm not sure I can, I'm at work most of the time. Fliss...' Panic rose in her throat. She'd always been there for him when her shifts allowed. Even when Fliss had been with her idiot of a boyfriend, she'd dropped Domino off when Jenna wasn't working, so he had company and she could walk him. She'd loved their walks, she'd loved having him, although she'd never admitted it to Fliss. She'd made it a game. She grumbled just to wind her sister up.

This, though, was different. The dog was injured. He needed care for far more time than Jenna had available. She needed Fliss, damn her.

'I'm so sorry about Fliss. Have you had any news?'

Jenna could only shake her head, her fingers trembled as she flexed them in Domino's fur, the thick ball of tears clogged her throat.

'I can recommend a good dog sitter. She'd probably be able to fit around your shifts.'

She didn't want a good dog sitter. She wanted Fliss.

She clenched her jaw, unable to meet Sarah's observant gaze. 'That would be helpful. Thank you.'

* * *

The dark expanse of him filled the doorway to her office, where he lounged with casual negligence. Under other circumstances, she may well have acted on the instinctive attraction to him. But she had nothing to give, no real interest apart from how to perform her job without getting into trouble. And that was the only function she required of him.

He was a seriously attractive man. And she was emotionally dead inside.

She caught the delicious aroma of strong coffee and her legs almost gave way with gratitude.

'So,' She snatched up the paper cup, peeped under the lid and sighed at the sight of the thick cream on the top of the cappuccino he'd brought her. She indulged herself in a long sip before she met his amused gaze. 'What brings you here today? I thought you had a court case.' She thought he trusted her not to interfere with her sister's case. She glanced at the paper bag on her desk, drew it towards her with one finger. 'What's this?'

Adrian's lips twitched as he slipped into the chair opposite, his wide shoulders in a dark burgundy cashmere jumper appeared to take up even more room than they had the day before. Despite his more casual dress, the man emanated class and money. Someone for her to definitely steer clear of.

Every penny she'd ever had, she'd earned herself. The financial struggle her mum had gone through when her dad left had never got them back on their feet again. Not until Jenna had joined the Force and Fliss had graduated with honours in her teacher's degree, initially working in a primary school in Birmingham until she'd fallen lucky enough to scoop a position in Ironbridge and Coalbrookdale school, much closer to home.

Adrian reached out and drew the package back over the desk. 'I figured you probably needed feeding this morning, as you'd have left the house without food.' He drew a chocolate twist and a croissant from the brown package and the sweet aroma filled the air. He twitched his eyebrows and gave a wide grin, so she noticed for the first time how straight and neat his teeth were. He took the plain croissant and pushed the paper bag back at her.

'Are they warmed?' The twist flopped against her hand, so he didn't need to answer as the warm gloop of chocolate smeared across her fingers and she pushed it into her mouth to take a bite. 'I had breakfast.'

His dark brows raised to crinkle his forehead.

'Yep.' She took another bite, enjoyed the sweet and savoury as she chewed. 'I'm not the type to do without food for long. I need to keep my strength up. There's work to be done.'

He leaned back in the chair, kept one hand under the croissant as he took a large bite. His jaw distracted her as it flexed, tight and muscular while he chewed. She'd not realised when he wore his suit just how toned he was. He smiled around his food. 'You didn't need to take it, you could have let me have it.'

'No chance. I had breakfast two hours ago.' She glanced at her watch. Nine o'clock. 'This is elevenses.'

He chuckled while he finished off the croissant and dusted his fingers, so the tiny flakes fell to the floor instead of on his neat jumper.

Jenna found her gaze staying on his hands. No wedding ring, but it didn't always mean something. His smart chequered shirt and burgundy tie showing through the V-neck of his fine knitted jumper was more of a give-away, especially with the razor-sharp folds in his slate-grey trousers. Married men had never been her thing, not since her dad had left her mum for a younger woman he worked with.

She leaned back in her chair, rested her elbows on the chair arms and linked her fingers in front of her. 'What can I do for you today, Adrian?'

'I thought I'd sit in on the brief, see where they've got to.'

Irritation skittered through her veins. 'I can't, I have to interview my rapist.'

'Alleged rapist.'

In one swift move, she came to her feet, pushed the last morsel of food into her mouth and swiped up her paper cup, the coffee still too hot to drink. 'No. He's a rapist. I can tell you that right now.' She touched her fingers to her cheek, where the bruise she'd disguised with a little make-up still smarted.

More leisurely than Jenna, Adrian stood, his own cup still on her desk.

His gaze raked over her as he stepped into her path and raised his hand to touch cool fingers against her florid cheek. 'He hit you?'

She tried to step back, but he slid his hand around the back of her neck, under her hair. Firm fingers held her captive while he inspected her face.

'It's nothing. He didn't hit me.'

He quirked his brow, doubt sliding over his face.

'He kneed me.'

The sharp hiss he sucked in accompanied the quick slam of his eyebrows across darkened eyes. 'He kneed you in the face?'

'Yeah.' She raised her hand to encircle his wrist with her fingers and pull it away from her neck, the fear of his sympathy too much for her to bear. 'It's what happens, Adrian. Sometimes I'm in the line of fire.' She wasn't sure how he managed to tangle his fingers in hers, but when she tugged away, he held on and drew her back.

'Jenna. Hold still.'

'I can't. I need to go.'

'Hold on just one minute. Did anyone check your face?'

'Yes. The duty doctor. There's nothing broken, he said he caught the fleshy part of my cheek. Hurt like hell.' She smiled up at him, but the effort was too much as anger swirled in his eyes and his lips dipped into a straight line. She didn't need his sympathy, didn't want anyone's sympathy. She was holding up just fine. Unless someone raked a gentle gaze over her or smoothed a tender hand from shoulder to elbow, then held onto her fingers again.

The constriction in her chest tightened to a painful wrench and the sob she'd held back escaped.

He opened his arms and wrapped her in the warm comfort of another human being while she encircled his waist with her arms and hugged him tightly, still gripping her coffee in one hand.

She couldn't remember the last time she'd had anyone hug her other than Fliss. Her mum had been all too frail at the end for anything other than a gentle stroke of her fingers across the back of her hand to reassure her she was still there.

This bear of a man made her feel so small and delicate, a rarity with her height. She gripped his soft jumper with her fingers and burrowed her nose into his neck to accept the comfort he offered. The desire to cry evaporated, but she simply stood in the circle of his arms and breathed long and slow.

He'd allowed her a moment of weakness and she appreciated it, but it was time for her to be strong once again.

She pulled back. 'I need to get to work.' Voice a husky whisper, she took another step back, so she could gain her equilibrium.

'Okay.' His slow nod jangled her heart. 'Me too. I'll sit in on the briefing and let you know what you need to. You go and carry out your interview.' He raised a hand and grazed a tender thumb over her cheek. 'Watch out for the little bastard this time, Sergeant. Don't let him get the upper hand.'

Heart already struggling to contain her feelings, Jenna swung open her office door.

'Morning, Sarg.'

That heart almost leapt out of her mouth as the scrawny kid stood at the entrance to her office, fist raised ready to knock. If he'd been just twenty seconds earlier, he may well have caught her in the arms of the Chief Crown Prosecutor.

'Ryan. What do you want?' She took large strides across the outer office, let him follow her. It wasn't that she was trying to escape, she convinced herself, merely that she needed to interview her suspect before time ran out and she was required to request an extension. Just another pain in the arse paperwork exercise she could do without. She suspected it would be frowned upon when her excuse was she was taking comfort from the newly assigned Chief Crown Prosecutor they'd sent to further torture her while she was completely helpless to find her sister.

'DC Ellis asked me to check on you. Said to tell you he's gone to the briefing and was there anything you needed him to ask?'

She whipped around with such speed the young kid almost skidded into her. 'Yes. I do have a question.' She leaned in close. 'Where the *fuck* is my little sister?'

His eyes sprang wide, showing a huge amount of white as the shock of her attack constricted his pupils to pinpricks. His ears flushed crimson.

Immediately regretting her outburst, Jenna bit her lip. 'Look, Ryan, just go along to the briefing.' She lowered her voice to soothe him a little more before he ran crying from the room. 'DI Taylor will be running the show. He's a quality boss. I trust him.' Ryan dipped his head in a slow nod. 'Keep your ears open, I know you've a bright enquiring mind, that's why you've been assigned to us. If you think of anything, anything you believe has the slightest impact on my sister's whereabouts, express it. This is not the time to keep quiet. Ask your questions. Collate your answers and write things down. Not everything sticks. Not everything means something to everyone, but if there's the slightest clue, anything, then speak with DI Taylor, or Salter and Wainwright. See how they got on with their questioning of Ed, Fliss's ex-boyfriend,' she qualified.

'They've done it.'

'What? They've done what?'

'Questioned the slimy ex.'

At her raised eyebrow, Ryan gave an idle shrug. 'Mason called him that.'

Impatient for the news, Jenna glared at the young DC. 'Ryan...?'

'He's got an airtight alibi.'

'Oh, right!' Sarcasm laced her words.

'Yeah, no. He has, Sarg.'

'How airtight can it be?'

'As airtight as not being in the country when the incident happened and evidence to confirm it.' He straightened his shoulders, puffing out his chest. 'I got to do the follow-up. Had to contact the airport and verify he was on the flight. It wasn't him.'

Disappointment warred with relief. In her heart, she'd known it wasn't him. It wouldn't stand true to the evidence already available. He was an arse, but she'd not put him down as a killer.

Most murders were conducted by people the victim already knew, but from the start this hadn't held the right elements. Ed had no reason to have followed Fliss into the woodland. Jenna touched the tip of her tongue to her injured lip. He didn't have the balls to cause Fliss physical harm.

No, this situation smacked of a stranger.

She shortened her stride as Ryan matched his to walk alongside her. 'Good work, Ryan.' She cast him a sideways glance as he flushed to the roots of his hair.

'Did anyone show Ed a photograph of the deceased victim?'

Ryan's head bobbed with enthusiasm. 'Yeah. We pulled a blank there too. He claimed never to have met her. No idea who she was. His eyes went kind of glazed as he stared at the photo. I thought he might spew, but he caught a hold of himself.'

Not entirely convinced Ryan's answer was the one she was looking for, Jenna shot him a tight smile. 'Keep an eye on the progress and let me know as soon as you hear any developments. I shot DI Taylor a list of Fliss's friends.' Jenna shook her head. 'It's a long list.' She ground to a halt, turned to face Ryan. 'Also, could you let DI Taylor know that I phoned the school head this morning, as agreed, and let her know Fliss wouldn't be in. I kept the details sketchy at this stage.'

Ryan bounced on his toes in his enthusiasm. 'Yes, Sarg.'

Tempted to pat the kid on the shoulder, she gave him a brisk nod instead and continued down the stairwell to the interview room, guilt making her feet move faster than ever.

The big bastard in there wasn't going to get the better of her this time. She'd asked for him to be shackled to the table next to his solicitor and two of her biggest PCs to be posted at the door. He'd got the jump on her once, but never again.

She slipped inside the door and took her seat opposite, noting the hate-filled narrow gaze that watched her every move.

25

'Nothing.'

Jenna rested her head against her hand and peered at Mason and Ryan from between her fingers, aware of Adrian's quiet presence in the corner of the room.

Still nothing. Not a clue.

'Brief me.'

'As I said. Nothing, Jenna.' Mason rubbed his fingers over his mouth, his skin had turned a dull grey during the day and the red rims around his eyes seemed to glow. Another full day and they'd still not found her. Time was ticking away. Mason looked as worried as she felt, and it occurred to her once more that his feelings for her sister were far stronger than he'd ever revealed.

Distracted by the incident room door being opened, Jenna paused as Frank and DI Taylor slipped into the office.

Surprise lightened Frank's eyes as his gaze caught hers. 'Sarg.'

'Frank. Hi.' Jenna cast her gaze over him. He appeared fresher than the rest of them. 'Have you just come on?'

'Mmmm. Nights.' He sipped his tea as he scanned the board. 'You?'

'I've been here far too long. I'm only here as an observer. I wanted a catch-up before I go off duty. Just to see if I can see something someone may have missed.'

Despite DI Taylor's presence, Jenna took the initiative and turned to Mason. He'd probably kept up to speed on the intel throughout the day.

'Take me through it, step by step.'

Ryan fidgeted and made her wonder if he was about to raise his hand again. Perhaps she'd take his enthusiasm over Mason's misery and Frank's quiet snuffles as he studied the paperwork in front of him.

She turned to face the younger man. 'Go ahead, Ryan.'

He shot up straight in his chair, his spine ramrod straight. 'It's a big area, but they've managed to cover a lot of the woodland today. The weather's not been too unkind, just a light drizzle, but some of the local Army pitched up and joined in the search. By lunchtime, we took local volunteers, keeping them as far from the crime scene as possible. The flood defences have been raised as the River Severn continues to rise.'

Jenna glanced at Mason. He held his head in his hands, elbows resting on his knees as he sat in the small chair he'd squeezed his frame into. DI Taylor leaned against the wall, arms crossed over his broad stomach. Frank shot a look in their direction, then ducked his head to scribble another note while Adrian tapped quietly into his tablet. He might appear oblivious, but she suspected nothing would get past him. She'd let him know she needed an update on her sister's case and, without a fuss, he'd been there. Ready when she was. Coffee in hand to offer her.

'What else?' She directed her question to Ryan again. She couldn't fault him for his ability to reel off facts and Mason hadn't disagreed with anything the boy had said so far.

'Dad said...'

She nodded encouragement at him as he hesitated for the first time. 'What did your dad say?' She'd known his dad for the past ten years; the guy was normally right.

'He said,' Ryan's voice gave a little warble, so Mason's head shot up, a deep frown streaking across his forehead. 'He doesn't think she's on the hillside. He's convinced she's been taken. He said if she was dead, then she'd been killed elsewhere, but there was no further evidence of another murder.'

'Okay.' She'd rather not have heard Fliss may be dead either in the gorge or somewhere else, but she had to face it. She may well be. She tried to keep her imagination from running wild, but experience and knowledge threw up thoughts she didn't want, making it hard to avoid them. Her police training exposed her to every possibility. 'Right. What else?'

'They've had the underwater search unit out all day. Nothing. They've scanned the waters and shore for as far as they can, taking in the rapid current, but the river's rising fast now and, as I said, the flood barriers have been erected in Ironbridge. The rain in Wales hasn't stopped for the past two days and rainfall has been heavier than normal today.' He'd started to sound like a weather forecaster, but she didn't stop him; he wasn't doing any harm.

She tapped her pen on the pad she had on the desk, glanced at Mason while he nodded in agreement and then let her attention wander across to the window. 'They'll probably have called off the search for tonight.'

'Yeah, Dad said for everyone's safety they couldn't risk searching the area overnight. If she's gone in the water, then it's reasonable to assume her body could have been swept downriver for miles. With the water so high, it's possible the body could have been swept as far as the Bristol Estuary. They'll check that far down, but it'll take time with the river as bad as it is and limited daylight hours.'

It stood to reason. It didn't make the desire to race out over the hills of Ironbridge and scream Fliss's name at the top of her voice until she answered any less. She couldn't let herself believe Fliss had been swept down the river.

Where could she be?

The reflection of the stark incident room stared back at her from the single small window, their images watery and blurred as night closed in.

'What about the dead woman?' she asked.

'Yeah, we visited the lab earlier. The pathologist had finished the autopsy.'

Jenna turned, a sneaking suspicion Ryan had turned a tinge of green was backed up by the quick succession of swallows he made.

Frank fidgeted, pushing a hand through his thinning hair as he nodded at Mason. 'I have an update. I just heard back from the pathologist. White female aged much younger than we initially thought. Around twenty-five to thirty. Height, five foot two inches. Weight, eight stone four pounds. Hair, short, light brown with a considerable number of grey streaks.' He studied his notes. 'No evidence of eye colour.' He shrugged. 'The animals, you know...' He waved his hands over his pale face, his mouth pulled tight.

'Is that it?'

'No. There's evidence that she recently gave birth.' Ryan, voice strong, came to his feet and stepped closer.

Jenna sucked breath in through her teeth and glanced around. Shock and disgust registered on every face.

'Fuck.' Mason swiped a hand over his eyes.

DI Taylor's voice lowered, strain tautening his features. 'There's a baby out there without a mother. This is desperate. We need to find it.' He turned to Ryan. 'What else have you got there DC Downey? Any more clues?'

Ryan shook his head. 'No distinguishing marks, other than the scars already mentioned. No tattoos, no birthmarks. She was underweight, with evidence of being malnourished. Her teeth.' He grimaced. 'Her teeth were not good. She'd very possibly not seen a dentist in quite some time.'

Mason handed Jenna a photograph of the corpse. Eyelids closed in death, skin purple-hued. 'There's a good reason to always floss, because if no one else can tell, the pathologist won't keep your secret.'

Jenna gave him a wan smile as Ryan gaped at him. Frank shuffled his papers and flashed a disapproving look Mason's way as though he didn't appreciate the disrespect.

'Was there anything further, Frank?'

He sat upright and leaned forward, the ceiling spotlights casting shadows over his face. 'She wasn't murdered in his opinion.'

'What?' She shot up in her seat, leaned over the table. 'What do you mean she wasn't murdered, Frank? We found her naked body at the bottom of the hill. Naked.' She whipped around to face her partner. 'Mason, did you explain that to the examiner when you saw him? She was naked when we found her. Bloody hell, Jim already gave her a preliminary examination.'

Mason held up both hands in self-defence. 'Yes, I know, and yes, I spoke with the pathologist about it, so there's no need for you to run off and find him. His experienced conclusion was, he thinks she broke her neck in the fall. He'll give a full report later, but this was just his initial findings while we were in attendance. When he did the nail scrape, there was nothing under there but dirt. No blood, no skin traces and there didn't appear to be any defensive wounds on her hands.'

'Okay.' DI Taylor nodded, making his presence known. 'I take it she was fingerprinted?'

'We have them, but I suspect there's nothing on file,' Mason replied.

'That's on my list to look into.' Frank fanned a sheaf of paper to indicate how much he still had to log.

DI Taylor pointed a finger at the board. 'We'll check all the anti-natal classes, hospitals. She must be registered if she was pregnant.'

Frank nodded. 'I'll get on to it.'

Jenna ran her fingers through her hair. 'Why was she naked?'

Frank shrugged and scribbled another note. 'We have no idea. Perhaps someone took the clothes from her body after death?'

'Uh-huh.' Ryan stepped up to the board and tacked the photograph of the deceased woman in the middle. 'Pathologist believes the body was moved post-mortem, dragged into the tunnel, presumably so no one would spot her during the day. The time factors seem to indicate she'd been hidden so that the perpetrator could come back and remove her in their own time. When Dad did the initial in-situ investigations, he found no trace of material from clothes, nothing to indicate that she was anything but naked when she was dumped there. But he could have stripped her elsewhere and dragged her body there. We've had so much rain, much of the original evidence would have been washed away or trodden into the mud.'

Jenna sat back and resumed tapping her pen on the pad, her gaze locked with Mason's as though they could create enough energy by their thoughts alone to explain why a naked woman with a broken neck would be at the bottom of the Gorge.

Ryan coughed, and Jenna shot him a quick glance, her eyebrows twitched upwards. He seemed to have plenty to say on the matter. 'Yes?'

'The examiner did say there was evidence of historical abuse.'

Frank shook his head. 'Not abuse, PC Downey. He never said abuse. He said there was evidence the woman had suffered several fractures in recent years, but it was too early yet to tell if this was from accidents or whether her bone density was too thin. He'll come back to us on that.'

'Nuh-uh.'

Frank's eyes widened at the audacity of the kid to disagree with him for the second time in so many minutes, but Jenna shuffled closer to pay attention. 'What else, Ryan?'

'There were scars on her skin, particularly the insides of her forearms.' He turned his arm, so the tender side was showing, and slashed his fingers diagonally across it. 'Several, as though she'd been slashed.'

'Or been self-abusing. That's what the examiner said.' Frank pushed his fingers through his limp hair and wrote something else.

Ryan dipped his head and mumbled into his chest. 'I've seen self-abuse. It doesn't look like that.' His head came up and he met Jenna's gaze full on, the maturity in his expression convinced her he knew what he was talking about. 'These scars looked deep. It was hard to work out which ones were from where she slid down the hill. The examiner will go through each one over the next few hours and let us know, but he pointed out a couple of deeper, older scars which seemed as though they'd been stitched, tiny dots still evident at the edges. There were several newer ones I noticed on her legs too.' He flicked Frank a cautious glance, evidently concerned enough not to want to undermine the more experienced man's opinion. 'You don't self-abuse and then stitch yourself up. Someone else had to have done it.'

'Someone else.' It made sense, but... 'Why hasn't she been reported as missing?'

The men shook their heads.

'Has anyone come forward since the press release?'

Mason shot her an uncomfortable look as DI Taylor shuffled through a stack of paperwork to snatch a newspaper from underneath. A full quarter page photograph of Fliss stared up at her. The photograph only the police had access to.

'Who the fuck authorised this?'

Adrian stepped close behind her to look over her shoulder.

'No one.' DI Taylor shook his head. 'I've spoken with the press office and confirmed what they issued. Someone leaked this to the press.'

She vibrated with anger as she stared at the front page of the newspaper. *Police Resources Stepped Up As Detective Sergeant's Sister Declared Missing.*

'Oh, god.'

The public would go wild. There'd be a frenzy of phone calls to the station, false sightings, concerned citizens with snippets of hearsay. Exactly the situation the police strove to avoid.

She read the name under the article. 'Kim Stafford. The bastard. How the hell did he get hold of this?'

DI Taylor pursed his lips. 'We're already looking into it. Someone on the inside obviously.'

'I bloody hate Kim Stafford. He must know what chaos this will cause. We're going to spend more time answering fake phone calls than chasing the culprit. For God's sake!' She paced across the small office, fingers gripping her hair.

Kim Stafford, slick bastard that he was. Same age as Jenna, they'd been in the same class at school together. She'd hated him then, she hated him even more now. If he was in the room with her, she'd kick his arse like she did when they were thirteen and he'd snapped her bra undone in assembly. She'd bloodied his nose and every minute of detention had been worth it.

There was nothing she could do about the situation. DI Taylor would have it in hand. She needed to move on, address the more pressing issue. She picked the newspaper up, gave it one last scan and tossed it on Frank's desk.

'What about the wedding ring? Wasn't it engraved?' They nodded their agreement. 'No joy on tracing it?'

Frank shook his head. 'We've sent out enquiries with the local jewellers but so far no one's recognised it. We thought about putting it in the Shropshire Star, see if it catches the attention of anyone locally.'

Jenna shook her head. 'I think we might want to keep this nugget of information to ourselves at the moment. We never know who might make a slip-up if they don't know about the ring. It could give us an advantage.'

Ryan almost bounced in his enthusiasm to impart the next piece of information. 'The pathologist confirmed it came from the deceased, as we suspected. Left hand, ring finger. From the wear on the finger, he estimated it had been there several years.'

'What was it doing off her finger further down the track?'

'No one knows. She never came from that direction, she came from above.' Mason came to his feet and wandered over to the board to stare at it for a long moment before he pointed. 'What if...' He puffed out small bursts of air from between his lips. 'This is a long shot. What if the woman fell, broke her neck because she was being chased and, for some reason, your sister was there.'

Jenna got to her feet too, to join him in front of the board. 'It makes no sense.'

'Nothing makes any sense, Jenna. Nothing. It makes no sense for your sister to disappear. It makes no sense Domino is virtually dead.'

'He's fine. I visited him this morning.' At his flash of annoyance, Jenna placed her hand on his forearm. 'I'm sorry, I should have mentioned it. The vet thinks he'll be fit to come home in a couple of days.' She shot him a wry smile. 'I may need your help.'

He raised one brow as he peered down at her.

'You know you love her dog.'

The other brow joined the first to wrinkle his forehead. 'I'm not having him.'

'No.' She didn't want that. Domino was hers now until they found her sister, and if they didn't... He'd be hers for the rest of his life. 'I didn't mean that, but he's going to need a lot of care. I wondered if you'd change your lunchtime. Take a different time from mine and visit him. I can visit him too. It means he won't be on his own too long.'

'I'm not damned well married to you, you know,' he grumbled under his breath.

She lowered her voice to match his. 'We'd have killed each other by now if you were.'

A reluctant smile spread across his face.

She touched the rough sleeve of his woollen jacket. 'You were always better suited to Fliss than me.' A rusty flush swarmed up his neck to pinken his cheeks and confirm what Jenna suspected. She rested her fingers on his arm a moment longer and gave a quick squeeze before she turned away, but her voice was a husky whisper when she spoke. 'I just need some help with him.' It strengthened as she continued. 'The vet recommended a dog sitter, but I want him to be with people he knows, and he knows you so well.'

'Yeah, I love the bugger. I planned to call in on my way home. See how he is. As long as he doesn't insist on sitting on my knee and sharing my bacon sandwich. I'm through with that,' Mason grumbled as he took his seat again.

Frank kept his head down, absorbed in his own work, but Adrian's cool observation never escaped her. His gaze held hers for just a moment longer than was comfortable before she glanced at Ryan.

'So,' she persuaded herself to ignore Adrian's attention while she recapped. 'You think this woman fell and broke her neck as well? For some reason, she was running naked on a freeze-your-ass-off October night through the woods. It's absurd.'

'You never know.' Mason leapt to Ryan's defence, already his champion it appeared.

'But I thought the examiner confirmed she'd been dead for between sixteen and twenty hours,' DI Taylor challenged.

'Yeah.'

DI Taylor crossed his arms over his chest and stared at the board, shaking his head. 'Which would place her there in the middle of the *previous* night.'

'I figured that, too.' Ryan nodded with enthusiasm.

'So why, then, would her chaser be there the following evening after she had been already dead for some time?' Jenna insisted. 'It doesn't make sense.'

'Maybe he was looking for her. Maybe he'd hidden her there, so he could come back for her for some reason. Maybe he was interrupted when it first happened.' Jenna wondered if Ryan was going off into the realms of fantasy, but she had no other possible explanation to offer. His take was as reasonable as any other scenario she could think of.

'Maybe he wasn't her chaser and the whole damned thing is some weird coincidence we'll never figure out,' Frank muttered.

Ryan shook his head, came to his feet and strutted across to the board, his scrawny neck swivelling within the wide collar of his ill-fitting shirt. 'No. Dad...' He coughed. 'Forensics say she fell all the way from top to bottom, there's evidence further up where her fall started. They found traces of her skin, blood and hair. She wasn't moved far from where she finally came to rest. Possibly dragged a couple of feet, so she was hidden under the archway.'

Jenna circled around Mason's chair to rest her backside on the desk while she studied the board, sideways on to Adrian. 'Naked female falls all the way down the Gorge. No one hears her.'

'Her neck may have been broken quickly,' Mason suggested.

'Possibly, but if I slipped, the first thing out of my mouth would be a scream.' She waggled her finger at Ryan to stop him bursting out with another comment, before she pointed at the board. 'Which is what happened when Fliss fell. She shouted Domino's name when he went down, which is why Molly's mum...' She clicked her fingers. 'Dina Whitby recognised the voice. Then Fliss screamed. According to the twilight walkers,' Jenna punched her finger on the photograph of the hillside, 'the scream went on, all the way to the bottom of the hill.'

At their nods of agreement, Jenna carried on. 'Fliss rolled into the naked body.' She tapped her sister's photograph, then the picture of the dead woman. It made sense. 'And the man, whoever he is, grabbed Fliss and took her away.'

Her stomach clenched, and hot bile rose in her throat as the thought struck her that she was dispassionately talking about her own sister. She swallowed it down. It was the only way she could be of any help.

'Why?' She glanced from DI Taylor, to Ryan to Mason to Frank, taking in Adrian's interest.

'Because your sister discovered the body.' Ryan's answer was so obvious, but there was a missing link, missing hours.

'Why was the body there? Why was he looking for it? If he'd committed a crime, why would he come back? Why not just leave it to chance that the body would never be found?' Jenna might as well push Ryan's enquiring mind and maybe spark something in her own, or Mason's, which would help.

'Because it's always the bloody dog walker who discovers the body.'

'Because,' at the sound of Mason's deep tones, Jenna turned to listen to him, 'he'd abused her. Held her prisoner for some considerable time, from the sounds of the amount of injuries she sustained. She escaped one night, ran through the woods, naked. She fell and broke her neck, or he broke her neck and pushed her. He had to leave her for some reason. Maybe he couldn't carry her. He needed transport. He'd followed her on foot and had to get back before someone noticed he was missing.' Adrian rose to his feet, his attention on the photograph of the victim. 'But he panicked for some reason and came back to the scene to retrieve the body. What if he believed she could be identified? He'd need to dispose of her body. She may have been reasonably well hidden, but her body was near the main path and, as Ryan pointed out, it's always the dog walker who discovers the body. Perhaps that's what he was afraid of. Once the stench of the corpse became obvious, she'd be discovered. And she wore a wedding ring with an engraving on it.'

Adrian peered over her shoulder at the photograph. 'So, he went back for the ring. And now he has your sister – as a replacement?'

Her heart quailed at his words. She didn't want to hear what he had to say. It was all too much. Her legs weakened, and she melted into a nearby chair, unable to make it to her own. Her hand came up to cover her mouth. 'Dear God.'

Mason squatted at her side, placed one large hand on her knee. 'No, I'm sure that's not it.'

She nodded. 'I think he's right. I think Adrian may be right. The man came back for the woman, his victim. Whether he murdered her or not, she has to have been his victim, and Fliss and Domino were there. There's the coincidence. I know in law we don't like them, but just once in a blue moon we get them.' She surged to her feet to study the pictures of the surrounding area. 'Fliss.' She closed her eyes and concentrated on centring herself. 'Of course, it would be Fliss. If there's danger in the offing, she'll be there. She's always been in the thick of things. Why wouldn't she just happen to be in the wrong place at the wrong time, with her crazy Dalmatian?'

'He's not crazy. He's a bloody lovely dog.'

She whirled around and flashed Mason a grin. 'Great, then you'll have no objection to helping me look after him until we find Fliss.'

He smiled back and flung an arm around her shoulder to give her a quick squeeze. 'You got me. Now it's time to go.'

DI Taylor closed the manila file he'd been studying and looked up. 'I agree, we've done as much as we can tonight, and we all need some rest to clear our minds. Night shift have their instructions and I'll be skinning someone alive, just as soon as I find out who our press informant is.'

As they walked to the incident room door, Mason cast a look over his shoulder at the young PC. 'Come on, lad. You've done well today. It's time to go home and get some hot food in your stomach. Night, Frank.' He nodded at DI Taylor. 'Goodnight, sir. Adrian, are you off home now?'

Adrian closed his tablet and came to his feet with indolent casualness, but his gaze never left Jenna. 'Yeah. Time to go home. Night, DI Taylor, Frank.'

Mason opened the door and waved Jenna through first.

'G'night sir, goodnight Frank.' She tossed over her shoulder as she walked through.

Frank grunted, keeping his head down as they left.

Hot food. The last thing she wanted and first thing she needed. Her stomach growled in protest as she made her way to her office to collect her coat. 'I'll see you in the morning. I'll be in by nine, I need to check on Domino again first.'

'Will you see him tonight?' Mason enquired.

She glanced at her watch. 'Yeah, I'll check on him on my way home again.'

'I'll probably see you there.'

Behind her, DI Taylor's radio burst out a scratchy buzz followed by an excited voice. 'DI Taylor, this is PC Donna McGuire.'

DI Taylor put his lips close to the Airwaves radio as he bumped through the doorway into the stairwell behind Jenna, Mason and Ryan. 'Go ahead, Donna.'

'I've been requested to inform you that SOCO have made a discovery at the crime scene at Ironbridge, sir.'

Jenna stopped four steps down and swivelled on her heel. She stared up at DI Taylor above her on the landing.

'What kind of discovery, Donna?'

Static echoed down the long stairwell.

'A baby's body, sir.'

26

Rain and misery poured down on their heads as they stood in a semicircle dressed in the pale blue PPE Donna had issued them with as they arrived on site.

DI Taylor and Mason flanked Jenna, their wide shoulders providing a little protection from the elements. Adrian stepped in close behind as they all peered up into the railway tunnel as Jim Downey crawled tentatively back out.

He gained his feet and turned to face them while he shook off the mud caked on his hands before he addressed them.

'Bloody awful situation.' He peeled off the first layer of gloves and dumped them in a temporary bin, leaving a second, clean layer underneath. 'I can't tell you much. I'm sorry.' His face drawn, Jim look around the group of observers. 'We'd removed the Jane Doe and climbed higher into the tunnel to check if there were any further traces of evidence. It's muddy up there, but there was a patch of earth that was softer than the rest. Felt like it had been disturbed. So, we started to dig.'

Jenna took a step forward and bent at the waist so she could peer through the brick entrance into the upward slope of the tunnel. A small figure dressed in PPE crouched in the darkened cavern over a shallow hollow. Without venturing further, Jenna couldn't see clearly enough to make out the tiny body with any clarity.

DI Taylor shuffled forward to join her. 'Any idea how long the baby's been there, Jim?'

Jenna came upright and backed away to allow Mason and Ryan to take a look.

'Not long, I'm afraid. Three, maybe four days. We'll have her out of here sharpish. I can't afford to keep the body in-situ with the weather setting in, we'll end up having a mud slide up there and losing all the evidence if we don't act quickly. Once we have the post-mortem, we can tell you more. Right now, my mind's struggling to even comprehend what the hell has been going on.'

Jenna nodded. 'Any thoughts on the baby's age?'

'Young. Very bloody young. A new-born, maybe a few hours old. A still-birth, possibly.'

As Jim advanced on them, they parted to let him through. He tugged the hood from his head and blew out a breath. 'This is not your ordinary, run-of-the-mill murder, DI Taylor. If these three events are all connected, and there's no reason to believe in this big a coincidence, then I'm sorry to say you have some kind of monster on your hands.'

The icy chill running through Jenna's veins couldn't be attributed to the weather.

27

Nausea rolled deep in her belly to fuzz her brain and liquefy her limbs, so she was helpless to move. Fliss rolled onto her side as the room spun in one direction, then jolted, turned and twirled the other way.

He'd drugged her. Again. The bastard. She knew he had, but she had no idea what with. Whatever he'd used, it could be lethal. Her stomach heaved. Each time he administered the drug, she felt worse. He'd possibly kill her next time, if he was overdosing her.

A kaleidoscope of colours splattered the walls and rotated maniacally before her eyes until she closed them in self-defence to shut out the attack.

When she cracked them open again sometime later, it was to the mild gyration of baby pinks, interspersed with yellow. A little easier on the brain than the previous profusion of violent colours.

A thick fog pressed down to suppress her feelings and deprive her of the capacity to formulate a single cohesive thought. With no ability to resist, she floated once more into an abyss she was incapable of escaping.

She blinked awake. Her stomach grumbled out a protest.

He'd left food for her. Water and food.

She reached out, misjudged the distance and flailed her hand into nothingness before she found she could focus.

If she could eat and drink, it may dilute the effect of the drug he'd administered. She rolled off the cot onto the floor, her already bruised knees taking the brunt of the cold flagstones to send shooting pains up her thighs.

She ground her teeth and concentrated on the bowl in front of her. She needed the food. She stretched her tethered hand as far as she could and managed to get hold of the spoon to scoop up the congealed, cold porridge. She leaned down as far as possible, stretched her aching neck until she could scoop the food into her mouth. Relief flowed gentle and calming as her stomach settled and the tasteless porridge served to coat it with the promise of no more sickness.

With small sips, Fliss drank as much of the water as she could, until her stomach sloshed, and she knew she'd fill the pants he'd put on her. She didn't care. There was no one to judge her. No one would in the circumstances. Just him.

She trailed her gaze around the place, only then realising he'd left the room illuminated when he left.

Although not warm, the small radiator had taken the threatening chill from the room, enough so she could sit on the side of the cot without the covers wrapped tight around her to restrict her movement further.

She chewed her bottom lip while she studied the instrument trolley he'd left behind. Neatly stacked with more pants, medical supplies, needles, vials of liquid she had no understanding of.

Strange he'd left it, but he'd been vaguely distracted, obviously anxious to go.

Fliss tipped her head to one side to better focus on the trolley. It made a small revolution around the ceiling and back before her vision settled again.

Mind slow to engage, she glanced from the trolley to her shackled wrist and back again. Trolley and shackled wrist.

She filled her lungs while she waited for her brain to clear. The trolley was too far away for her to reach, but while she stared at the handcuffs the foggy trace of an idea formed.

If only she could move the bed nearer the trolley, she could reach the instruments there.

She slipped to her feet, the icy floor freezing them until her toes curled up in self-defence. She focused on the bed. Aware she could only put pressure on one hand, she wavered before she grasped the iron cot with the handcuffed hand. A wave of weakness flooded her system, sending her legs to jelly until she had no strength left to brace herself to make the pull.

She dropped to her knees by the side of the cot, breath soughing in and out of her lungs as the room swayed. Tears of frustration trailed down her cheeks. Dammit. Dammit. She didn't have time to fall back to sleep. The man would return. He'd gleaned such pleasure in hurting her. She needed to escape. She had to get out.

The icy stone floor chilled her knees to remind her she was half naked. She swayed against the bed, leaned there to gain her equilibrium. Too heavy to hold up, she flopped her head onto the mattress. Only a moment. That was all she needed to get her strength back, but as the freezing numbness spread up her legs, Fliss used her remaining strength to haul herself back onto the bed. She yawned until her jaw cracked, then laid her head down on the thin pillow, just to take a few minutes and recuperate.

Her eyelids fluttered closed and the gentle swirl wafted her off into sleep.

* * *

Jenna blinked her eyes open and stared at the blackness surrounding her, darker than behind her eyelids. She reached out and groped for the lamp switch and banished the darkness with a golden glow of light.

She swiped the wetness from her face. Her own pitiful sobs had woken her.

She was powerless to do anything to help Fliss. No one would let her join in the investigation. She could watch from afar and make a few small suggestions, but she'd been banned from making any true contribution.

Aside from knowing more than a member of the general public would be allowed to, her hands were just as tied.

Jenna tossed the sheets back and leapt out of bed, her restless legs refusing to let her brain settle. She edged back the curtain and leaned her forehead against the cold window while she stared out at the moonlit landscape of her back garden, filled with ghostly shadows spiking cruel fingers into the darkened corners.

The next-door neighbour's cat slipped an elegant tightrope walk across the top of the fence, slithering down to melt into the darkness and leave Jenna wondering what had become of him.

The same thing had happened to Fliss. She'd disappeared into the night to be swallowed up by the shadows and no amount of searching was going to peel her out of them.

Jenna scanned the empty garden, but the harder she tried, the more difficult it became to discern the light from the dark. She dropped the curtain back into place and stepped away from the window.

She shouldn't still be awake. Exhaustion tugged at her. She needed sleep so she could function the next day. She needed to stay aware so she could find Fliss.

Jenna climbed back under the covers and tucked them under her chin, a mild shudder trembled through her at the chill in the room.

Fliss hated the cold. She always moaned about the winter. She was a bit like that dog of hers. A sun worshipper. They could lie out and sunbathe all summer long, but when winter came, they'd be huddled in front of the fire, whining about how cold the house was and Fliss would ask to turn up the heating. When the rain set in and they went for walks, the pair of them were like an old couple, each huddled in their own jackets.

Jenna huffed out as she flipped over in bed again, creating a draught down her back as she did.

She rolled over again, as the vision of the baby filled her mind. Poor little soul. Had she belonged to their Jane Doe? Is that what had lured the woman there?

Her eyes popped open.

What the hell was a naked woman doing running through the woodland? The question had been asked time and again, but the answer was the baby.

Jenna sat up, drew her knees up tight to her chest.

Where had she come from? The naked woman. Had she buried the baby?

Jenna flung back the covers and swung her legs out of bed. As she placed her feet on the floor, she stared at them for a long moment before she jumped up once more, making her way in the dark to the bathroom. Her mind full of questions. Questions she couldn't remember anyone else asking. Perhaps they had, but she'd never heard the answers, and the Ryan kid, he'd been detailed in relating all the events of the day to her.

She flicked on the light and grabbed the thick black jumper and jeans she'd left on the small chair at the end of her bed earlier. She glanced at her watch. There should be someone at the coroner's office to answer her questions by the time she had driven there, she could stop on her way to grab a coffee and by then there was bound to be someone available.

Back in the bedroom, she scooped underwear out of her drawer, and flung on her clothes, bounding down the stairs while she yanked the jumper over her head.

It was cold. Damned cold, and despite her hurry, she swiped up her thick, winter coat and grabbed her handbag, slamming out of her front door while she dialled Adrian. His sleepy voice mumbled a greeting.

'Adrian, I need you.'

Voice suddenly more coherent, he replied, 'There's an offer I don't get every day.'

She flung open the passenger door of her car and stuffed her coat and bag on the seat before she made her way around the bonnet to climb into the driver's side. The chill of the leather hit her system while her breath puffed out small white clouds. She shoved the key into the ignition as quickly as she could so she could start the car and get the heater going. It made one hell of a noise, but it worked well. Within minutes it would blast out hot air and fill the car with the warmth she desperately needed.

She chose to ignore his comment. 'I'm on police business. I need to get to the coroner's office, and you need to meet me there.'

'They only work nine to five.'

She pulled the seat belt around her as the phone kicked into her car Bluetooth. 'You're kidding me. People don't only die nine to five.'

'When have you ever had to visit a coroner in all the time you've worked for the police?'

Inborn habit had her looking over her shoulder before she pulled out into the deserted street. 'Normally between the hours of nine and five, but only because most of my admin time is during those hours.'

His annoying 'Uh-huh,' like he knew what he was talking about, had her flooring the accelerator and zipping out into the early morning traffic.

'Are you kidding me?'

'Yeah.' She could hear his movements as she evidently had managed to get him out of bed. 'They're twenty-four hours, but admin staff are normally nine to five.' He let out a quiet grunt. 'What did you think of that had you up so early?'

'The victim's feet.'

'Her feet?'

'Yeah.' She unwrangled her thoughts so they didn't just blurt out the mess they'd formed in her head, but she needed to know. It was important. 'The victim was naked and barefoot. I need to know how far she'd travelled barefoot, how badly damaged they were. Adrian.' She glanced through the steady downpour of rain. 'She's local. She wasn't dumped. She was escaping like you and Ryan said earlier. She was looking for her poor little baby. I need to know how bloodied her feet were.' She rubbed her fingertips across her lips as she contemplated the situation. 'The only reason you would run naked through the woods in the middle of winter is if you were out of your mind, crazy. Which we can't rule out yet. Or you were so desperate to escape, you never waited to pull on clothes and shoes. You had a window of opportunity to go and you took it. Ran in sheer terror. So, the question is: how far did she run from a possible monster?'

His quiet sigh floated through the silence of the Bluetooth. 'Jenna, you have to go back to DI Taylor and do this officially, you can't take off on your own investigation. It's one thing to study the incident board and check all the information over for accuracy and fact, but you can't run amok just because you have a thought no one else has yet had.'

'But we're running out of time. The longer it takes for us to find Fliss, the more likely...' A soft sob escaped her throat as she gripped the steering wheel until her fingers ached. She couldn't bring herself to face the fact that there was a possibility Fliss was already dead. Except she'd hoped whoever had taken her wasn't a murderer. That theory had just been blown wide apart. Defeated, she pulled the car into the feeder lane, circled a roundabout and headed for the station. 'You're right. I can't compromise the case.'

'What were you supposed to be working today?'

She shrugged. 'Lates.'

He sighed. 'I'll meet you at Malinsgate in twenty minutes. It's going to be a long day.'

Without his low, comforting tones, silence consumed the car as she focused on the road ahead. Unable to bear it, Jenna tapped the volume switch on her steering wheel until Radio Two blared out the sounds of the eighties while she drove to Malinsgate.

She flicked the switch to open her window, snatching in a shocked breath as the cold wind whipped into the car. A thin layer of ice covered the button on the access barrier to the car park as she punched it, tapping her fingers against her steering wheel while she waited for the barrier to raise up and then drove through.

When she slipped from the car and slammed the door behind her, the icy air froze the clouds of breath she puffed out.

She huddled tighter into her coat while she considered the naked woman who'd risked everything to escape someone. What would drive a person to run naked and barefoot through a forest in the pitch dark?

A monster.

A monster who'd killed her child.

A monster who possibly now held Jenna's sister.

It wasn't the outside temperature that froze the blood in her veins.

She stepped into the station and spotted Frank by the front counter.

'Morning, Frank.' She scanned the intel officer as he gave her a gritty-eyed blink. 'Long night?'

'Yeah, and Sonya called in sick. I'm covering until six.' He patted his hand to his thinning, dark hair. 'Then I'm going home to my wife and I'm going to sleep all day.' His tight smile told of his tiredness, but his red-rimmed eyes met hers. 'You're early though. I didn't think you were on until this afternoon.'

'Yeah.' She floated past the front counter and stepped through into the open stairwell. 'Something came up.' She took the stairs two at a time leaving Frank to follow at a more sedate pace, still bouncing with energy by the time she reached the top.

She flung open the door into the incident room, already abuzz with people. Surprised to see DI Taylor there already, she strode over to where he stood in front of the board, while Frank slipped into the incident room behind her.

DI Taylor shook his head, the thick roll of muscle at the base of his neck flexed under his short grey hair and bulged out over the top of his brilliant white shirt. An officer approaching retirement, he still bulled his boots until they reflected their surroundings. If his collar was a little tight, it was because he refused to order brand new shirts when his wife kept his stock of them perfectly starched and ironed and he could eke them out until he retired, saving the force a small fortune.

'You're early. How are you holding up?' Voice gruff, he barely spared her a glance.

She didn't expect a display of sympathy from the man, but she knew she had it as he took his perfectly pressed handkerchief from his trouser pocket and blew like a trumpet into it.

'I'm fine. I had a thought.'

He gave one last swipe of his nose, tucked his handkerchief into his pocket, and then grazed his astute stare over her. 'And what might that be?'

'The victim's feet.'

He nodded as though he understood and despite her respect for him, irritation unfurled at the time he took to reply, and she found herself elaborating before he prompted her to.

'She can't have come far, naked and barefoot. Surely, sir. She's got to be local.'

He nodded again and turned back to the board. 'I have extra photographs to put up.' He reached out, picked a pile of them off the windowsill and gave her the one off the top. 'Here.'

She studied the dark russet slashes across the woman's feet, the caked on mud which gave a clue as to her descent, and golden-brown leaves depicting where she lay for several hours.

Taylor stuck the first picture on the board before he handed her the second. After the coroner had cleansed her. The slashes on her feet still cut deep, dark purple several of them, leaving her flesh swollen and grey, but it didn't look so bad that she could have come far.

'Have we visited all the houses at the top of the Gorge?'

'We have. There aren't many. No one reported hearing anything. Nobody recognises the dead woman.'

'The victim.'

'I'm not sure she is a victim. If the coroner says her neck was snapped accidentally by her fall, then we're hardly looking for a murderer.'

Jenna shot a sideways glance at DI Taylor. 'Oh, we're looking for a murderer, sir. There's no doubt in my mind. Her snapped neck may be the cause of her death, but she'd been abused. She was naked and running from danger. And the baby was murdered.'

'Quite possibly by her.' He tapped the photo of her. 'We have no idea how that baby died, we can't assume a dead person's motive. She may have killed her own child.'

'Possibly. But it doesn't sit right.'

He chewed his lower lip. 'No. None of it does.'

They studied the board, side by side, going through each photo, each link.

Aware of the moment Adrian entered the room, Jenna stretched out her fingers and almost like magic, he placed a tall cappuccino in her hand.

'Frank,' Jenna glanced behind her, and Frank shouldered his way to the board. 'Have you got any further with the ring?'

'Ring?' Frank blinked red, watery eyes at her. 'What about the ring?'

Jenna knew she'd have more patience if her own sister wasn't the one who was missing, but why did Frank have to choose now to be obtuse? 'Yeah, you know we were going to look into the initials on the ring.'

Face blank, Frank shook his head. 'I'm sorry, I thought I was told not to progress anything further with the ring so we didn't attract attention from the public.'

Jenna raised her hand to her forehead and then dropped it down by her side. It wasn't Frank's fault. She probably hadn't been clear enough. 'No. We said not to make it public about the ring. We still need the script to be checked out. We need those initials identifying for definite.' She kept her speech slow and controlled as Frank frowned at her, his lips moving as though he wanted to say something.

Not so subtle, DI Taylor leaned in. 'Would you get on to that, Frank? It's urgent.'

Jenna turned from them and stepped close to study the woman's face, bloated in death. 'Who could she be? Why has no one reported her missing?'

'Because someone doesn't want us to know she's missing.' DI Taylor leaned in with her.

'But surely someone has to know who she is? Isn't she on an antenatal list somewhere?'

'We've got someone on that now,' DI Taylor confirmed. 'It's slow work.'

"Have we checked the local hospitals, mental institutions?"

DI Taylor focused on the photograph. 'We have. Nothing.'

She tapped the picture. 'Someone knows she's missing, dammit. She can't have got pregnant on her own. We just have to find out who the father is.'

'The baby's DNA will give us that, but we can only identify him if his details are held on the system.'

'God,' she growled. 'We need to find him.'

DI Taylor rested an easy hand on her shoulder. 'It may not lead us to your sister, Jenna.'

Her gaze swept up to the photograph of Fliss in the top right-hand corner of the board. 'It may not.' But in her heart, she knew the two were connected.

28

TUESDAY 30 OCTOBER, 05:30 HRS

Silence bore down in a thick, heavy blanket she welcomed. It meant he wasn't back. He'd been gone forever again. Whatever he did, it kept him away from home for hours at a time. Not a normal office worker. At least twelve-hour shifts. He'd mentioned paramedics. It had to be something like that. Although it was difficult to tell with the amount she'd slept. By the desperate pangs from her protesting stomach, he had to be have been gone a long time.

Fliss stirred. She needed to move. How long had she been out this time? It was hard to keep track. There was no natural light, just the single bulb burning.

The man would be back, and she'd still be lying on the cot with soaking-wet incontinence pants and the humiliation of him changing them again. Touching her.

A shiver of revulsion raised goosebumps over her flesh. She screwed her eyes shut and waited for the nausea to pass. In the silence, the gentle lap of water soothed her until she floated on a sea of tranquillity.

Her eyes shot open. Water? Why the hell could she hear water?

She jerked herself up onto one elbow and peered around the room. The dark stench of rancid water infiltrated her battered nose and filled her mouth. Liquid filth oozed under the doorway to coat the floor in a mixture of river water, soil and sewage. The dank, ominous odour of it triggered her senses. Fliss stared at the previous tide mark. If it reached there, she'd drown. She needed to get out before the water rose further.

She flopped back onto the bed, gathered her energy while her mind raced. She pushed back the fog that had engulfed her brain and forced it to work.

He couldn't have taken her far. They were by the River Severn. The flood defences were up on the north side of the river. They didn't use them on the south side. It was impractical and the amount of properties affected probably not worth the outlay for extra defences.

The rising waters eddied in little whirlpools across the uneven surface of the floor. If she didn't move before the waters rose higher, she doubted she'd drown, but she may just die of hypothermia.

She stared at the swirling currents. It was even possible she'd die of some disgusting disease brought through by the sewage seeping in.

Fliss glanced at the radiator. Electrocution wouldn't be the ideal way to go either. She judged the height of the electric socket against the rate the water slid under the door. She had no idea how long it would take for the waters to rise two feet.

Gathering her resolve, she ground her teeth and rolled onto her side to stare at the metal trolley. She needed an instrument, something she could pick the lock with. Ed had shown her how to do it. He'd bragged of how easy he found it to pick a lock and become a burglar as he often reminded her, just to spite her sister. He'd thought it hilarious that he had a skillset to boast of. One which could easily let him slide into the criminal world.

She'd never seen what an arse he was until her mum became ill, and all he wanted was to demand more of her attention and keep her away from her sister once her mum died. His jealousy had never been an issue, or so she thought, but once she'd seen it, every last thing Ed had done made her feel like a fool for ever believing she was in love with him. Self-centred and needy, he'd clung to her, so she'd believed she was indispensable, worshipped. When, in truth, all she'd been was a victim of his emotional abuse.

Well, she was no longer a victim. She refused to be.

She sat up, grasped the bedframe between her legs with her good hand

and and bunny-hopped, dragging the bed inch-by-inch closer to the trolley until she could reach out and drag it closer. Sweat popped from her pores and she dropped her head to her knees, exhaustion giving her no other choice but to rest for a minute.

Determined, Fliss raised her head and stretched out her plastered arm to grasp a pair of scissors, the scream of pain tore through her elbow into her shoulder as she flexed her fingers closed around them. Quiet whimpers sneaked from her lips, but she ignored them as she transferred the scissors to her other hand.

She needed to move to take a better look. Fine though they were, the scissors were too large to insert into the tiny lock.

She raced her swirling gaze over the trolley again. A hypodermic needle. She reached out, forced her damaged fingers to clutch it and brought it close to the handcuffs. The shake in her fingers stopped the end of the needle from going into the lock as her vision hazed in and out of focus.

Frustrated, Fliss took a moment to decide the best course of action. She held onto the needle as she rolled off the cot onto the freezing, wet floor and braced her tethered arm against the bed to hold it still. The slosh of icy waters eddied around her knees. As the clouds chased across her mind, her vision centred on the metal rail she was cuffed to.

She dropped the needle on the floor and leaned in closer, desperate to focus on the fine fracture line she could see in the metal. She cast her gaze the length of the cot, inspected the connection she could see there. It was feasible. It had to be. Her only hope was to break her way free of the bed frame.

Heart pumping, she staggered to her feet, twisted her hand so her fingers could grasp the cuff, then she slid the manacle as far along the rail as she could get it. Hope gave a vague flutter while she halted to listen for a hint of noise. She sniffed the air to detect any fumes. Nothing. He wasn't home yet.

She fought the terror that gripped her stomach, tightened her grip on the cuffs and gave a one-handed yank as hard as she could. Her feet swept from under her and she slapped down on the silt-covered floor, thankful for the thick pants which gave a soggy slap but protected her backside from too much damage. If ever her sister got to rescue her before she escaped, she'd never live down the humiliation of the incontinence pad.

She took inventory of her condition. She had no idea of the state of her hand, possibly strained or broken wrist, definitely broken fingers, gashes along her legs, cuts and bruises, swollen ankle, swimming head. God, her head swam. And she was stiff. Stiff from the cold and the battering she'd taken, but she was alive. Normally fit, healthy and pretty strong, she had the strength to do it. She had to.

Whatever happened once she got out of that hellhole, at least she could run. She glanced around. She had no shoes. He must have taken them. She could only hope to hell she didn't have to go far before she was spotted, picked up, or she found her way to civilisation. She knew how damned cold it would be out there, but determination would see her through.

She wanted to go home. It was time.

A wild, desperate sob broke free.

Domino wouldn't be there. He was dead. Without him, she had no idea how she would cope. Tears tracked down her cheeks and she swiped them away, anger driving her onwards. She couldn't dwell on the negative, she needed the strength to rescue herself.

Breathless, she worked her way to her feet again. She stared at the thin line on the rail, unsure whether the hairline crack had widened. She braced herself to try again. Froze.

Was that a noise? A creak of a door? Was someone coming?

Fliss tilted her head to listen. No further sound came from the old house.

She focused on the rail, the small fissure that could possibly have widened.

She wasn't going to let fear stand in her way.

She was going to escape.

She raised her foot against the bed frame and then jerked back with her whole weight. The top end of the frame burst apart and the connection ruptured, the cuffs snapped free, flinging her backwards. She let out a howl of agony as her plastered arm smashed elbow first into the floor, chasing away the white, sticky clouds in her brain and replacing them with bright sparks of firelight.

With soft whimpers, Fliss rolled to her knees. She struggled to her feet and made a stumbling dash for the door. She grabbed the handle with her right hand and yanked. It never moved. Pulse thundering in the base of her throat, she tried again, but the door was locked.

Tears dashed into her eyes, but she blinked them away. She needed a clear mind and clearer vision. She smelled the air. Nothing. No evidence yet of his return.

She scanned the room as the water eddied around her feet, determined to bring her panic back under control. If she could think straight, she could get herself out of the situation. She'd done it before with Ed. She'd left him without her big sister's help. She could do this without Jenna too.

God, but she wished her big sister was there. If only she'd burst through the door and rescue her just like she had a hundred times before.

Fliss sniffled and dashed the tears away as they streamed down her cheeks. Last time Jenna had tried to help, Fliss had told her to butt out of her life. That was before she'd realised what a grip Ed had got on her.

Fliss swiped at her cheeks again, pulled her shoulders up straight. She could do it. She was halfway there. She'd got herself free of the bed, now she needed to get out of the room.

She glanced down at her bare feet, curled her blue toes up against the cold, the thick sludge of dirty water whirling around her toes while her vision wavered. Whatever drug the man had given her, it hadn't worked its way out of her system. Her feet grew larger as she stared, expanded to fill her vision and the hot acid of nausea rose in her throat and clenched her stomach in spasms. She gulped away the excess water in her mouth, tightening her lips against the threat of sick rising up her gullet.

She needed to focus on something else.

She forced her gaze higher, tracked it up her bruised and battered legs and then stared in revulsion at the pants she wore. Damned if she was about to be found in a soaked, shitty incontinence pad with the stench of piss and menstrual blood. She ripped them down her legs with her one good hand, her cuffs rattled in protest, but a smile of satisfaction curved her lips when the pants gave a loud soggy slap as they hit the floor.

Naked from the waist down, Fliss sploshed through the water to the trolley, snatched a fresh pair of pants and made her way back to the cot. Her breath wheezed out as she slumped onto the bed, lifted her feet and scrubbed them against the mattress until they were almost dry.

One-handed, she wrestled the pants up her legs and hefted them over her hips. With her heart pounding, she flopped backwards and waited for her breath to even out before she rolled off the bed onto her feet.

Fliss snatched the thin blanket from the mattress and wrapped it around herself, wedging up against the cot so she could hold it in place while she struggled one-handed to tuck the end in at her waist.

Exhausted and dizzy, she panted out desperate breaths before she shoved herself away from the cot.

With one last glance around, Fliss bent to retrieve the scissors. They might be her only defence if the man returned while she was trying to escape. At this point, there was no way she could leap back on the bed and pretend nothing had happened, the place was too much of a shambles.

With a wild grimace, she pulled her lips back from her teeth and let out a frustrated howl.

She'd rather kill him than remain his prisoner for however long he wanted. He'd obviously kept the other woman. She weighed the scissors in her hand. Mentally she was prepared, emotionally she hardened her heart. If he died, so be it. Whether she was physically capable was a whole different matter. Her only way would be to take him by surprise. Shove the scissors in his neck and run like hell.

With studied determination, she made her way to the door on the opposite side of the room, paused to listen. She couldn't remember which way he'd left, she'd already been under the influence of the drug he'd administered. Her hand wavered in front of her face as she reached for the handle, grasped it.

Shock rippled through her over-sensitised system as the door swung open to reveal a short passageway to a set of stairs.

Without another moment's pause, Fliss raced along a hall and up a flight of stairs, ignoring the small stumbles from her tortured legs. Her swollen ankle shot fire into her frozen foot, but she charged on regardless. She wrenched open the door at the top of the short flight and hesitated.

Instinct told her he hadn't returned, but she paused to listen, to smell.

He wasn't there. Nor was anyone else, she was certain.

She peered around his empty, silent hallway, every ancient wooden door leading from it closed to give it a cold, heartless feel, but the front door had a tiny half-circle of bright painted glass. She closed the stair door behind her and slipped along the hall, her toes sinking into the thick patterned runner on the floor. She curled her toes into it to steal even the smallest amount of warmth.

She cast her gaze around, sorely tempted to peep inside one of the rooms to see if she could grab a pair of shoes or trainers, anything to slip onto her feet, but she didn't dare take the risk.

As she reached for the door handle, the dull rumble of an approaching car stopped the breath in her throat. The vehicle was coming her way.

He was back.

Oh god, oh god, oh god!

29

Exhaustion ramped up the irritation until the prospect of getting home left him trembling with anticipation. Work had his temper frayed and his patience with others teetering on the brink of breaking. He needed a holiday. Some time away.

He licked his dry lips, every moment away from her a torture. He'd take some time off and spend it teaching Fliss the way of things in his house. Discipline is what she needed.

He pushed his heavy glasses up his nose and cruised the old black Astra into his drive in front of the cast iron up-and-over garage door.

Once he'd settled in, poured himself a small glass of whisky and eaten the pre-packed roast beef dinner, he'd pay her a visit.

Unbidden, the rage rose in him. If she'd disobeyed him again, he'd teach her a lesson. He'd yank her hair out, twist her broken hand until she begged for mercy. Mercy he'd given his wife once she'd learnt her place.

He switched off the car engine and sat in complete silence while he looked up at the dark, imposing Victorian house he'd come to loathe.

A reluctant smile curved his lips. Still, he had something to come home for now.

30

TUESDAY 30 OCTOBER, 06:45 HRS

Fliss clutched the scissors to her chest. Her only weapon. Her heart quailed at the thought of using them, but she may have no choice. The bastard deserved it.

The floor trembled beneath her feet as the car passed by, its headlights flashing through the coloured glass panels in the front door to briefly illuminate the dim hallway.

Panic sent adrenaline spiralling through her, but she held firm at the front door while she listened above the pounding of blood rushing through her head.

The engine quietened but the vibrations continued, low and threatening.

He was there. He'd come in. She'd be stood in his hallway.

She stepped to one side of the door, placing her back against the side wall. With the scissors clutched tight in her fist, she raised her arm, reassessed and changed her grip. Better to go in low and surprise him than give him the opportunity of grabbing her wrist and wrenching the weapon from her grasp.

As the silence stretched out, she darted her gaze around, determining her best route. What if he didn't come in through the front door?

Breath hissing through her teeth, Fliss forced herself to listen. The distant reverberation of the garage door reached her ears while the memory of fumes reminded her he would go through the garage into the cellar where she'd been.

Frantic, she threw a quick glance over her shoulder at the aged bolt on the door to the stairwell.

She limped back to the door, slid the bolt home and backed away before she shuffled through the hallway to the front door with its little glass panel of hope.

The deadlock grated as she turned it and she froze before she swung the door open.

An icy blast hit her as a wild gust of wind greeted her at the door. No idea until she made the move whether it was day or night, relief washed over her as the blanket of grey dawn light gave her hope she might escape without him being able to see her.

Petrified, she stepped out, paused, and then pulled the door closed behind her, cringing at the shotgun crack of it in the silence.

She crouched and took a tentative step away from the house, swivelling her head from side to side to check for movement as she focused through the thin drizzle into the semi-light.

The hard flint of small stones bit into the soles of her feet and cut into the gaps between her toes. Numbing herself to the searing pain, Fliss ground her teeth and slid her feet one step after the other over the loose stones while a kaleidoscope of vicious colour daubed her vision as the drugs reacted to the kick of adrenaline.

The hard surface turned soft and slippery, a relief to her feet as she shuffled along a dirt track, every moment vital, every breath soughing through her throat in hitches of panicked air.

Fliss scanned the area, her hope of recognising some landmark scuppered by the curtain of murky dawn. She narrowed her eyes and peered into the distance. Tiny specks of light and optimism wavered through the darker outline of swaying trees to her left.

The soft whoosh of water confirmed that she was near the river.

She glanced behind, held onto her breath while she listened.

'Get off the track, Fliss,' she muttered under her breath. 'He'll see you.'

With one step forward, her feet shot from under her, her backside hit the ground, and she slithered down a short, steep incline. Her breath rushed out of her in a fierce grunt as she slammed into a tree trunk. She curled into a tight ball, holding onto the tree while she sucked in feeble gasps of air until the burn in her lungs subsided.

She forced her head up and peered above her, scouring the shadows for sound or movement, puffing out a silent breath as the silence lay heavy.

She braced herself against the tree and pushed to her feet, determination lending her strength. She wasn't about to let him capture her this time. She was no longer a victim. She straightened her spine, empowered by fear and determination. 'I'm not a victim!' But she kept her voice at a husky whisper.

She swiped her hands over the thin blanket to wipe the mud away, then scraped her matted hair out of her eyes, tangling her fingers through it, only to have it flop forward again in a straggle of wet locks. She raised her face to the sky, closed her eyes and welcomed the soft wash of rain to cleanse her skin.

She swayed on her feet. Her eyes popped open and the adrenaline rush she needed to push back the after-effects of the drugs charged in.

Three steps forward and the terrain changed again. Her naked feet skidded over a wooden fishermen's landing. The dash of water rushed underneath, and she died a thousand deaths as she teetered on the edge. She wind milled her arms and staggered back away from the edge, her breath heaving in her chest.

She bent over at the waist and leaned her good hand on her knee, tucking her plastered arm against her stomach to hug in the warmth.

Dear God, she didn't need a maniac to kill her, she was about to achieve it all on her own.

She raised her head while her world spun with triumph.

The soft glitter of fading moonlight sprinkled over the tar-black river a footstep in front of her. The current rushed the water onwards as the strength edged back into her trembling legs.

She knew where she was. Not the exact location, but upstream, where the light glimmered, was Ironbridge.

Filled with hope, she scrambled a few steps away from the small dock and turned right to follow the narrow pathway along the edge of the river, ankle-deep in the floodwaters. No sound but the rush of water and her own desperate breaths filled her head, but as the sky lightened, her heart burst with courage and she picked up speed as each footstep drew her closer to the distant lights.

The burn in her chest spread so each breath scraped at her raw throat with the effort of staying upright.

'I'm coming, Jenna. I'm coming home.'

Tears streaked her cheeks to mix with the rain and the mud and her own hair straggling across her face. She gasped in another breath and forced her wobbling legs onwards.

Fliss stumbled, slammed her plastered arm against a tree and sent a fresh spike of pain in a fiery heat all the way to her shoulder. Wheezing, she leaned against the tree. Icicles filled her lungs as she laboured to pull in oxygen.

With legs of jelly, she sank to her knees, swiping away the icy slime of snot from her upper lip with the back of her hand and then rubbed it off onto the dirty blanket.

She pushed up from the ground and staggered onwards, the river on her right. One foot in front of the other.

'Almost there, Jenna, almost there.' She puffed in rhythm with the fast, erratic slap of her feet against the muddy track. 'Almost there.'

She jerked to attention as she left behind the icy squelch of mud and her feet hit the concrete at the edge of Ironbridge car park.

Fliss spared the few houses shrouded in darkness to her left further up the Gorge a quick perusal and made for the bright lights of the Ironbridge instead. Dizzy and weak, she had no idea where she'd come from, but the safety of the dense population of houses drew her to the opposite side.

'Jenna.'

Fliss clenched her teeth and blew out short, sharp puffs of air past dried, flaking lips. She turned right out of the car park and stumbled past the Tollhouse on her left. Her bare feet scraped onto the pebbled surface of the Ironbridge. Oblivious to the pain, she gripped the blanket around her waist, scissors still in her grasp, and forced her feet to move.

One step at a time.

One foot in front of the other.

Closer.

Her head bobbed in a drunken wobble and she reached out with her right hand to lean against the thick iron girders of the Ironbridge as the angry waters swirled below.

She clamoured for breath, drawing it in through her mouth as her nose burned in agony. The weight of her head too much, she dropped it down below her shoulders, tucking her left arm safely around her waist while she almost shook herself apart as the tremors hit her.

With a slow roll of her head, Fliss glanced to her left, barely able to keep her eyes open.

Fear bolted through her at the vision of a dark shadow in the lee of The Tollhouse and she turned and fled in a staggering hobble.

31

TUESDAY 30 OCTOBER, 07:00 HRS

The man stared into the distant lightening dawn coming from the east.

His teeth ground together. 'Fucking bitch!'

She'd be seen by anyone out and about on early-morning business.

Nosy bastards.

Fury bubbled beneath the surface, but he could control it. He'd always controlled it.

He leaned against the wall of the ornate gates leading to the Ironbridge and swiped sweat from his forehead, focusing on the burn in his thighs from running so hard. She'd had him racing along the fucking muddy lane from the house, then back again to check before he'd turned himself around yet again and managed to track her. Straight down from the front of his house to the river. Fury raged. The bitch.

If only he'd not been delayed at work. A few minutes earlier, he would have caught her before she'd even got out of the front door. Instead he'd wasted precious moments looking for her in the small cellar room. Not that there was anywhere for her to go. Except upstairs where she'd locked the fucking door into the house on him.

Once he'd realised his mistake, he'd dashed back through the cellar and out through the garage door into the ever-lightening dawn and the persistent rain, heart exploding from his chest.

He stood in the shadows of the Tollhouse at the entrance of the Iron-bridge as she leaned against the deep railings, her body seeming to melt as she appeared too dazed to move on.

It wouldn't take much to heft her over the railings into the river below, then all evidence of her existence would be washed away. Her body would be found and they'd be left with another puzzle to solve as her time of death would never relate to their timelines. His lips twitched in wicked amusement. She probably wouldn't reach the Severn Estuary, miles downriver, but with the swell of the river she'd get a long way towards it.

He rubbed his hand over his mouth, temptation poking at him to dash across the bridge to where she still leaned against the side.

He scanned the area, narrowing his eyes. With no one in sight, no movement that he could detect on the opposite side of the Ironbridge, he took a tentative step forward, keeping to the darkest shadows to get a better view of her.

As though she sensed his presence, she glanced his way, her head jerked up as her shadowed gaze met his. She pushed upright, then stumbled, going down on one knee before she found her feet and ran in an unsteady stagger.

A reluctant wisp of admiration curled in his chest at her strength.

'I'm going to kill her. Stupid cow.' Her death would be a pleasure.

He glanced around.

Fog snaked low across the River Severn, dulling any noise.

The man stole forward again.

'Morning!

The swift rush of a bike sweeping past from behind almost stopped his heart. With swift instinct, the man melted into the shadows of the Toll-house, breath rasping through his closed throat.

He'd been seen. Fury kicked and struggled to burst free, but he held on to a thread of reason which kept him from leaping forward.

Almost on top of Fliss, the cyclist slewed his bike sideways and leapt off, running the last few steps to her inert body.

A shout went up from the cyclist and the man froze against the wall of the Tollhouse. He needed to go. But he'd find her again, and he would kill her. There was no doubt in his mind. She could identify him to her fucking supercilious fucking bitch of a sister. But he had a little time.

Fliss would have hypothermia. She'd be in shock. Not enough to die, but enough so she wouldn't be able to think straight to start with, wouldn't know enough about him under the thick layer of drugs he'd administered to her. It was a risk, but he'd have to take it. He had no choice.

The man flattened himself against the wall of the Tollhouse to take one last look before he slunk away, keeping low along the stone wall, alert for every giveaway movement of people. He comforted himself with the thought that the man on the bike never took the time to look back, never connected him with the woman on the ground. Every ounce of the cyclist's attention pinned on poor, pathetic Felicity.

The man shivered, the cold cutting into his flesh as he passed through the old gateway and made his way along the river path, to the east, where the weak rays of sun broke through the clouds and cast fingers of apricot and lilac through the persistent drizzle.

Panic pressed a heavy weight on his chest. He was surprised she hadn't run full tilt straight through to the police cordon without going over the bridge. Shame she hadn't. He could have disposed of her then, wrung her neck and dumped her body where she'd originally fallen. Irony. Justice.

He glanced over his shoulder. She would have done better to have kept going. Three police officers stood guard outside the cordon. She'd have run straight into them.

Stupid bitch. He snorted. Too fucking stupid to know which way to run.

He worked his way up the small incline to his house, his boots crunching across the shingle driveway. If anyone saw him now, they'd assume he'd just arrived home from work. Lucky none of his neighbours lived in close proximity and he had very little to do with them anyway. Hardly knew their names.

He hadn't even closed the garage door, or the front door she'd left wide open in her bid for freedom. A bid she'd won. Hate scratched a deep furrow in his heart.

A tension headache throbbed behind his eyes as he pulled the front door closed and then worked his way around to the garage. He stepped inside and heaved the heavy iron up-and-over door down, plunging himself into darkness. Punching the light switch, the man made his way through to the small cellar room to study the mess she'd made of it.

She'd pay. He'd make her fucking pay.

He sloshed his way through the four inches of floodwater, knowing it would rise still further before it receded, leaving its stinking, foetid mud behind. He was sick of it. Sick of the place his mother had left him. The trap she'd left for him to rot in because he'd never sell it. Never be able to. Who'd want a virtually derelict, uninsurable house, with a garage and cellar that flooded and the mostly decomposed body of someone's mother buried beneath the false concrete floor?

Exhausted, he panted out irritated breaths. He needed to sweep the room, remove any evidence of Fliss's visit, her existence. Just in case.

He kicked the broken cot bed with his booted foot as he passed it and made his way through the room to the stairs beyond. He had to force himself to calm down. He needed his wits about him if he was to deal with Felicity Morgan before she let her sister know who'd taken her.

He smacked the heel of his hand against his forehead in an effort to focus his mind. They'd take her to the hospital first. DS Morgan probably wouldn't even be allowed to see her in the first instance, which could be to his advantage.

He ignored the visible shake in his fingers as he reached for the door into his hallway. His plans had fallen apart. He needed food, then he'd clean up the cellar and sleep before he made a new plan to get him out of the situation she'd put him in. It was her fault. But he'd formulate a plan. It was his forte. Planning.

He pulled at the door handle, but the door stuck fast. He clenched his jaw so hard, his head pulsed with pain. He'd forgotten she'd locked it from the other side. He'd never thought to unlock it before he came through the garage.

He reared his head back and with a roar of fury kicked the thin door with all of his might, splintering it off its hinges to send it crashing through into the hallway of the house.

With a slow intake of air through his nostrils, the man smoothed his fingers through his fine hair as he made his way to the kitchen without a backward glance at the fallen door.

32

Jenna leaned her backside against the desk, taking a life-saving sip of black coffee from another takeout cup Adrian had pressed into her hand, while she studied the latest progress on the board.

Shoulder to shoulder with DI Taylor, she shrugged. 'It doesn't make sense. What the hell is the link? There just doesn't appear to be one.'

He nodded his agreement and then turned away, picking up a file of papers as he made his way to the end of the conference table and took a seat. Head in hands, he studied the file in front of him in silence while Jenna continued to scrutinise the board.

Misery weighed her down. 'She's been missing more than eighty-four hours now. Any leads we might have had have gone cold.'

As a police officer, Jenna knew those first few hours were vital in tracing a missing person.

DI Taylor shook his head, his lips pursing. 'Jenna, we've covered so much in so little time.' He counted off on his fingers the points they'd covered. 'We still have an unidentified body despite looking through every missing person.' His mouth dipped down at the edges. 'A baby, literally hours old when it died, buried under the tunnel that the woman was found at the mouth of. DNA results that confirm they were mother and son.' He shot her a sideways look. 'As you know, we deal in facts and evidence, but somewhere along the line, we have to accept the coincidences are too strong. So, who killed the baby, because we know he didn't die of natural causes, he was suffocated.'

In pain, Jenna worked her way around the room to stand over him. 'What monster could do that to a baby?'

DI Taylor leaned back in the chair and crossed his arms over his wide chest. 'Well, either the woman did it, and then committed suicide by flinging herself off the hillside...'

Jenna shot him a doubtful stare.

He shrugged and continued, 'or there's a monster out there who has kept this woman for years and when she gave birth, murdered her child. Their child. And buried him in a shallow grave.' He raised his arms, linked his fingers and, leaning into his hands, cradled the back of his head. 'That would be my take.'

Jenna pulled in a sharp breath. They'd known it was a possibility, almost bet on it, but having it verified hit a chord in her heart. 'Poor baby.'

'Poor mother.' DI Taylor scratched the top of his head, the short thick hairs rasping in the quiet of the room.

She studied the photographs of the woman. 'Why naked?'

DI Taylor shrugged. 'Her only chance to escape? He didn't allow her clothes?'

'What about the door-to-door? Surely someone knows her, recognises her?'

'They turned up nothing. No one saw anything, no one heard anything.'

'But she was pregnant. Didn't she go to antenatal?'

'Evidently not. We've checked all the records.'

With a quick glance to where Adrian worked on his laptop at the opposite side of the room, Jenna sank into the chair next to DI Taylor. 'Where did she come from? I mean, what about her footprints? From the night she died? Where were they?'

'Difficult. We found his, which could have been from either night, but none of the victim's. Mainly we assume because of the torrential rain. It would have washed them away. We haven't found anything further up the hillside that may have belonged to her, but forensics are still on it and will be for some considerable time. There's a hell of a lot of ground to cover.'

'And Fliss...'

DI Taylor touched her arm. 'I'm so sorry, Jenna, but we're no further forward with that part of the case either.'

Airwaves radios sizzled to life.

'Control from Golf Bravo 13. Woman found in Ironbridge, believed to be Felicity Morgan.'

Jenna shot upright, her coffee sloshing over the rim of the cup. She whipped her head around to stare at DI Taylor.

He held up a hand, demanding silence. 'Go ahead, Golf Bravo 13.'

Excitement laced the deep male tones on the radio. 'We've found her, sir. We've found her.'

Terror paralysed Jenna while she watched the room move in slow motion, officers jumped from their chairs, Adrian headed across the room to join her, his hand tightened on her shoulder.

DI Taylor turned his gaze on her, pure professionalism in his stance as he raised his radio to his lips again. 'What's her status?'

'Alive. She's alive, sir.' The exhilaration in the officer's voice bounced down the Airwaves and released Jenna from her statue-like state.

'Where is she?' She grabbed at her bag, dug inside for her car keys while she waited for an answer.

'Golf Bravo 13, what's the location of Miss Morgan?'

'Ironbridge, sir. She's here. We have her. She's weak, and confused, sir, but she's alive and conscious.'

'Golf Bravo 13, have you called an ambulance?'

'That's a positive, Control.' A moment's hesitation crackled the line before the officer returned. 'The woman in the newsagent called them. We were just passing through and she shot out of her doorway. Miss Morgan had fallen coming over the Ironbridge. A cyclist helped her to the shop doorway, the woman was still on the phone to the ambulance service when we passed by.'

The buzz of sirens sounded in the background as Jenna raced for the door, heart skipping in her chest.

She was alive. Fliss was bloody well alive.

Dammit, she was going to kill that sister of hers when she got hold of her for putting her through hell and back. Her heart skipped a beat and a sob hiccupped out of her mouth.

'Has she confirmed her name, Golf Bravo 13? Do you have confirmation of her identity?'

'Negative, Control. She's unable to talk. We have her wrapped in our coats. She's almost naked, Control, suffering from hypothermia at a guess. But it has to be her, Control. It has to be.'

Jenna's feet skimmed the stairs as she shot down the three flights. She gave a firm push to the door at the bottom and continued headlong through to the outer door without pausing for breath, until she skidded to a halt just outside as a car lurched to a stop in front of her, brakes squealing in protest.

The door was flung open and Jenna bent at the waist to peer in.

'Get in.' Tension tightened Mason's mouth as his sharp gaze met hers. 'I heard it over Airwaves as I walked in. I knew you'd want to drive, but it's my pleasure.' His grin was fast and feral.

Her fingers shook as she grasped the door and pulled it closed once she'd flung herself into the seat.

'What if it's not her?'

The voice from the back seat took her by surprise when it expressed the fear she'd already raised in her own mind. She craned her neck to stare at Ryan, who leaned forward, his hands braced on the back of the driver's seat.

When had she stopped being so young and passionate? She'd never stopped caring, she just paced herself better. Considered the world in a different light. With cool cynicism, instead of hot enthusiasm.

Well, that keenness had raised its head and there was no way she was about to be negative or cynical about this. 'It's her. They said it has to be her, who else could it be?' She'd deal with the desperate disappointment if it wasn't, but right now, she needed to remain positive and focused. It was Fliss. It had to be.

Adrian flung open the rear door behind her and launched himself inside the moving car as Mason floored the accelerator. 'Not so bloody fast, you're going nowhere without me.'

Jenna whipped around and pinned Adrian with a deadly stare. 'Don't try and stop me seeing her. I will mow you down if you get in my path.'

His lips twitched. 'Wouldn't dream of trying, DS Morgan. I'll merely act as a professional witness of any encounters.'

Mason took the first right at the roundabout and Jenna almost swallowed her tongue in desperation.

'Where are you going? It's Ironbridge, Mason, Ironbridge.' Panic gripped her throat as she flapped her hands around to indicate he should go back the way he'd come, but he raised one hand from the wheel and pointed ahead.

'The hospital. They'll take her straight to the hospital. Priorities, Jenna. Her physical welfare is the most important thing right now. The paramedics will take her straight there. They won't wait for anything.'

Her mind cleared to zero with a sharpness she'd always utilised in her job. He was correct. It may be her sister, but she still had to do things right, otherwise they'd end up chasing ambulances through the grey light of dawn. She gave a curt nod and stared out of the window, counting the minutes until they arrived at the casualty department.

Mason negotiated the roundabouts with nauseating fluidity until she gripped the passenger door, her fingernails digging into the plastic handhold. Reluctant to make any criticism, Jenna grit her teeth until her jaw popped.

As the car came to a skidding halt, Jenna leapt out, air sticking in her lungs as she hitched in strained breaths.

Quiet at that time of the morning, there was only one ambulance in the emergency bay, back doors open to reveal its emptiness.

She wound her way through A&E to the check-in desk, flipped out her warrant card and dangled it in front of the nurse. 'DS Morgan. I believe a Felicity Morgan has been brought in by ambulance this morning.'

Unfazed by the badge of authority, the nurse took a moment to study Jenna's warrant card before she scanned the computer screen in front of her.

Jenna's heart stuttered. One part of her wanted to race down the hospital corridors screaming out her sister's name, while the cool professional side had to batten down the desire and swallow the lump in her throat as she waited for the nurse to respond.

'I'm afraid we have no one of that name here.'

Jenna ground her teeth and forced herself to smile. 'Could you check if she's on her way in by ambulance?'

'Of course.' The nurse took even longer, and Jenna resisted the temptation to tap her foot. It wasn't the nurse's fault, but where the hell was the ambulance? It should have had its blues and twos all the way there. They should have arrived before Jenna.

Worry had her whipping around to meet Mason's intent gaze. 'Where is she?' She pointed her finger at his nose. 'If they've taken her to Shrewsbury instead...'

Ryan fidgeted, tugging at his already loose collar, while Adrian stood cool and observant, towering over the young PC.

'Okay.'

Jenna swung around, avid attention pinned on the nurse's next words.

'She's in the ambulance that's just pulled up to the doors.' As Jenna turned to sprint back along the corridor, the nurse called out. 'Stay here, DS Morgan, and I'll get someone to escort you through when they're ready.'

Desperate, Jenna whipped around. 'You don't understand. She's my sister.'

The nurse came to her feet and let herself out of the side door to reception. 'I do understand.' Her low soothing tones, and the hand on Jenna's arm, calmed the skittering of her pulse. 'Come through here, and as soon as she's ready, we'll let you through.'

'Thank you. Thank you.'

Aware of the other three following her, Jenna sank into a hard, plastic chair and glanced at the time. Mason had got them there pretty damned quick.

She crossed one leg over the other and thumped her foot rhythmically up and down in the air, glancing at the clock again. Two whole minutes had passed, and it felt like a lifetime.

She jumped out of her seat as the automatic door slid open and DI Taylor marched into the room. Suit immaculate. Shoes shined to a high gloss.

'The ambulance has just arrived,' she blurted. He probably already knew, but it was something for her to say.

'You, DS Morgan, sit back down and stay exactly where you are.'

She slumped back into the chair as his penetrating stare held her gaze.

'I just broke the land speed record getting here so I could stop you from seeing your sister before you broke every rule in the book.' He ranged his hawk-like stare around the room, taking in the other three. 'I would have radio'd you, but it appears not a single one of you had the foresight to pick up Airwaves when you hauled your arses out of the station, leaving me to tie up the ends before I could leave someone in charge on the ground.' His thick eyebrows dipped low over his eyes. 'Do we all need to be here?'

'Yes, sir,' Mason spoke without hesitation. 'Jenna's here as family. I'm here as she can't take Fliss's statement because it would be a conflict of interest, and Ryan's here for the experience.'

Adrian leaned against the door frame, gaze unruffled and indolent. 'I'm with DS Morgan.' His tone brooked no argument.

The line between DI Taylor's eyebrows deepened, but he said nothing, just slipped into the chair next to Jenna's and turned so he addressed only her. 'We have no idea what state your sister's in, Jenna, I'm advising you to stay here.' At the fast shake of her head, DI Taylor leaned in close to growl in her face. 'I bloody well know you won't stay put.' As she took a breath to interrupt, he pointed a finger at her. 'I understand she's your sister and you want to make sure she's safe, but as a professional you know exactly what will happen if you compromise anything about this case. She is to tell you *nothing*.' He stabbed his finger in the air, circled it around. 'You are to ask her *nothing*.' He thumped his thumb against his chest. '*I* will be her first point of contact until we get the team in place. A team that would have been in place had you not shot out of the station like shit off a shovel, leaving me to zip after you.' He slapped his hand on his knee, let out a long groan. 'I'm getting too damned old for this. I almost had a heart attack catching up with you.'

'Well, at least you're in the right place, sir.'

Taylor turned dead eyes on Ryan. 'You want to go back to uniform, son?'

Ryan's face flushed all the way through from his skinny neck poking out of his loose collar to his hairline. 'No, sir. I mean no, DI Taylor. No, sir.'

One side of Taylor's mouth kicked up. 'Learn to process your thoughts before you let them escape through your mouth. It's an acquired skill, but one you'll need if you ever make it through your probation and pass your promotion exams.'

'Yes, sir.'

Jenna slumped over to dangle her hands between her knees and flopped her head forward over them. If she could smile, she would. She always appreciated the DI's humour, but she simply couldn't muster up a single stroke of emotion. Everything was on hold.

She may not be as tough as she'd always thought herself. The hollow grind in her stomach served to remind her. Every emotion she'd been put through in the last few days had stripped her and left her vulnerable. She'd been plunged into the abyss. Nerve endings scraped raw, she had no other choice but to pull herself out, inch by painful inch.

Jenna raised her head to cast her gaze around the room at the four men staring back at her. She filled her lungs, straightened her shoulders and addressed them all. 'I'm prepared for anything. I've seen just about everything there is to see in my service and my main concern is to make my sister feel safe and secure.'

Proud of the strength of her voice, Jenna met Taylor's stare with a direct one of her own.

33

Gentle female tones soothed as Fliss floated on the tranquillity of safety.

'Felicity? Felicity Morgan?'

'Hmmm.' They call me Fliss, she normally told people, but she had no hope of opening her eyes or making her vocal cords work. She'd used every last molecule of energy to get over the Ironbridge with the absolute conviction the man was close behind her. Breathing down her neck.

She tried. She really did, but her eyelids gave a brief flicker and her tongue was so dry it stuck to the roof of her mouth. That would be the drugs. And the lack of fluids she'd had over the previous god knows how many days.

'Felicity.' Cool fingers touched her cheek. 'You're in good hands. They've brought you to The Princess Royal in Telford. You're safe now.'

The woman was so kind. The effort might be worth it.

'I know.' The gravel in Fliss's throat barely allowed the words to pass through. 'I'm so tired.'

'I understand, but I need you to help me, Felicity. Can you open your eyes for me?'

Try as she might, her eyelids wouldn't obey. 'Mmm.'

'Not to worry, Felicity.' Soft hands took hold of hers, held on to her, grounded her. She was safe. 'Felicity, I'm Lana Gill.'

Lana. Lana Gill. Fliss ran the name through her mind. Was she supposed to remember it? Was it important? The thick sludge in her brain swallowed up the name and let it float away.

'Felicity. I'm a forensic nurse.'

Forensic. Did that mean she was dead?

'Do you understand what that means?'

Short of a shake of her head, she flopped it from one side to the other, aware of the crackle of the hospital pillow. She cleared her throat. She needed to speak up. Make herself understood.

'It means I'm here to examine you, to help you understand what's happened and to collect any evidence or DNA as soon as I can.' Fliss took the words in as the nurse continued. 'Here. Have a sip of water. But that's all for now. Just a sip, until the doctor examines you and agrees what we need to do.'

Fliss took two greedy pulls of water from the straw the nurse slipped between her lips.

'That's all, I'm afraid.' Lana removed the straw from Fliss's mouth. 'I'm here to examine you, Felicity, and to answer any questions you might have. I'm aware you're very sleepy, so I'll go slowly, and we'll stop whenever you want.'

''Kay,' Fliss mumbled. 'Drugged.'

'Drugged?' There was no surprise in the woman's voice, no change to the gentle sympathy of her tone.

'Yes.'

'I'm going to take your blood pressure now and do some other tests to check your status, then if you're in agreement I'll need to do toxicology tests on you. Blood and urine. Is that okay?'

'Yes.'

Strong, cool fingers grazed Fliss's skin as the nurse wrapped a cuff around the upper part of her undamaged arm. As the band squeezed tighter, Fliss's eyes shot open, panic slicing through her chest.

'It's okay. You're safe.' Lana gave a gentle squeeze of her fingers at the same time the cuff relaxed on her arm. The thunder of Fliss's heart filled her ears as she puffed out panicked breaths while her gaze centred on the cool blue gaze of the nurse. Lana.

'I'm sorry. I...'

'It's okay. I understand.'

Lana continued to hold her hand until Fliss's breathing ratcheted down to reasonably normal.

'I'll talk you through what I'm going to do. First, we're going to do your obs – observations. Blood pressure, we've done.' She released the cuff from Fliss's arm and slipped it off. 'Stats.' She raised a clip and showed it to Fliss before attaching it to her middle finger. As she took hold of Fliss's wrist, Lana glanced at her watch. Her slow, even breathing calmed Fliss as she stared at the woman.

She was safe. He might still be out there, but right now she was safe.

The swift surge of energy drained just as quickly from her and Fliss rolled her head on the pillow to stare through heavy lids out of the window while Lana continued with her obs.

'Here.' Lana held out the glass of water with a straw poking out of the top. 'Have another sip of water. I think it did you good. You seem a little more alert.'

Fliss sipped at the water, then grimaced as Lana took it away all too soon. She pushed her voice out, aware of the heavy slur. 'The cuff – it squeezed.' She dragged in a breath. 'Too much.'

Lana touched her arm, her face a mask of serenity. 'I'm sorry. I didn't mean to upset you.'

'You didn't. He did.'

'Do you want to tell me about it?'

Barely able to move her head, Fliss gave it a slow roll on the pillow. 'He didn't rape me.' At Lana's encouraging nod, Fliss continued. Her lips wobbled with the effort of speaking. 'I may be wrong.'

'We can check. Would you like me to check?'

Fliss inhaled. She didn't want Lana to check but understood the necessity. She let go of the fear that held her rigid. 'I'm on my period. It disgusted him.' The memory of his harsh intake of breath flashed through her mind.

Lana simply nodded, her quiet presence a gentle reassurance.

'Do the tests.' She was sure she'd know, that there'd be some sign, but she'd rather know for definite and this was the only opportunity to find out, once that narrow margin of time had passed, the evidence would be gone for good.

'Right.' Lana shot her a compassionate smile as she removed the clip from her finger and noted down the results. 'First, though, we need to get your clothes off, bagged and tagged for evidence.' Lana came to her feet, removed the nitrile gloves she was wearing, dumped them in a bin and pulled on a new, fresh pair. She reached over and picked up a sickly-looking green gown and placed it on the chair she'd been sitting on. 'Would you like to take your clothes off yourself, or should I help you?' Lana flicked open a large plastic bag and looped the top over a trolley.

'I think I can manage.' Fliss pulled herself upright, every muscle in her stomach protesting. Her arms screamed in agony as she struggled to yank a pullover the cyclist had covered her with up her body, but gentle helping hands reached out to assist, persuading the item off over her head.

Exhausted, she flopped back against her pillows, aware of the soft puff of air they let out as they deflated under her weight.

'Rest a moment,' Lana murmured as she stuffed the item of clothing into the open bag. As she turned, she picked up the ugly green gown, opened it up and rolled it until the neck hole showed. She offered it.

Fliss took a moment to gather her strength before she leaned in and allowed Lana to slip it over her head. The clean, clinical scent wafted over Fliss to underpin the safety she felt.

Lana placed her hand on Fliss's back. 'We'll slip your bra off before you put your arms through.' Lana slipped the bra into the first bag. 'I have paper knickers for you.' She flicked a pair loose and Fliss stared in horror at them. Lana chuckled. 'I know, they're more like a bloody nappy, and one size fits all.' Lana touched Fliss's arm.

Fliss shrugged. 'He made me wear a nappy. As good as. He said I was incontinent.'

'That doesn't sound nice. I'll take this blanket.'

'It's his. I took it from the bed.'

Lana tugged the ends from underneath Fliss's bottom and thighs and slipped the blanket from her, her gaze skimming over the incontinence panties. She rolled her lips inwards. 'I'm sorry, perhaps my nappy remarks were inappropriate.'

'No.' Fliss closed her eyes, black clouds swarmed in to blot out her vision.

Her hearing the only sense still functioning, she listened while Lana carried on with her job and gently removed the incontinence panties from Fliss's body. The hushed rustle of plastic bags and shuffle of Lana's shoes the only noise in the room.

Aware of the total silence now, Fliss forced her eyes open. Lana sat in the chair next to the hospital bed, her slow, steady hand writing up her notes. She raised her head and offered a gentle smile as she caught Fliss's stare.

'Do you need any sanitary products?'

As fire blossomed over her chest and spread up her neck to flame over her face, Fliss swallowed hard. 'Yes. No. I don't know. I may have finished.' She stared down her body, opened her thighs and screwed her eyes shut at the sight of smeared blood. 'Yes. I guess so.'

Unruffled, Lana handed her a sanitary towel. 'I'm sorry, but no tampons until we finish the tests.'

Humiliation scalded Fliss's cheeks while the nurse started her step-by-step examination of Fliss's body, taking swabs, examining cuts, marks, bruises and noting them all down in her file. Despite Lana's absolute discretion and compassion, Fliss lay in mortification until the nurse was almost done.

'I need to take some bloods now. Are you ready?'

'Yeah.'

Fliss turned her head away as Lana searched for a decent vein. 'I'm going to take the one on the back of your hand. You're quite dehydrated, so when I've done this, I'm going to get a line in and rehydrate you.'

'Right.'

At the touch of the needle to her flesh, Fliss flinched and whipped her hand away.

'I'm sorry. The man... he...' Fliss tucked her knees up to her chest and rocked.

The rational part of her mind soothed her, but her pulse rate bumped up.

'Felicity. It's okay. We don't have to do this now.' Lana touched her shoulder and Fliss swallowed.

Relax. You can do this. She sighed out. *Relax.*

'We do need to do it, don't we?'

Lana smiled and nodded. 'We do, Felicity, because we need the toxicology and because you're dehydrated so we need a line in. But if you can't, I understand. I can wait.'

'The longer you wait, the less of the drug will be in my system though?'

'Yes, and the more dehydrated you'll become. I'm going to use a cannula.' Lana picked up a small, plastic tube with a tiny valve on the end to show her. 'And I'll use this spray to numb the area first. Okay?'

'Okay. Let's do it.' Fliss unfurled herself and offered her hand to Lana.

'You don't have to look.'

'I think I do. When I closed my eyes before, it made it worse. Perhaps we'll talk. Or... or I could sing, not that I'm good at singing, but I could sing.' She was rambling, but her tongue took control from her empty brain.

'You can sing if you wish.'

'What though, what can I sing?'

Lana held her hand as she waited for Fliss to begin.

Fliss turned her head to stare out of the window as weak rays of sunlight broke through the thick black clouds. For no reason she could think of, other than the regular assemblies she attended, Fliss began to sing 'Morning has broken'. She angled her head and gave Lana a nod.

Quicker than she thought possible, Lana had the cannula in the back of her hand, three phials of blood taken and a line in with saline washing into her veins.

Exhausted, Fliss slid down the bed, her body melting across the mattress until she was liquid wax. 'I'm done.' She closed her eyes and drifted, letting the sound of Lana's movements wash over her.

34

She may have thought she was prepared, she certainly knew the process, but Jenna's heart hammered so hard she thought it might burst from her chest.

The sight of her little sister flat out, her skin as white as the sheets tucked under her arms, her hair a ball of manic frizz, made a liar of Jenna. Something gave way inside and her knees turned to water. She hated that she was going to cry. A ball of fear and anger burned in her chest. She wanted to be strong for her little sister. She needed to be the super-bitch she'd become in order to survive the job. Cold, logical.

She ran her gaze over her younger sister and every ounce of super-bitch deserted her. Fliss's beautiful face was a fragile mess. Despite the clean-up, blood still caked her nostrils, the break in her nose gave it a twist to the left and black encircled her eyes, slipping down to her cheeks in an olive and mustard smudge.

It wasn't possible to remain detached. Jenna's heart hammered in her chest until it threatened to explode. Who did this to Fliss?

She covered her mouth with both hands to keep in the sobs, no longer caring if she was being watched. As Fliss lay asleep, Jenna cruised her gaze over her, checking every scrape and bump. She'd never seen anything like this, because it had never been her own sister in a hospital bed before. Grazes and deep scratches marred the beauty of Fliss's skin, bright crimson stark against the alabaster of her cheeks.

Confused, she stared at the plaster cast on Fliss's arm. Where had it come from? She'd been ages with the forensic nurse, a lifetime, it seemed, but there's no way the hospital had put a cast on her sister in that time.

Despite the agony, Jenna's enquiring mind fired up. Where the hell had Fliss been?

Fliss turned dull eyes on her, but she still raised her good arm for Jenna to lean into.

The sweet cloying smell of mint and thyme clung to her sister, but nothing could make Jenna let go of her death-like grip on her.

Hot tears soaked into her shirt from where Fliss rested her cheek on Jenna's neck, but she didn't care. She didn't care about her own tears rolling down her face into Fliss's mangled hair, she just clung, the ball of fear rolling in her chest. It didn't matter. She had her sister, safe in her arms. Alive, if damaged.

She sniffled again, drew back to inspect Fliss.

'Christ, you're a mess. Did your mother teach you nothing?'

Fliss spluttered out a tearful laugh. 'You don't look so hot yourself.'

The door was flung open and a short, slender nurse stepped inside the room Fliss had been assigned. 'Only two in here at a time, please.' She gave a long, hard stare at Mason and Ryan until they pushed themselves off the wall they'd leaned on and ambled out one after the other. Ryan a close imitation of the older man as they both dipped their hands in their trouser pockets and hunched their shoulders in a show of juvenile recalcitrance. Adrian had already been abandoned in the waiting room, his nose deeply buried in work since the DI had assured him he was no longer required while Taylor was there.

Mason paused, glanced over his shoulder, his gaze skimmed over Fliss and he opened his mouth as though he were about to speak, then shrugged. With a regretful smile kicking up one corner of his mouth, he headed for the door. 'I'll be back.'

He closed the door behind him and Jenna came to her feet. Left with no option but to release Fliss's hand, she moved her chair back out of the way, so the nurse could get closer. Taylor never moved.

'The doctor will be here in just a minute.' With a tilt of her head, the nurse pinned Taylor with an inquisitive stare. 'And you are?'

He almost stood to attention, coaxing a smile from Jenna. 'DI Taylor, nurse, I'm one of the investigating officers.'

The nurse turned to Jenna, her gaze filled with empathy. 'You're Felicity's sister?'

'Fliss, we call her Fliss.' Jenna nodded, her throat almost too tight to swallow. She didn't need sympathy, she needed to remain in control. 'Yes.'

'I'm Lana, Fliss's forensic nurse. I'm here for as long as she needs me.' Lana made her way to the opposite side of the bed and touched Fliss's arm as she handed her a glass of water. 'You look so alike.' Jenna shot Fliss a quick look. Some people saw it, others couldn't. 'It's the shape of your eyes, although they're not the same colour, they tilt up, and your jawline.'

Jenna forced a smile and nodded at Lana. A clever woman, obviously experienced in her field, she'd engaged both sisters with surprising ease, reducing the speed of Jenna's pulse before it took a foothold.

Fliss closed her eyes, but a ghost of a smile hovered over her mouth. 'I think it's because we both look as rough as hell.'

Jenna gurgled out her laughter and sank back into the chair, exhaustion taking hold of her. Fliss was safe. It didn't matter what had gone on before, she was here now, she'd escaped. Jenna would sleep for the first time in days.

Lana took the glass from Fliss and placed it on a bed trolley and then turned to check the IV fluids. When she turned back, she made direct eye contact with Jenna. 'Fliss tells me you're a police officer.' At Jenna's nod, Lana continued, 'I've carried out all the required tests on Fliss, with her permission, and now we're waiting for the doctor. Once he's been and checked her over, Fliss will be allowed to shower and then we'll get her into a fresh gown. As far as I can tell, there are no life-threatening injuries, but the doctor will verify everything I've done.' She touched Fliss's shoulder. 'Hopefully, he'll let you go home once we X-ray your arm.' She picked up the file and with clinical professionalism took a seat in the corner of the room, silently studying the information she had.

'Felicity.' DI Taylor drew a chair close into the bed and sat down, his lined face calm and placid and Jenna remembered why she respected the man so much.

'Fliss,' Jenna corrected.

Taylor inclined his head. 'Fliss, I need to ask you some questions while we wait for the doctor. Are you okay with that?'

Jenna drew back but kept hold of Fliss's good hand while she sat in the chair.

Tears swamped Fliss's green eyes, turning them almost neon in the bright lights of the hospital. 'He killed Domino, Jenna. He killed him. Have you found him?'

Close to tears herself, Jenna leaned forward into Taylor's line of sight, but she didn't care. He might be her senior officer, but this was her sister. She clasped Fliss's hands in hers to warm the icy chill from them. 'No, he didn't. Domino's alive, Fliss.' Her voice caught on a sob. 'He's as beaten up as you, but he's alive.'

'Oh God. Really?' Fliss screwed her eyes shut, tears leaking out of the corners to trickle into her hairline. Pitiful keening broke from Fliss's lips to make Jenna's heart tremble.

'Would I lie to you?' She raised one hand and smoothed her sister's wild hair back from her face to give herself comfort as much as Fliss.

'No.' Fliss swiped at the tears on her cheeks and flopped back on the pillows, all the strength she had appeared to have melted from her. She covered her mouth with her plastered hand and then drew it away, her lips curling with distaste, and rolled her head, so her gaze met Taylor's. Her jaw clenched while she swallowed several times, her delicate nostrils flaring. 'Where do you want to start?'

Taylor drew an old-fashioned notebook from his jacket pocket and poised his pen. 'At the beginning, Fliss. Tell me what happened from the very start.'

'I was walking Domino.' Her voice slurred, and her eyelids slipped shut. She licked dried and cracked lips before she continued. 'It started to get dark, and stupidly I'd taken the narrow path.' She opened weary eyes and flicked Jenna an apologetic glance. 'I wanted to be alone, and I thought I was safe with Domino.' She shook her head. 'Poor Domino. When can I see him?'

Jenna smoothed her thumb across the back of Fliss's good hand. 'He's at the vets' right now, but when you've been checked over, we'll see him. He's due home tomorrow anyway.'

Only the soft puff of Fliss's breath greeted her.

35

TUESDAY 30 OCTOBER, 13:10 HRS

The door swung open, admitting a young, fresh-faced doctor. He glanced around the cubicle, surprise flickering in his dark stare, then his gaze landed on his patient.

'Felicity Morgan?'

Fliss gave him a vague nod, then stuttered through her date of birth and address when asked.

'I'm Doctor Ahmed.' Softly spoken, the doctor sank into the chair beside Fliss's bed that Jenna vacated and touched her arm in a gentle reassurance. 'Are you comfortable with me asking you questions in front of the police, or would you rather I ask them to leave?'

'No, I'm okay.' Fliss's eyelids flickered closed and she rested her head back on the pillow, her nose pinched with stress. 'DS Morgan is also my sister.'

The doctor gave Jenna a cursory nod and then returned his attention to her sister as he wound a cuff around her arm and pumped it up. 'I've spoken with the paramedics, and Lana,' he nodded towards the nurse, 'but would you like to tell me what happened?'

White around the mouth, Fliss clenched her teeth as the cuff tightened for several long seconds and then deflated. As the doctor jotted down the results on her medical notes, Fliss chewed her bottom lip. 'I was walking

Domino, my dog.' She hitched in a breath and glanced at Jenna. 'I thought he was dead,' her mouth twisted in a crooked downward grin. 'But he's alive.'

Jenna's chest burned as she held onto every ounce of her self-control.

'And then the man was there. Just there, above us in the woods. He killed Domino. I thought he had.' She screwed her eyes shut. 'I heard something. He came from the hillside above us. A huge branch in his hands, he hit Domino.' She paused, breath heaving. 'And then I stepped over the edge of the path and fell, and fell, and fell.'

She went silent, her breathing evened out.

Just as Jenna thought her little sister had fallen asleep, Fliss mumbled. 'I told Lana I didn't think I'd been raped.'

Hot relief flooded Jenna's system. She couldn't think of anything worse than Fliss being kidnapped, raped and murdered. Two of those had been discounted and now they needed to get to the bottom of why she was kidnapped.

The doctor leaned in closer. 'We're waiting to see what drugs are in your system, because Lana told me you said you believed you've been drugged.'

'I have been drugged. Several times. He used a needle.'

Doctor Ahmed jotted something down, all the time nodding. 'I believe Lana has already arranged samples of your urine and blood. This will give us a better idea of what he might have used, and if you're at risk of any needle-associated diseases.'

Jenna swallowed hard. She'd not given consideration to the after-effects. She'd focused on Fliss being safe. But she may not be. The man may have ruined her sister's life in other ways.

Fliss rolled her head from side to side, her skin almost as white at the pillow. 'No, I don't think he used dirty needles. From what I remember, the couple of times he stabbed me, he used gloves and removed them from the packaging. He was very precise. His actions were so weird, like he thought he was a doctor.' She rubbed her furrowed brow, her speech so slurred Jenna leaned in to hear her better. 'He said he'd had training. I can't remember clearly, but I'm sure he said he'd trained as a doctor.'

Jenna's gaze clashed with Taylor's. His eyebrows winged up before he gave a brief nod and made another note.

Doctor Ahmed made a humming sound in the back of his throat as he wrote some more. 'I see Lana has also carried out rape tests.'

Taylor continued to write without looking up.

With a weary sigh, Fliss passed her gaze around the circle of spectators. 'We don't think I was raped. I was drugged heavily, but the man showed signs of disgust because I was on my...' she stared at Taylor's bowed head for a long moment as he scribbled, 'on my period.'

Taylor raised his head, his soft gaze filled with understanding and Jenna's heart stumbled. She'd always respected him, but now she was just a little in love with him for the way he treated her sister.

Fliss's cheeks flushed, but she continued. 'Lana says there's no sign of damage.'

'That's good news.' Doctor Ahmed lifted Fliss's uninjured wrist and placed fingers against her pulse. 'We'll have a much clearer idea once we have all the results back. We've put a rush on them.'

Fliss closed her eyes, her strength almost gone. She licked her lips. 'There's something else...' She took two long drawn-out breaths, then licked her lips, her quiet voice barely there in the silence. 'I can't remember if I've mentioned this before. My mind is a little hazy.' She paused again for a long moment, then drew in a breath, the words carrying as she expelled it. 'He said he knew me.'

A ripple of fear shuddered through Jenna. Unable to contain herself, she shuffled closer to her sister. 'Was it Ed?' He might have an alibi, but the question still had to be asked.

Fliss shook her head. 'Definitely not. I may have been drugged, but there was a world of difference between them. His smell alone was different.' She wrinkled her bruised nose. 'I have no idea who the man was, but he took me because he believed I recognised him.'

'Okay.' Jenna nodded. 'We had Ed in for questioning, but Salter and Wainwright were convinced he had an airtight alibi. At least it rules him out for certain.'

Taylor leaned in, his voice honed steel. 'Thank you, DS Morgan. I'd appreciate it if you allow me to follow through. Perhaps you would like to track down a cup of coffee for us all?'

Jenna breathed in until the thud of heartbeats slowed in her head. 'I'd like to stay, sir. I won't say another word.'

With a soft snort, Taylor turned back to Fliss. 'Could you describe him, if we get you a police artist?'

Fliss's face went blank. 'I'm sorry.' Her voice slurred and she raised her right hand to her forehead. 'I can't think straight.'

The doctor continued his obs, checking the screen for each of her vitals.

Jenna almost called a halt as the silence stretched out, but Fliss continued, her voice a soft whisper.

'His eyes were...' Her forehead crinkled. 'Dark. Dark and dead. He wore glasses. Really thick glasses. When he was angry, spittle came out of his mouth.' She touched her cheek, revulsion rippling over her features. 'His teeth weren't nice. He had a horrible smell. As though he lived in mothballs.' She rolled her head to look at Jenna. 'You know the smell at Grandma's house, down in the cellar? We used to call it the spider room. I always think of spiders whenever I smell it. An old-fashioned smell.'

An image of their grandma's cellar formed in Jenna's mind, the overpowering scent of dust and dead things hung in the air to remind her. Jenna gave a shudder and restrained herself from checking if there were any spiders in the room.

'I was in the cellar.' Her breath came in fast snatches. 'The cellar, with one light bulb and the river water rising. I had to get out. I had to escape.'

Taylor placed a hand on Fliss's arm but withdrew it immediately when she flinched. Instant responsiveness, which Jenna could only admire.

With an automatic move, Jenna linked her fingers with Fliss's good hand. Her sister may not have been raped or murdered, which to everyone surrounding her would be an excellent outcome, but the impact of what had happened to her was already taking its toll.

Fliss sniffled. 'I want Domino. I want my dog.'

Jenna studied her sister. She was fragile. They'd mend together. All three of them.

Tears lodged in Jenna's throat and she leaned in to take Fliss into her arms. She rocked her like she used to when Fliss was a baby, like she had when their mother had died, and again when Fliss had left Ed, the bastard.

'Let's get you seen to and once we're finished up with the questions, we'll ring the vets, see what they say.'

'Okay.' Fliss gave her a one-armed squeeze, then lay back down, weary lines streaked her face. She rolled her head on the pillow to look at Taylor. 'I slipped down the embankment, and I scrabbled around to find Domino so I could get him away from the man, but instead I found...' Her eyes flew wide, she slapped her hand over her mouth, dry-heaved for a moment while Lana reached for a cardboard bedpan. Fliss accepted it and laid it on her lap and then shook her head, removed her hand from her mouth and sucked in great gulps of air. 'What I touched was dead. Oh my god, cold and clammy and very obviously dead.' A tear slipped from under her eyelashes and trickled down her cheek.

'It's okay. We found her.' Taylor scribbled for a moment longer before he glanced up. 'She'd been dead some time. The coroner believes a snapped neck.'

Horror filled Fliss's face as memory flooded back. 'She was naked.'

'Yes, she was. Do you know anything about that?'

'No. Just, she was naked. I touched her hand. It was icy.' She rolled her head to one side, her eyes still closed.

'It's time for Fliss to rest.' The doctor stepped closer to the bed, but Fliss opened her eyes again and gave her head a shake.

'One more minute,' Taylor requested.

'Just one,' Dr Ahmed agreed as he finished writing his notes and hung the clipboard on the bottom of the bed.

'As I grabbed her hand, a ring came off.' Fliss raised her hand and rubbed her fingers together as though she still felt the ring in her grasp. 'I held on to it as long as I could.'

'We found it, too, thanks to you. Well done. It could prove invaluable if we can identify it. You dropped it along the trail, near the car park.' DI Taylor's eyebrows dipped low as he took in both medical staff. 'This is information we haven't made public, so I'd appreciate your discretion.'

Dr Ahmed and Lana nodded in agreement and DI Taylor continued.

'What else can you tell me?'

Fliss raised shaky fingers to her throat. 'He tried to strangle me, but my fingers were wrapped in the dog lead.'

'Dog lead?' Taylor enquired.

She threw Jenna an apologetic glance. 'Yes, I'm sorry. I normally loop his lead around my neck, save holding on to it while we're walking.' She demonstrated with a weary wave of her hand around her neck. 'I snap the clip onto the metal ring to keep it from sliding off.' She dipped her head, defensiveness slipping into her husky voice. 'It's easier.'

Jenna leaned in and growled, the desire to make a better job of strangling her sister brewing just under the surface. 'Bet you won't do it again.' The amount of times she'd told Fliss not to wrap the lead around her neck, but her younger sister always thought she knew better. Well, not on this occasion. She'd say it served her damned well right, but it didn't, it never would. Fliss shouldn't have to worry about maniacs wanting to strangle her.

Fliss cast Jenna a sheepish glance as though she could read her mind and stuttered out. 'I somehow managed to get my hand snagged in the lead.' She raised her plastered hand, the fingers poking out were purple and bruised.

Jenna's heart stumbled.

Fliss cleared her throat and Lana passed her a glass of water. After several small sips, Fliss returned the glass to her and continued. She held her plastered hand with the other one and frowned down at it. 'I felt the bones snap,' she sucked air in through her teeth, nursing her arm. 'It crunched. I felt it grind all through my body as he twisted and wrenched the lead and I knew, just knew, I couldn't let go. If I did, it would be my neck.' She let out a soft sob. 'I should be dead, but instead I have a mangled hand.'

Dark clouds washed over Jenna's vision as heat clawed its way up her neck at the horror Fliss had suffered. Jenna had never reacted this way to a victim telling her their story, but this was different. This was her sister. The heat of bile rose in Jenna's throat and she wondered if she could make it through the rest of her sister's statement without dashing from the room to throw up in the ladies' toilets.

Dr Ahmed's gentle tones washed over her as waves of blackness receded. 'We're about to take you to X-ray to check the damage. Then we'll be able to make an assessment of what needs to be done.'

Aware of Lana's gaze on her, Jenna wondered if she'd turned the unhealthy shade of green she felt. With long, slow pulls of breath, Jenna managed to get herself under control and tuned back in to Fliss's story.

'When I woke, I was in some kind of cellar, handcuffed to a bed.' She raised her good hand and the dark bruises encircling her wrist drew Jenna's attention. 'He visited a few times. I'm sorry, my head... it's not clear, he drugged me, several times, and the pain was unbearable.' Fliss jiggled her plastered hand. 'He snapped my hand back into place, one finger at a time. It felt worse than when he broke it. I fainted. I know I did. I must have been out for some time because when I woke, my arm was like this. He'd plastered it.'

Jenna surged to her feet as surprise whipped through Fliss's gaze. 'I'm sorry.' She stared at the nurse as pinpricks of light sparkled in her vision. 'Could I possibly have some water?'

Instead of Lana going to fetch water, she stepped in close and guided Jenna back into her seat. With a cool, gentle hand on the back of her neck, she pushed Jenna's head down, in between her knees. 'Stay there while I get you some water. You can't faint if you stay like this.'

'I'm sorry,' Jenna mumbled, ashamed of her reaction, when her sister lay in bed, battered and beaten yet still able to function. Heat rushed through her chest to suffuse her neck and cheeks. 'I'll be all right in a minute.'

'That happened to me when he did it, only I crashed and burned. Fainted dead.'

Jenna raised her head to meet the amusement in her sister's stare. How could she joke about it when the matter was so deadly serious?

As the light-headedness faded, Jenna shucked her jacket to try and cool off, grateful to accept the plastic cup of water Lana offered her. Taking small sips, Jenna glanced at Taylor. 'I'm sorry.'

Gentle empathy softened the hard planes of his face. 'You need a break?'

'No, please, carry on.' Mortified at her own weakness, Jenna took another sip of water and nodded for Fliss to continue.

'He stitched up some of the bigger gashes.'

'I took a look at these earlier.' Lana nodded. 'In my opinion, whoever carried out this work did a pretty adequate job. I would say it looks like the work of a first or second year student, fairly good, but not as precise and neat as a surgeon.' Her lips quirked up in a smile. 'Or a nurse practitioner.'

Dr Ahmed nodded in agreement. 'I don't think we need to do anything more with these. They're clean, there's no infection and if we unstitch them just to stitch them up again, the likelihood is your scarring will be worse. What I would like to do shortly is take you to the plaster room, so they can cut the plaster off your arm; we'll have it x-rayed. Depending what he's done to it, we may have to operate to set your fingers straight again.'

At Fliss's cringe, Jenna looked askance at the nurse. 'Can she have some painkillers?'

'She already did when the paramedics brought her in.' The nurse smiled at Fliss. 'Don't worry, when they reset it, they'll put you under anaesthetic first.'

Fliss gave a weary nod, her eyes fluttered closed.

'Okay, that's enough for now.' Dr Ahmed's tone brooked no argument. 'You can stay.' He nodded at Jenna. 'You're a relative.'

Taylor came to his feet and made his way to the door of the side room. 'Let me know when she's all right to continue. I'll be in the canteen. Jenna, if you need anything, anything at all, just let me know.'

'She'll need a mug of coffee.' Fliss's faint voice faded on the last word, but Taylor's lips kicked up in a crooked smile.

'I'll make sure that's seen to, don't you worry.' His gaze trapped Jenna's, his dark brows pulled low. 'If she wakes, no questions, Sergeant. Make sure of that. You're here as a relative only, not a police officer.'

Jenna laid her head back on the chair and gave him a nod. She was incapable of forming questions, she just wanted to sit and watch her sister, wallow in the self-pity and delirium of having Fliss back.

As they all left, Jenna stared at her younger sister. Fliss was alive and that was the best she could ask for. She would recover, her scars would heal, and Jenna would make damned sure she was there to help her move on. She'd never complain about the damned dog again. She smiled to herself. She'd arrange to have him taken home, surprise Fliss when she got there, provided Domino was well enough. Perhaps Mason would take him back to her house if she gave him the keys.

Jenna squirmed in the hard chair, then came to her feet to peep out of the open doorway. Surprise curled through her at the sight of Mason on the other side of the room, arms crossed over his chest, brow furrowed as his gaze clashed with hers.

Jenna stepped outside the room and gave him a weary smile. 'She's okay.'

He nodded. 'So I heard.'

He'd taken it very hard, she could see that, could see the worry swirling in his gaze. 'You can go if you want.'

The slow shake of his head and tightening of his lips stopped her. 'No. We have no idea who this man is and what he wanted with Fliss in the first place. As we don't know his whereabouts yet, or whether there's a possibility he'll come back for her, there's no way I'm leaving her alone.'

Jenna flashed him a feral smile, jiggling her eyebrows at him. 'I'm here.'

He nodded, her attempt at lightening the situation bypassed his sense of humour. 'I'll not risk either of you.'

'Thank you.' She touched his arm for a brief moment before she stepped back into the room, surprised to find Fliss awake and staring at her.

Her voice weak, Fliss narrowed her eyes at her as though the light in the room had become too strong. 'I remembered something.' The deadly seriousness of her voice had Jenna moving in closer. 'He knows you.'

'Pardon?' Jenna stepped closer to the bed and bowed her head, so she could hear better, an anxious flutter filling her chest.

'He knows you. That's why he took me, because he thought I recognised him. That I know him through you.'

Jenna's mind flew into overdrive, a million possibilities racing through her head. She leaned in. Nose to nose with her sister, she peered deep into her exhausted eyes. 'And do you?'

Fliss's death-filled gaze held hers as she gave a slow shake of her head.

36

'Nooo!' Fliss lurched upright, heart leaping from of her chest. She gulped in great mouthfuls of air as she choked on her tears. Dark shadows shifted in the room as she blinked in furious desperation. She was still there. Trapped.

'Shhhh, Fliss. You're safe. You're home. I've got you.'

She crumpled into Jenna's arms, petrified this was the dream and the reality would be that she was still incarcerated in the cellar of a madman's house. She clung even tighter, her chin on Jenna's shoulder, and let the tears roll into the soft pyjama top Jenna wore.

'I thought I was there.'

'I know. Shhh. You're not. You're safe.'

'Where's Domino?'

'Don't say his name, he'll only jump...'

As the weight of the Dalmatian bore down on her legs, Jenna huffed out a breath, but Fliss reached out to curl her fingers around his satin ear and take comfort from his familiar presence as he did a slow kamikaze crawl from the bottom of the bed until he lodged himself between them. With a contented sigh, he lowered his head and snuffled his cold, wet nose into the crease of her elbow.

Despite the comfort he offered, the dream still swirled in her mind.

'He came back.' Tears stung her eyes as she blinked at Jenna through the lavender pre-dawn light. Her voice thick with terror, she made a desperate attempt to control her horror. 'I saw him. He was so real. He breathed his mint breath in my face.'

With one arm wrapped around her, Jenna stroked Fliss's face. The soothing rhythm of it calmed her, but the shot of adrenaline still had Fliss's heart racing.

'Do you think you'd be able to give a clearer description of him?'

Fliss took several beats to reply while the shudders wracking her body died down. 'Yes. His eyes were... hollow. He seemed so large.' She closed her eyes and a vision of him sprang into her head. 'But it was always dull grey in there. Almost like twilight. I could barely see. I never knew if it was night or day. There were no windows. But when he came in, he always switched on the light. It was bright. A bare bulb dangling from the ceiling and he always stood in front of it. I don't know whether it was contrived so I couldn't see him, or to make him appear scary. His face was shadowed. He was always angry. His face... strained.' Calm layered over her panic as she talked.

She leaned back against her pillows, taking Jenna with her, her shoulder nudging the comatose Dalmatian snuggled tight to her side to elicit a long-suffering groan. He wasn't supposed to come upstairs, but what could she do? They were both recovering from emotional and physical trauma. It would have been a cruelty to both of them to leave him downstairs. He needed her as much as she needed him. Even if he took up two-thirds of her double bed. She laid her hand on his shoulder, the heat of him an instant comfort, but the fear of the dark could no longer be dispelled by him alone.

'Will you stay?' she whispered to Jenna. 'Just for a while?'

Jenna smiled against Fliss's cheek. 'Of course. For as long as you need me.'

Warmed by her sister's presence, Fliss took comfort, her eyelids drooping as sleep tried to claim her. 'I'll always need you.'

Jenna's voice thickened. 'I know.'

Conscious of the police officer posted downstairs in the living room, Fliss shifted her weight on the bed and lowered her voice. 'When will the police decide not to provide protection any more?'

'Hopefully not until they catch him.'

'What if you don't? What if you never catch him? It can't go on forever.'

'We'll catch him.'

'But you have nothing to go on.'

'We have plenty to go on.'

She twisted so her face almost touched her sister's. 'Like what?'

With an impatient shuffle, Jenna hissed through gritted teeth. 'You know I shouldn't talk to you about this. I could lose my job.'

'Nobody would know. I won't say anything.'

'Fliss!'

'I promise. I won't whisper a word. I may be able to help. Knowing something is being done will help me sleep.'

Jenna's breath puffed out across the top of Fliss's head and their hands nudged each other as they both stroked Domino. 'They're following any leads they can. The ring has distinctive markings. They're looking for the jeweller who might have made it or inscribed it.' Jenna wriggled further down the bed, her voice low and soothing. 'We're trying to find a link through her dental records.'

'Hmmm.'

'We're collating all the door-to-door evidence, but there really isn't much, and as you know, we've put out an appeal in the newspapers.'

Plastered all over the internet and papers, news of her attack dominated. She'd closed down her iPad when she'd arrived home, refusing to look at Facebook. Many of the comments sickened her.

Fliss turned onto her side to spoon Domino, placing her damaged arm on top of the duvet cover, tucking it closer to ward off the chill. Her eyes drifted shut again. Anaesthetic still buzzed around in her system from the four hour operation she'd had to endure. At least they'd reset her bones.

Her fingers gave a convulsive twitch inside the cast, a shimmer of heat prickled over her skin as a sharp reminder of the damage she'd suffered. Damage which she prayed had been rectified by the operation. The X-rays had shown less damage than they'd expected. Her two middle fingers were broken, where they'd twisted in the lead, but her hand, rather than being broken, had suffered deep bruising to the tendons. Her fractured wrist had already started to heal. The light, flexible splint they'd fitted gave the support she needed without the heavy weight of a cast.

Six weeks the surgeon predicted. No driving. How the hell was she supposed to work?

'Are you asleep, Fliss?' Jenna's voice whispered over her.

'No. I was thinking about my hand.'

'Does it hurt?'

'Yeah, hurts like hell.'

'Do you need any painkillers?'

She raised her head and turned towards her sister. 'Can I have some? How long has it been since I took the last ones?'

The bedcovers rustled as Jenna sat up. 'It's almost five o'clock. You took them when you came to bed at ten last night, so yes, you can have whatever you like.'

'Paracetamol, I think.'

'You don't want something stronger?'

'I don't like codeine, it makes me feel weird. It reminds me of the stuff he gave me. I feel sick and dizzy with it.'

Jenna slipped out of bed and, in the dark silence of the room, Fliss let her mind drift, so when Jenna returned, she had a question ready. She struggled to sit up, pinned by the weight of the dog on the covers.

Jenna leaned over her, blocking out the light. 'Let me help you.'

'I feel so pathetic.'

Jenna wrapped her arms around Fliss and hauled her into a sitting position.

'I should be able to do this myself.'

'It doesn't matter, you soon will. You've been through a lot, Fliss, and your hand was badly damaged. It's not surprising you can't do anything yet. And the anaesthetic will take a while to get out of your system.' Jenna perched on the side of the bed, shuffling Fliss over so she had more room, then she picked up the glass and the paracetamol and offered them to her.

Fliss tossed the paracetamol onto her tongue, grabbed the glass and washed down the tablets while eyeing her sister as she remembered the question whirling around in her head. 'What about the cyclist who found me?'

Jenna squinted at her. 'What about the cyclist?'

'Did he see him? Did he see the man? I know he was there.' The memory was screened in mist, but the sensation still prickled her skin. 'I could feel him watching me.'

Jenna stilled. 'You never mentioned this before.'

'It's only just come back to me. I was sure he was behind me, and then I was on the ground and the cyclist was there.'

'Keith Fellows.'

'Keith. He was so kind.'

'According to Salter and Wainwright he was a nice man. Quite trauma-tised by the event. They've interviewed him.' Jenna picked up her phone and started tapping in information. 'I'll check if they enquired whether he saw anyone else. I'm sure they would have asked him. But just in case.'

'Yes.' Fliss's jaw creaked as she yawned. She slipped back down the bed, inhaling the freshly laundered scent of the bedlinen, antiseptic and warm dog, no longer able to keep her eyes open. 'See, I told you I could help.'

Jenna gave her an affectionate cuff on the head, and they lay in silence for a moment, Domino's soft snores filling the silence while another thought nudged at Fliss's conscience. There was something else she had to say to her sister.

'Jenna?'

'Hmmm?'

'Thanks for picking a decent photograph of me for the newspapers "missing" item. I'd have been really peed off if you'd picked a bad one,' she mumbled as the darkness took her down into a deep slumber.

37

WEDNESDAY 31 OCTOBER, 18:45 HRS

The man gave a vicious stab of his fork into his meal-for-two dinner. He raised a slice of processed chicken to his face to stare at it for one long moment before he shovelled it into his mouth and chewed. Enjoyment wasn't expected. The fury bubbling in his stomach soured the taste.

He slapped the tinfoil container on his kitchen table, sending it skittering across the wooden surface to the other side. The bottle of whisky at his elbow, still uncorked from his last slug, proved too much of a temptation. Bypassing his usual crystal whisky glass, the man took hold of the bottle and upended it, catching the waterfall in his mouth. The liquor burned all the way down to his gullet, but he only stopped when the last of the whisky was gone, before he slammed the bottle down on the table. He stared at the dark green bottle, fury vibrating through him. He snatched it up again and launched it across the kitchen into the sink. The shatter of glass did nothing to satisfy his bloodlust.

The stupid cow. Stupid, stupid cow. She'd deprived him of so much. Was about to deprive him of still more when she remembered. When they came for him.

He rubbed his fingers across his dry, cracked lips, bristles rasping. Two days he'd been off work. Two days of lying in a virtual stupor, waiting for the doorbell to ring and the cops to arrest him. Stupid bastards had done

the initial door to door, even accepted a cup of tea while Fliss lay underneath their feet in the cellar. They'd chatted about the tragedy of the
missing woman, of the dead body. Clueless, they'd never asked to check
further. Dopey sods had tripped off to the next house to grab another cup
of tea.

With a bitter smile, he knuckled his fist into his forehead. He'd waited
for them the previous day, but no one had come. Nothing had happened.
Due back to work the following morning, life had continued as normal.

Normal. He snorted. Nothing would ever be normal again. If only the
little slapper hadn't crossed his path. He stretched across the table and
dragged his dinner back towards him. The room lurched, ceiling and floor
meeting in the middle, then parted to whirl around in a mad kaleidoscope.
His mouth watered as the oily contents of his stomach bubbled up.

With a fast dash to the cramped downstairs toilet, he spewed thirty-five
pounds' worth of whisky into the toilet bowl, over the floor and splattered it
up the walls. As his knees turned to water, he melted onto the floor, his
head too heavy to hold up. He slumped in the confined space, rested his
head in the crook of his arms and let the riotous swirling take him down in
the knowledge he couldn't fall any further.

The sour stench of vomit filled his nostrils as he reared up to dry-heave
into the bowl again, sharp knives piercing his stomach as it gave a spas-
modic clench. He puffed his lips out as he breathed out in a desperate
attempt not to suck in any more of the rancid odour of his own sick and
piss.

Filled with self-disgust, the man lurched to his feet and staggered out of
the toilet. He negotiated the stairs, determined not to touch the walls with
his puke-smeared hands. He stumbled into the shower and turned it on full
force. The icy blast wrenched a pained howl from him, and he dropped to
his knees again as he waited for the water to warm up and soak the ice from
his veins. He peeled the layers of clothing from his body, allowing the
powerful gush of water to sluice away two days' worth of dirt and body
odour. His hate-filled heart beat thin and thready.

He flipped the water off and stepped out of the shower, reaching for the
thick brown towel he kept on the heater. With his hands digging into his
soaking hair, he stood naked, his face screwed up as the vague recollection

of a puke-filled towel in the kitchen rolled through his memory of the previous night.

He padded barefoot across the landing and opened the airing cupboard door. He reached inside to grab the first towel he could, fingers of ice trailing down his body. Goosebumps skittered over his skin as he tossed the towel around him and started to rub while he made his way back to the bathroom, a fusty odour from the airing cupboard thick in the air, triggering his vomit reflex again.

He rubbed the towel over his body until his skin smarted, then he swiped the steam from the mirror. Red-rimmed eyes greeted him as he stared back at himself.

Women. Bitches, all of them.

He'd given Mary a wonderful life, hadn't he? She'd have still been snivelling, curled up in a ball in a back alley, if he hadn't saved her eight years before, probably prostituting herself and living on drugs. It was no life for a teenager. Her parents had never missed her. Never tried to find her. Alcoholics, both of them, according to Mary. Why would anyone look in the backwater that was Shropshire? She'd jumped on a train from London, with only enough money to get her as far as Telford, she'd said, a new town, a new life. And he'd saved her. Ungrateful cow. Look how she'd rewarded him.

At first life had been good. Mary had been content to live with him and his mum. She'd not wanted to go out. Why would she?

His mum hadn't been out for years. She had no friends. No one she cared to go and see. He'd been enough for his mum. He'd been her keeper.

But he hadn't been enough for Mary. She'd wanted to go out. To see and be seen. She'd been young back then, malleable, and he'd made sure she didn't go out. Promised his mum she'd settle down, make a good wife, when he'd locked her in the cellar for her own safety. Away from his mum's vicious jealousy.

He leaned his hand on the wall to stop the world from spinning.

If only his mum hadn't wanted to visit Mary. If only he hadn't pushed her from the top of the cellar steps. He cradled his head in his hands. Ignorant bitch. Life hadn't been the same since his mum broke her neck in the fall. Inconsiderate bitch. Stupid, clumsy woman. She'd ruined his fucking life with one mis-step. Literally. It had been entirely her fault.

He dragged his fingers down his face.

He couldn't go into work like this. If they didn't already know, they soon would. He never went to work looking anything other than sleek and professional.

He pushed back his stringy, wet hair and raised his chin. Ignoring the roiling nausea that threatened to overwhelm him again. He would not be sick. Not again. Mouth grim, he drew air in through his nostrils, determined to conquer the alcohol still streaming through his veins.

A shave. He would shave and that would make a difference.

He reached for the razor and hoped he didn't slit his own throat.

He should have slit Mary's throat and buried her in the cellar along with his mother. No one would have ever found her. She'd been quite content until she'd become pregnant. Once the baby had been born, she'd been consumed by it. Completely overwhelmed. It had only taken a slight pinch to the baby's nose and he'd gone. Too easy really, and not his fault, if only the baby's cry hadn't pierced his soul. If it had stayed silent instead of yowling and distracting Mary from her duty. She was supposed to look after him, not a fucking baby.

He'd buried the baby under the brick tunnel along the Gorge. Far enough in so no one would ever find him.

Only, she tried. Perhaps he shouldn't have taunted her with the knowledge. He'd underestimated her attachment to the baby, never realising how much she'd miss him.

It wasn't his fault, of course.

It was her fault.

And the stupid bitch had lost her mind and made a break for it. She'd rather have been found naked than stay with him any longer. He'd arrived home to find the cellar empty. Mary gone. He should have realised how strong the bond to her baby had been. Strong enough for her to go in search of him. Her mind had been addled by then. Whatever they called it, baby blues, post-natal depression, she'd been affected, and he'd been left with no option but to follow her and put an end to it. An end to her. It hadn't taken much to break her neck, though it hadn't been deliberate. If only she'd come back with him, but with no good reason other than the damned baby she'd refused to acknowledge had died he'd been unable to persuade her to come home. And that godawful caterwauling she'd started. He'd needed to stop the noise. Just stop her before the entire town came out to investigate.

He hadn't anticipated losing her down the Gorge either. Stupid carelessness as he'd flung her naked body over his shoulder and overbalanced, surprised at the dead weight of her as she flopped over him.

The only good thing to come of it was the stupid examiner had declared the death an accident – another bloody woman, they should all be strangled at birth – he'd broken Mary's neck with such skill it appeared she'd done it on her long slide down the Gorge. Pride nudged away the nausea. He'd never thought they'd mistake murder for a simple nudge down the Gorge.

Fingers still shaky, he lifted the razor to his face, making the job a dicey one but, in the end, the two day growth of mottled grey and black whiskers were removed and his clean-shaven face glowed a healthy pink, enough to deceive most people. The ones who never saw beyond the outer shell. Bitches like Detective Sergeant Jenna Morgan who pretended to care but had no interest really.

Shame he hadn't killed her sister. It would have been interesting to watch Jenna deteriorate. She thought the world revolved around her and her little fucking perfect family, but it didn't. He'd had nothing to do with the demise of her mother, but the pleasure he'd experienced watching DS Morgan's desperate misery had soothed his soul.

The man peered at his watch as it swirled before his eyes. If he was lucky and fell asleep straight away, he'd get five hours rest before he needed to return to work.

He squeezed toothpaste onto his electric toothbrush and did precisely the recommended two minutes, glancing at the little timer each time the toothbrush jigged every thirty seconds, just to make sure.

He grabbed the glass on the edge of the sink and filled it with water. As he gulped down the third refill, his gaze, swirling with alcohol and superior satisfaction, stayed on the mirror.

They didn't know. Fliss hadn't told them. For whatever reason, she'd decided to hold on to the information that could ruin him.

The man placed the empty glass back on the sink, a glimmer of a smile danced on his lips. There had to be a reason she'd not told the police who he was. Perhaps Felicity hadn't really wanted to escape. Had he made a mistake drugging her too much? He'd confused her. Maybe she regretted fleeing. She'd changed her mind and wanted to belong to him. Let him keep her again.

38

'Hey, Frank. How's it going?'

Frank's bony shoulders jiggled. He rubbed his hands together, stare firmly fixed on the incident board. 'Nothing. Just nothing. It's a dead-end.'

Jenna stepped closer, narrowing her gaze to see what he could. Still nothing. Every time she came in that's what she was told. No little nuggets of information. Anything they'd found so far related to Jane Doe and her baby.

'Essentially, we've got no leads.' He shook his head and met her gaze, his own filled with a peculiar, satisfied gleam. 'A perfect crime.'

'No crime is perfect.' She sipped at her coffee as she turned her attention back to the board.

'I didn't think you were allowed in here without that guy.' He turned away from the board and his gaze bored into her.

'I'm allowed to look. I'm just not supposed to do anything.' Frustration rumbled through her voice. 'I just like to think something will "pop" and I'll see what no one else has.'

'If you do, be sure to let me know first. I'd hate to see you lose your job over it.'

Jenna shrugged. Frank was unusually gritty. He'd obviously had a bad day. 'She's my sister, Frank.'

'Not worth losing your job over.'

'I'd give up my life, if it meant she was safe.'

His dark eyes swirled with uncomfortable intensity. 'Would you really?'

'Yeah, of course.'

'How is she? Back home? Recovering well, I hope.'

'Early days yet, but, yes, I think she'll be okay.'

'Good.' He nodded as he picked up a stack of papers and handed it to her. 'As you're here, you might as well have a look through these.'

'What are they?'

'People you've arrested since you began your career who fit your sister's description of her... kidnapper.'

Disappointed, she flicked through the dozen or so sheets of paper. 'Not many.'

'No, I guess your sister gave a reasonably generic description.'

'I guess "murdering-bastard-sleaze-ball" doesn't show up on our search engine?'

His mouth kicked up at the sides, but his expression stayed flat. 'I guess not.'

Jenna reached out and squeezed his arm. 'I'll run through them. I'll let you know when I'm done.' She turned and wound her way through the tables towards the door when a thought occurred to her. He had issues with his wife's mental health. With her own problems, Jenna hadn't given him a thought. Last she'd heard, his wife had been going through a better time, perhaps the situation had changed again. 'Frank?' She swung around in his direction. 'How's your wife?'

Surprise shot his eyebrows up. 'She... left.'

Staggered, Jenna stopped in her tracks. 'What?'

'She left me.'

'Oh, Frank, I'm so sorry.' She took a few steps in his direction. 'You should have said. I feel terrible. I thought she was so much better.'

He gave a tight smile. 'So much she decided she didn't need me any more and left.'

As Jenna came closer, she lowered her voice so the others in the room couldn't hear. 'Did she say why?'

He hesitated, then puffed out a sigh of resignation. 'No. She just walked out the front door, leaving it open.' He stood with hands on hips.

'How long ago was this? Have you heard from her?'

He dipped his head, shaking it so a hank of thinning hair flopped over his face. 'No, but I'm sure she's happier where she is.'

Before Jenna could voice a reassuring reply, her radio fizzed. 'Juliette Alpha 76. This is Control.'

She patted Frank on the arm, mouthed 'I'm so sorry.' And then spoke into Airwaves. 'This is Juliette Alpha 76, go ahead, Control.'

'Hey, Sarg. I have some information for you regarding the rape case you're dealing with.'

'Go ahead.'

Her mobile phone rang, and she glanced over at the number. Not recognising it, she nodded at it and mouthed to Frank, 'Could you get it?' as she listened to Control.

Frank raised her phone to his ear. 'DS Morgan's phone, Frank Bartwell speaking.' He waited, his brow crinkling with consternation as he held the phone to his ear a moment longer and then lifted the mobile away from his face. He shrugged before he put it back and spoke again. 'Hello, this is DS Morgan's phone... can I help you?' He stared at the display again and then stabbed the call end button. 'Some stupid kid messing around, or a heavy breather.' He placed her phone on the desk, raised his hand to give a quick wave. 'I'm off home now. See you tomorrow.'

39

THURSDAY 1 NOVEMBER, 18:25 HRS

'Fuck. Fuck.'

Sweat popped out of every pore on his skin as Frank's foot shot from underneath him and he almost went head first down the police station stairwell in his haste to get out.

'You all right there, Frank?'

He reared his head up and glared as Mason trotted up the stairs towards him. Bastard. If he said another word, he'd fucking smack him on the nose. Teeth gritting, he forced himself to reply. 'Yeah.'

Mason paused on the step below him. 'Are you sure? You don't look so good.'

Staggered by the genuine concern on the other man's face, Frank paused. *Be nice. Be nice to him and he'll never suspect.* 'I'm fine. It's been a long day.'

Mason moved up a couple of steps. 'It's been a long week.' He reached out to pat Frank's shoulder and it was all Frank could do not to flinch at the sickening display of manly bonding. Mason was a fucking dick. Everyone thought he was funny, but he wasn't. He was just a juvenile prick.

Frank ducked his head and continued down the stairs, slower this time. Better not to attract attention.

Mason called out from above him. 'You seen Sergeant Morgan?'

Cold sweat pooled along Frank's spine, but he forced himself to pause and look up, so his gaze met Mason's. 'She's in the incident room.'

'Cheers, pal.'

Frank dipped his head to keep the vicious retorts running through his mind from spilling out of his mouth. *You're no 'pal' of mine, you fucking twat.*

Frank raised his hand to the duty sergeant as he passed the public service counter and then dipped his fingers into his pocket to wrap his fingers around the set of keys he'd removed from Jenna's handbag. When would women learn that it was the easiest crime in the world to just swipe keys, purses, credit cards, fucking money from the top of their handbags? Not even a crime, just an invitation to take when they left the bag on the back of a chair, with its top gaping open like a yawning mouth.

He slid into the driver's seat of his car and rested his forehead on the steering wheel. Control. He needed to get back his control or he'd ruin everything.

She'd already nearly ruined everything for him. Fucking woman. He rued the day her path had ever crossed his. Each time he formulated a plan, she managed to bugger it up.

He scraped his trembling fingers through his hair and then buckled up.

He'd planned everything so well. He'd even managed to change Donna McGuire's duty using Taylor's profile, so when it was investigated, no one would suspect him.

He blew out a breath as he turned the key and fired the engine.

Cornered, he had no choice but to carry on. Strategy was his thing, provided he didn't panic. Discipline.

Follow the plan. It was still his intention. Everything had fallen into place, just the way he needed, except the timing. Even so, he could handle it. The window of opportunity would be tight, but he could do it.

He reversed his car out of the parking space, glancing over his shoulder at the concrete and glass monstrosity that was Malinsgate Police Station. His heart pounded. He'd never set out to deliberately kill anyone before. Life had just happened and his mum and Mary had both been accidents. Even the baby had gone quicker than he expected. A weak, pathetic life that had snuffed out in the blink of an eye. He'd never meant them any harm. Each one of them had contributed to their own demise. Stupid, stupid women. It wasn't his fault. He couldn't be held to blame. And now he had to clear up this mess that she'd created.

40

As she finished her conversation with Control, Jenna glanced around. Frank had left for the day, but the pile of identities was still on the desk in front of her. She glanced at her phone, the last number on it not one she recognised.

Adrian had slipped into the office while she discussed her case and leaned over his laptop, too deep in concentration to notice her.

She glanced over at DI Taylor, absorbed in conversation with Salter and Wainwright.

Mason swung through the doorway, pushing food into his mouth as he approached.

'What's going on?'

'Unfortunately, nothing. The leads are all cold. Not a single decent connection to the dead woman and her baby, and Fliss.'

'Huh.' He slumped into the seat next to hers, giving her a shoulder bump so her chair wheeled a few inches away from the desk.

'Where have you been?' She shot him a quick glance while she shuffled through the papers in front of her, pressing her fingers into her furrowed brow as she tried to imagine one of the unlikely suspects kidnapping her sister.

'I took the kid to do some investigating.'

'Investigating? You took him for something to eat, didn't you?'

He grinned and swallowed the last of the burger bun, swiping the back of his hand across his mouth to rid himself of any crumbs. He shuffled his chair forward and leaned on the desk next to her, earning a quiet look from Adrian from across the room.

'Did you bring me anything?'

He snorted. 'Nah, you're off soon. Won't Fliss have something ready for you?'

Doubtful, but they had microwave meals.

Jenna flicked through the photos and discarded three of them, showing them to Mason. 'Too young.'

Mason nodded his agreement.

'Fliss placed her kidnapper as older than those three.' She put another two in the discard pile. 'There's no way they were capable of kidnapping Fliss, let alone tossing her over their shoulders and walking the two hundred metres or so to the car park.'

'I'm going to tell her you said so.'

'Do, and you die.'

'Then you'd have to arrest yourself.'

'No one would blame me, I'd probably be congratulated.' She turned back to the photographs, bumped the heel of her hand against her forehead as she stared at the next one. 'Does he look familiar to you?

'Yeah, nasty piece of shit.' Mason slipped the photograph from her fingers. 'He beat his mum black and blue, put her in hospital when she refused to give him the last of her pension money so he could buy a packet of cigarettes.'

Jenna glazed her eyes until they went out of focus and the image blurred in front of her. 'Fliss said the guy wore dark-rimmed glasses. Thick lenses so his eyes appeared piggy behind them. She was very clear about that.' She tossed the image on the desk in front of Mason. 'This guy doesn't wear glasses.' She let out a long sigh. 'It'll be worth interviewing him. He's the right height, fits the weight parameters and his face matches Fliss's description closer than most of the others.'

'No glasses.'

'Contact lenses?'

He nodded.

She set another one aside. 'He's serving time at Her Majesty's leisure.'

She stared at the last two. Not much joy there either.

Mason tapped his finger on the first one. 'He no longer lives in the area.'

Jenna pushed the second one in front of him. 'Last I heard, he'd found God and spends most of his time helping the homeless.' She gazed at his picture a moment longer, then placed it on her 'maybe' pile. You could never be certain someone had truly turned that corner in life. She scribbled down his name. She'd pass him on to Salter and Wainwright to investigate.

Jenna reached for her coffee, took a sip and pulled a face. It didn't even have the decency to be tepid. She grimaced again and shot a quick glance at the wall clock in the comms room. After 19:00. already and she'd promised Fliss she wouldn't be late home. Jesus, where had the time gone?

She flicked her gaze around the room as Donna McGuire's softly spoken words reached her ears.

'So, a guy as good looking as you, you must be married.'

Startled by the other woman's frankness, Jenna tuned in to Adrian's low reply.

'I am indeed.'

Jenna's gaze clashed with Mason's as she whipped her head back around. Ignoring his inquisitive stare, she flung him a tight smile. It was none of her business. None of Mason's.

'I need to get home.'

She pushed up from the desk just as Donna wandered towards her. 'Hey, Sarg, how're things going?'

'They could be better.' With a vague sense of disappointment, Jenna closed the avenue her mind wanted to wander down and thought instead of her sister safe at home with Domino to keep her company and a police officer posted outside. 'They could be worse.' She glanced at the clock again and then back at Donna. 'I thought you were on shift at my place tonight?'

Donna shrugged. 'I thought so too but it looks like Matt Dingles is down to cover.'

'Matt? I thought Matt was off sick.'

'Is he? I don't know. I just checked the duty rota because I thought I was there today, but it definitely says Matt's covering.'

With a curl of unease, Jenna glanced around. The DI was no longer in the office. She picked up her Airwaves radio and called person to person. 'DI Taylor?'

'Sergeant?'

'Can you tell me who is on duty at my house now?'

'Certainly, Jenna. It's Donna.'

Jenna met Donna's wide-eyed stare.

'No. Donna's with me in the incident room. She says the rota has Matt Dingles down for this evening.'

'Matt Dingles is off sick.'

Jenna nodded, the twist of doubt tightening her stomach. 'That's what I thought. Can you check the rota?'

Through the long silence, Jenna kept her gaze on Donna.

'Jenna.' The radio hissed back at her. 'Some idiot's changed it. Just wait until I find out who. I'll have their guts for garters.'

The sliver of panic rose to her throat to tighten it. 'Sir. Who is currently with my sister?'

'John Sivitar was on until 18:00 hours. Bear with me a moment.'

Airwaves clicked off as he changed channel and Jenna's adrenaline kicked up a notch while Donna stood beside her, transferring her weight from foot to foot as though she were about to take off on a marathon.

The radio shot to life again. 'Jenna, John left at 18:00 on the dot. He signed off from your house as he has an appointment this evening. We all assumed Donna would be there.'

'It's 19:10 now, Sir. Fliss hasn't phoned to say no one has turned up.'

'I'm sorry.' Donna's soft whisper drew Jenna's attention. 'I'm so sorry.'

Jenna shook her head and spoke back into the radio. 'Sir, Donna and I are going straight around to my house now. I'll check in when we get there.'

'Acknowledged.'

She swiped up her mobile, her fingers not quite steady, and checked the last call. The unidentified number. She hesitated for a long moment, a feeling of unease winding through her stomach. The last time she'd ignored a call it had been her sister in trouble. She could have been there so much sooner if only she'd answered the damned call. She could have saved her sister.

Frank had said a kid or a heavy breather. She considered the number for a long moment before she stabbed her finger on the call-back button. She could always block them if it turned out to be some prankster. Get their number traced. More likely it was that dick, Kim Stafford, trying to wheedle information out of her.

Jenna waited for six rings and was about to hang up when the phone was answered. As Frank had said, a breather. Not a heavy breather though, just soft, hesitant breathing as though someone was waiting for her to speak.

Jenna lowered the tone of her voice to give it a kick of authority. 'DS Morgan here. Identify yourself.'

'Jenna?' The tremor in her sister's voice pulled her to a stop halfway to the door.

'Fliss?'

'It was him. I'm sure it was him.' The hiccupping sob on the other end of the phone stopped Jenna's heart dead in its tracks.

Confused, Jenna ran a distracted hand through her thick hair, irritated when it flopped back against her forehead. 'Fliss? Fliss! What's going on?'

'It was him, Jenna. I swear it was his voice.' Breathless, Fliss could barely be heard above the soft crackling background noise.

'Stop! Felicity Morgan, I cannot understand you. Stop crying and explain because I have no idea what you're saying.' Aware of the sharpness of her tone, Jenna glanced around as a few heads lifted and eyebrows raised. She used her mum's voice. A tactic her mum always employed if the girls were upset. It settled them, made them respond. Jenna only hoped it would work for her.

The long breath on the other end of the line shuddered to a halt until her sister's disembodied voice came across the line. 'The man who answered your phone. Who was it?'

Jenna took a moment to comprehend. 'Frank. Frank Bartwell, our intel analyst.'

Fliss's voice whispered from the phone. 'Is he still there?'

Jenna glanced around the room even though she already knew the answer. His shift had finished at 18:00 hours. She'd seen him go. 'No.' With studied patience, she questioned her sister. 'Fliss? What's going on?'

Hoarse with fear, her sister's voice rasped down the phone. 'It's him. Jenna, he sounded just like the man who took me.'

Disbelief held Jenna paralysed, her brain unable to comprehend what she'd heard. 'What?'

'I'm sure.' A thread of doubt licked into her voice. 'The man who answered your phone sounds just like the guy who took me.'

As her legs weakened, Jenna slipped into a chair, putting her fingers against her forehead, aware of Donna's intense scrutiny and Mason's puzzled frown as he moved in closer. Adrian came to his feet and made his way over the room towards her.

'Fliss, where are you?'

'At home.'

'Whose phone is this?'

'Mine. My new one. That's why I was phoning you. I had it delivered today and I wanted you to know the number... and then he answered. I was too scared to phone you back in case he picked up again. I didn't know what had happened to your phone. I called Mason, but his phone kicked to answerphone.'

Jenna's gaze clashed with Mason's. 'Who's with you now, Fliss?'

'John left a while ago. I thought Donna was due, but she's not here yet.' There was a moment's silence. 'There's no police car outside either.'

Jenna shot to her feet, her limbs moved slow and dreamlike as though she was stepping through thick treacle. She made her way to the door, conscious of a trail of people following her.

Trying not to panic her sister, Jenna kept her voice flat. 'Fliss. Check the doors are all locked. I'm on my way.'

'They're always locked.'

'Good. Check them just in case. Go to the bathroom. Take Domino with you. Lock yourself in.'

'Jenna, you're scaring me. Why are you scaring me?'

'I'm just being cautious.' Her feet were now racing as she dashed through the rabbit-warren hallway. 'What did you say to Frank?'

'Nothing. I said nothing.'

'But you made a noise. Did you say anything?'

Fliss's soft intake of breath sighed down the phone. 'Your name. I whispered your name.'

'Fliss I'm on my way. I need to hang up now, but I'll be there shortly.' She whipped through to her office, signed out the keys for a police issue vehicle and headed for the stairs.

'Don't hang up, Jenna. I'm scared. Don't hang up.'

'I'll be there. I need back up. Hold on.'

Jenna lifted her Airwaves radio to her mouth. 'Juliette Alpha 76. Control, has Frank Bartwell left the building?'

'Signed off shift almost an hour ago Juliette Alpha 76. Looks like you've missed him.'

'Thanks.'

Jenna fumbled with her mobile. 'I'm still here Fliss. Hang on.' Mouth to Airwaves, she called DI Taylor person-to-person again. 'Sir, DS Morgan here. I have my sister on the phone. This may quite honestly sound mad, but Frank Bartwell just answered my phone to her.'

'Bartwell?'

'Yeah, the intel analyst.'

'I know who he is. And...?'

'And, sorry about this, but Fliss tells me that Frank sounds like the guy who kidnapped her.' Coming from her mouth, it sounded stupid.

Static crackled through the momentary silence. 'What the hell are you talking about?'

'Frank Bartwell answered my phone, sir. Fliss was on the other end.' She panted as she trotted down the stairwell, past the front counter, aware that every step was being dogged by Donna, Adrian and Mason. 'Fliss believes Frank is her kidnapper.' Jenna flung open the station door and headed for her vehicle, Donna hot on her heels.

Calm and patient, DI Taylor's voice came over the Airwaves. 'Jenna, how can you be sure? Your sister has undergone a huge trauma. You need to slow down.'

'I need to be home right now, sir. I'm going home, and I'd appreciate back-up.'

'Jenna, hold on. Take a step back a moment.'

'I can't.' She wrenched open the car door and flung herself into the front seat. 'He has to know she recognised his voice.'

Donna flopped onto the passenger seat next to her, whipping the seat belt around her and slamming the buckle into the housing.

'DS Morgan. Frank Bartwell is the least likely person to be a kidnapper...' He paused for a long moment as the impact of what she'd told him processed. 'Or killer.'

Frustrated, she ground her teeth. 'It's always the fucking least likely.' She'd pushed too far, swearing at him on a recorded line.

Silence followed, then Airwaves crackled to life.

'DS Morgan. Go with your gut. You have my backing. I'll arrange for DC Ellis to meet you at your house.'

She glanced in her rear view mirror at the back seat. 'He's with me, sir. As is PC McGuire.' She glanced at the vehicle behind her and swore blind she saw Ryan leap into the passenger seat of Adrian's Land Rover.

Jenna clenched her jaw while she considered. Was she letting Fliss's panic get to her? Were they both overreacting?

She raised her mobile to her ear. 'Fliss, I'll be there shortly. Don't open the door to anyone. You hear me? Not anyone.'

'What about Donna?'

She glanced across at the calm determination on the other woman's face. 'Donna's with me. We'll be fifteen minutes. Do not open the door. Go to the bathroom. I have a key to let myself in.'

'Okay.'

The quietness of her sister's voice unnerved her. 'I won't be long. I promise.'

'I'll see you soon.'

41

The soft sound of Drivetime on the radio murmured through from the kitchen radio. Jenna would be home soon. With a quick flutter of her heart, Fliss checked the lock on the front door, just as she had at the back door, and then moved into the sitting room. Breathing through her panic, she cast a quick glance around. She'd already closed the curtains when darkness dropped at around 4.30 p.m. It didn't make her feel any safer, just claustrophobic.

On fluffy, pink-slippered feet, she stole to the front window and pushed aside the cream brocade curtains to scan outside.

With soft pants, Fliss got a grip on her fear and wrestled it back down. She was home. She was safe.

Nothing moved, not even the neighbour's cat made an appearance. She dropped the curtain back into place and stepped back.

She drew slow, measured breaths in through her teeth. Jenna wouldn't be long now.

Flames licked up from the teepee of wood Fliss had stacked in the wood burner. By the time Jenna arrived, it would be a roaring inferno. Jenna always told her off for putting too much wood on, but she'd appreciate the comfort tonight.

Just as Domino did.

His tail gave a lazy thump against the soft cushion of the pale grey sofa. Funny how Jenna hadn't made a single objection to him climbing on the furniture since his misadventure.

Fliss paused beside him to scratch his ear, her heart pounding so hard she could barely hear anything above the raging torrent of noise in her head. To console herself and him, Fliss spoke out loud. 'Jenna's on her way home, lad. She'll be fifteen minutes. Just fifteen minutes.' She peered at the screen on her mobile. Only three minutes since she'd spoken with her sister.

Her throat clenched in a tight fist, so constricted she could barely swallow never mind murmur sweet endearments to Domino. 'Come on lad, let's go upstairs.' Into the bathroom where she could sit on the floor and hold onto Domino behind a locked door until Jenna arrived.

She squeezed her eyes shut. What if she was wrong? Jenna would kill her for wasting her time. Wasting police time. Accusing some poor man. Worse still, she'd send her to a bloody psychiatrist for imagining things.

But she hadn't imagined it.

His soft, whiney voice curled through her memory and shot wild panic through her veins.

She breathed in through her nose. It was okay. Everything was going to be okay. Jenna was on her way. She knew who the man was. She'd have him arrested.

Domino came reluctantly to his feet while Fliss's gaze was drawn back to the wood burner and the small set of iron fenders next to it. With an instinct borne of fear, she reached over with her right hand and selected the short-handled poker. Rather than hold it by the end, she gripped it in the middle. When Jenna arrived, she'd think she was a damned ninja.

Heart thrumming in her chest, she ushered Domino to the stairs and checked the front door again before she touched his rump with the side of the poker to encourage his slow progress up. The long, metallic zipper on his side oscillated as he climbed upwards. Another two days and the vet would remove the staples, leaving a deep scar she hoped would be covered eventually by his fur.

Fliss followed him, breath sticking in her lungs.

Jenna had said go to the bathroom, lock the door. She'd be ten minutes now. Only ten. White noise consumed Fliss's hearing as she mounted the stairs one slow step at a time behind Domino.

Halfway up, Fliss froze at the rattle of keys in the front door as Domino stopped mid-step, a low growl rumbling through his deep chest. She glanced at the time again. Only five minutes since Jenna had said she was on her way. Even Jenna's wild driving couldn't get her there in that time.

Convinced it wasn't Jenna, Fliss turned her head so she looked directly at the front door as the man stepped through it, his hollow eyes tracking up the stairs until he met her gaze.

The air wedged in her throat as Fliss drew in snatches of breath.

'Oh, Felicity.' His brows drew down over the thick frame of his glasses. 'You disappoint me.'

The man pushed the door to and leaned against it until it clicked closed, a sickly-sweet smile on his face.

Domino's deep, guttural growl snapped her out of her trance, and she turned to scramble up the stairs, pushing Domino before her.

Fear propelled her upwards.

On her before she could even draw breath, the man snatched at her ankle, fingers digging deep into her flesh, and she slammed face first into the stairs, her cheek going numb. White-hot pain shot through her fingers, sending black spots to cloud her vision. Terror gripped her as she yowled in agony, scrabbling up another step, fingers around the thin poker gouging at the carpet to gain traction.

In panic and sheer desperation, she lashed out with her foot, only to have him snatch at it and drag her down another step, closer to him.

Fliss closed her fingers around the poker and spun onto her back, arm pulsing in agony, heart pounding so loud she could barely hear Domino's savage growls as he snarled in her ear, trying to get past her.

As the man came up the stairs at her, she reared up to scream in his face. 'Fuck you. *Fuck* you.'

She gripped the small poker in her hand and swiped at the man's head. Blood exploded from his nose to splatter up the wall and his glasses flew from his head to clatter on the hallway floor below. With an ear-piercing yell, he reared back, covering his face with his hands and gave her the opportunity she needed to escape.

But the adrenaline that shot through her system was no longer fuelled by fear. Red-hot fury fired her blood.

She wasn't going to escape. She didn't need to. She needed to stand and fight.

Blind with rage, she lifted the poker again and while he staggered backwards down two steps, she launched herself at him, smashing the poker across the side of his face with another explosion of blood spraying Jenna's magnolia walls. She clenched her jaw and followed him down the stairs. She lashed out a third time, catching him under the chin. His head snapped backwards, and he teetered on the third step from the bottom.

Oblivious of the pain that whipped through her arm and up into her shoulder, Fliss pushed him. As he flipped backwards onto hallway floor, she scrambled down until she towered over his inert body, poker gripped in her right hand, vengeance in her heart.

Apart from the sound of her own ragged breathing, silence reigned.

She angled her head as a bright flash of silver at his throat caught her eye. Without hesitation, she leaned in and snatched her angel from his neck, snapping the delicate chain she could always replace.

'Thanks, but I'll have this back.'

She brought her hand to her mouth, uncurled her fingers and placed a gentle kiss on the tiny angel.

She raised her head.

Domino stood beside her, lips drawn back in a silent growl, eyes flashing with fury.

With a suddenness that had her heart leaping into her throat, the front door exploded inwards, the sound of breaking wood like gunshot.

With a wild snarl, she let her knees go soft and crouched, the poker gripped in a fist of iron.

In a burst of dust and splinters, Mason staggered through the open doorway, almost toppling over her and Domino. Jenna shot in behind, slamming into him, unbalancing him so his right foot smacked onto the wooden floor, clipping the man's head.

As Donna, Adrian and Ryan bowled through the doorway, the young PC's eyes went wide.

'Fucking hell!'

Heart pounding in her throat, Fliss glanced down at her pink slippers and the body of the man lying beside them.

She raised her head, her gaze trailing past the blood splattered walls to the four police officers in the front hallway.

'I killed him.'

42

Head in hands, Jenna sat in an uncomfortable plastic chair outside the treatment room, waiting for her sister.

She wasn't sure if the blood had returned to her brain yet after witnessing something she never wished to see again in her life.

The dead man, Frank Bartwell, stretched out on her hallway floor; eyes wide in a blank-eyed stare. Until the moment he blinked. His chest expanded outwards like a pair of bellows, he heaved a desperate cough and rolled onto his side to spew up on her wooden floorboards.

Jenna raised her head and rubbed her hands over her face, pushing back in her chair to straighten out her spine. The crackle and pop of her neck only served to remind her she'd been there for more than five hours.

This time she wasn't even allowed in her sister's room until Fliss had been interviewed. This time, though, Jenna put her worries to one side. DI Taylor was with Fliss. There was no doubt in Jenna's mind that Fliss would be fine. It appeared she'd found herself. In those few moments they'd had together before the cavalry arrived, energy had pulsed from her little sister.

Empowerment.

She'd saved herself.

Pride surfaced over the worry and Jenna settled back to wait.

Mason slumped in the chair beside her, his face still chalky white. 'I thought she'd killed him.'

She had no words. Several little bobs of her head was all she could manage. The weight of her limbs anchored her to the chair.

'I thought he was fuckin' dead, I did. Fuckin' dead.' Ryan bounced on his toes in front of them.

Mason's lips kicked up at the edges at the enthusiasm of his young partner. 'We all thought he was dead, Ryan. Jesus, I don't think I've ever seen anything like it in my life. The guy was dead. For thirty seconds, he was definitely not of this world.'

Jenna tilted her head back to rest it against the grubby wall behind her and closed her eyes.

Frank had been dead. The vision of his wide, staring eyes hit her again and she closed her eyes. Her little sister could have been arrested for murder. Salter and Wainwright were with DI Taylor questioning Fliss about the events leading up to Frank's comatose body lying on Jenna's floorboards at the bottom of the stairs.

The door clicked open to the private hospital room and Jenna shot to her feet.

Salter met her frantic gaze with a wry twist of his lips. 'Your sister, she's got some balls, I can tell you.' He raised his notepad and waggled it at her. 'Pure self-defence. Fucking Frank got everything he fucking deserved. I've got everything for now. You can go in. If she remembers anything further, let me know. I'll be right here.' He pointed his notebook at the short line of plastic chairs and grimaced.

Jenna rubbed damp palms down her black trousers, then pushed the door open. Heart fluttering in the base of her throat, she stared down at her younger sister. Eyelids purple and bruised, Fliss lay against the white pillows surrounded by a cloud of her blonde hair.

'Hi.'

Jenna slipped into a seat beside the bed and took hold of Fliss's pale, delicate hand. 'Hi to you. How are you?'

Fliss bestowed Jenna with a weak smile. 'Not bad for someone who battled a psycho murderer and came out on top.' She gave a delicate snort. 'Literally.' She shot a glance towards the open door and lowered her voice to a whisper Jenna barely caught. 'I thought I'd killed him.' She rubbed her fingers across her dry lips, doubt swirling in her gaze. 'At the time, I wished I had.'

Jenna squeezed her sister's hand, understanding swarming through her chest. 'He'll still pay, Fliss. At least his death won't be on your conscience.'

Fliss gave a low gurgle of amusement. 'I don't think I have a conscience. I really didn't care if he was dead.'

'You would have. Eventually.'

'Maybe.' With a sigh, she closed her eyes. 'One thing I do know, I just wanted to beat the hell out of him.' She winked open one eye. 'And I did.'

Jenna flicked a worried glance at the open doorway and lowered her voice. 'I hope you didn't tell them that.' She could lose her job for saying it, but Fliss had suffered enough without being prosecuted for attacking the man.

Fliss held her look for a long moment, a ghost of a smile played across her lips. 'Of course not. He pulled me down the stairs by my ankle. I couldn't get away. My broken hand...' she raised it to face level. 'I defended myself.' Her mouth curved in a weak smile as her energy visibly drained from her.

Fliss rolled her head on the pillow, her eyes closing.

In the lengthening silence, Fliss's fingers slipped from Jenna's.

'You're tired. Would you like me to go?'

'No, stay a while longer. They gave me drugs for the pain, but it's nice having you here. I feel safe.' Her voice trailed off.

'You'll always be safe, Fliss.'

Her mouth twitched up in a smile. 'And Domino defended me too.'

'He did. Bless him.'

'I bloody love that dog.'

'Me, too.'

'He's going to be fine.'

'Yeah, Mason and Ryan took him to the vets for a quick check-up. Sarah declared him fit. He'd done no further damage, but she gave him some painkillers which will make him sleep. We're going to spoil him rotten from now on.'

A little hiccup caught in the base of her throat and she blinked away the quick rush of tears, grateful Fliss still had her eyes closed. Jenna's voice was threaded with huskiness as she pushed out the next words, hoping Fliss wouldn't call her on it. 'They only just got back from delivering him to Mason's place where we're going to stay for a few days.'

Fliss's eyes gave a drowsy blink open. 'Why can't we go back to our house?'

Jenna patted Fliss's hand. 'Because I have no front door, and it's a crime scene. SOCO will be in there for a couple of days.'

'I'm sorry.'

'It's not your fault.'

'It's not every day a psychopath comes after you.'

Jenna narrowed her eyes at Fliss. 'Twice in one week is a little extreme.'

A small bubble of laughter burst from Fliss's lips. 'I'll try not to let it happen again.'

'I'd appreciate it.'

Fliss raised her plastered arm. 'I was lucky. Apparently, nothing moved when I fell on the stairs.' She gave her fingers a cautious wiggle. 'They said to watch it in case it swells, but otherwise I'm good to go.'

Jenna pushed out of the chair and wandered over to the window over-looking the car park. She watched while visitors came and went, absorbed in the movements of people on a mission. She raised her hand and rested it on the chill of the windowpane. 'Whoever would have believed Frank Bartwell capable of something so vile?'

Fliss's voice when it came was heavy with fatigue. 'How ironic. I never knew him. I didn't recognise him at all and yet that was why he took me.'

At the quiet knock, Jenna turned to the door as Chief Superintendent Gregg stepped inside the room.

'DS Morgan.' He gave her a smile and then turned to her sister. 'Felicity. I hear you've been through the mill for a second time.'

'Fliss. Call me Fliss.'

Her sister struggled to sit up, but he waved her back with a casual flick of his fingers as he squeezed his large frame into a small bucket chair at the side of the bed. 'Just relax, Fliss. I'm not here to question you, just to give you an update of the situation.'

Jenna perked up, curiosity shimmering below the surface. Chief Superintendent Gregg giving an update to a victim? How unusual.

She leaned against the windowsill and crossed her arms over her midriff to hug herself as Mason and Ryan edged into the room.

Mason raised an eyebrow as he propped himself on the edge of Fliss's bed, his attention on Chief Superintendent Gregg. Ryan stood rigid, as though he was on parade.

Gregg quirked him an easy smile. 'Easy, son.' He turned to Fliss. 'I hope you don't mind, I've asked DC Ellis and DC Downey in as they're also working on the case.' He cast his gaze around the room to take in all of them. 'When Wainwright and Salter questioned Frank Bartwell earlier this evening, he gave them information which led them to believe there was further reason to investigate Bartwell's house, other than to look for Fliss's DNA, fingerprints, clothes fibres et cetera in the cellar.'

Jenna's heart skipped a beat and she pushed away from the windowsill to stand next to the bed and take hold of Fliss's hand, the iciness of her own fingers tangling with her sister's warmth.

Gregg rolled his lips inwards. 'DI Taylor is on his way there now with a scenes of crime officer. Bartwell confessed to murdering his own mother somewhere in the region of eight years ago, which would coincide with the timing of when he claims to have come across his wife. A young runaway who he purports to have saved from a life of prostitution and drug abuse. He claims not to have killed the baby, but post-mortem shows the poor little soul had suffocated. It's something we can address further down the line.' His gaze touched on each one of them in turn and came to rest on Fliss again. 'We're working on identifying Mary from the information he gave us. He was a little vague. It appears he may have been knocked out in the fall he took down your stairs, Fliss.'

Fliss gripped Jenna's hand as a bloom of colour stained her neck, creeping over her ears and cheeks.

'The blow certainly seems to have loosened his tongue. It appears he'd like us to know everything. He's made a full confession.'

Fliss's grasp loosened but she never let go. 'What happened to his mother?'

'SOCO are working on locating the body he claims to have buried in the cellar. They've used imaging. It'll take some time to exhume her as it looks as though he poured a new concrete floor over her body and, to further complicate matters, the cellar is currently flooded. Almost up to the two foot mark. We've had to get a team in to pump out the water before we can even begin to exhume the body.'

The rosy pink colour drained from Fliss's face to leave her a deathly pale hue.

'Oh God.' Fliss's voice thickened. 'I was right there. Right where he buried the poor woman. His own mother.' She raised her head, tortured gaze darting around the room to encompass them all. 'She was there. Her body buried beneath where I lay.'

If she could have spared her sister the pain and shock, Jenna would have. A dead body in the cellar wasn't exactly what Jenna came across every day, but her reaction wasn't as visceral as Fliss's. Perhaps it would have been had she slept in the dark, dank cellar with a body buried beneath.

Gregg gave her sister a moment longer to compose herself before he continued. 'I'm sorry to distress you, Fliss. I needed to know if it jogged a memory from the time you were down there.'

Fliss shook her head and struggled upright. 'He never spoke about his mother at all.' She narrowed her gaze. 'Apart from when he talked about the incontinence pads. I'm sure he told me they were his mother's one time, and then said they belonged to Mary.' She scrunched her face up. 'No.' She shook her head. 'No, I can't remember any more. I was too hazy when I was there.'

Gregg nodded, a twitch of regret slanting across his lips. 'Right. Thank you all the same.' He glanced around at all of them. 'Time to leave Fliss in peace now. She's had enough excitement for tonight.'

'To last a lifetime.' Fliss's eyelids drooped as the adrenaline rush left her body. Her hand sagged onto the covers.

Gregg came to his feet. The small bucket chair clung momentarily to his hips, then clattered to the floor and Fliss's eyes popped open, fear racing through them.

Jenna laid her hand on Fliss's arm as she took the seat next to her bed again. 'It's okay. Nothing to worry about.' It had already been a long night and promised to be even longer.

Jenna's head drooped as relief robbed her of her remaining energy.

As the others filed out, Gregg turned in the doorway. 'I assume you'll stay.'

Without hesitation, Jenna nodded. 'Yes, sir. I'm not leaving her.'

He nodded. 'I'll arrange for a cot to be wheeled in. Can't have one of my officers too exhausted to perform their duty.'

She threw him a grateful smile, the edges of her lips wobbling with the effort. 'Thank you, sir.'

'No. Thank you, DS Morgan. Good job.' He paused for a moment longer, then glanced at his watch. 'I'll see you in the morning, sergeant. We have work to do.'

ACKNOWLEDGMENTS

Thanks to my wonderful family for their unwavering support. My sister, Margaret, the first person to ever get to read my manuscripts. My most dedicated fan and toughest critic.

My daughters, Laura and Meghan, who are quite comfortable with me killing people off.

My husband, Andy, who I grill for his policing knowledge. Despite listening, any errors in techniques and law are totally my own, because I don't always take notice...

Although I have used real place names to give my story authenticity, all characters and their names are entirely fictitious.

Finally, to the Boldwood team for putting their trust in this series. They have inspired me and driven me to produce stronger and better storylines.

MORE FROM DIANE SAXON

We hope you enjoyed reading *Find Her Alive*. If you did, please leave a review.

If you'd like to gift a copy, this book is also available as an ebook, digital audio download and audiobook CD.

Sign up to Diane Saxon's mailing list for news, competitions and updates on future books.

http://bit.ly/DianeSaxonNewsletter

Some One's There, the second instalment in the DS Jenna Morgan series is available to order now.

ABOUT THE AUTHOR

Diane Saxon previously wrote romantic fiction for the US market but has now turned to writing psychological crime. *Find Her Alive* was her first novel in this genre and introduces series character DS Jenna Morgan. She is married to a retired policeman and lives in Shropshire.

Visit Diane's website: http://dianesaxon.com/

Follow Diane on social media:

facebook.com/dianesaxonauthor
twitter.com/Diane_Saxon
instagram.com/DianeSaxonAuthor
bookbub.com/authors/diane-saxon

ABOUT BOLDWOOD BOOKS

Boldwood Books is a fiction publishing company seeking out the best stories from around the world.

Find out more at www.boldwoodbooks.com

Sign up to the Book and Tonic newsletter for news, offers and competitions from Boldwood Books!

http://www.bit.ly/bookandtonic

We'd love to hear from you, follow us on social media:

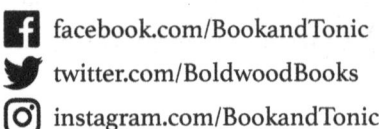

facebook.com/BookandTonic
twitter.com/BoldwoodBooks
instagram.com/BookandTonic

Milton Keynes UK
Ingram Content Group UK Ltd.
UKHW041532010424
440364UK00002B/7